Harmonics
Harmonic Magic Book 2

P.E. Padilla

Crimson Cat Publishing

This book is a fictional story and as such names, characters, and events are fictitious. Any resemblance to persons, either living or dead, is coincidental.

The reproduction, sale, or distribution of this book without the permission of the publisher is illegal and punishable by law.

Cover Art by Damonza (https://damonza.com/)

Published by Crimson Cat Publishing

Copyright © 2016 by P.E. Padilla

All rights reserved.

ISBN-13: 978-1-943531-02-8

DEDICATION

For Alejandra.
Your example inspires and motivates me, my friend, and makes me want to be a better person. Thank you for being.

CONTENTS

Maps	vii
Prologue	1
Chapter One	7
Chapter Two	16
Chapter Three	32
Chapter Four	39
Chapter Five	45
Chapter Six	53
Chapter Seven	61
Chapter Eight	68
Chapter Nine	75
Chapter Ten	84
Chapter Eleven	91
Chapter Twelve	97
Chapter Thirteen	104
Chapter Fourteen	112
Chapter Fifteen	121
Chapter Sixteen	129
Chapter Seventeen	134
Chapter Eighteen	140
Chapter Nineteen	149
Chapter Twenty	156
Chapter Twenty-One	162
Chapter Twenty-Two	169
Chapter Twenty-Three	180
Chapter Twenty-Four	187
Chapter Twenty-Five	200
Chapter Twenty-Six	206
Chapter Twenty-Seven	217
Chapter Twenty-Eight	225
Chapter Twenty-Nine	235
Chapter Thirty	242

Chapter Thirty-One	249
Chapter Thirty-Two	254
Chapter Thirty-Three	261
Chapter Thirty-Four	267
Chapter Thirty-Five	274
Chapter Thirty-Six	284
Chapter Thirty-Seven	295
Chapter Thirty-Eight	305
Chapter Thirty-Nine	313
Chapter Forty	321
Chapter Forty-One	327
Chapter Forty-Two	339
Chapter Forty-Three	348
Chapter Forty-Four	357
Chapter Forty-Five	365
Chapter Forty-Six	372
Chapter Forty-Seven	381
Chapter Forty-Eight	388
Chapter Forty-Nine	397
Chapter Fifty	405
Chapter Fifty-One	418
Chapter Fifty-Two	426
Chapter Fifty-Three	432
Chapter Fifty-Four	440
Chapter Fifty-Five	450
Chapter Fifty-Six	461
Chapter Fifty-Seven	469
Chapter Fifty-Eight	480
Chapter Fifty-Nine	490
Chapter Sixty	498
Chapter Sixty-One	506
Epilogue	511
Glossary	516

MAP OF GYTHE

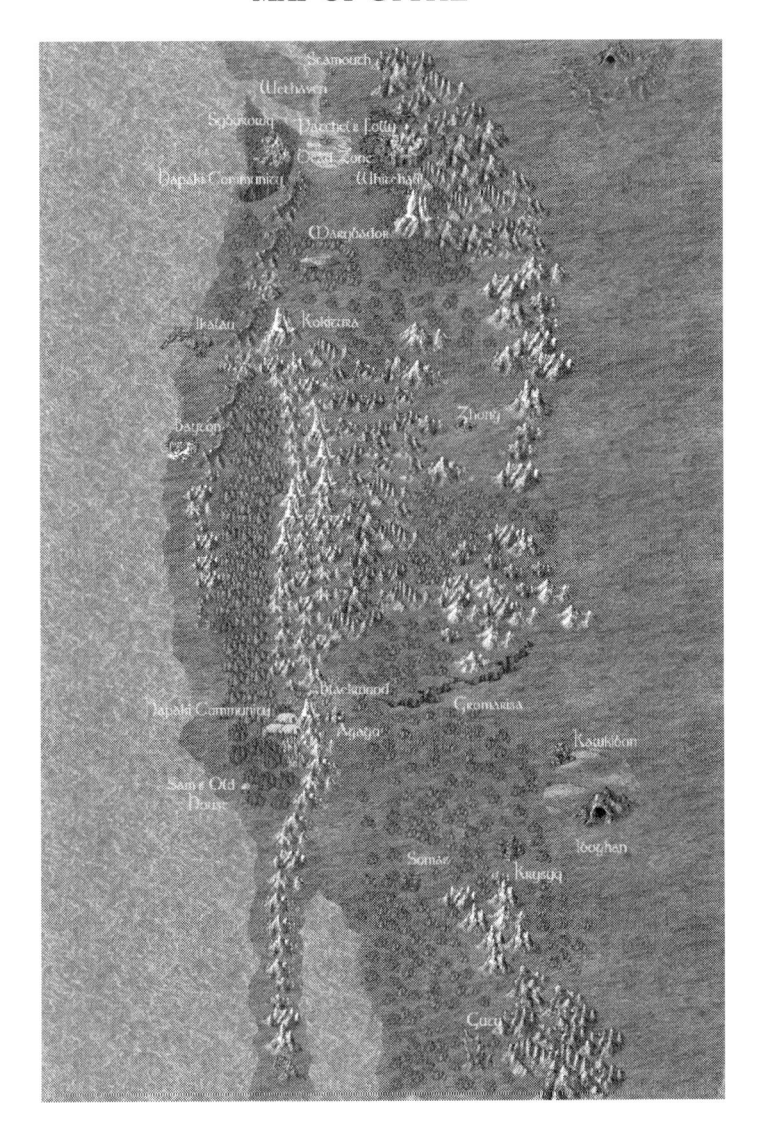

MAP OF GYTHE
Detail – North

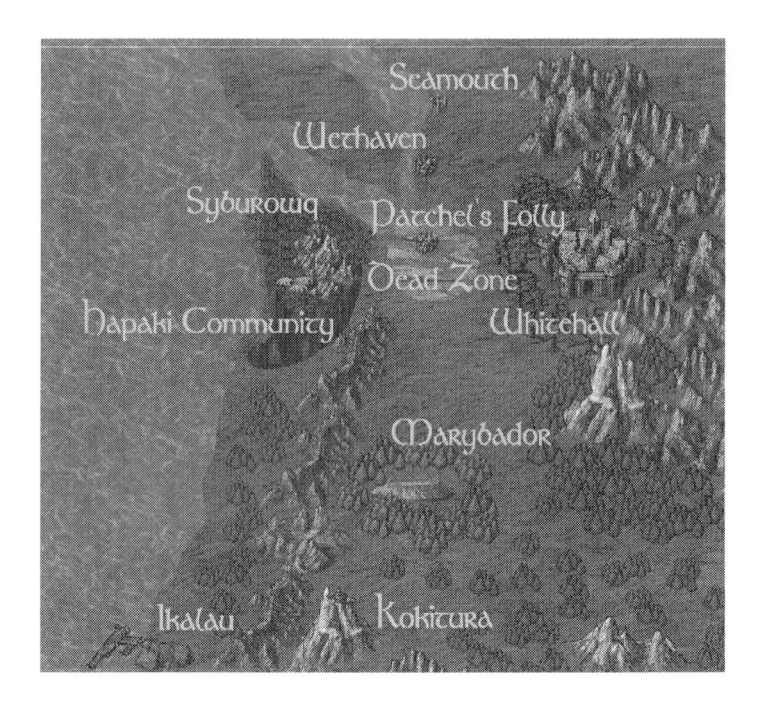

Seamouth
Wethaven
Syburowq *Patchel's Folly*
Dead Zone
Hapaki Community *Whitehall*
Marybador
Ikalau *Kokitura*

MAP OF GYTHE
Detail – Central

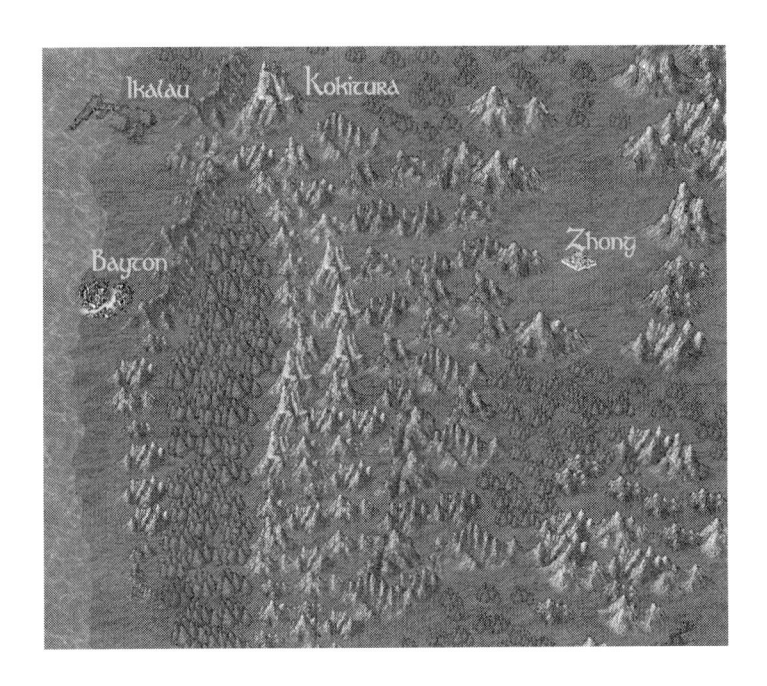

MAP OF GYTHE
Detail – South

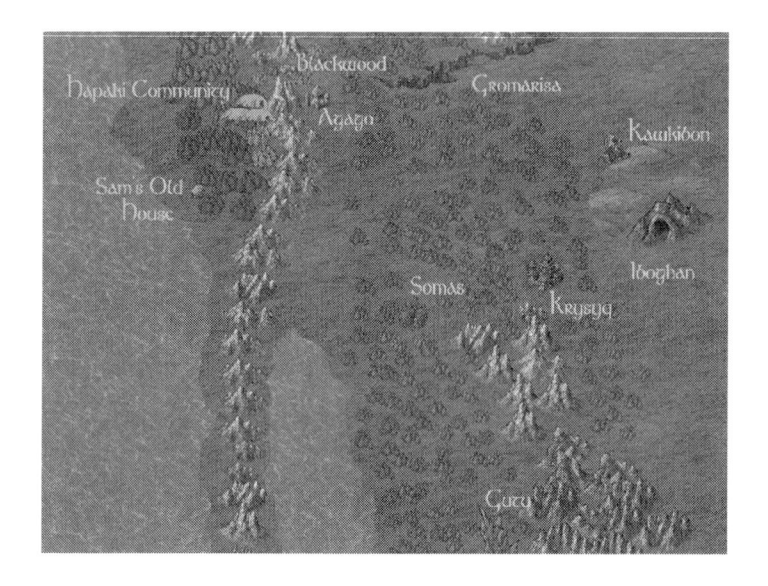

*Darkness is a part of life, as much a part as light is
Embrace the darkness as you embrace the light
and it cannot gain mastery over you.*

> Zouyim Master Chetra Dal,
>
> *The Twelve Forms of the Wind*

*The fool stumbles about in the dark, but the wise man
lights the candle.*

> Zouyim Master Rindu Zose

Prologue

The cold stone was implacable as Ayim Rasaad pushed her body against it, trying to melt into the wall. The more she thought about it, the more the sound she had just heard seemed to have been a scream. Not a woman's scream, though. A man's. It was full of pain…and terror. Somehow, she knew it wasn't just someone being tortured in the dungeon. Her senses were tingling. Something was not right.

Swallowing hard against the dry lump in her throat, she edged her way down the hallway, sticking to the shadows lest she be seen and become prey, like the screamer. She didn't plan on making her first night in the Arzbedim fortress her last in this world.

That was who she was here to see, the Arzbedim, the a group of powerful energy users who were once Zouyim monks. Their craving for power had caused them to split off from the Zouyim temple and form their own order. Both groups used the *rohw*, the vibrational energy that the common people called magic, but while the Arzbedim pursued their own selfish goals, their former brothers always put others first, protecting and serving the citizens of Gythe. Leaving the Zouyim to join the Arzbedim was betrayal of the most serious kind. But that was unimportant right now. Danger was about.

There was a feeling in the air, an awkward hum, almost like the entire fortress was shaking so subtly that one could only catch it on individual hairs, such as the fine strands on Ayim Rasaad's arms that seemed to be standing on end and waving in a non-existent breeze. She didn't like it.

Rasaad looked down the darkened corridor, just a few feet from the secret door she had used to enter the fortress. Silicim Mant, leader of the Arzbedim himself, had given her instructions on how to secretly enter the fortress. He had promised to meet her and welcome her into the order, to discuss with her at length what she would be expected to do. But he was not where he should have been, not waiting where they were to meet, at the opening into this hallway. What could have held him up?

The Zouyim defector was probably being paranoid, even silly. Silicim Mant was a busy man. If he was running late, so what? It was meaningless. She could be patient and wait for a few minutes before searching him out. She had met several of the Arzbedim before as they groomed her for inclusion into their order. She would not be accosted for remaining here and waiting for her contact.

But what about that feeling? What about the scream? What about the unnatural silence that punctuated and emphasized the shrieking like someone shouting directly into her ear? What of that? She could argue herself in circles, but she didn't like it. Her instincts were telling her that there was danger, death stalking the cold, drafty corridors of the Black Fortress.

Ayim Rasaad's fingers were going numb, the cold radiating into her wrists, making them ache. She pulled her hands from the wall and brought them to her mouth, silently breathing on them and rubbing them together. She could feel the stone leaching the warmth from her body where her back still touched the corridor wall, even through the clothing and cloak she wore.

This was getting her nowhere. She would simply stride down the corridor until she found someone and then demand to be shown to Silicim Mant. She had been invited by the Arzbedim leader, after all. Yes, that was what she would do. She would not skulk in the shadows awaiting his pleasure.

Taking a deep breath, she rocked herself into a straighter posture several inches from the cold stone. She lifted her left foot to begin walking and froze. Was that a footstep? Did she actually just hear a sound, or was she imagining it? Maybe it would be best to wait for the owner of the foot to come to her. Yes, that would be the best option. She was not afraid. It was just logical that she not jump out and scare the person coming toward her. She leaned back against the wall once more, slipping back into shadow.

The soft footfalls came closer. Rasaad thought that maybe she saw a darkness projected on the rough granite, but it was difficult to tell in the dimly lit corridor. There. She was sure she saw something, the penumbra of a shadow, a slight darkening and distortion of the straight lines of the wall. A breath later and she saw the bald white head of Silicim Mant coming from an intersecting corridor. She breathed out a sigh of relief and started to step from the deep shadow in which she stood.

The red-rimmed black eyes of Silicim Mant went wide and he made a sound that was somewhere between a gasp and a wheeze. Then, he dropped onto his face on the stone and remained motionless. Ayim Rasaad froze, standing still as a statue in the shadows. She had seen a glow just before Mant fell, the telltale sign that *rohw* was being used. By reflex, she used a talent that had served her well in the past, a little trick that she was born with. She folded in on herself mentally, becoming invisible to vibration-sensitive sight.

She had learned early on in her training in the Zouyim temple that she was able to do this. It was a little thing, and useless for the most part, but she had played with it, practiced it, and refined it to such an extent that when she was younger, she was never found in the games of hide-and-seek the masters had the disciples play to increase their *rohw* sensitivity, the sensitivity to the vibrational energy used by the Zouyim and the Arzbedim.

When she used her ability, she showed virtually no vibration or any hint of vibratory powers that could be recognized by other energy users. She had come a long way from hide-and-seek champion to where she was now, and this small ability might just save her life this night.

"It's nothing personal, you understand," a rich voice, laden with vibratory power said to the body lying on the floor. "It is merely something necessary, though if there was one with whom I would take my time in prolonging his suffering, it would be you."

Hiding in a shadow that seemed much too thin to act as the shield she needed, Ayim Rasaad looked carefully toward the visible piece of the speaker, peering out of the corner of her eye to prevent him from seeing the white of her orb. He looked similar to the other Arzbedim—pale and completely hairless from manipulating dark energies—but more ragged. He was thin and wearing clothes that were too baggy on him, as if they belonged to someone else entirely. She had never seen him before, but that wasn't saying much. She had only seen a handful of the Arzbedim.

The tense seconds dragged on. The man cocked his bald, white head slightly, as if listening. No, as if catching the barest hint of a scent. His eyes softened and went out of focus, then flared briefly. With a slow, soft nod, he turned on his heels and headed back the way he had come, quick footsteps retreating down the hallway. Before

Rasaad was able to take a step, she heard another surprised grunt and scream, cut off as immediately as it had started.

She was not sure what was going on, but she had just seen the leader of the Arzbedim, the most powerful enemy of the Zouyim order, killed in less than a second with barely more than a thought. Some foe, it seemed, was going through the fortress and purging it of life, if what she had heard was any indication. This was no place for her to be.

Slowly, ever so slowly, she inched her way along the wall, pressing her body up against the shadows while trying to ignore the cold that not only radiated from the stone but now came from within as well. Her breaths came in stuttering gasps, threatening to make her hyperventilate, but she wrestled them under control and forced herself to breathe in, breathe out, and try to relax. She was almost to the secret door now. It was her escape, her salvation. A few more inches.

She had never been so scared in all her life. During her fifteen years at the Zouyim temple, she had prepared for every situation, always with the focus on remaining calm, at peace. Life-giving breath was a staple for a Zouyim monk, and she had thought that nothing could phase her, nothing could cause fear to sink its paralyzing tentacles into her as long as she could breathe deeply of the life-giving air. She had been wrong.

When an agent of the Arzbedim had contacted her three years earlier, she thought she would finally be able to learn all the secrets that had been kept from her. She was pushing, always pushing, trying to learn more and more, but the masters held her back. When the Arzbedim offered her a place among them, she jumped at the opportunity. She had proven her worth, her loyalty, over the last three years by spying on the Zouyim activities, informing the Arzbedim and now, tonight, she was finally to join them officially.

She had left the Zouyim temple to join her new

brotherhood, and had been given instructions on how to find the secret passage and directions to meet with Silicim Mant himself. She thought she had finally achieved her goal, finally found a way to unlock the secrets to the *rohw*, the vibratory energy she had been learning to use for so long. She would truly become a master now.

But it was clear that was not to be. In fact, if she couldn't get to the secret passageway and escape, she too may end up face-down on the cold stone floor like the ex-leader of the Arzbedim. Anyone with the power to kill such a powerful *rohw*-user instantly was not someone she wanted to deal with. She would escape and figure things out after she was safe. Just a step or two more now…

She reached out and swung the secret door—which she had not closed all the way—open. Quickly slipping inside the passage, she closed the door behind her and made no sound as she shuffled a dozen feet before leaning hard against the corridor wall. She closed her eyes and took a very deep breath, held it, and then exhaled. The ex-Zouyim repeated this three more times before she stopped shaking so violently that her teeth were chattering. Now she was merely trembling.

Taking one more deep breath, she straightened her back, softened her gaze so she could use her aura to guide her in the pitch black corridor, and made her way back outside the walls of the fortress. She knew she had narrowly averted being killed in the most ignominious of ways and she was thankful. With the Arzbedim dead and the Zouyim no doubt aware of her betrayal by now, she did not know what she would do. She was alive, though, which meant she had at least a little more time to figure it out.

1

As was his habit, Sam Sharp was up before the sun rose. Sitting on the back porch of his small home, he greeted the sunrise in meditation. Eyes closed, his breathing deep and regular, he heard the sounds of the forest waking up behind the buffer of his almost-trance. *Khulim* was what his teacher, Rindu Zose, had called the condition. It was just shy of being in a trance, body completely relaxed, mind focused inward on nothing, awareness of the surroundings complete but muted so as not to distract. There was no better way to start the day, Sam thought.

Half an hour later, the sun was visible just above the horizon and Sam rose to his feet. He took a deep breath, the scent of the cold forest filling his nose. Wet leaves, moist earth, pine bark, and fresh clean air. Smiling, he started slowly jogging toward his destination.

It was not quite spring, so by all rights it should have been colder, but he was glad it wasn't. It had been relatively warm and dry lately and there was not much left of the snow that fell a week ago. His muscles quickly warmed up as he plodded around his training area for one, two, three laps, gradually increasing his speed. When he stopped and stretched his now-warm muscles, there was a sheen of perspiration on his skin that reflected the diffused morning light.

Feeling loose and warm and powerful, he began his daily routine. He had built a training area on the forty acres of forested land he owned. The area included obstacle courses, martial arts training devices, and general fitness equipment, some of which he had invented and built himself.

It had been about a year and a half since he had returned from his adventure and his life could not have been more different than before he left. He had been living in the desert in Southern California; now he was living in a forest in Southern Oregon. He had been working at a warehouse; now he didn't need to work because of the gold he had been given. He had always enjoyed physical activity, but now he had brought it to a new level.

His adventure had taken him to another world, Gythe. It was another dimension, really, sharing the same physical space as his own world but vibrating at a different frequency. It had been an accident that he was even able to go there, but once there, he had learned many things, not the least of which was combat. He had learned about vibrational energy, too—it was called *rohw* there—and had come to realize that he had a knack for it. When he had finally come home, he knew that things for him would never be the same as they had been.

Bringing his mind back from its wanderings, he paid closer attention to what he was doing. Jumping up on the first of two dozen wooden posts set in the ground—their height above the ground differing—he hopped one-footed from post to post. He flowed smoothly over them, barely breaking stride. Jumping off the final post high into the air, he tucked into a tight ball and turned a perfect flip, landing lightly on his feet. As his feet touched the ground, he collapsed his right knee and smoothly turned his momentum into a shoulder roll, coming back up almost instantly, running to the next obstacle.

He dove through the small opening between movable bars—they could be adjusted vertically and horizontally to increase or decrease the opening size and the window was set so it was just barely bigger than his body—not even grazing the bars, landing in a roll and regaining his feet.

Next was a series of horizontal bars. Sam jumped up and grabbed the first. His forward momentum was enough to allow him to swing, release immediately, and grab onto the next, higher bar. He swung his body up, pulling at the perfect time while bending his body around so that he ended crouched with his feet on top of the bars and his hands still gripping in between them for balance.

Pushing away strongly with his feet, he launched himself to the next bar, which was at the same height as the one he was standing on, ten feet from the soft forest floor. He kept the nearby trees trimmed carefully so as not to interfere with his obstacles, but their height and lush foliage made it so that the entire area was normally heavily shaded. It was only partially so now, since fully half the trees had lost their leaves for the season. Only the evergreens sprawling overhead showed their verdant hues, though some of the other trees seemed to be sprouting.

He landed with his feet on the next bar and immediately sprung to the next, and the next. He jumped precisely, landing on three more bars until he dove at another, this one vertical. He grabbed it with both hands as he passed. Spiraling around the bar, he released his grip and flew back the way he had come, toward a crowd of hanging wooden targets in the shape of small logs. The targets were two feet long, hanging from ropes at different heights. He struck them as he passed, a side kick to this one, a punch, an elbow strike, a crescent kick, followed by a spinning back kick as the small log swung away from him.

Making it through the targets, he jumped onto the balance rail. It was three feet off the ground and twenty-five feet long. There were three such rails, all parallel and spaced five feet apart. He ran quickly down the first and, when he got to the end, jumped over to the next one. On this one, he planted his right hand and began a series of cartwheeleds until he reached the end. Instead of leaping to the next one, he dove up into the air and across to it, landing with both hands on the two-inch-wide rail in a perfectly balanced handstand. Shuffling his hands while holding the handstand, he moved down the length of the rail. When he got to the end, he stopped, tightened his body, and then lifted his left hand in the air, holding a one-handed handstand for ten seconds. Flipping gracefully to his feet on the ground, he moved on.

When he finished the remaining obstacles, he moved over to the striking target area. Here, he had bags of differing weights set up for power training, along with many moving targets to practice precision strikes. Before long, he was sweating profusely and felt his muscles burning.

Sam dropped to the ground and sat motionless in a loose cross-legged position. He paused there, breathing and slowing his heart rate to a more normal pace. Just a moment before he caught movement out of the edge of his vision, he sensed a presence. His adversary moved silently, but he had trained himself to sense and notice things that were out of the ordinary since he had returned to this world. He would not be caught unaware.

With lightning speed, he vaulted to his feet in time to meet his attacker before a blow could be struck. Kicks and punches came at him with blinding rapidity but he parried the first few aside and then stepped out of range to render others harmles. He slipped a few of the subsequent blows, letting them barely graze his skin, before he attempted to trap the striking arm. However, his assailant was too skilled to be trapped.

Realizing defense would not give him victory, Sam went on the offensive. Twisting to avoid a front kick that transformed into a side kick in the blink of an eye, he jabbed with his left hand and then came around with his right in a hook punch that should have been outside the attacker's field of vision. A flick of the combatant's elbow deflected the punch so that it narrowly missed the head, going up and over and putting Sam at a disadvantage.

He immediately shifted the course of the punch to strike the assailant's face with his elbow while throwing an uppercut with his left hand and attempting a knee strike with the right leg. His adversary, using the arm that had deflected the hook punch, punched his elbow, sending electricity shooting up his arm; caught the uppercut with the other hand; and shifted slightly so that the knee strike passed harmlessly to the side.

Then, without hesitation, the assailant grabbed Sam's tingling arm, twisted it up with the failed uppercut, and spun Sam around like a top, causing him to spiral outward because of the force and pain in his shoulders. He spun in the air and landed hard on his back with a loud huff, looking at the bright blue sky and the wispy clouds passing by, just visible through a break in the pine boughs above him.

"Ow," he said, when he was finally able to get his breath back. "That was awesome. Can you show me that?"

Nalia reached her hand out and helped him up. "If I showed you, then how would I use it against you again? Do not be ridiculous."

Sam came to his feet with a smile and a groan. He wrapped his arms around Nalia and squeezed. "Fine. I'll just have to think it through. I'm sure I'll figure it out."

She smiled at him, flawless white teeth flashing in the morning sun. Looking at her, he was struck again, as he had been thousands of times before, by how perfect she was. Her chestnut-colored hair was gathered in a pony tail hanging down her back to keep it from getting in the way. Her eyes, blue one moment and pale green the next, looked into his own blue-gray eyes. Her delicate face, oval-shaped and the perfect mix of soft curves and strong features, still took his breath away. Her nose, which he found adorable, crinkled slightly as her perfect lips formed a smirk.

Yeah, he had it bad. She could have asked him to walk into a bear trap and he wouldn't think twice about it until it snapped around his leg. He smiled back and took her hand.

"So, now that we've had our little workout, what's on the agenda for today?" he asked as they turned and walked toward the house.

"We must go into town to get some things. And we need to talk about returning to Gythe."

"Yeah." Sam stopped, forcing her to stop or release his hand. She stopped. "We'll have to talk to my mom. I'm not sure how she'll react to it."

Those perfect lips made a straight line. "Sam, I do not think it will be as big a problem as you predict. We will get the things we need and then talk to her when we return."

"I know you don't think so," he said, "but *I* think it's a big deal. I'm the only one she has, the only one in the world. She didn't know I was gone that last time I was in Gythe because time flows differently in the two worlds and it hardly passed here while I was there. If it was the same, I would have been missing for months and it would have killed her."

"Yes, but that is because you simply disappeared. We will tell her this time. She will know where you have gone. It is different."

"Maybe." He ran his fingers through his hair, as he always did when worrying about something. "I'm just nervous about it. What if she really takes it hard, feels like we're giving her no choice? Or abandoning her? I love her, Nal, but she sometimes reacts to things differently than I'd ever think. Just look at what she did when my dad died when I was very young. She cut all ties with every friend and family member we had and moved us to the other side of the country."

"Oh, Sam," Nalia put her hands on either side of his face and looked into his eyes, "do not worry overmuch. Your mother is not as she was back then. We will discuss it with her and then you will see if there are problems. Does that not sound reasonable?"

"Okay," he said. "I guess that sounds good to me. Do you mind if I stay here while you go to town? I have some work to do."

Nalia pulled him toward her and drew him into a hug. "We will do the shopping. Do your work and we will talk with your mother later. Do not hurt yourself doing your work. You are a clumsy oaf, after all."

It was an old joke, one that made him feel warm inside. "I know. It's a good thing I have you and mom to look after me."

*****

Nalia Wroun watched Sam head out to his workshop. She had spent almost the last two years with him, first in her home on Gythe, and now here. He was precious to her and became more so every day. She loved to look into his blue-gray eyes, to run her fingers through his short blond hair. Well, she liked to run her fingers through it if he did not put the sticky stuff in it to make it stay in place. She still could not understand why people here did things like that.

The point, though, was that she was happy here with him. Happier than she could remember being for many years. She felt as if she belonged with him, wherever that may be. Yet, she missed her father. And truth be told, she missed Dr. Walt, too, that lanky old scholar.

"Are you ready to go?" Nicole Sharp asked Nalia, interrupting her memories.

"Yes, I am."

The other woman looked around. "Uh-oh. Sam isn't

going, is he? How did he get out of it this time? What's his excuse?" She winked as she said it.

"He has work to do in his workshop."

"Ah, the workshop." She laughed, her voice tinkling like the wind chimes Sam had made for her.

Nalia liked her laugh. She liked Nicole. She had become almost as a mother to her, as well as a cherished friend. She looked over at the older woman. For a woman of fifty years, especially in this world, she was in fantastic shape. She did something called yoga that kept her body firm and slender. Her hair, almost as dark as Nalia's, framed her face in a pleasing way, much like the round picture frames Sam had scattered throughout their house. Her skin, taut with but the smallest of wrinkles around the eyes and the corners of her mouth, was cream-colored and flawless. Her blue eyes were expressive, much as Sam's were, and that lopsided half-smile Sam often wore could trace its roots to his mother. Her face reminded Nalia of the pixies Sam had told her about and shown her pictures of in some of the old mythology books he had, and her personality was pixie-like, too. Yes, Nalia had great affection for this woman with whom she had spent the last year and a half.

"What?" Nicole Sharp asked.

"What, what?" Nalia answered and then paused. "Oh, I am sorry. Was answering your question with another question disrespectful?" She had adopted some mannerisms and phrases since she had been on this world that probably would have been frowned upon by her father and the other Zouyim. It was difficult to know if "slang" was respectful or rude sometimes.

"No, it's fine. You were looking at me quizzically just then. Do I have something on my face?"

"No, no. You do not," Nalia rushed out. "I was merely noticing your smile when you teased me about Sam. He wears that smile often."

Nicole sighed. "I know. It's infuriating, isn't it? Makes

him look like he's always up to something. His father had a smile like that, as did my brother. It must run in the family."

Nalia was at a loss at what to say. "Uh, yes. Perhaps it is so."

Nicole laughed and hugged the other woman. "Oh, I'm just teasing you. I know I wield that smile like a sword. No disrespect to those of you who actually do wield swords."

Nalia laughed. She was one of the *Sapsyra Shin Elah*—the name meant "dagger of God" in Old Kasmali—an order of women warriors on Gythe, called the finest combatants in the world by those who knew of such things. As far as she was aware, she was the last of the Sapsyra still alive. Nicole knew her background and had seen the swords that were her favorite weapons.

The two women climbed into the truck and headed off to the small town fifteen miles away, chatting amiably. Sam would see, Nalia thought. There would be no problem with discussing their trip to Gythe with his mother. She was sure of it. Mostly.

2

Sam put the finishing touches on his current project and took a shower just in time for the girls to get back from town. He helped unload and put away what they got and helped in the kitchen while his mother made them some dinner. She didn't normally allow him to cook because it was one of her great loves. She always said she would die in the kitchen, and would do so happily.

An enjoyable, relaxed meal followed and when everything was put away and cleaned up, the three sat around the living room to talk.

"I had a confrontation today with one of the men in town," Nalia said without preamble.

Sam looked at her blankly, not quite knowing what to say. "You...you had a confrontation? What exactly does that mean?" He looked back and forth between his mother and Nalia. He was sure the confusion was evident on his face.

Before Nalia could say another word, Nicole spoke. "Harold, that guy I told you about who has been asking me to go out on a date with him, he was there are the grocery store."

"Oh, yeah, I remember you talking about it. He's what, in his mid 30s? He's a good-looking guy. I don't know why you won't give him a chance. I think it's a compliment that someone so much younger is interested in you."

The look his mother gave him told him volumes about what he had just said and how wrong it was. Her arched eyebrows and furrowed brow made him feel uneasy, like he was a child in trouble. He swallowed loudly. "Sorry," was all he could think to say.

"As I was saying," she eyed him sternly and he caught a small smile on Nalia's face to the side and behind his mother, "he has been more and more insistent. He's got a crush on me, that's plain. And yes, it does feel nice that men, much younger men at that, are interested. He's not the only one, by the way, but it's a small town and maybe their options are limited."

She waved the idea away. "Anyway, he was bugging me about going out on a date—again—and I was politely declining. I told him we had to go and he grabbed my shoulder. Not hard, just a soft, pleading action."

Sam saw where this was going and feared for the worst. "Oh no," he whispered.

"I did not hurt him," Nalia said, then added, "much," as if she were saying she bought lettuce while at the store.

Nicole laughed. "Don't worry, what she says is true. She grabbed his arm, did something where she twisted his fingers, and his feet left the ground as he did a complete flip and landed flat on his back in the grocery aisle. Still twisting his fingers, which seemed to cause him more than a little pain, she made him apologize for touching me and then promise never to do so again unless specifically asked by me."

Sam shook his head and then put it into his hands. "Did you seriously hurt him?" he asked Nalia.

"No, it is as I said. I merely subdued him. He was surprised and the joint lock on his fingers caused him discomfort, but after he got up, he walked away without too much limping. He will be fine, but he will think again if he ever intends to touch Nicole in the future."

Sam's mother looked fondly at Nalia and then shifted her gaze to Sam, eyes softening and mouth twitching into a subtle smirk. "He's fine. While I think maybe it was a bit extreme, it had the intended effect. I don't think he'll be bugging me anymore. Definitely not when Nalia is around. She's my bodyguard." She squeezed Nalia's shoulder and smiled at her.

Nalia's firm nod was Sam's cue that this conversation was over. "Okay, well, now that that's out of the way, we need to talk about something."

Sam looked at his mother and started. "Mom, you know the whole story about how I met Nalia, how I accidentally transported myself to Gythe, how I traveled that world that occupies the same space as ours but in a different dimension, with a different vibratory frequency." Her nod was almost imperceptible.

"Well, Nalia and I have been talking about it. We've been back from Gythe for almost a year and a half now and we both love it here in our little house in the trees, but she misses her father, Rindu. With the way time passes differently in the two worlds, she's afraid that he may be close to death from old age.

"After all, I was there for about seven months and when I returned here, only a few hours had passed. How many years have passed since we left there?"

He ran his fingers through his hair and sighed. "Basically, what I'm trying to say is that we want to go back to Gythe. What's more, we're thinking maybe we won't just go to visit. We're thinking we may want to stay there. Live there. The only thing is…"

Nicoles eyes widened and her face lit up with her smile. "I think that's a great idea. Can I come too?"

Sam stopped mid-breath and looked at his mother, then to Nalia, and then back to his mother. "Come again?"

Nicole took Sam's hand. "I asked if I could come too.

You know, go to Gythe. Live there. With you."

"I...um...but...it's kind of primitive there." He saw a sharp look from Nalia and hurried on. "I mean, technologically. There aren't any modern conveniences. Electricity, stoves, cell phones. None of it."

Squeezing his hand, Nicole continued softly. "Honey, I know what it's like there. We've talked about it enough. You and Nalia have told me all about it. I do like my modern conveniences, but anywhere we're together is home to me. I love the trees, love living in them here. According to all you've told me, Gythe sounds like a huge forest. I think I could adapt."

"That's great," Sam said with a sigh of relief. "I was afraid that you'd stay here and I'd feel bad about leaving you. I don't know why I was so nervous about talking to you about it. I think maybe my guilt just made me afraid."

Nalia mouthed, "I told you so" from across the room. Sam made a shooing motion with his hand.

"I'm sure you knew I'd want to go. You always have overanalyzed everything." She kissed the top of his head. "So, when do we leave?"

Sam, Nalia, and Nicole bustled around the house, packing things and trying to figure out what they would need close at hand and what could be packed away for later use. Sam had given it a lot of thought and decided that he would be able to, with Nalia's help, transport his house and workshop both to Gythe. It was a matter of including the structures and the air around them, as well as everything within the radius of the vibratory field he would set up. He hoped it would work.

As he got ready for his trip, he thought back to the last sixteen months or so. He had quickly melted down the gold ingots they brought back from Gythe—gold was worthless there—and formed it into smaller chunks that could be sold. The last several years, places were popping up everywhere offering to buy gold jewelry and other gold scrap for cash. With the money, Sam paid off his mother's house.

His own house he sold with just a touch of sadness. He loved that little place, but he would no longer need it. They would be moving to where there were more trees, to Southern Oregon, very near where the Sapsyra headquarters were on Gythe. That area was approximately where Crater Lake was here on Earth. In Kasmali, the language spoken on Gythe, the world from which Sam came was called Telani, meaning "shadow." Apparently, people on Gythe had known about Earth and had named it accordingly, a shadow to their own world.

While his mother stayed home and prepared to rent her house out to a close friend when she moved up north with Sam and Nalia, the two took a road trip to look for property.

Along the way, Nalia marveled at everything Telani had that Gythe didn't. The desert, a strange thing to her because her world had much more forest, was fascinating to her while the beautiful ocean views from the highway they traveled didn't seem to be all that interesting because she had seen the same coast in her homeland.

The cities were a wonder to her. She literally walked around with her mouth open, staring at the structures, the numbers of people, the clothing. She had gotten used to the thought of electricity, appliances, transportation, and other conveniences, but the sight of the Golden Gate Bridge spanning the familiar narrow opening to the bay in San Francisco made her goggle.

Sam could understand. When they passed through the city of Bayton on Gythe, he had the same reaction, but for the opposite reason. He could only stare at where the bridge he was used to seeing in Telani sat, but in Gythe, there was no hint of any structure ever having been there. It was unsettling.

Sam suggested to Nalia that they visit Chinatown in San Francisco, wanting to pick up some things. She agreed excitedly and they set out to wander the streets.

They made their way down the street, gawking at the buildings, the people, the different world that was nothing like anything Nalia had ever experienced. Even Sam, who had lived in this world his whole life, recognized this was like no place he'd ever been. It wasn't even like the rest of San Francisco, which he had visited before.

As they made their way under the Dragon Gate, Nalia tightened her grip on Sam's hand. Her head darted back and forth, taking in the sights, sounds, and smells. Sam looked into her eyes, which were alight with excitement. He squeezed her hand and started them down Grant Avenue, toward the heart of Chinatown.

There were many shops that had exotic items, but they both agreed that their favorites were martial arts related. When they walked into one small shop and saw the weapons lining the wall, Nalia's sudden inrush of air made Sam look at her quizzically. "What? What's wrong?" he asked her.

"Are those shrapezi? Do they exist here, too?" She was pointing toward a pair of weapons mounted on the wall, crossed and glinting dully in the overhead light.

Sam knew they were called hook swords here on Telani. They were about as long as the distance from his shoulder to the tips of his fingers if he spread his arm out straight. They were swords, yes, but different in form than what most people would consider a sword to be.

The longest part of the sword was straight with a curved section of blade on one side, looking somewhat like a shepherd's crook, but with sharpened edges. The other side ended in a triangular sharpened point. A hand span above the spike was a crescent that guarded the hand and provided more sharpened edges and two wicked points. The handle consisted only of thick cord wrapped around the main section of the sword underneath the crescent. Other than the wrapped handle, every other surface on the sword was sharpened. At least, it could be. Sam could tell that these hook swords were sharpened only on a few areas, such as the hook itself and one side of the main section of the blade.

Nalia's shrapezi, the weapons she used on Gythe, looked exactly the same as the hook swords, but they were very high quality steel and razor sharp. Sam had seen her remove limbs and even heads from enemies with those weapons. She was a master with them.

"They're called hook swords here," Sam told her. "I've seen very skilled martial artists use them in demonstrations, but none of them have near your mastery of them."

Her mouth quirked into a smile and she hugged him briefly. She knew she was a master at combat, but it never hurt to remind her that he knew it, too.

Realizing that the weapons were much inferior to hers, she moved on, studying the other weapons displayed. When she got to the glass case with the more conventional swords, she turned to Sam.

"It is amazing to me how much steel there is in this world. Just the items in this shop alone would be worth enough to buy a large city on Gythe."

Sam knew what she was talking about. Because of the unique vibrational frequency of the world of Gythe, steel was…problematic to make. Iron was softer on that world, for some reason, and it did not readily alloy with carbon sources to make steel. Her swords alone were worth enough to buy a village, or to live in luxury for a lifetime. Most edged weapons on Gythe were made of either bronze or a ceramic glass that was much stronger than should be possible, staying razor sharp for years, and durable besides.

"Steel is common here. There are people here who would pay a lot of money for the ceramic blades from Gythe, though. Each world has its benefits."

She was already moving on. "Oh, those swords are magnificent!" Nalia said, pointing toward a pair of classic twin Chinese broadswords. They had wide curving blades, sharp on one side, shaped somewhat like a pirate cutlass. The wooden handles were separated from the blade by a large half-oval handguard and had a bright red scarf attached to the end. The swords fit together so they could be wielded as one sword and fit into the same scabbard. "May I see them?" she asked the clerk, a small, older Chinese man with a mole on his face that had three wiry hairs at least six inches long coming out of it. Sam had trouble keeping his eyes focused on the man's eyes without them straying to the hair quivering slightly in the breeze of the fan sitting on the counter.

"Of course, of course," the man said with a strong accent. "Very good steel. Very sharp. Old swords, antiques."

Nalia picked up the sword the man offered to her. "They are balanced well and the handle is firm, not loose."

"Full tang. Sword is hand-made, in the old way. Very good blade. Belonged to Master Ho Win Po. You know Master Ho? Very famous."

Sam studied the man as he talked with Nalia. He expected a hard sell, having visited the Chinatown in Los Angeles several times. This man was sincere, though, Sam thought.

"I am sorry," Nalia told him, "I have not heard of Master Ho. Why were his swords not handed down to his sons or daughters?"

The man's long white hair, swished as he bowed his head toward Nalia. "Very sad. Master Ho had cancer, died at only fifty-five years old. Had no sons, no daughters. He came to America and so there was no temple, no school to leave weapons to. They were sold to pay medical bills."

"That is unfortunate," Nalia told him, her eyes softly holding the man's. She seemed to have no trouble in keeping eye contact. The man saw her sincerity and bowed his head to her again. Sam decided he liked the man.

The two stayed in the shop for half an hour, chatting with the store clerk and looking at his wares. When they left, they were carrying the two broadswords and had significantly less money. If Sam hadn't trusted the man by the time they left, he never would have spent so much. He departed satisfied with the purchase. They were magnificent swords.

As Sam and Nalia left the shop, Sam narrowly avoided colliding with an older Chinese man on the crowded sidewalk. "Pardon me, I'm sorry," Sam told him as the older man deftly dodged out of the way.

Sam stopped and looked at him. He seemed familiar in some way. Realizing he had been staring at the man for a good ten seconds, and that the man was staring back at him, he felt himself flush. He couldn't place what it was, but he felt some sort of connection, a kinship to the man. Embarrassed, he turned and started to follow Nalia down the street.

"Excuse me, sir," the man said to him. "Are you a Sifu, a Sigong?"

Sam turned back to him. The man was probably not even five and a half feet tall, had a full head of pure white hair, cut short, and a kindly face. His Asian features; the eyes, nose, and cheekbones, were softened somewhat from others he had seen during the day. Sam thought he was probably not full-blooded Chinese, but had other ethnicities mixed in. He still couldn't place why the man looked so familiar. "I'm sorry, what?" Sam said.

"Oh, I was wondering if you were a kung fu master. Your chi is strong. I can feel it from where I'm standing."

"Chi?" Nalia asked.

"It's the name we use here for *rohw*. It's how kung fu practitioners here refer to internal energy," Sam answered her. "Chi, ki, mana, prana, they're all names for the same thing, the 'breath' or internal energy." Sam had researched the subject in the past, when he first became interested in meditation.

Turning back to the man, Sam answered him. "No, I am no master. I have studied chi and have tried to develop it, but I am no master."

The man brought his hand to his face and rubbed his chin. "I see. Yet, you have strong chi. Both of you. It's rare to find such power in two who are so young. To my eyes, you are glowing brightly among the throngs of people flooding the street."

He considered for a moment, then continued, "Would you do me the honor of sitting and having tea with me? I would like to talk to you of your training. Perhaps we can trade information, if anything a lowly old man like myself can offer is worthwhile."

Before Sam could say anything, Nalia bowed formally to the man. "We would be honored to share tea with you. Would it be amiss to ask your name?"

The man returned her bow, holding his hands one inside the other in a salute. "Of course not, my apologies for my rudeness. I am Li Jun Fan."

After Sam and Nalia introduced themselves, they followed the man as he headed out of the tourist area and toward the part of Chinatown where the locals both lived and did their business.

The man was silent, moving with a grace and elegance that was almost mesmerizing. "Look at how he moves," Nalia whispered to Sam. "He is a master at combat. Do you see him glow, the power of his *rohw* ability?"

Sam could. He was surprised at first when he came back from Gythe and found that his *rohw* abilities and sensitivity were severely limited. He thought something had happened to him, but Nalia commented on it also. They decided that because of all the technology and the destruction of much of the natural forests in the world, the vibrational energy on Telani was suppressed. They could still sense the *rohw*, use it, but it was weaker than on Gythe. Even with it weaker, he found that he could see a glow now, when he softened his gaze and tried. Maybe that's why he felt a connection to the man. Maybe he wasn't really familiar but Sam was drawn to him because of their connection to the universal energy. Still, there was something about his face…

"Yes, I can." Sam smiled. The man reminded him of Rindu, Nalia's father, a Zouyim monk and master with the internal energy. The Zouy was the one who had taught Sam to use his *rohw*. He was looking forward to conversing with this man.

They made their way to a narrow street with buildings that rose up sharply on either side. Entering a small doorway, they headed up a rickety staircase to a hallway so cramped that Sam could barely walk without brushing one of his shoulders against the wall. Li Jun Fan stopped at the third door on the left, took out a key, and unlocked the door.

"Please," he said, gesturing for them to go in.

Sam's eyes widened as he stepped through the door. The room was not what he expected based on the hallway and stairway. It was spacious, as large as his living room at home, with the entry to the kitchen tucked off in a corner and a hallway to another part of the apartment off to the right. It was decorated in a classic Eastern style with furniture consisting of graceful curves and lines, with heavy lacquering. The chests of drawers, display cases, and benches covered by soft-looking cushions were arranged to leave the central area clear.

A small table contained a large pot-like incense holder filled with sand. Sticks of incense, some half-burned, protruded from it like tiny sentinels. On the floor, an ornate woven rug completed the picture, its red and black designs swirling around each other in a pleasing pattern. The peaceful energy of the room flowed over Sam. He smiled. It reminded him of his meditation room.

Sam realized he hadn't said anything for a long time and felt himself flush that he was scoping out the room. He looked over to see the man considering him carefully.

"I'm sorry," Sam said, "the amount of space in here surprised me. Is this your meditation area? It feels…peaceful."

"Yes, it is, amongst other things. It's arranged in harmony with feng shui. There is good energy here."

"I can feel it," Sam said.

The man dipped his head in a half-bow. "I will heat the water for tea. Please, make yourself comfortable." He left the room to go to the kitchen. Sam could see him through the doorway as he moved around taking things out of cabinets.

"I like him," Nalia said. "He reminds me of my father. He has a quiet mastery that only comes from one who has achieved balance with the universal energy."

Sam nodded his agreement, walking around the room and looking at the various pictures displayed on the walls and on frames spread on tables and shelves. Many of the pictures contained people who were recognizable to Sam, martial artists from forty or fifty years ago who made up the "Who's Who" of the American martial arts community when it was just getting started. He had seen pictures of them in old magazines and books. There were plenty of pictures of movie stars from that era as well. Somehow, Sam wasn't surprised. He wondered why there were no pictures of Master Li.

"Here we are," the old man said, carrying a tray with a tea pot and three small cups. "Do you like my photographs?"

Sam took the tray and set it carefully on a small table. "Yes. I recognize many of the people in the photographs. They're all very famous. You seem to have many of Bruce Lee. Did you know him well?"

Li Jun Fan waved the comment away. "I knew him well enough. They are all just men and women, just as we are. Back then, our opinions of ourselves were much too high. It is unbecoming a true martial artist. But let us talk of other things."

He poured tea into the cups with such grace and elegance that it reminded Sam of a carefully choreographed dance. "For example, may I ask where the two of you studied? It is very rare to find ones so young with such strong chi. Did you study in China?"

Sam saw Nalia glance at him out of the corner of her eye. He nodded to her slightly. "No," he said. "We actually trained with Nalia's father. They live in a remote land far away."

The old man handed the other two their cups of tea and then took his, nodding over it thoughtfully. "I see. Was it kung fu you studied? What style?"

Nalia took a sip of her tea, so Sam continued answering the man, "It wasn't kung fu. It is sort of a family art, not really like any other art or style I've seen."

The old man looked at Sam, considering. "Well, I don't want to pry into secrets of a family martial art. Suffice it to say that I am glad to see two young people such as yourselves focusing on the internal arts, on the mental aspect of the warrior's art, instead of just concentrating on the physical fighting styles. It is a rare thing nowadays."

Trying to change the subject, Sam asked, "Master Li, what about you? It's obvious you have been training for decades and have rubbed elbows with legends here in America. What style did you study?"

"Oh, no particular style, and many particular styles." He laughed softly, almost like a sigh. "When I was young, I was obsessed with being the best, with making a name for myself. I wanted to be famous. I studied with a master, learned from other masters, and then created my own hybrid art. Then, one day, quite suddenly, I realized that my energies were misplaced. I went on a search for the true martial arts, true mastery. I traveled widely and learned from yogi in India and masters of internal kung fu in China, as well as the wise in many other nations around the world. I learned what it is to truly be a warrior, what it is to truly be a person. Now, I am happy living in the community, conversing with masters who have decades of training and life experience. I no longer want to be famous. I simply want to be in my place, in balance with all things. But I'm sure you know what I mean." He looked at Sam meaningfully.

Sam smiled at him. "I think I do."

Finishing his tea and putting down his cup, the old man rose to his feet. "Would you do me the honor of doing some chi exercises with me, Sam? I have to admit I'm curious as to just how strong your chi is. Would you humor an old man?"

"I would be honored, Master Li, but I don't know your forms."

"Oh, no, it's nothing so formal as that," the old master said to him. "It is merely exercises of pushing and pulling and moving with the flow. I'm sure you will slip right into it."

Sam agreed and soon they were standing a few feet apart, facing each other. "I will gently push toward you, palms to palms. Once you have recognized my energy, then you can push back toward me. Simple enough?"

"Simple enough." Sam immediately began to control his breath, to become more aware of the energy surrounding him. He realized, with surprise, that the room he was in was fairly saturated with it. It was obvious the old master meditated and performed chi exercises in the room often.

The power coming from the master was different than what he felt when doing similar exercises with Rindu. It was just as implacable, just as solid, but instead of feeling like he was being slowly pushed back with a massive stone block, it felt like he was being buffeted by a soft feather mattress. It was obvious the small man in front of him was skilled beyond measure.

When he became comfortable and the flow seemed to allow it, he rechanneled the energy coming at him and directed it back at the master. He imagined the force coming out of his palms and projecting toward the other man. After several minutes, he felt Master Li relax and allow the energy to dissipate into the room. "That was marvelous, Sam," he said as he bowed with his hands in the salute in front of him, one fist inside the other. "Thank you. It was…invigorating."

Sam took a deep breath and relaxed, his body slumping. It felt like he had been wrestling, but he was tired in a good way. Peace radiating throughout his body. "Thank you, Master Li. I'm honored to be able to do those exercises with you."

"The honor was mine. Sam, please do not blame an old man for trying to share a bit of wisdom he has learned from many years of study, practice, and mistakes, but may I make a suggestion? My masters believed that to impart the gift of knowledge to another was the most precious gift of all."

Sam was confused for a moment. "Yes, please. I would appreciate any corrections or suggestions you could make."

"Thank you," the old man said. "I noticed that you were having a little trouble in melding your energy with mine, with truly coming into harmony with my energy and the energy of the room. It may be that it feels different than what you are used to, I am not sure. I would suggest that you meditate upon what it means to truly be one with others and with your surroundings. On that path lies true mastery. It is something I learmed late in my training, to my detriment. It is believed that to be strong, one must have strength within oneself, but I have found that strength comes through cooperating with others, no less so with internal energy than in everyday life."

Sam wasn't sure exactly what he meant, but he would consider it more later. "I will try to think on it, Master Li. Thank you for your guidance."

Sam looked over to Nalia, who had been quietly watching them the whole time. "What about you," he asked her. "Do you want to give it a try?"

"No, thank you," she answered. Watching you two do

it was sufficient." The old master nodded to her, dipping his head in an almost-bow.

The three talked for a while longer, about energy and philosophy and the state of the world. Sam showed him the swords he had bought, which Master Li recognized as Master Ho's weapons and told them a short story about them and their former owner. When Sam and Nalia left, it felt like they were leaving home.

"It was a pleasure to meet the two of you," Li Jun Fan said. "If you ever happen to be in the neighborhood again, please stop by. You have lightened my old heart that there are yet people without gray hair who realize the importance of the internal arts. Please continue training. I can only imagine the things you will be capable of doing with another decade or two of practice. Focus on developing harmony and you will attain a new level of proficiency."

The old master bowed formally to each of them, politely asked Nalia if he could give her a hug—she agreed and he did so—and then bade the two of them farewell. Sam was halfway to their car before the idea struck him that he had known who the old man was all along.

Sam smiled warmly as he recalled the experience. He took the wrapped bundle of the swords he had bought and replaced them in the wooden case he had made for them. He had plans for those swords and the idea made his smile grow larger.

3

"I guess that's it," Sam said to Nalia and his mother. Everything was finally ready and all that was left was to leave.

Stoker, Sam's gray cat, was weaving in and out of his legs, rubbing himself against Sam with every pass. When Sam looked down, the cat looked up and meowed at him. "Well, buddy, are you ready for an adventure?" The cat meowed again and resumed his rubbing.

"What do we need to do?" Nicole asked him. "You two have gone back and forth to the other world, but I haven't. What's my part?"

Sam hugged her. "You don't have to do a thing, Mom. Just sit down and relax. You may want to close your eyes. I'm not sure how it'll feel for you, but when we have traveled to and from Gythe in the past, it was a rough ride."

Once his mother sat down, holding the cat, Sam and Nalia seated themselves on the floor of the meditation room, both in cross-legged positions and facing each other. "I think I know how to direct what gets transported now," Sam said. "I'm going to try to make the house and the workshop, and everything in them, go with us."

Sam began breathing in and out methodically. Air softly flowed in through his nose and out through his mouth. It was second nature to him now, and he slipped easily into the almost-trance, called the *khulim* on Gythe. After a few moments, he was relaxed and at peace, ready to continue.

In his mind, he pictured himself sitting cross-legged on the floor, a mere few feet from Nalia, facing her, as it was in reality. In his inner eye, he saw her look at him and nod. Together, they conjured up the image of just the two of them, sitting in complete blackness. Then, off to his left, a pin prick of light appeared and grew larger. It resolved itself into a tunnel of swirling colors, twisting and shifting around the opening.

Sam let Nalia take the lead, fixing firmly in his mind the vibration necessary to cross through the tunnel, the vibratory signature of Gythe. They slipped and slid, turning summersaults and twisting, moving their way through the tunnel. It was disconcerting, but it didn't make him dizzy, just disoriented. When it all suddenly stopped, he felt as if he landed hard in his body. Slowly opening his eyes, he saw his meditation room and Nalia, just as they were when they started.

"That was…different," he said to her. "In fact, it hasn't ever really been the same twice. Each time, there are some things that are the same, but others that are different. I wonder why. It seemed easier this time, too."

Nalia opened her eyes and looked into his. "Yes, easier. I do not know why it is different each time, though I have only done it twice now. Perhaps my father would know. Did it work? Are we in Gythe? The energy here feels different than when we started."

"Let's see. Mom, are you okay? How about Stoker?"

Nicole Sharp was still sitting on the chair, as she was when they started. She was breathing heavily, but didn't seem any the worse for wear. "Wow, that was intense." She dropped the squirming cat to the floor. "I don't think he liked it much, but we're both fine."

Smiling, Sam got up and went toward the front of the house. His steps were quick as he hurried to see if they had returned to Nalia's world. Throwing open the front door, he surveyed the landscape.

He was in the middle of a forest, but then the land on which his house was built in Telani was forested. This wasn't his normal forest, though, and it felt colder. The trees were different, unfamiliar, and more crowded. The final piece of evidence, though, was that there was no road, no driveway to his house. It was gone, completely. "Nalia," he said, "I think you're home."

"I think *we* are home," she said, hugging him from behind.

"I have given it a lot of thought," Sam said as they sat on the back porch of his house looking out on the unfamiliar forest, "and it seems to me that we should be able to adjust the vibrations of the house to send it fully back to Telani. When I came to Gythe the first time, and the second, I think my house was partially in this world and partially in the other. If we're going to stay here, I should send it all the way back to where it belongs."

"Then why did you bring it here in the first place?" his mother asked.

Sam's face reddened. "Well, you know how you always say I overanalyze stuff? I wasn't sure if I could transport all of us as individuals. I figured it would be easiest if I simply brought the whole house with us because I'd done that before and knew that it worked. Besides, if anything happened and we had troubles when we got here, it seemed good to have a house full of food."

Nicole looked at him blankly for a moment, then smiled. "I can accept that. It was good thinking, I guess. We should probably make sure things are how they're supposed to be before we send it back, though."

The other two agreed. "But first," he turned to Nalia, "I was hoping you would show me where you grew up," he looked at her expectantly, "that you would show me Marybador. We are close to it."

Sam watched Nalia's face as it went from surprise to tension, to sorrow, and finally to stern resolve. "Yes. I think it would be good for me to see what is left of my home. If I am to rebuild the *Sapsyra Shin Elah*, then I must see what I have to work with. I will take you there."

Sam nodded and began rummaging through the closet where he kept his outdoor gear. In just a few minutes, he had taken out three sets of cross country skis and poles, backpacks, and assorted sets of gloves.

"Luckily, it looks like there is fresh snow out there. We should easily be able to get there within a couple of days, three tops." He pulled out the custom, ultra-light snowshoes they had bought just a few months ago. "We better take these, too. I'm not sure what we'll run up against and they may come in handy."

Nicole eyed him, nodding her head gently. "Is that why you insisted I try cross-country skiing? Have you been planning this trip all along?

Sam squirmed under his mother's scrutiny. "Ummm. Well, yes and no. I thought the skiing would be great exercise, which it is, but I had planned on going back to Gythe at least for a visit. Honestly, though, I had always thought it would be in the spring or summer. I guess we just got impatient." He smiled weakly at her and was relieved when she smiled back. "Still, it probably wouldn't have mattered when we left home because we don't know what time of the year it is here. It could be the same season as on Telani or it could be another. It's obvious that it's not summer, and there's more snow than there was this morning in Telani."

"It's a good thing you are a planner. It will be much faster to ski than to walk. How far is it?"

"Marybador is the name of the Crater Lake region here on Gythe. Actually, it's the name of the island itself, but people refer to the whole region by that name. So, I'd say it's probably forty or fifty miles from here, if we go straight toward it. There aren't many roads to speak of here. Is that accurate, Nalia?"

The Sapsyr had become very quiet. When Sam looked at her, he saw her face, scrunched up as if she had eaten something that disagreed with her. "Yes, that is true, but perhaps I can find an old road."

Sam went to her and drew her into a hug. "We don't have to go if you don't want to," he said. "I know it'll be tough seeing it again."

She raised her chin and looked him in the eyes. "No, it must be done. As my father would no doubt say, 'You must clear out the brambles before you lay down your bedroll.'" She forced a smile, and he almost believed it was real. For a moment.

Squeezing her again, he set about packing things into his backpack.

The trip was uneventful. The crisp air was invigorating as they shushed their way through the trees until they found what was undoubtedly a road at one time, evident from the lack of large vegetation along the path. Though they couldn't see the ground, the treeless snow made for easy traveling. Before he knew it, Sam was standing on the edge of the caldera that made up the border of the lake.

The bowl of the crater lay out before them, ringing in a lake with the bluest water Sam had ever seen. He thought it was even brighter in Gythe than when he had seen it in Telani when he was younger, when he and his mother had driven up to visit it. The sharply jutting walls surrounding the water were covered with snow, the green of the sparse trees poking out here and there in all their evergreen glory, breaking up the vast white landscape.

Sitting there in the middle of the deep azure of Zyrqyt Lake was the island. It was called Wizard Island on Telani, but here, it was Marybador, former home of the *Sapsyra Shin Elah*. The cone rising up on the far side of the island seemed to be stark and forbidding in the blue background.

The water, so still that it displayed a perfect mirror image of the island, the caldera walls, and the wispy clouds that lazily crawled across the sky, made Sam thirsty.

"Oh my," he heard his mother say from his right. "That is just beautiful!"

Nalia, as still as a statue, stood to his left and stared longingly out toward the island. Sam went to her and hugged her to himself, kissing the top of her head. "Are you all right?" he asked.

"I am…fine. It is just a shock to see it again after so many years. Can you see the shapes, just there," she pointed to a flat area on the island where there appeared to be some rock formations under the snow, "the ruins of some of our buildings?"

Sam studied the shapes. He could see that maybe they could have been buildings rather than stone formations. "Yes." The word seemed inadequate, but he didn't know what else to say.

"I would take you to the island, but I am sure none of the boats have survived all these years. Perhaps we can come back at another time and I will show you where my home used to be."

Sam squeezed her again. "No," he said.

She tensed in his arms and her hawk-like eyes burned into his. "We can come back another time and you can show me where you will rebuild your former home, where you will rebuild the headquarters of the Sapsyra."

She smiled then, like the sun breaking through clouds on a somber day. "Truly? You would have me rebuild my order?"

"Of course. I'll help you in any way I can. The Sapsyra are too great a force of good on Gythe to let them disappear. The Zouyim temple needs to be rebuilt, too. It's one of the main reasons I wanted to come back as quickly as we could. We'll get started on it as soon as possible."

Then she was kissing him, pulling him into her arms and making him forget who he was, where they were, and everything else that seemed to be important just seconds before. "It is not for nothing that I love you so, Sam Sharp," she said to him, nuzzling against him as they looked out toward the ruins of her home.

"Ahem," Nicole interrupted. "That is very sweet and I love to see it, but I'm getting kind of cold now that we've stopped. I enjoy the beautiful scenery, but are we going to set up camp or something? I'm not sure I have it in me to go all the way back home right now. I'm not used to this kind of exercise. I'm sore all over."

Sam smiled at his mother. "Mom, have I got a surprise for you. Give me a few moments to prepare and I'll show you what I mean."

Sam went off to a flat rock a dozen feet away and scraped the snow from it. Climbing onto it, he sat there, cross-legged, and controlled his breathing, quickly attaining the khulim. He was motionless for several minutes, looking outward in his mind's eye, recognizing the place in which he sat, learning the unique vibrations there.

After a quarter hour, he opened his eyes slowly and looked to his mother and Nalia, softly chatting while sitting on another rock close by. He began to speak when he saw the man sneaking out of some trees three dozen feet away, coming right toward them.

4

Sam saw Nalia's eyes widen and then she was somewhere else, having drawn her shrapezi and moved toward the man more quickly than seemed possible. No one was able to react, least of all the intruder.

"Wait," was all that Sam could get out.

While the word was still in the air, Nalia had swept the man's legs out from under him, causing him to fall backward into the show. Her twin swords were there in a flash, unwavering at his throat.

"Do not move or it will be the last thing you ever do," Nalia told him, keeping her head still but moving her eyes about to look for others. The man stayed exactly where he was. In the meantime, Sam had crossed the distance and Nicole was moving toward them, breathing heavily as if she was going to hyperventilate.

"Are there more of you?" Nalia asked. The man remained silent.

"Nal, pull the swords back a bit," Sam said. "If he tries to talk, you'll cut him with how close they are." She grimaced at him and continued shifting her eyes, searching. After several seconds, she nodded stiffly and pulled the swords back. An inch.

"Answer me," she said.

"Nalia?" the man said, his voice quivering. "Nalia Wroun?"

The Sapsyr was taken aback, her eyes widening again. Then they narrowed and she glared at him. "What do you know of that name? Speak."

"I…I…I'm Shen Nan. You remember, right? Shen. Eoria's husband."

Nalia lowered her shrapezi and a look Sam had rarely seen played across her face. It was the face she wore when she spoke about her mother. And about her sister Sapsyra who had been killed in the assault on the Gray Man all those years ago. She turned and took three steps toward the trees, her eyes losing focus. She didn't say a word.

"Nal?" Sam said, but she didn't respond. He looked at his mother, who was already putting her arms around Nalia. She nodded toward the man who was still on his back in the snow. Sam understood. He went over and helped the man to his feet.

"That is Nalia, isn't it?" he asked Sam softly. "I didn't recognize her without her mask, but it must be her. No one could have taken the shrapezi from her."

"Who are you?" Sam asked the man, helping him dust the snow off his clothes.

"Shen Nan. My wife, Eoria, was one of the Sapsyra who went with Nalia to bring justice to the Gray Man for destroying the Zouyim temple. Nalia was the only one who survived, and only because the Gray Man wanted her to deliver his message to the remaining Sapsyra. He finished the job after we had all dispersed and a few of our number broke his agreement and attacked his soldiers. He hunted down any Sapsyr left and killed them. Again, all but Nalia."

"That was a long time ago," Sam said. "Why are you here, Shen? What were you doing when Nalia knocked you down?"

The man flushed even redder than the cold and his

short-lived battle had already made him. "I was going to try to steal your packs while you were distracted. You have to understand, it's tough to survive out here. I wasn't going to hurt anyone, just steal some food, that's all. There are a few children and food is scarce this year. It's not even winter yet and we're already starving."

"You are welcome to any food we have," Sam said. "How many more of you are there?"

"There are three men, four children, and one girl who I suppose should be called a woman by now."

Nalia had regained her composure and was stepping back toward Sam and the man. "Shen Nan," she said, "my apologies for attacking you. I thought you meant us harm. It is good to see one who lived with us at Marybador." She gave him the formal salute used on Gythe, the right fist cradled in the left hand. The man returned the salute.

Nalia turned to Sam and Nicole. "Perhaps you do not know because I have rarely spoken of it, but Marybador was more than just a military compound. As the home of the *Sapsyra Shin Elah*, it also housed the families of those sisters who were married and had children. There were two main sections of the compound: one where the single sisters lived, some in a dormitory-style, and one where the sisters lived with their families. "

Nalia's eyes became unfocused, as if she was looking far away. "There were always family members moving about the compound, and children. Oh, seeing the children playing was a joy when so much of our lives revolved around combat and warfare.

"When the Gray Man killed all the sisters who assaulted the Gray Fortress—all except me—their families were left in the compound to grieve their passing. After I delivered the message the Gray Man forced me to take and our leader commanded us to disperse, I never again saw any of the former residents of Marybador. I suppose I assumed that they were eliminated by the Gray Man as were the remaining Sapsyra. I can see now that my reasoning was faulty."

She turned to Shen Nan. "I am sorry I did not search out the families of my sisters and lend aid when I could.

The man ducked his head and wrung his hands. "No, Nalia. We heard rumors of the Faceless Sapsyr and the Lone Zouy—I'm assuming that was your father—and how the Gray Man's minions were constantly searching for them to kill them. You would have put yourself at risk to find us. We would not have wanted that."

"I understand," Nalia said. "Thank you. Now, please tell me how it is that you are here so many years after our home was destroyed. When my father and I heard of the destruction of the compound by the Gray Man, we came and saw the wreckage but found no one here."

"That's easy enough to explain," Shen Nan said. "When everyone dispersed, we went as well. With no other relatives, I stayed within fifty miles of this place. I worked for some of the local farms when the harvest required extra hands and generally moved around. Rumors spread fast and when I heard of the destruction of Marybador, I came to see for myself, much as you and Rindu did. I wept for days after seeing it. It was my home for many years.

"I tried going back to the life of a wanderer, tried to find a place where I felt comfortable, but my thoughts always returned here. Months after the compound's destruction, I found myself standing here, looking out over what had been the heart of the Sapsyra order and I decided I would stay here, for better or worse."

He looked longingly at the island. "I was too scared to try to stay on the island iself. What if the Gray Man's troops came again to make sure it remained desolate? Instead, I found an area I thought suitable and I began to make a home there. I was an accomplished traveler, so I had a fine tent, some useful tools, a bow, and a long knife.

"When I found the first of the others, the girl who is now a woman, she was half-starved and unsure of anything other than that she knew this was her home. Her mother, one of the few Sapsyra who did not go to the Gray Fortress, was found and killed by the Gray Man's assassins while she hid nearby and was not detected. The others trickled in as well, and we have made a permanent camp of a sort. We live day by day, trying to survive, not sure of what the future will hold."

Nicole had a sorrowful look on her face. Nalia's was stern, jaw clenched, as if she was angry...or as if she was tamping down emotion.

"Where is your camp?" Sam asked.

Shen Nan pointed to the north. "Just over there, a mile or so. We didn't want to be too close in case others came. It was only chance I was here today. I stand and look out over what used to be my home often, remembering."

"We have tasks we must complete," Nalia said, "but once we have made sure it is safe, we will come back for you. For all of you. You said you were hungry enough to steal food. Will you be able to stay where you are for a few more days if we provide what food we have?"

"We can. There is nowhere else for us to go. Eat or starve, we will stay here."

"We will give you what food we brought," Sam said. "Within a few days, we will return for you. We plan on making sure Marybador is rebuilt, but until then, I believe we will have a place for you."

The man grabbed Sam's hands. "Thank you. Rebuild Marybador? Just that news alone will keep us from starving for a month. I must go and tell the others. Will you come and meet them?"

Nalia answered, "We cannot. We must see how things stand at the Gray Fortress as soon as possible. We will return soon, whatever the situation there."

"Alright," the man said. "I will tell the others to expect you. Be cautious. We will look for you in two days, and every day thereafter, at noon." He bowed to Nalia, who returned his bow, then he did the same with the other two. With one more look at the island sitting in the middle of the calm, azure lake, he headed off toward his camp.

Sam watched the man go. "It looks like we already have a start to repopulating the new compound." Nalia smiled at that."Okay," he said to them, "let's go. We have things to do."

His mother sighed and started to put her skis back on, but Nalia touched her arm, said something Sam couldn't hear. The two of them walked with him to the flat rock on which he had been meditating.

The women climbed up onto the rock with him and sat. "Just sit still for a minute, please," he said to them and closed his eyes, resuming the controlled breathing he did now as second nature.

He fixed firmly in his mind the vibratory signature of his home. Adjusting his own vibrations within his mind, he pictured himself and the two women encircled by a glowing field, his aura. With a final push from his mind, he made the vibrations of all three of them the same as those of his home. He felt the world lurch slightly and then stop.

When he opened his eyes, he saw his mother's face light up with excitement, tempered a bit by confusion. They were back in the living room of their home, skis and boots dripping snow.

"Oh, Sam," his mother said, breathless, "that was fantastic. I know you have told me the stories about Gythe and how you learned to teleport, but wow. I never really thought about what it would be like to do it. That was amazing!"

"Yeah," Sam winked, "I'm just full of surprises. Let's hope I continue to be so."

5

After a good night's sleep, the three worked at moving everything they wanted to keep from the house into the workshop. Sam had been moving things to the storage section of his workshop for more than a month, so it didn't take long. The largest portion of the task had been putting shelves in one part of the storage area and moving his books there. He definitely wasn't going to leave those behind.

"Do you hear that?" Sam asked as he was walking back toward the house to make one final sweep for anything they may have forgotten but may need.

"I do," Nalia said. "What is it?"

Sam walked around the house slowly, listening intently. There. Something was making noises toward the rear of the house. He got down on hands and knees and put his head near the large firewood bin. The soft sounds of mewling floated in the air and then faded into nothingness, almost too softly to be heard. Sam looked at Nalia and she back at him.

Carefully and slowly opening the door to the bin—it was old and didn't fit well, with gaps as large as Sam's hand—Sam looked inside. "Yep, just as I thought," he said, lifting the lid completely and swinging it out of the way.

There was a cat nestled in the space, lying on her side. She was long-haired, white with multi-colored patches all over her body. Five tiny kittens were nursing and one other, seeming to have lost its way, raised its head, eyes still closed tight, and mewed pitifully.

Sam reached down and pet the mother while gently nudging the straggler toward the source of food. It found an opening and started to eat voraciously.

Nalia had grown silent and still. Sam looked at her and saw in her face wonder and excitement. "They are babies? That is how cats begin their life?"

At first surprised, Sam realized that until she came to Telani, Nalia had never seen a cat. At least, she had never seen one smaller than a pantor, Gythe's version of a panther or a cheetah. Even though she had become used to Stoker, she had never seen newborn kittens with their eyes still closed and their fur bedraggled and sparse.

"Yes," Sam answered. "They must have just been born. We can't send them back to Telani with the house. It would feel too much like abandoning them. How do you feel about adopting a bunch of cats?"

Nalia's eyes had not left the kittens as they spoke. Sam took her hand and brought it down to the mother's fur, guiding her to pet the cat. Her furry face turned toward Nalia, eyes squinting tiredly, and she began to purr as her head dipped back down. Sam enjoyed the sight of Nalia's smile growing on her face. "Yes, I think that is a wonderful idea."

Nicole found the two fawning over the cats and soon the three of them had transferred all seven into a shallow basket filled with towels. Sam carried the basket to the workshop and put it near a well-stocked food dish and bowl of water. He introduced Stoker to the newcomers and, to his surprise, his old tom sniffed at them, looked up at Sam, and then set about cleaning the mother cat's fur. The male cat shied every time one of the kittens made a move, but it was a relief that he didn't react violently. He would have to lock his cat in with the kittens while he sent his house back to Telani.

With the cats secured in the workshop so that they wouldn't get in the way, Sam and Nalia sat on the ground in front of the house. Sam nodded to her and then closed his eyes and attained the *khulim*. They linked with each other, and sent the house fully back to Telani. Sam felt a small pang of sadness as the home he had grown to love over the last year and more vibrated out of existence from the world he was in.

"That was strange," he said to her. "Even though it was partially in Telani, it felt like it was fighting to stay here. Or fighting not to return there. It was much harder to do than bringing us, it, and the workshop here."

"Yes," Nalia agreed, "it was odd."

"Anyway, now that we've finished with that," he said to both of the women, "do you want to go see what everyone's been up to at the Gray Fortress? Hopefully our friends are still alive. I don't know how much time has passed here since we were gone. We probably should have asked Shen."

The women both agreed. Sam leaned back and forth in his cross-legged position in front of the workshop to get more comfortable, preparing to teleport. He angled the staff he called *Ahimiro* across his knees. "You know, I should really practice this more so I don't need to sit down and take so much time to travel. It could more useful if I could do it more quickly." Nalia simply nodded.

"I'm going to teleport us to the road outside the Gray Fortress first," he continued, "so we can look around. I don't want to take the chance of appearing in the middle of the keep if there are people there who won't recognize us. It could be dangerous." Nalia nodded again.

A few moments later, the three were standing on the

road cut through the foliage surrounding the fortress, a place he had memorized while here the last time. Sam had almost forgotten how pale and creepy the strangled, twisted trees of the Undead Forest looked. He saw his mother's concerned look and gestured toward the Gray Fortress. Her eyes went wide.

It was a massive structure, more imposing by the fact that it was sitting on top of high cliffs. Two hundred feet above where they were standing, the main gate yawned like a terrible beast. Leading up to it was the only practical way to the top of the sheer walls, a series of switchbacks that zig-zagged up the face of the plateau, every inch of the path paved with perfectly cut and fitted stones. Seeing the sight again took Sam's breath away and made him think once more of how powerful energy must have been used to build the structure and even the road to it.

On top of the cliffs, massive gray walls jutted up, perfectly straight. Sam knew from experience that the huge blocks from which the walls were made were fitted to precisely that they left no reasonable handhold or foothold for climbing. They were nearly impenetrable. Nearly. Thrusing up above the walls was the immense keep itself, the Gray Fortress proper. There was where the Gray Man had held his domain. There was where Sam and his friends had infiltrated and put an end to the villain. There it was that Sam had learned all the terrible truths that still haunted him, that the Gray Man was actually his uncle, brought to Gythe against his will and transformed into someone else, something else.

He pushed the thoughts out of his head and looked toward his mother. She was still standing there, eyes wide and mouth open, craning her neck to see all of the fortress in front of her. "This…this was where Grayson lived?" she said of her brother. "This was his fortress? The one he gave to you?"

"Yep," Sam answered. "Kind of cool, huh?"

She didn't answer, only kept staring.

"The good news is that there doesn't seem to be anything different, though I'm not sure what we could see from here if it had changed. What do you say we try to go inside?"

Nicole remained silent, but her mouth twisted into a grimace as her eyes followed the tortuous path upward. Nalia answered instead. "Yes, let us go inside."

Sam reached around his mother and hugged her with one arm. "We won't use the path. Come on, mom. I'll teleport us to the room I used to have. Hopefully we won't surprise anyone, but if we do, at least we can be sure there won't be too many people in the chamber. It's not that big."

He sat down in the middle of the road in his cross-legged posture with the other two closeby. He recalled the unique vibratory signature of the room, the first place he had ever teleported to, and in a few moments they were in the Gray Fortress.

The three appeared in Sam's old room. He was glad it was unoccupied. It would have been embarrassing to suddenly appear in someone else's room. Or dangerous.

Adjusting his backpack as he came to his feet and moving his grip on the staff he carried, Sam looked over at the two women. Nalia's expression was grim, her eyes darting around the room for any hidden dangers, her shrapezi out and ready. She looked prepared for anything. Nicole's eyes were slightly glazed, trying to catch up with what was happening. They seemed to be scanning the stone walls and the closed heavy wooden door.

"Are you okay, Mom?" Sam asked her. "It's kind of a lot to come to another world and then to jump around until you land in an old-fashioned castle."

Her frantic eyes met his and she purposefully took a long, deep breath. "I'm fine. It's just…different."

Before Sam could do so, Nalia put one arm around her and gave her a quick hug. "It is to be expected that you would be disoriented. We will be using our own feet for now, so there is nothing to worry about."

Nicole nodded and exhaled loudly.

Sam went to the door and listened for a moment. "Let's be careful. We don't know how long we've been gone and we don't know what the situation here in the fortress is. We'll go to the main library. If Dr. Walt is still alive, he will be there."

The other two nodded and they went through the door into the wide hallway. It looked as it did before, plain stone block, the walls sparsely decorated with tapestries of landscapes and battles. The cloth of the tapestries was faded and fluttered weakly in the slight breeze. Only every third torch was lit, so the three moved from shadow to warm yellow light and back into shadow again as they headed toward where Sam remembered the library to be.

When they arrived at the massive double doors to the library without having seen another person, Sam was chewing his lip, unsure what he would find. He noticed that his palms had started sweating and his fingers twitched unconsciously. He firmed his grip on *Ahimiro*. "Are you ready?" he asked Nalia.

"I am," she replied.

"Mom, why don't you step back a bit. If there is trouble, I'd just as soon not have you in the middle of it."

He waited until she nodded and stepped back toward the opposite wall of the hallway before grasping the door handle and pushing the door inward.

The heavy door groaned in protest as it moved away from him. Sam, staff at the ready, stepped inside and scanned the cavernous room for enemies. Nalia was at his side, shrapezi up and reflecting the firelight.

Movement on the outskirts of the room caught Sam's eye and made his heart jump. He held his staff in a guard position and prepared to defend himself.

"Oh, Sam, Nalia, what a surprise!" the voice rang out. Dr. Walt got up from the chair he was in and set aside the book he was reading. "You've come back so soon? Telani a little too boring for you?" He laughed.

The lanky old scholar was a welcome sight. He was just as Sam remembered, tall and thin, with a permanent hunch, no doubt from bending to read and look at the artifacts that were his life's obsession. His hair and neatly trimmed beard were white, not for the first time making Sam think of Colonel Sanders. He did not appear to have aged since he last saw him, just less than a year and a half in Telani time.

"Dr. Walt!" Nalia said, sweeping the man into a bone crushing hug. "We were not sure if you still lived. We have been gone so long."

Dr. Walt looked at them, puzzlement on his face. "Nonsense. You have been gone less than three weeks. You just barely left after our…ahem…adventure with Grayson."

As he spoke, he noticed Nicole as she slowly came through the door. "Ah, you have brought a visitor." Sam thought he saw a look of confirmation cross the doctor's face, but it disappeared so quickly, he assumed he had imagined it. The doctor bowed slightly to Nicole and introduced himself. "I am Dr. Walter Wicket, my dear, but everyone just calls me Dr. Walt."

Confusion painted Nicole's face. She looked from Sam to Nalia to Dr. Walt. "I'm sorry, but I don't understand you," she said. Sam realized that Dr. Walt had been speaking Kasmali.

The scholar gave his head a shake. "My apologies," he said in English, with his English accent. "Habit, you know." He introduced himself again.

Nicole's confused expression changed to one of surprise. "Oh. Sam has told me all about you, Dr. Walt. I'm Nicole Sharp, Sam's mom. It's a pleasure to meet you." She crossed the distance and shook his hand firmly.

"Sam's…mom? Surely you are just teasing me. You must be a sister, a cousin, possibly an aunt. You couldn't possibly be Sam's mother. You're so young."

Sam caught his mother's eyes rolling at the compliment. "Sam didn't tell me that you were such a charmer. I'm his mother. If you don't believe me, wait until he steps out of line and you'll get irrefutable evidence." She winked at him.

Sam interrupted. "Dr. Walt, did you say we were gone less than three weeks? We were in Telani for almost a year and a half. When we got back last time, even though almost seven months had passed here, less than a day had passed on Telani."

Dr. Walt's eyebrows looked like bleached caterpillars trying to escape by running up his forehead. "Really? Hmmmm. I suppose that's logical. As we discussed when you were here before, I believe that the timeframe for the two worlds progresses at the same rate overall, but perhaps it occurs in fits and starts. It is possible that sometimes time goes faster, relatively speaking, here in Gythe, and sometimes it's faster in Telani. I'm sure that's what happened. How fascinating."

Nalia fidgeted, waiting for Dr. Walt to finish. When he did, she spoke up. "Dr. Walt, where is my father? Is he well? I would like to see him."

"What? Oh, yes, Rindu. It must seem like a long time since you've seen him, though it hasn't been long here at all. Yes, of course. He and I are actually supposed to meet in one of the audience chambers shortly. If you would like to come with me, I'm sure that would be the easiest way to get to him. Perhaps you could help us, you and Sam. And Nicole, of course. The more the merrier."

6

A few minutes later, Sam, Nalia, Nicole, and Dr. Walt entered a small audience chamber several corridors from the main library. They were the last to arrive. Seeing her father, Nalia rushed to him and pulled him into a hug. He tolerated it stoically, making a clumsy attempt to put his arms up to encircle her.

Sam thought about how Nalia had changed in the last year. When he had first met her, she was tough, all-business, a warrior who apparently had no soft side. After being in Telani, though, and especially after spending so much time with his mother, she was much freer with her affection. She had actually become a hugger. He made the mistake of mentioning it one time and the backlash kept her from showing affection for a solid month. He hoped Rindu didn't say anything or she may revert to her former ways.

The father and daughter spoke quietly for a few minutes, Sam just waving to Rindu from across the room so they could have their time together. He looked exactly the same as when he left. His off-white colored robes swished with his movement, providing glimpses of the soft boots he wore, laced all the way up his calf. His salt and pepper hair, pulled back into a pony tail, framed his angular, asymmetrical face. His eyes were slightly tilted, giving him an exotic look, and sat to either side of his very flat nose that seemed to dominate his features. He showed little expression, as was typical, but the little he did show was enough for Sam to see he was happy to be with his daughter again. The man waved back to Sam and a tiny smile appeared on his face before it was wiped away as if it had never been there.

Sam thought about the difference in how beauty was perceived in Gythe compared to Telani. In this world, Rindu was accounted as handsome while Nalia was considered hideously ugly. In fact, she had worn a mask her whole life to hide her features so as to prevent showing disrespect to others. In Sam's world, Nalia's beauty was beyond compare.

"I'm sorry for being late," Dr. Walt said loudly, "but it appears that everyone we expected to be here is here, and a few more besides." He nodded in Sam's direction. When he did so, two of the other people in the room noticed Sam for the first time and their eyes grew wide.

Sam whispered to his mother, "Mom, we'll all be speaking in Kasmali. I'll try to translate as quickly as I can for you, okay?" She squeezed his elbow and watched as Dr. Walt continued.

"I'm sure Sam Sharp and Nalia Wroun need no introduction. Beside Sam is his mother, Nicole. They will be listening in, if that's all right." Everyone in the room nodded enthusiastically.

Sam looked around the chamber. Besides his friends, there were four other people, two men and two women. He wasn't sure if Dr. Walt would introduce them or explain what the meeting was about, but he hoped so.

Almost as if reading his mind, Dr. Walt began speaking again, "Just so everyone knows everyone else, let me give a brief introduction."

"Here," Dr. Walt said, motioning toward a very large man tightly wedged into one of the sturdy wooden chairs at the table, "is Georg Santas, Principle Man of Wethaven." The obese man nodded his great head firmly, causing his jowls and his four chins to quiver. His piercing blue eyes, looking much too small for his enormous head, seemed to drill into Sam.

Sam waved at him. The man smiled then, and seemed a completely different person, more like a lovable Santa Claus—Sam did catch the coincidental last name—than someone more intimidating.

"From Seamouth," Dr. Walt motioned toward an impossibly tall woman sitting ramrod straight in her chair, "Fulusin Telanyahu. She serves as of Mayor of that city." The woman displayed a smile, just wide enough to appear friendly, but not so much as to seem informal. Sam noticed that it didn't reach her eyes.

"And," Dr. Walt turned to face the other two leaders, sitting next to each other, "Let me present to you Raire," the man waved happily, "and Akila Gonsh." The woman nodded sternly. "They are husband and wife as well as co-Ministers of the city of Patchel's Folly."

Sam waved to the two, to the delighted smile of Raire and to another small nod from Akila.

"Sam, it's a great honor to meet you," Raire said. "I would like to be the first to thank you for all you did in ridding the world of that monster, the Gray Man."

He noticed his wife's mouth compressing into a straight line.

"What?" he asked her. "I'm just saying what everyone else thinks. We owe Sam a great debt and I, for one, want to let him know we appreciate it." Sam got the sense that the man wanted to stick his tongue out at his wife. She just shook her head.

"That very kind of you to say, Minister Gonsh—"

"Oh, please, call me Raire. No need to be so formal."

"Raire, then," Sam continued. "That's very kind of you

to say, but my friends did much more important things than I did. I was just along for the ride."

"Nonsense," the man said to him. "I do appreciate the hard work and sacrifices of all of your associates," he nodded to Nalia, to Dr. Walt, and to Rindu, "but you were the one who made the difference, Sam. Why, if it wasn't—"

"Enough Raire," his wife interjected, not unkindly. "We have business to discuss. You can tell them all about it later." She patted his hand affectionately.

"Of course," he said. "My apologies."

Dr. Walt cleared his throat. "Right. Well, the purpose for which I have invited you all here is an important one." He scanned the room, making eye contact with each person there. As his eyes reached Sam and saw him translating what he was saying for his mother, he nodded.

"With the defeat of the Gray Man, there has been a bit of a hole left in the power structure on Gythe, a hole that unsavory types no doubt are planning to fill. I believe we must fill it first.

"The cities and towns all have some form of local government. Even villages have their elders or councils. That is good. Remember, though, that all those forms of local government were in place when the Gray Man began annexing them and using the locations for his own purpose. Some he would simply destroy while at others he would install his own people to rule. Small or large, these local governments were not strong enough to stand up to his forces, let alone his own power."

"But," Fulusin Telanyahu said, "The Gray Man is no more. There is no one with his power to step in and take the reins. I don't believe we need to worry about it. I have my own city to run and cannot, will not, waste my time thinking about what other cities are doing. No offense meant to your distinguished guests.".

"Ah, but you are mistaken." It was Rindu who spoke. "It used to be, ten or more years ago, that the Zouyim and the Sapsyra were a safeguard. Their whole reason for being was to protect the common people from dangers such as the Gray Man, to prevent any tyrant from becoming too powerful.

"Sadly, the Zouyim and the Sapsyra are no more, not in any strength." He nodded toward Nalia. "If a charismatic leader from one of the larger cities decides to begin a campaign of conquest, taking over smaller towns and villages, consolidating power, who is to say that there will not be another like the Gray Man within not so many years?"

"Granted," Akila Gonsh said, "there is no group of people to protect everyone. But do we need such a thing? My city will not be taken easily. We have forces of our own. Even the Gray Man didn't try to overcome us."

"Ah, but he did, my dear," Raire said to her. "We are still trying to find the people of influence in the city who were bought and paid for by the Gray Man." His wife wore the face of someone who had eaten a bite of food that had gone rotten.

"I, for one," he continued, "think it is a good idea to prepare for the next tyrant who will come along. If our history is any indication, this will happen sooner rather than later. I'd hate to be the one who prevents our fine city from being part of a coalition made up to protect its members."

Akila Gonsh glared at him for a moment and then dropped her gaze to the table and allowed her shoulders to slump. "Maybe you're right," she said quietly. He smiled and squeezed her hand.

Georg Santas filled the silence. "If I may ask, what is it that you're proposing, Dr. Walt? Are you proposing to become a ruler in the Gray Man's place?"

"What?" Dr. Walt's eyes widened and he put both hands up as if warding off something dangerous. "Oh no! No, I would never do that. The simple fact is that as a historian, I have seen this situation play out countless times during history. In fact, I have seen it play out on two different worlds. I am simply bringing it to the attention of those in power," he swept his arms out as if to include them all, "you."

"It seems a sound idea to me," Georg said, wheezing slightly as he attempted to pull in a full breath, "But remember that we are only three of the cities closest to the Gray Fortress. There are many others who would have a say in this matter."

"Agreed," said Dr. Walt. "I have sent messengers to all the major cities, directing them also to stop at towns and villages when possible to spread the word. Whatever form of government we end up with, everyone should have a say in setting it up."

The four leaders nodded, the Gonshes whispering softly to one another.

"So," Dr. Walt continued, "if we are in agreement, then I would ask that you think about my proposal while we wait for the other leaders to respond. Once we have more of them all together, we can begin to hash out the details, to talk about specifics."

"One further question," Fulusin Telanyahu said. "Where would this new government be located? If hosted in a particular city, there would be unfair pressure to do what was best for that city."

"Those are my thoughts exactly," Dr. Walt said. "Forgive me if I have not had time to ask permission, but Sam, would it be all right to use the Gray Fortress as a seat of government? You were bequeathed the entire fortress by the Gray Man. It's yours to do with as you will."

Sam started as he translated that last part for his mother. He hadn't thought he was going to be part of the conversation.

"I…uh…yes. Yes, of course. That sounds like the perfect use for it. There's more than enough space here and it's neutral territory, so to speak. It's a great idea."

"Splendid!" Dr. Walt said. "Well, then, if there is

nothing further, I will allow you to get back to your busy schedules. I will send messengers when the next meeting can be held. I am hopeful there will be other representatives by that time."

With that, the formal meeting was over. Raire Gonsh immediately came up to Sam, his thin body weaving between chairs to reach him. Sam was occupied for the next few hours discussing many things with him, repeating an account of the battle with the Gray Man and answering questions. When the city leaders had finally retired to their own rooms until dinner, Sam clasped Nalia's hand, put his arm around his mother, and went off to their rooms. Sam and Nalia reatained their old rooms while Nicole took the room next to Nalia's.

The newcomers took some time relaxing in their rooms before meeting again for dinner. As Sam entered the dining hall with his mother by his side, he saw Rindu and Nalia discussing something.

"I do not understand, *Iba*," Rindu said to her. "Why will you not don your mask once again? I can understand not wearing it in Telani, where you are not considered ugly, but here, your features offend others' honor. I mean no disrespect, of course, but as a Sapsyr you must be mindful of how your actions reflect upon your honor."

"I no longer believe that to be true, father," Nalia said. "My experiences in living in another world have allowed me to see some things more clearly. I know how ugly I am to the eyes of people of Gythe and it is unfortunate if looking upon my face causes discomfort. However, I do not believe it is my honor and respect that is at issue.

"I believe that this mortal shell I wear is not of primary importance. A misshapen rock may still be used as a perfect tool if no other weapon is available. Is it any less honorable an item than a finely crafted sword? I do not think so. I will not cover my face again. If onlookers take offense, then perhaps they should search their own motivations and their own honor for flaws."

"But *Iba*—" Rindu noticed Sam and Nicole then and stopped talking. "We will discuss this more later," he finished.

"Is everything all right?" Nicole asked Nalia in English.

"It is fine," the Sapsyr answered. "My father disagrees with my actions. It is nothing."

The three settled into a nice meal, joined partway through by Dr. Walt. Some of the leaders Sam met earlier, as well as some of the servants, were also eating. After dinner, Sam and Nalia remained in the dining hall talking with Rindu, Dr. Walt, and Nicole. It had been a full day and Sam was tired, ready to turn in.

"Sam," Dr. Walt said. "I wonder if I may impose upon you further and ask you to accompany me. There is someone I would like you to meet."

Okay, so maybe he would not go to sleep just yet.

7

"Sure," Sam told Dr. Walt, "as long as I don't have to talk any more about our quest to confront Uncle Grayson. I'm pretty tired of that."

When Sam was in Gythe before, stranded with no clear way to get back home, he had battled all the way to the Gray Man, in this very fortress. At the end, his friend Skitter saved the day by using his telepathic powers and bringing to light memories the Gray Man had forgotten, memories that he was actually Sam's uncle. His name had been Grayson Wepp, and because of years of torture by the Arzbedim, the group of evil users of the *rohw*, he had become the Gray Man. When it was all made clear, Grayson chose to end his own life rather than to live with what he had done, what he had become. Sam referred to him now as Grayson, not wanting to forget his uncle and the sacrifice he made.

"No worries at all," Dr. Walt said. "In fact, you'll find that you probably don't have to answer any of this man's questions."

Sam wasn't sure what that meant, but agreed to go. Nalia and his mother came with him. Rindu politely excused himself, saying he wanted to meditate and go to bed.

Their footsteps echoed in the wide hallway. That is, Sam's, Nicole's, and Dr. Walt's footsteps echoed. Nalia, as always, made no sound.

As they passed corridor after corridor, unwanted memories assailed Sam's mind. He had spent a fair amount of time in the fortress after Grayson's death, but he could never shake the memories of running through the halls and fighting for his life. He saw sprays of blood along the walls, stains that were no longer there. He saw bodies lying where he had put them. The ghosts of his frantic flight through the fortress to reach the Great Hall would not leave him alone.

"Are you okay, honey?" his mother said, snapping him out of his visions. "You look a little pale."

He smiled at her weakly. "I'm fine. It's just—" he cleared his throat, "it's just hard to remember. So much blood, so much death. I'm okay."

She kissed him on his cheek. "I'm so sorry that you had to go through that."

He was sorry, too.

"It's just a bit farther, up this way," Dr. Walt interrupted.

It made Sam drop his other thoughts and think about where he was going. "Dr. Walt, who is this man you want me to meet?"

"His name is Lahim Chode. You might remember him. He was the only prisoner in the Gray Man's, I mean Grayson's, dungeon who survived.

"Oh, I remember him," Sam said. "When I left, he still couldn't speak, still wasn't conscious."

"Yes, yes, that's him. Well, he is conscious and speaking now, though he is still weak and bedridden. Ah, here we are." They were at a wooden door that looked like the dozens of other wooden doors they had passed on their way.

Dr. Walt knocked softly on the door, then opened it. He walked into the room followed by Sam and the two women. It was a moderate-sized chamber, with a large bed off to one side, a bookshelf and night stand flanking it. There was a small dining table with four chairs to the right of the room. A large wooden wardrobe finished the furnishings. In the fireplace, a fire glowed merrily, chasing away the chill that seeped out from the stone walls. A large window was on one wall, shut against the night.

The man was sitting in his bed, pillows behind him to prop him up. He was sickly, very thin, and pale, almost as if Sam could have looked right through him to the wall behind. His long auburn hair was in disarray and looked not to have been washed for a very long time. He turned his sunken eyes toward the newcomers and Sam noticed what he thought was a small smile play across the man's face.

"Sam Sharp," the man croaked, voice raspy with disuse. "It's an honor to finally meet you. Please forgive me for not getting up, but as you can see," he motioned with his hand, calling attention to his skeletal frame, "I have seen better days."

"Hello, Master Chode," Sam answered. "You are in much better shape than last time I saw you, just a few weeks ago."

"Yes." The man coughed, took a long drink from a cup he picked up from the night stand, and then cleared his throat. "Yes, a few weeks for me, but more for you. Many more."

Sam looked to Nalia and then to his mother. Finally, he turned to Dr. Walt, who seemed content to let the conversation go along as it had started.

"Dr. Walt tells me that you wanted to talk to me?"

The man looked into Sam's eyes. Sam thought he saw something there, some type of recognition, almost as if he had just confirmed something. It made him uneasy.

"Actually, I just wanted to meet you. I wanted to make

sure it was you that I saw." He took another drink from his cup. "It was."

"Sam, Lahim here has a talent. He is able to view things. He sees other places, other times. He told us two days ago that you would be arriving today. He said Nalia and someone else would be with you. We wrote it off as feverish dreams, but here you are. Here you all are."

Sam laughed, but then cut off again immediately when no one seemed to be laughing with him. "Are you kidding with me?" he asked. No one else was smiling. "Come on. Telling you that I would show up is a very good guess, a large coincidence, I'll give you that, but things like that happen all the time. No offense, Master Chode, but I don't think it proves that you're a seer or an oracle."

"A viewer, actually," the man said.

"A view…wait, what?" Sam looked to the others for support, but none met his gaze.

"Sam," Dr. Walt said, "Lahim is a viewer. On our world, the skill was known as remote viewing. It's sort of an out-of-body experience that allows the viewer to project himself along the path of time and space to view things. The United States government actually had a sophisticated program to train and utilize remote viewers for espionage. There are numerous accounts of viewers looking forward into the future or even viewing other planets. It's fascinating, really."

"I…I—" Sam couldn't think of what to say.

"Sam," Lahim Chode said. "It's no problem. I didn't ask to see you to make you feel uncomfortable. I just wanted to confirm that it was in fact you that I saw. When you were here last, I was unconscious and so never really had a chance to see what you look like." He took another drink from his cup and re-adjusted himself on the bed.

"More than anything, I wanted to make sure my talent still worked, that I was not fooling myself into thinking some fever dream was a viewing. The torture the Gray Man subjected me to has had a serious effect on my body.

And on my mind. I wanted to be sure I could still use my skills. Thank you for coming to see me. It was very nice meeting you. I hope to see you and have a proper conversation with you when I'm not so weak."

The others turned to leave, but Chode spoke up once again. "Sam, I wanted to tell you that earlier today, I had another viewing. This one was not so clear as when I saw you arrive, but where it lacks clarity, it makes up for in its ominous nature. The viewing was jumbled, but I saw a woman in a corridor. I believe it was this very fortress. She witnessed a murder but escaped unharmed. Another image came to me, showing her learning, training in some way, becoming more powerful. Finally, she came into her power and began to use it for selfish ends. I could almost hear someone speaking as I watched her planning, 'She is coming for you, she is coming…'"

The man coughed weakly, took a drink, and was silent. No one else moved or spoke for seval long moments.

"Why don't we allow Lahim to rest now?" Dr. Walt said. "Even conversation is taxing to him in his weakened condition." He shepherded the others toward the door. He stopped when he was about to go through into the hall.

"Did you need anything Lahim? Some food, more drink, anything?"

"No, Dr. Walt, but thank you. The servants have been doing a fantastic job in keeping up with my needs. You are much too kind to someone such as I."

"Nonsense. You were subjected to horrors beyond our imaginings. The least we can do is to help you heal. Be sure to let us know if there is anything you need."

On the way back to the part of the keep where their rooms were, Dr. Walt told Sam about Lahim Chode.

"He used to hire himself out to the wealthy, using his talents to help them make decisions. He made quite a name for himself and he was pampered and paid well by many different families.

"Apparently, the Gray Man, or one of his minions,

heard about his skill. Your uncle was always on the lookout for more information, so he had his Collectors apprehend Chode and bring him to the Gray Fortress.

"He was asked to describe exactly how he did what he did. When it made no sense, the Gray Man...I mean Grayson...no, the—"

"It's fine, Dr. Walt," Sam said, patting the doctor's arm, "don't get too tense about it. I know who you mean. Thank you for caring enough to try to remember to call him Grayson."

"Oh, yes, yes my boy. I understand the trauma in learning he was your uncle. It must be difficult. Anyway, Chode was tortured so that the truth could be extracted from him. The problem was, Chode really didn't know how to explain it. How can you explain to a fish how to breathe air? So, he was tortured off and on and left to deteriorate in the dungeons. If we hadn't found him when we did, he would have died like the rest of the prisoners."

Sam thought about what the doctor had told him. "So, you really believe he has some talent, that he can actually see across space and time?"

"I don't know, Sam. I have seen things in my research that boggle the mind. I have seen you yourself do things that seem impossible. What is one more unexplained mystery? If Lahim Chode can actually get information that could help us in anything we do, I think we should listen."

Nalia, quiet up until this point, spoke. "Sam, it is a little thing to hold off on judging if this thing is real or fantasy. It will cause no harm to keep an open mind. Have you not learned this in your studies?"

Sam felt his face grow warm. One of his ongoing problems with learning to use the *rohw* was his disbelief in things he could accomplish with it. Nalia and Rindu had demonstrated to him pointedly that his doubting mind was a large hindrance to progressing in his training.

"You're right, Nalia. Sometimes I'm just cynical. I'll try to 'empty my cup,' and keep an open mind."

To him, her beautiful smile was better than a gold medal.

8

The next morning, Sam found a spot tucked out of the way in one of the smaller courtyards near one of the doors into the keep. He spent some time learning the vibratory signature of the place and then teleported back to his workshop. Within minutes, he teleported the entire structure and everything in it to the place he had learned. Now all his belongings would be near at hand.

He opened the workshop and checked on the cats. Stoker meowed enthusiastically, explaining all the terrible wrongs he had suffered by being locked inside for an eternity. The mother cat, which Sam had decided to name Molly, looked less haggard than the day before. She was lying down and allowing the kittens to nurse again. She purred at him when he stroked her fur. All of the felines seemed to be doing well.

Stoker exited the building warily, realizing it was not an area he recognized. He sniffed, his head swaying back and forth, then went back into the familiar workshop. Sam knew the cat would get used to the new location, but it was just as well he wanted to stay put for now. Topping off the cat's food and water and picking up a wrapped bundle from one of the benches, Sam closed the door again.

He found Rindu in his room, the same chamber he had in the weeks following Grayson's death. When he knocked on the door, he heard the Zouy say, "Come."

Sam entered the room, carrying his bundle, which he leaned against the wall near the door. The chamber was simple, as Sam imagined Rindu's room at the temple must have been. Everything was in its place—the few things that the monk had—and it was immaculate, of course. The man himself sat at a low table on a thick rug. He was sitting on his knees, in a formal posture with his back straight. The Zouy was doing something, but Sam couldn't tell what it was because Rindu's back was to him. When he moved around the side, he saw that there was a large piece of paper in front of the monk, an inkwell sitting off just to the right of the paper, and a thin brush in his hand.

The Zouyim held the brush perfectly vertical with his right hand. With his left, he held the sleeve of his robe so it would not drag across the wet ink. He was drawing what looked like Chinese characters on the paper.

Sam silently watched as Rindu maneuvered the brush with expert precision, laying down lines of ink, creating characters on the page. He was mesmerized by the fluid motion, the grace with which the brush moved. He felt a lump in his throat. It was beautiful, a perfect blend of speed, grace, and patience. Rindu finished one final stroke, pulled back his arm, and cleaned the bristles with the same grace with which he had written the characters.

"Calligraphy?" Sam asked. He saw surprise register on Rindu's face.

"Yes. How do you know of calligraphy?" the Zouy asked him.

"It's done in my world. Chinese and Japanese calligraphy is an art form. Some famous calligraphers sell their works for great amounts of money."

"I see."

"Not only that, though. It's supposed to develop

supple wrists and fine coordination that help with swordplay and with other martial endeavors."

"Ah, so you have heard of the value of the practice." Rindu nodded approvingly. "It is more than that, however. It strengthens the connection with the *rohw*. It develops qualities that are important for a warrior."

"What language is that?" Sam asked. "What are those characters?"

"The language is called Syray. It is no longer spoken. A great Zouyim master taught me the language and how to wield the brush when I was a young disciple in the temple. When he died during a mission, the masters gave the brush set to me, as per his instructions. I hid them when Nalia and I were fleeing from the Gray Man. I just retrieved them a few days ago. It was an eight-day journey to do so.

"This character is wisdom," he said pointing to one of the characters. He pointed to the other three in turn. "These are power, harmony, and strength."

Sam thought about it a moment. "How does calligraphy help the connection to the *rohw*?"

The Zouy looked into Sam's eyes. "Ah, that is a fascinating tale, one my master told me when I was a young disciple in the Zouyim temple.

"It is said that when the Supreme Being created the universe, he pondered how he would teach humans to tap into the energy he had provided, the *rohw*. After much thought, he decided that a written language would be ideal. The formation of the letters, or characters, of the language would emulate the movements necessary to take in the universal *rohw* and thereby cause the writer to be in harmony with the energy and with his surroundings.

"The first humans were taught the language, the remnant of which is Syray, so they were, at the beginning, much more a part of the balance of the universe. As time passed, however, people began to forget the correct writing of the characters as they developed new dialects, new languages, until calligraphy was forgotten almost completely. So it is that people are no longer balanced in their oneness with the universe."

Sam looked at the Zouy, waiting to see if there was any more to the story. Rindu looked back at him, a satisfied look on his face, as if his short story explained it all. "Uh, that's a nice story, but it still doesn't really tell me how your calligraphy helps with connection to the universal *rohw*."

Rindu looked as if he might be offended, but then a thoughtful look crossed his face. "I suppose you are right," the monk said. "The history does not tell the mechanics."

Rindu stood and faced Sam. "Do you recall the *kori rohw* exercises, Sam? They are the movements that help to bring one into harmony with the universal *rohw*. You observed Torim Jet and me performing them at Tramgadal when you were last in Gythe."

"I remember," Sam said, not wanting to discuss that Nalia had been teaching him some of the movements while they were in Telani. That bit of news could wait.

"Attend me," Rindu said, as he assumed a stable stance that Sam recognized from watching the monk perform the *rohw* exercises. "Watch my movements carefully, especially those of my hands."

Rindu moved slowly and smoothly. His body turned and gyrated, but Sam focused on the monk's hands and saw that there were tiny movements and positionings that he never would have picked out if watching the entire set of exercises.

"Now," Rindu continued, "watch my hands and wrists as I wield my brush to draw characters in the air."

Sam did so and noticed that the tiny movements and the exact positioning of the monk's appendages matched perfectly with those of the *kori rohw*. "Wow," he said. "I see it now."

"Good," the Zouy said, becoming still once more. "There are, of course, other facets, such as meditative aspects and the meanings of the characters themselves, which are important for us to think upon, but you can see that, altogether, calligraphy is helpful in finding balance with the *rohw*."

"I can," Sam said. "Thank you, Master Rindu. But before I forget why I actually came to visit," he picked up the wrapped bundle he had leaned against the wall, "I wanted to give you a gift. Nalia and I found these in our travels. They belonged to a master who had died of disease. You would honor me if you would accept them and use them as your own."

Rindu carefully took the bundle from Sam's hand and bowed over them toward the younger man. His deft hands lifted the covering and set it aside, eyes going wide. That was equivalent to jumping up and down screaming for most people, so controlled were the Zouy's expressions in normal situations. As the monk unsheathed the blades, ingeniously fitted together in the single scabbard, Sam thought he saw Rindu's eyes go liquid for a brief moment.

"Sam," the older man said. "They...they are magnificent. They are the finest broadswords I have ever had the privilege to hold."

"They're spring steel, so they are flexible, but not so flexible as many of the broadswords I've seen. These are a bit heavier weight, thicker. Technically, I think they're classified as 'battle broadswords,' though I suppose that's just to distinguish them from thinner blades used for demonstration purposes on Telani."

The monk separated the swords and held one out straight, sighting down the blade. Stepping back, he whirled it in a circular motion, blade whistling through the air as he slashed with it, rolled it around his shoulders and whipped it out for another strike. A rare smile lit up the Zouy's face. "They are exquisitely balanced and the hilt is very firm."

Sam smiled back. "Yes, there is a full tang in the hilt so there will be no loosening and no rattling even with heavy use. When we saw them, Nalia and I both thought of you.

They are fitting weapons for the man who will rebuild the Zouyim Order."

Rindu expertly put the swords back together so that they looked like one blade and then, in one smooth motion, sheathed them in the black-lacquered scabbard. "Sam, this is a spectacular gift." Holding the scabbarded sword in his right hand while bringing it together with his left in a salute, he bowed formally. "Thank you. It is my hope that I will not have to use them except for training, but if the need should arise, they should prove to be valuable indeed."

Sam returned the bow, his heart swelling within his chest. "I'm glad you like them. Hopefully Nalia won't be upset I gave them to you without her here."

"I will let her know how much I appreciate the gift. Did this master of whom you spoke name the weapons? Is that a custom in your world?"

That threw Sam for a moment. "I didn't think to ask. I'm sorry. It didn't really occur to me."

"That is fine," Rindu said, still eyeing the scabbard as if he could see the swords within. "I saw markings on each blade, but I believe those to be the maker's mark. I will call them Sunedal, Teeth of Dal, in honor of my great master Chetra Dal, who was lost to us trying to accomplish a dangerous mission. Master Dal's wisdom often clove through falsehood and confusion and made clear the truth of things. It is fitting, I think."

"I think so too. It sounds like a perfect name to me."

Near noon, Sam and Nalia teleported to Marybador. As promised, Shen Nan was there waiting, his smiling face greeting them as they appeared. He was not alone.

"I told the others that you may not show up for several days, but they insisted on waiting with me each day, with all their belongings," Shen said to them. "As you can see, we don't have much."

Nalia busied herself in greeting each and every one of the refugees. The children had not been born when their families had left Marybador, or were very young, but the adults all recognized her even without her mask. They greeted her with respect and affection that made Sam's heart glad. These were her people and it did her good to know there was still a remnant left, even if none of her sisters had survived.

It took only a few minutes to bring the group back to Whitehall, where stewards were waiting to show them where they would be living. There was more than enough space in the keep, so they would be given rooms near each other and found work to occupy themselves.

Nalia smiled at Sam as the bedraggled group was led away to their room so they could leave their possessions and head to the dining hall. They waved at her, smiling, as they left.

"When we rebuild Marybador, they will be given a choice to return there or to stay here," Sam said. "Or to go wherever else they want to go. They're long past due for being able to move on with their lives."

"Yes," the Sapsyr said. "It is good that we can help them. They will be happy, as I wish all Gythe would be happy. Maybe with the new government, all people will have a chance at that dream."

"I hope so, Nal," Sam said. "I really hope so."

9

Sam spent the next several days re-acquainting himself with the fortress and all its many corridors, chambers, and features. One day, as he and Nalia were heading out toward one of the many training yards to spar, Dr. Walt chanced upon them. He looked exasperated.

"Hi, Dr. Walt," Sam said. "You look kind of frazzled. Is everything all right?"

"Oh, good morning Sam, Nalia. I'm fine. It's just that dealing with the leaders and trying to get them to agree on anything for the new government is driving me batty."

"What is it this time?" Nalia asked.

"Oh, several of the leaders want the seat of government somewhere else. They say that the reputation of the Gray Man will taint any government that is based in the fortress. They say even the name 'Gray Fortress' will call to mind the things that were perpetrated from here." He shook his head and sighed, looking at the stone floor. "I can't say I blame them. It's all so fresh in everyone's mind."

"Do you think maybe it'll pass, that people will forget about it in time?" Sam asked him.

"I'm sure it will, but how much time is needed? Starting a new government is tenuous work. Something like this could prevent it from starting at all, keep the general population from ever supporting it."

"What other location could be used?" Nalia asked. "There is no place that is suitable. Not one outside of the cities. The leaders of the other cities will never stand for that. Trying to find a location where a new headquarters can be built will be as difficult to agree on."

"You are exactly right," Dr. Walt answered. "Thus our dilemma."

He patted Nalia's shoulder and smiled a thin, sad smile at Sam. "Thank you for letting me complain to you. We'll figure something out. It's just all so frustrating. Anyway, don't let me hold you up. Go and enjoy the day. We'll talk later." He hurried down the corridor, muttering to himself.

Sam looked to Nalia. "Nal, I have an idea. Can we postpone our sparring for a little while? I need to find your father and ask him about something."

"Of course," she said with a smirk. "I know you are afraid to spar with me, even after all this time. It is to be expected."

Sam laughed and kissed her on the cheek. "Exactly. You want to come with me?"

"I will leave you to it," she said. "I will take the time to continue your mother's lessons in Kasmali. She feels uncomfortable having only three people with whom she can speak. When you are ready to be bruised, come find me."

Sam hurried to Rindu's small room and found him there, reading.

"Master Rindu," Sam said. "I was wondering if you would help me with something."

The monk placed a piece of ribbon on the page he was reading and closed the book gently. "Of course, Sam. What is it that you need?"

"Please come with me, and I'll explain as we're

walking."

The two started off, Sam to the right and just slightly ahead of the Zouy.

"Dr. Walt has a problem with the leaders and the new government," Sam started.

"He has many problems with them, yes," Rindu added.

Sam laughed. "I guess you're right. Well, this particular problem involves using the fortress here as the location for the government. People are concerned that in the citizens' minds, they will connect the new government with Uncle Grayson's…atrocities."

The monk looked thoughtful. "Yes, I have heard this brought up. It is a valid point, I think."

"I agree," Sam said, "but what if we could do something to separate the place from the man and his actions, make it so that it is clear that things have changed and it is a different place, a different world now?"

"I would think that would ease matters. What is it that you propose, Sam?"

"Well, when I was reliving Uncle Grayson's memories, when Skitter was broadcasting them into my mind as well as my uncle's,"—Sam turned right at an intersection and began climbing up a set of stairs—"there was one thing that happened that I think is important.

"In the memory, Uncle Grayson was unhappy with the color of the Black Fortress, not wanting to be thought to be just another Arzbed. He used his *rohw* and changed the frequency of the fortress stone, just slightly, so that it reflected gray color instead of black."

"Hmmm." Rindu made the sound, obviously seeing where the conversation was going.

"The memories were played back in my mind as if I was living them. I could see, hear, taste, smell, and feel everything as if I was the one experiencing all those things. I can 'remember' changing the color of the fortress. I think I can work out how to change it again."

"To a more suitable color, I assume?" Rindu asked.

"White."

"Ah, that would be very good. Are you sure you can do such a thing?"

Sam moved onto a short landing that led to a narrow corridor. "I think so, but I figured I'd need you to help me, to guide me."

"I know nothing of this technique, Sam, but I will do what I can."

"I think," Sam said, "it's like when you helped me with the teleportation thing. We both read how it should happen and then you were able to guide me through it. I never would have been able to do it without your help. Or, at least, it would have taken me a long time to figure it out."

"Yes, that is true. Between my experience and your raw power with the *rohw*, we will do this. It is a very good idea, Sam. I am proud of you."

"Maybe you should reserve being too proud until we figure out if we can actually do it."

"Oh, Sam," Rindu said, eyes downcast, "have we not discussed this many times before? 'When a man decides firmly to do a thing, the universe conspires to make it happen.' We have but to apply ourselves wholly and we shall overcome all obstacles."

Sam tilted his head and scrutinized Rindu. "Have you been reading the books I brought for you? Was that a quote from one of them?"

Rindu's eyes twinkled but his expression remained neutral. "Dr. Walt has been kind enough to translate a few short passages for me. I am rewriting them in Kasmali. I will learn your language so I can read them myself and set the words down in the language of Gythe. There is much wisdom in your gift. I thank you once again for them."

He bowed to Sam.

Sam spoke through the lump in his throat. "I'm glad you like them. As I was moving my books I chose them out because I know your love of quotes and parables.

Maybe you can merge the wisdom of both our worlds and make Gythe a better place."

"It will be so."

Sam had given Rindu a handful of his books. Some were compilations of quotes from many different sources, but others were standalone classics, such as the Tao Te Ching, the Analects of Confucius, and the Bhagavad Gita. He knew if there was anyone who would appreciate them as much as Sam, it would be Rindu, though now that he thought about it, Dr. Walt may appreciate them solely because they were books. He was glad the Zouy appreciated his gift.

They arrived at the high battlement where Grayson, in the memory, changed the color of the fortress. Sam supposed it didn't matter if it was the same location as far as actually performing the action, but he thought it might help him concentrate and remember more clearly.

He spent a few minutes discussing with Rindu every second of what he had seen and felt in the recollection. When they felt they were ready to attempt their task, they sat facing each other on the cold stone, legs crossed, knees almost touching.

The wind screamed through the crenels, striking the merlons on the other side of the battlement and swirling around Sam and Rindu, tugging at their clothing. Both were well-practiced at concentrating, however, so they were able to ignore the biting blasts almost entirely.

"Your focus has grown better, Sam," Rindu said. "That is good. I am glad you continued to practice and progress. Now, you must attain the *khulim*, the 'almost-trance.'"

Sam did so, slipping into the soothing, light-headed feeling he was so familiar with. Immediately, he saw in his mind's eye the energy swirling around him. It almost shocked him out of the *khulim*; he had never seen the energy of the wind before. His *rohw* sensitivity was so much keener in Gythe than in Telani. He felt Rindu in front of him, felt his energy reach out to Sam's.

"Now, Sam," he heard Rindu's voice as if it as coming from the bottom of a well, "fix in your mind the feeling of the vibrations Grayson used to change the stone's color."

Sam recalled the specific feeling of the frequency of the fortress, how it was changed from black to gray. He nodded.

"Now picture the snow as it floats in the air, as it covers the ground. Feel its vibration. Can you identify it? Are you intimately familiar with it?"

Sam was. Living through the winter in his forested home, he had meditated outside in the snow many times. It was a means to increase his focus, ignoring the cold and the wet, becoming one with nature and feeling its call.

One day in particular stuck in his mind. He had been meditating for over two hours and the snowfall was becoming heavier. He had lost track of time but was still deeply in the *khulim*. Suddenly, he felt himself melt into his surroundings. There was no other way he could describe it. It felt like he became the snow, really became part of the natural world. At that moment, he understood the frozen water in a way he had never thought possible. He came out of his meditation to find he had several inches of snow covering him from being immobile for such a length of time.

Sam remembered that feeling now. He understood the component of the snow that determined its color, what light it reflected. He realized the precise vibration he was looking for. He tried to apply it to the wall, reaching out and touching it.

Nothing happened.

He cracked an eyelid and looked at the stone he was touching, looking for any sign of a change. There was none. He was so sure he had remembered it correctly. What was wrong? He let his hand drop.

Taking an extra deep and long breath, he relaxed his mind for a moment, then latched firmly to the vibration of the snow he had experienced. He tried to become that vibration, tried to become the snow. He felt something shift within him and recognized in a distant way that his body no longer felt the chilling wind at all, as if it was going through him.

Sam felt one with the snow. Not just the snow from his memories, but the snow he saw in the surrounding landscape. He turned it over in his mind, becamse intimately familiar with it, even more so than before.

He felt Rindu smile. There was something in his energy that fairly screamed the expression much more accurately than outward expressions.

"Good," Rindu said. "Now, make the stone vibrate at that frequency. Start at one location and let the energy transmit though all the fortress, changing it all to the color of snow."

Sam reached out his hand again and touched the frigid rock of the battlement. When he did, he felt a slight resistance at first, as if it was going to impose its immovable nature and resist Sam's changes, but it lasted only a brief moment. He felt energy transfer from his hand to the battlement and begin to spread, picking up momentum as it went, building on itself. It was, he thought, like a snowball rolling down a hill, becoming larger with each turning.

He opened his eyes and watched with wonder as the dark gray stone turned white, the bleaching radiating out from him in a wave. It looked like the demonstrations his science teacher used to perform for the class when he was in school, using a large beaker of colored liquid then adding another compound which prompted a color change, the shift moving down from the top in a wave until all the liquid was the new color. He wished he could have filmed the fortress changing.

It took very little of his own energy to continue the color change. He could feel the whiteness spread, going throughout the entire keep and its walls, moving along to other buildings, reaching the fortress walls themselves.

When it was done, mere minutes later, he felt that it was finished and dropped his hand to his lap. He was tired, but not nearly as tired as he thought he would be.

He looked over at Rindu. "It is done," he said simply.

"Sam, that was remarkable," the Zouy said to him. "Until you told me of it, I had never heard of anyone doing such a thing, let alone doing it on such a large scale. Come, let us see what your handiwork has wrought."

Rindu helped Sam to his feet and they both looked out over the crenels to the rest of the keep, the grounds, and the walls. Though it was an overcast day, the walls shone white, reflecting the diffuse sunlight and causing a glare. It looked like an entire castle made of ice. It was simply beautiful.

"That ought to make people think about whether this is the same place the Gray Man resided in or not," Sam said, feeling the face on his skin stretch tight in the cold wind. "Maybe we should go tell Dr. Walt it was our work so he doesn't spend the next year investigating how it happened."

Rindu clapped Sam on the back. "I believe you have the right of it. Please, after you." He opened the door back inside the keep and motioned for Sam to enter.

The two found Dr. Walt frantically looking through books, obviously trying to understand why he was now standing in a room with white walls when everything had been gray just a short time ago.

"Dr. Walt," Sam said as they entered the library, "it was us. You can stop looking for a reason."

The old man's head snapped up, not having heard them enter. "What? Sam, Rindu, have you noticed anything odd about the color of the walls?"

"It was us," Sam repeated. "We changed the color of all the stone in the fortress. We thought it would help people to forget who lived here last. We thought it would help them accept the place as the seat of the new government."

"You…" Dr. Walt forced out, "you changed the color

of the stone?"

"Yes," Rindu said. "Sam remembered how the Gray Man, Grayson, had done it when he changed it from black to gray. Sam changed it to white. Our apologies for not warning you beforehand."

"Wha—" the scholar stammered. "Ah, no. No worries. It was just a surprise, that's all." He rubbed his chin in thought. "White, eh? Yes, that could help. Shining fortress and all that. I think perhaps this could make a difference. Wonderful, Sam, simply wonderful. Thank you."

"You're welcome," Sam said. "There's one other thing. I was kind of thinking about it and maybe I have a good name for the place, since White Fortress seems kind of lame after it was the Black Fortress and then the Gray Fortress."

"Ah, yes, I hadn't thought of that," Dr. Walt said. "What would you suggest, Sam?"

"Whitehall."

10

"You did that?" Nicole asked Sam. "You turned an entire fortress, millions of tons of rock, a different color just using that energy stuff you're always talking about?"

"Yeah, Mom," Sam said. "It's called *rohw*. It's much more powerful here than back home, probably because there isn't all the interference from electromagnetic fields and because there is more of a natural setting here. There are actually forests. Not the relatively small pockets of forest like on Telani, but ones that stretch for hundreds of miles. At least, that's why I think it's more powerful.

"Besides, you've seen me use the *rohw* before. I used it to teleport us here, after all."

"I know, but…it's just…I don't know." She shook her head. "It's kind of crazy, almost scary. It's a big fortress."

Sam laughed. "I know. It's strange to me, too, I only knew how to do it because I shared the memories of Uncle Grayson changing it to gray, and Rindu had to help or I never could have done it. The power he held, and the knowledge of how to use it—that was scary. Anyway, do you like the new color? I think it's kind of cool."

Nicole came over and hugged him. "Yes, Sam, it's kind

of cool." She laughed.

"That was good thinking, Sam," Nalia said, smiling at him. "Renaming the fortress and changing it to shine like a beacon for miles was just the thing Dr. Walt needed to convince the leaders that this is the appropriate location for the new government. I am proud of you."

"Thanks, Nal," he said. "It just kind of came to me. I hope it helps. We need all the help we can get to make everyone agree on things."

"Are you ready to spar now that you are finished solving everyone else's problems?" she teased.

"Absolutely, let's go."

An hour and a half later, as their sparring session was winding down, Rindu appeared, watching them. Sam had, as normal, been beaten to a standstill. As much as he felt like he was improving, Nalia was always so far above him in skill that he could hardly see her from where he stood. When they finished, the monk came over to the two.

"Your skill has improved, Sam," the Zouy said.

"Thank you," Sam returned. "Nalia has been working me hard, trying to make me improve. It has been a year and a half since we were here. At least, it was that long where we were."

"It is true," Nalia said, "and we have practiced constantly in that time. Sam may become a warrior yet. Maybe." She winked at him, causing his heart to flutter.

Rindu nodded. "It is good. Sam, Nalia has mentioned that she taught you some of the movements of the *kori rohw*. Would you show me?"

Sam felt his heart speed up even more and felt the movement in his stomach, as if there was a creature waking up, trying to get out. "Um, I guess. I haven't practiced them that much, though."

"That is fine. I would like to see the first thirty movements, if you please."

Sam gulped. He thought he performed the movements well, but showing them to Rindu made him nervous for some reason, especially after seeing the precise hand movements Rindu demonstrated earlier. Still, he handed his staff, *Ahimiro*, to Nalia, walked a few steps away from the duo, and began.

The *kori rohw* was a set of exercises meant to increase *rohw* sensitivity and to enable the body to become one with the surroundings, with the universe. It was obvious that some of the movements represented strikes, blocks, and evasions, but others seemed to serve no martial purpose at all. The motions were performed slowly, with no force, as smoothly as the exerciser could manage. It was more about flowing through all the parts of the exercises than showing power or speed.

As always, when Sam started, he felt a heat generate in his body, especially in his palms and the soles of his feet. A warm, glowing feeling soon centered just below his navel and radiated out, empowering him while at the same time relaxing him. Half the time, he kept his eyes lightly closed, just because it seemed that he could concentrate more fully on the energy surrounding him, as well as his own, without the distraction of sight. He knew Rindu didn't keep his eyes closed when he did the movements, but Sam chalked it up to his own inexperience.

Sam soon finished the thirtieth movement and stopped. He looked to Rindu for some kind of expression, some kind of response. There was none. Rindu, as normal, wore a completely emotionless look on his face.

The silence stretched on.

Sam began to get fidgety. "Master Rindu?" he said.

"I am trying to determine where to begin," the monk said.

"That bad, huh?"

Rindu's expression softened a tiny bit. From diamond to stone. "No, Sam, it is not that. You have learned the movements, but we must work on improving them. Please do the first five movements again, very slowly."

Sam had only gotten through the first two movements

when Rindu interrupted him. "Slowly, Sam. Do them more slowly."

Sam tried again. After the first movement, Rindu stopped him. "You must perform the *kori rohw* more slowly. The skill in perfect movement requires freedom from hurry. Not only must you maintain correct posture in order to move as slowly as required, but you will collect more of the surrounding *rohw* doing so. Please observe."

The Zouy went into the starting stance, standing straight up with his feet next to each other, hands at his side. He stepped into the first posture, bringing his hands up as if cupping a ball between them. He did it so slowly that it took almost a full minute just to shift his weight and place his foot precisely where it belonged. He performed the second movement as well, taking just as long as the first. Then, he stepped back into a normal standing posture. "Do you understand, Sam?"

"I do, Master Rindu, but I am having trouble moving so slowly."

The monk's face grew contemplative. "I have an idea. Please come with me."

Sam and Nalia followed Rindu around a portion of the keep, to a door Sam had never opened. After going through the portal, they had only a short distance to another. When Rindu opened it and motioned Sam to go through it, Sam's eyes widened in surprise.

They were in a massive greenhouse. Sam couldn't even see the far walls of the chamber. It was much warmer inside than out in the fall air from which they had come. Plants of all kinds were everywhere. He saw movement and noticed that there were birds, insects, even the occasional squirrel.

"This is amazing," Sam exclaimed. He looked at Nalia, who had a look of wonder on her face as well. "I didn't even know this was here. I didn't get to this area of the keep when I was here before."

"It is a favorite place of mine, since I found it. I enjoy

coming here to meditate amongst the plants and animals. It is much closer than going down to the Undead Forest, and more peaceful as well. But we are here for a specific purpose. Come."

He led them to another area of the greenhouse. Sam clasped Nalia's hand as they followed her father, head swiveling left and right, trying to take it all in. In a moment, Rindu stopped at the edge of a field of wildflowers.

"Wildflowers? It's getting close to winter. How is it that there are flowers here?"

Rindu tilted his head slightly at Sam. "The great glass panels above bring the sun in, and magnify it, but I think they do more than that. I can feel a strange power here, related to the *rohw* but not quite the same. I believe this place was infused with some energy, some 'magic,' that makes it possible to simulate the spring or summer. Dr. Walt, right after we found this place, searched for references in the many books here. He found only mention by the Arzbedim, that they were unable to affect the greenhouse's function. They tried, but were unsuccessful. Finally, they accepted it for what it was and instead used it to breed bees so they would have a supply of honey. They used it to make mead.

"But," the Zouy continued, "we are not here for lessons in greenhouses. We are here for the *kori rohw*. Sam, please come with me. Nalia, stay where you are. We will only be a few feet away."

Sam wondered what the master was going to do. He followed obediently, moving through the tall grass and the flowers of many different colors. There were bright yellows and oranges, deep blues and purples, too many different shades of red to count, and even some white flowers punctuating the landscape. As he passed, grasshoppers and butterflies moved at his approach, some landing on him. He laughed as a tiny grasshopper landed on his arm and tickled him with its minuscule feet.

Rindu stopped him in a patch of tall grass almost devoid of the flowers. "Wait here for a moment, Sam," he said, and moved toward a brightly colored patch of low plants with blossoms everywhere. Sam waited patiently, delighting in the butterflies that flew up and came to rest on him, slowly pumping their wings as if in greeting.

Soon, Rindu returned with his hands cupped around something.

"Do not move," he said. He waited for Sam's affirmation and then slowly uncupped his hands, revealing nearly a dozen butterflies within. The monk put his hands near Sam and carefully allowed each butterfly to walk off him and onto the younger man. When it was all done, Sam had close to twenty of the insects resting on different parts of his body, including those flying in to land on the perch Rindu's butterflies had taken.

Sam was confused. "Um, Master Rindu?" Sam said, "What's going on?"

"This will help your training," he answered. "You must perform the *kori rohw* with your new friends perched upon you. If you do so slowly, as you should, they will remain on your body. If, however, you cannot complete the movements at the proper rate, they will be disturbed and fly off. Then we will have to catch more and place them on you."

Sam looked at the Zouy with exasperation, trying his hardest not to move. Two butterflies that had been on his face flew away. Rindu, in a perfect mixture of speed and fluid motion, intercepted the butterflies, one with each hand, and gently placed them on Sam's shoulder. Then he stepped away carefully.

"Now," Rindu said, "perform the first five movements of the *kori rohw*. Do so without causing the butterflies to flee."

For the next hour, Sam tried to go through the exercises at such a glacial pace that his colorful friends would not be shaken and fly away. He was mostly unsuccessful. When Rindu told him that it was enough, Sam released a breath he had not known he was holding, causing five more butterflies to leave their landing places. Only three stubborn insects remained on him.

"That was very hard," Sam told him as he was walking back toward Nalia with Rindu. "I never knew it was so hard to move slowly."

"Indeed it is," the monk said. "It is said, 'a movement in its slowness will reveal the skill of the man' and also 'the unskilled student makes a show of striking quickly, but the master needs not speed to prevail.'"

"Okay," Sam said, "I get it. I'll try to practice more slowly."

"Good," Rindu said. "It will also make it easier for me to correct your many errors in position." The monk winked at him.

Sam sighed. Just when he was feeling good about his progress, here he finds out that he had not even really started yet. They turned to leave the greenhouse, Sam saying a mental goodbye to the creatures there. He knew he would be spending a great deal of time here in the future, if Rindu had anything to say about it.

"I can't wait," Nalia said with a smirk, "to tell your mother that you are so sweet that the butterflies came to you instead of all the beautiful flowers. She will like hearing that."

Sam sighed again.

11

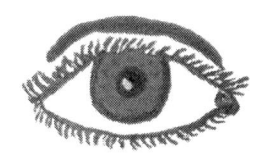

Life had become for Lahim Chode one nightmare after another. He had hope for the future, now that the bastard who called himself the Gray Man was dead and his vanquishers were in charge of the fortress, but he wasn't sure how far-reaching the effects of his previous treatment would be.

He had been tortured and neglected for what was probably months. The seer had lost track of time in the dungeons beneath the Gray Fortress, never knowing if it was day or night. If he hadn't been rescued when he was, he knew he would have been just one more prisoner that had died. As it was, he was the only survivor, and that just barely.

It was frustrating that he was still bedridden, though he supposed three weeks really wasn't too long a time as far as these things were concerned. He was feeling better each day. A little better. The pain of his injuries was more bearable and he was able to sleep a few hours uninterrupted each night. He looked forward to being able to get a full night's sleep. Eventually.

When he rang the bell frantically this morning, desperate for one of the servants to answer his call, he may have been a bit too insistent, a bit too presumptuous in commanding the young woman to go and get Dr. Walt immediately. What he had to tell the old scholar was important, there was no doubt, but maybe he should have been kinder about his delivery. There was nothing to do about it now. He would apologize to the woman for screeching at her when he got a chance. For now, it was important to tell someone about his viewing.

He heard footsteps in the hallway, several sets of them. Good, it wasn't just another servant. Dr. Walt had come to answer his call. Now he would be able to prove his worth. He would be able to feel better about the care given and the cost incurred to nurse him back to health. He would show he had something to contribute.

The door opened and Dr. Walt stepped in. Right behind him, Sam also came into the room. That was an unexpected, but fortuitous, occurrence.

"Lahim," Dr. Walt addressed him, "I was told you had an urgent matter, something you must tell me immediately."

"Yes, Dr. Walt. I had a viewing." Sam's eyebrows raised slightly before he smoothed his brow and put on a neutral expression.

"A viewing? I see." The doctor scratched his chin and pondered for a moment, no doubt lost in his constant ruminations about the nature of the viewings. The old man shook his head slightly, as if to shake off the thoughts, and looked back to Lahim.

"Oh, I almost forgot. Sam was discussing something with me and offered to come along. I hope that's okay."

"Of course," Lahim said. "I would like for Sam to be involved. The matter affects him also, maybe more strongly than most."

"Well, then," Dr. Walt said, moving his hands in a circular motion to indicate he wanted to get on with it, "what have you seen?"

Lahim Chode looked into Dr. Walt's eyes, face set and

serious. "I have seen a new threat, a new evil in Gythe." He caught motion from the corner of his eye and was sure he saw a small smirk on Sam's face, quickly hidden in a soft cough.

"A woman named Ayim Rasaad, an expert energy user, is building forces to take advantage of the confusion, the 'hole' in the power structure since the Gray Man's death."

Sam spoke up. "How do you know this?"

"I have viewed it, heard her in conversation with one of her colleagues. I heard the other say her name. She will track down three items, ancient artifacts. I witnessed her reading an ancient manuscript, but not out loud. I couldn't see the words, but she described these items as being very powerful. She intends to use them to obtain complete control over Gythe."

"Where is she?" Sam asked.

"I'm afraid I don't know," Chode admitted.

Sam looked to Dr. Walt and then back to Lahim. He didn't say anything further.

Lahim knew when someone thought he was hallucinating but was too polite to say so. He felt his hopes shrink and disappear.

"I'll try to find more information, but my viewings don't work that way. Most often, the information I get is not that which I'm looking for. I'll try, though."

Dr. Walt looked sincerely sorry for him. "Don't overdo it, Lahim. You are weak yet. Let yourself heal and then you can search for more information. If you tax yourself, your health will suffer. We will take what you say under advisement and I'll see if I can find records of the artifacts you mentioned. Thank you for telling us. Get some rest now."

The two exited the room, leaving Lahim Chode with only his failure. He would have to make them see. What he had witnessed scared him to his core. If the Gray Man was bad, this Rasaad was worse because she would have powerful artifacts at her disposal. He had to find more information, find a way to convince them.

He took a sip of water, adjusted the pillows on his bed so he was more comfortable, and began to breathe rhythmically. Soon, he was in a state of meditation that was necessary for his mind to relax and become receptive to the information from the matrix, the stream of time and space which included all things. He would find more information. He had to.

*****

After leaving Lahim Chode's room, Sam looked at Dr. Walt as they walked along. "What do you think? Is Lahim just dreaming things up for attention or does he believe that he actually sees the future?"

"I do not believe he does it for attention," Dr. Walt said. "He does not see the future all the time. What he told us just now seems like it is happening in the present, but far away. From what I have read of remote viewing, that is the way of it. Sometimes it is distant, sometimes forward or back in time, sometimes both."

"But do you actually believe there's something there? I don't understand this whole time and space matrix stuff he talks about. I know I said I'd try to keep an open mind, but really, it seems like prophecy, like in fiction. Sometimes with the things that can be done with the *rohw*, it seems like magic, but prophecy? That's kind of a lot to swallow."

Dr. Walt stopped walking and looked at Sam. "It is, I agree. I still tend to base my opinions on things I learned in Telani. Things that are possible there are obviously possible here, even more so I think. The reading I have done on remote viewing says that such things can be done.

"At different periods of time, governments of one nation or another did research into extra-sensory abilities, trying to get an edge in reconnaissance or combat. Germany, the Soviet Union, the United States, all of these and more had programs to use these types of abilities.

Their development and use is documented. If such things are possible on Telani, how much more so on Gythe, where the natural world holds more power. You yourself have said that the *rohw* is much stronger here. Why not these other things?"

"I guess you're right," Sam said. "It sounds far-fetched to me, but I suppose it's possible. I don't know why it bothers me. Maybe it's because I feel like I'm being manipulated, like my choices aren't my own. I don't like anyone telling me how I must live my own life."

Dr. Walt slapped Sam on the shoulder. "I totally understand, but I don't think this has anything to do with free will. Lahim claims to be able to see things in the stream of time. The things he sees don't seem to be prophecies in the sense that they are unchangeable. For all I know, they are just a possibility. When he sees something in the present time, though, I think we would do well to consider it. At least until we have more evidence one way or another."

"I suppose." Sam was silent as he started walking again, Dr. Walt following. "Dr. Walt, why have you not trained in using the *rohw*? You've been here so long, studying everything here, I would have thought you'd try it out. I know not everyone has an affinity for it, but my understanding is anyone can meditate and feel the *rohw*."

"Quite right, Sam. I have tried, on occasion, to learn to use the vibratory energy and to come into harmony with it. Because I have no natural talent for it, learning is very slow and, well, not to put too fine a point on it, I'm lazy. I will go through phases wherein I meditate and practice, but then one thing or another happens and I stop. Now that I am settled in one place, not on the run from some enemy, perhaps I will take up the practice again and try it out."

"I see," Sam said. "I understand that. It's hard to create a habit. I bounced back and forth with meditating when I first started doing it in Telani. I'd be good for maybe a month but then I'd drift away from doing it daily. It took a good long while to make it a habit. In fact, it still wasn't something I did all the time until I came here and started training. Let me know if I can help in any way when you decide to start up again."

"I definitely will, Sam. Thank you. As for Lahim and his viewings, I think I'll see if there are any books in the library talking about artifacts of power. Can't be too careful, you know."

As they split up, Dr. Walt going to his library and Sam to his room, he thought about that. The scholar was right, of course. Better to heed the warnings and then have them be false than to ignore them and be stuck with the consequences. Pondering the strange powers in the world, he made his way back to his chamber to think on it properly.

12

This world of Gythe was fantastic, confusing, frustrating, and scary all at the same time, Nicole Sharp thought. *Yep, just like home.*

She had only been here a couple of weeks, but the things she'd seen were amazing. Sure, technology was primitive here, but even the relatively small sample she'd seen of the landscape was beautiful. She thought she might really like to stay here. As if she had a choice.

Truth be told, she did have a choice. Sam could bring her back home and leave her there if she wanted, but he was firm in his conviction that he would stay here from now on. She had nothing for her back on Earth. No, she would stay with her son and see all the wonders of this new world. At least there wasn't some maniacal villain like her brother had become, killing people and seizing whole villages.

Grayson. She still could hardly believe he had been here all that time, had become the most powerful man in the world, had become a murderer. She hoped he was at peace now, after all those years. Sam swore to her that he was lucid and reasonable in the end. He had regained his humanity. She believed Sam. Wanted—no, needed—to believe him.

"Are you ready to go?" Nalia asked in English. Nicole had been trying to learn Kasmali, but didn't know much yet.

"Sure am," Nicole said cheerfully. She smiled at Nalia, already calling her "daughter" in her mind, though she wasn't even sure if they had such a thing as marriage in Gythe. She really did love this beautiful, deadly warrior. Well, beautiful to anyone from Earth—she guessed she should refer to it as Telani. Here on Gythe, based on popluar notions of attractiveness, Nalia was horribly ugly. Nicole still found the difference hard to believe. Not for the first time, she wondered if she was pretty or ugly here and what that really meant to her Earthborn sensibilities.

"Sam went to the workshop to get something out of the storage area," Nalia told her. "We will meet him at his room and then we will go on to our destination."

"Sounds good to me," Nicole answered. The two left the room and headed toward where Sam's was.

He was just stepping out of his door with a sack in his hands when the two women got there. Nicole looked at her son. He had changed from the clothing he had worn when they came here into more Gythian attire: rugged britches tucked into calf-high boots, a sturdy tunic over some type of linen shirt, staff in hand, all wrapped up in a forest green cloak. *When did he get so tall, so regal?* He looked so much like his father had. Not really physically, though she saw similarities, but in his manner, in the way he held himself. Her heart ached as she looked at him.

"Mom," Sam said, "are you okay? You look faint."

"Yeah, I'm fine. I was just wondering when you got to look so much like a movie hero. Just look at you, with your magic weapon and your cloak."

She watched him look down at himself and blush. "*Ahimiro* isn't really magic, just porzul wood, harder than steel and great at channeling *rohw* through. And it's cold out there. These cloaks are awesome. I always thought they'd get in the way, but they're warm and functional and pretty cool looking, huh?" He turned in a circle and laughed, cloak flaring out from him as he did so.

She grabbed him mid-spin and hugged him tight. "I love you, you know. I'm glad you were willing to bring me with you when you came back here."

He hugged her back. "Of course. I don't ever want to be in a different world from you. Again."

He looked to Nalia, got a mischievous look in his eye, and grabbed their hands, one in each of his. "C'mon, I can't wait to show you where we're going. I think you'll like it." He dragged them down the corridor.

Sam checked in with Dr. Walt, who was in one of the libraries, of course. "We're going to head south for the day. We should be back by dinner time."

He absently waved at them. "Splendid. I'll see you then." His eyes never left the book he was reading.

Sam brought Nalia and Nicole to the room next to the library, a small meeting chamber. "This will do," he said. He set the sack he had brought with him on the ground and directed them to sit on the floor with him and hold one of his hands each. He seemed to breathe more deeply and slowly, and within moments they disappeared from the room.

As Nicole opened her eyes, all she saw was vegetation. They were sitting in a clearing, a meadow of some kind, in very thick forest. The grass of the meadow was dying out with the season, as were the ferns between the trees. There was a mix of evergreens and trees with most of their leaves gone, leaving skeletal shapes that seemed to complement their lusher cousins. She looked up and saw the bright blue of the morning sky overhead. It was also a bit warmer here than where they came from. Still chilly, but not so much as where they had left. The scent of the living forest wafted in front of her nose. It smelled…green. Like life itself.

"Oh, Sam, it's beautiful. I've never seen a forest this thick back home."

He smiled at her. "That's not all. This spot, the very spot on which we're sitting, is where my meditation room was on Telani. This clearing," he swept his arms out wide to encompass it all, "is where my old house is, the one in Southern California. This is where I first came to Gythe."

"But," she said, "there are so many trees. It's all desert back home."

"I know. Imagine my surprise when I found out it was the same location. It's kind of crazy, right?"

"Definitely," Nicole said.

"But that's not nearly all," Sam continued. "Come on, there's more."

The three stood and Sam took off into the trees. He had a look of concentration on his face and she wondered what he was thinking so hard about.

Within a few minutes, Sam had slowed and then stopped. Nicole swore she could hear words in her mind, though she knew it was probably just the sounds of the animals and insects in the foliage. Aside from those sounds, it was very quiet here, without all the noises she had always taken for granted back home. She thought about how it was always more quiet in Gythe, without all the background buzzing, roaring, hissing, and other such distractions from modern technology. That was one of the things she loved about this new world.

*It…been…weeks…not…see…*Words *did* seem to be entering into her mind, and they seemed to be getting louder.

*Nalia…mother…yes…meet…*Nicole shook her head, trying to ignore the words. Was she starting to hear voices? She grew concerned.

Nicole noticed then that Sam had stopped and that he was focusing his attention on the forest floor just ahead of him. There was some activity there, the sound of something moving about.

"Mom," Sam said, "I'd like you to meet Skitter, my best friend on Gythe."

A small creature covered in reddish-brown fur emerged from the undergrowth just ahead of Sam. It had a wise little face with a sharp nose and large green eyes without pupils. Its face looked almost raccoon-like. No, more like a lemur or some type of small monkey. Its body was shaped like a badger or possibly a raccoon, but with a stiff bottle-brush tail that looked to be wagging. He was the cutest thing she had ever seen.

"Oh!" she exclaimed. "He's adorable. Do you think it would be okay to hug him, maybe pet him?"

Sam looked a little uncomfortable.

Okay...mother...must nurture...saw...in...mind. The words were insistent in Nicole's mind.

She answered the voice with her own voice, within her mind. *Who are you? Why are you talking in my mind?*

The small creature froze.

Sam? the voice in her mind said. She finally understood what was happening.

No, it's Nicole, she sent back.

There was silence, both outside and inside her mind.

"Mom," Sam said, "can you hear Skitter in your mind? Can you speak with him?"

"Yes," she said, laughing, "I think I can."

Can...hug...you? she sent to him.

Okay, the answer came.

She carefully picked up the hapaki and hugged him to her chest, stroking the fur on his head. Feelings of contentment leaked out of the little creature into her mind.

Nice...meet...you, she sent.

After returning the hapaki to the ground, she and Sam discussed her apparent ability to communicate with Skitter.

"I guess it makes sense," Sam said. "The only

other human Skitter had ever been able to communicate with was Uncle Grayson. It must be something that runs in the family. That's great!"

"Is it always that difficult to communicate?" she asked. "I can only get every few words and some feelings."

"That's the way it started with me, too. Within a couple of weeks, we were communicating much more fluidly. It just takes some getting used to."

Nalia had knelt and was scratching Skitter behind his small round ears. "Now I feel left out," she said in a fake pout. "Everyone can speak mind-to-mind except for me." She exaggerating puffing her lower lip out like she was a child. Nicole thought it was adorable.

"You're even beautiful when you throw a tantrum like a child," Sam said, kissing her cheek. "You don't have to feel left out. We won't talk about you. Much." He winked at her and kissed her again.

Nicole liked to see the interaction between the two of them. They had an easy, teasing relationship filled with humor. It reminded her of when she was young and newly in love with Mark, Sam's dad. She swallowed the memory, noticing one of Skitter's eyes opening to look at her knowingly.

It's...nothing, she sent to him. He nodded slightly and closed his eye, enjoying Nalia's scratching.

Sam took out the gift he had brought Skitter: a whole case of granola bars. The excitement in those large green eyes made Nicole giggle. After a moment of silence, with Sam wearing the look that apparently indicated he was communicating with Skitter mind-to-mind, he spoke.

"I'm going to carry these to Skitter's community. The dwellings there are too small for us to enter and he's not sure how afraid the other hapaki will be, so if you two could stay here, we'll be back in a little while. Is that okay?"

Both women nodded. Skitter left, leading Sam, who was carrying the case of food for him. It was much too heavy and unwieldy for the hapaki to carry. As she watched them leave, she wondered why she couldn't hear Sam's thoughts if she could hear the hapaki's without trying. She'd have to ask him later.

Nicole and Nalia sat quietly chatting, watching the small animals and insects in the forest move about. Soon, Sam came back. Skitter was with him, as well as another hapaki. This one was smaller than Skitter and had dark brown fur banded with a lighter tan color. Sam had told her that hapaki really had no gender—they had a fascinating ability to begin gestation of offspring within themselves, at will—so it wasn't really a "he," she supposed, but Nicole didn't like the thought of calling the intelligent creatures "it." "He" would have to do.

"Skitter has decided to come back with us to Whitehall," Sam said. "He is also bringing his favorite nephew. The community decided that it was time to reach out to other communities and to other species. If a new government is going to be established, they want to have their say in how things are run."

Nicole sent to the younger hapaki, *Hello. Nice...meet...you.* She watched him look around for the source of the sending, finally letting his large, luminous blue eyes rest on her.

You...talk...me...in mind? he sent.
Yes...but need...practice.
We...practice...together.

She sent him a feeling of happiness and affirmation. When she looked up, Sam's smiling face was right in front of her. "Well, are you ready to head back home?"

"Yes, I am. I have a lot of language practice to do. Kasmali *and* Hapaki."

13

Sam knocked on Rindu's door, wanting to ask him about a particular movement in the *kori rohw*.

"Come," he heard the Zouy say.

Sam stepped into the room to find Rindu at his small table, books strewn about and paper scattered over the surface.

"Master Rindu," Sam said, "I was hoping to ask you a question."

"All of the things in the world, Sam, and the one you hope for is to ask me a question? It seems that you do not dream largely."

Sam looked into Rindu's eyes, searched his face for any sign of emotion. There was none. He didn't know what to say.

"It is a joke, Sam. Perhaps staying in your own world for too long has ruined your sense of humor. No matter. What was your question?"

"It's about the twenty-fifth movement of the *kori rohw*. I still can't seem to get it right. Can you help me?"

"Of course," Rindu said. "Show it to me."

A few minutes of Rindu pushing and pulling different

parts of Sam's body as he tried to assume the correct body position and he had it.

"I'll practice it," Sam said. "Thank you." Turning to Rindu's desk, he asked, "Master Rindu, what are all those papers and books?"

Rindu looked forlornly at the table. "They are my attempts at learning your language. I do not want to rely on Dr. Walt or you to translate the fine books you gave me as a gift. I want to learn your English—" he sounded the word awkwardly "—so that I may translate the words myself and thereby become more intimately familiar with them."

"Oh, that sounds great!" Sam exclaimed. "Please let me help you, as you helped me to learn Kasmali."

"That would be much appreciated, Sam," the Zouy said. "It is difficult with just the few passages Dr. Walt has provided to translate others."

"We can start right away," Sam said with a smile, "but instead of doing it like we did when you taught me, we can tackle the written word at the same time. I bet my mom would even help, and Nalia."

"I am anxious to see if your world follows the *wireh* as the Zouyim and the Sapsyra do here."

"The what?" Sam asked.

"*Wireh.*" Rindu looked at him, confused. "The path, the way. You know, *wireh.*"

"I'm not really sure what you're talking about, Master Rindu. I don't think you ever taught me about that when I was here before."

"Ah," the monk said, "perhaps I did not name it, but I taught you of it. What we call *wireh*, Old Kasmali for road or path, is the manner in which a man should live. It is the way through which we fulfill our cosmic significance, through honor and in harmony with the *rohw*. Does not this sound familiar to you?"

"Oh," Sam said, "Tao. On my world, it's called Tao. The way. At least, that's one name for it."

"It is the way to an enlightened existence, to an honorable and harmonious life?" Rindu asked.

"Yes, all of those things. It's not the only such philosophy, though. There are many that declare they know the only true 'way.' Several of the books I gave you are about those philosophies, including the Tao."

Rindu's eyes lit up. "Truly? Sam, again I must tell you how great a gift you have given me. I must learn your language right away to unlock the secrets of the wisdom of your world."

Later that evening, everyone was gathered for dinner in one of the dining halls. There seemed to be more people trickling in from the cities and villages in the surrounding areas. Dr. Walt's messengers were keeping busy, no doubt, in inviting the leaders to the grand summit at Whitehall to design the new government. The dining hall held more than thirty people besides Sam and his friends.

Skitter and his nephew had moved into the park area in the greenhouse temporarily, until they found another suitable location, perhaps in one of the gardens elsewhere in the keep. The two of them were sitting on benches near the table where the others sat, eating the vegetables provided them, including onekai. It wasn't just Skitter's favorite, it seemed, but also that of his nephew.

When, in idle conversation, Sam brought up Lahim Chode's viewing of Ayim Rasaad, Rindu interrupted him.

"Did you say Ayim Rasaad?" the monk asked.

"Yes. That's the name Lahim used to refer to the woman he saw in the viewing."

"That is…interesting, and a little troubling," Rindu said. "Ayim Rasaad was one of the Zouyim. She betrayed the order to go to the Arzbedim, but that was at the same time the Gray Man had come into his power and destroyed all the rogue *rohw* users. We had always assumed she had died with the rest of them. Perhaps she did not. It is probably of little matter, but it is unexpected."

Conversation at the table stopped for a few moments

as everyone wrestled with their own thoughts. The buzz of conversation from the other tables continued.

Sam kept noticing people watching him and they seemed to be talking about him. When he looked toward a group that was pointing and whispering, they immediately averted their gaze. It was disconcerting.

"Dr. Walt," Sam said. "Is everyone staring at me or am I just imagining it?"

Dr. Walt swallowed the food he was chewing and looked up. "Well, my boy, you are famous. It seems that the soldiers who fled and some of the servants who left the fortress spread tales of what happened here that fateful night. Too, rumors have trickled in from other areas, places we passed through on our journey north. You know how stories grow in each telling. Gythe has been so long without a hero, they have decided that you would be theirs."

"But I did the least amount of any of my friends," Sam said. "I was trapped in a force field while Rindu and Nalia fought. Even at the end, it was Skitter who made the difference and reminded Uncle Grayson who he was. I didn't really do much of anything."

"Be that as it may, they have decided that you are the face of the new Gythe. You are the one they pin their hopes on. I'm afraid there's no talking them out of it. You're the closest thing to a celebrity that Gythe has. Don't despair, though. Rindu, Nalia, and even Skitter are also famous heroes. If it makes you feel better, they are looking at and whispering about them as well. All of the heroes of Gythe at one table. It's something to tell their grandchildren about."

"Do not forget that you also are highly respected, Dr. Walt," Rindu said between stuffing forks full of food into his mouth. "You are the genius from another world who masterminded the operation from within the fortress, after you cleverly allowed yourself to be captured to lull the villains into a false sense of security."

Dr. Walt's eyebrows climbed half way up his forehead. "What? I haven't heard that. Are you sure?"

"I am," Rindu said, winking at Sam when Dr. Walt looked away.

"Anyway, anyway," Dr. Walt stammered, "what I'm trying to say is that many of the leaders are calling for you to be part of the government. Many are calling for you to *head* the government."

"That's ridiculous," Sam protested. "Even if I did everything they have told tales about—and I didn't, mind you—that wouldn't make me qualified to lead them. These people are crazy!"

"No crazier than back home, Sam," his mother added, in English. Nalia had been translating for Nicole throughout the entire conversation. "Look at the presidential elections. Often it devolves into a race for who is more popular. Why would it be different here?"

"I guess you're right," Sam admitted, "but I am not going to be a leader or government official. I don't know the first thing about governing and even if I did, I'm not cut out to do that sort of thing."

Nalia patted his hand and smiled at him. "Do not worry, Sam. If they ask me, I will tell them you can hardly manage to walk and talk at the same time so they should not expect you to be a leader. I will make them understand."

Sam made a face at her. He was tempted to stick his tongue out. "Thanks a lot."

"So, Sam," Dr. Walt continued, "I have been thinking about what we discussed earlier, about having Nicole and Skitter's nephew act as emissaries to other hapaki communities. I think it's a great idea, but communities are hard to find. I have told you how hapaki haven't really been seen for hundreds of years."

"I know," Sam said. "I talked with Skitter about it and he doesn't know where to find them, either. He has never seen a hapaki that was not of his community, nor does he know of any who have. I don't know what to do about it."

"I mentioned it to Lahim a couple of days ago. Perhaps he will find some clue as to where they may be."

Sam looked to the doctor and sighed. He wasn't going to get into this subject again. Dr. Walt seemed to understand from his expression.

"Sam," Dr. Walt said. "when I was still on Telani, I read a fair amount about what was later called remote viewing. It's something that has been reported through the ages, by different names. Seers, oracles, people who have out-of-body experiences, they all seem to be related. I know as a scientist perhaps I should not believe in such, but what scientists actually believe in the *rohw*? Let's just see—"

A servant interrupted Dr. Walt and handed him a message. The old man read it, folded the small piece of paper, and looked up.

"Speak of the devil. Lahim Chode sends a message that he has seen something. Would you care to go with me, Sam? Nalia? Rindu?"

"I'll go," Sam said.

"I too," Nalia said.

"I must review the English lessons Sam gave me earlier," Rindu said. "Please excuse me."

Nicole was communicating with the hapaki, by the focused look on her face, so Sam told her quietly they would be back later and left with the others.

Soon, all three were at the door to Lahim Chode's room, knocking.

"Come in," he said. His voice sounded a little stronger than the last time Sam had seen him.

The man looked less pale than before, but he was still sickly and appeared exhausted. Sam saw him try to look Nalia in the eye. When he was unable to look at her face, he averted his gaze to her body, but then realized what that would look like, so he dropped his gaze to the floor. It was this type of thing that caused Nalia's parents to make her wear a mask as she was growing up. It was embarrassing to all involved.

"I just wanted to tell you," he said quickly to chase away the awkward silence, "that I have located two hapaki colonies."

"Communities," Sam corrected.

"Ah, yes," Chode said. "Communities. My apologies."

"That's wonderful, Lahim," Dr. Walt said. "Where are they?"

"I have drawn rough maps. They are not close, and both are in areas not frequented by men, thus not near any roads." He handed a piece of paper to Dr. Walt.

The drawing were crude, but there were landmarks that allowed them to determine a general location for each of the communities.

"This one," Sam said, pointing to the marking far to the south of where they were, "seems the best bet. If we start from the site of my old house, it will be less travel time than the other location west of us, since I don't know any locations to teleport to near that one. It looks like it is near where Barstow would be on Telani. Are you sure about your viewing? I don't want to spend several days hiking only to find nothing."

"I'm sure," Chode replied. "Sam, I know you don't believe in my talent and I can't really blame you. It's different than what you are used to. But please think of your work with the Zouyim 'magic.' To me, that power is hard to understand, hard to believe. Can you at least try to be impartial and see what evidence is presented to you, for and against?"

Sam felt as if the pressure in the room increased, closing in on him. "I'm sorry," he said. "I know with all I've been through and all that I've seen, I should be more willing to give you the benefit of the doubt. I'll try to remember to do so."

Lahim Chode smiled at him, the skin around his eyes crinkling in amusement. "That's all I ask. My talent will prove itself."

"It's all decided then," Dr. Walt said, defusing the tension. "All that needs to be done now is the preparations. When will you leave, Sam?"

Sam considered for a moment and then answered. "I think first thing tomorrow morning would be soon enough. I'll have to talk to my mom and to the hapaki and gather supplies. I have an idea that may make traveling much easier."

14

The morning dawned bright and crisp. Sam started the day in the same way he had for the last week, meditating on the top of a short tower. He had found the location while looking out from a higher battlement and searched for half a day to find the stairs that reached it.

It was a roughly circular—perhaps more octagonal—platform twenty feet across, surrounded by a low parapet which reached just above Sam's waist. Though it was lower than many of the surrounding towers and walls, it was not crowded by them so it provided a view of the bailey and courtyards, even of some of the gardens. Most of all, it was away from the general hustle and bustle of the keep, so it was ideal for quiet thinking or meditation.

Sam slowly came out of the *khulim*. He opened his eyes over the course of several breaths—all of them puffing little clouds in the cold air—allowing them to adjust to the glare of the sunrise off the surrounding snow. The fluffy white flakes had fallen during the night, covering all surfaces within sight.

It still amazed Sam when he saw the snow up against the battlements and walls. Though he had used it as a reference when he changed the color of the fortress, the stone seemed to shine brighter, making the snow look almost dingy by comparison. He thought it might be that the "magical" nature of the fortress accepted what he did and made it just a little bit better.

Rising to his feet, he sighed as he looked out over the keep and its surroundings. It was breathtaking.

He heard the door to the platform stairs creak open. *Speaking of breathtaking*, he thought. Nalia made her way silently toward him, her dark hair glistening in the morning light.

"Good morning, Sam," she said as she came close and embraced him. "I thought you would be here."

"Yep. I like it here. It's peaceful." He held her for a moment more, just enjoying the warmth of her, the scent of her. The feel of her.

"Mmm," she hummed. "It is." You can't even hear the other people in the keep. I might have to steal this place from you."

Sam laughed. "There's no need to steal it. We can share." He paused for a moment, and then winked. "Just don't make too much noise."

She squeezed him one more time, then punched him in the arm.

"Come on, lazy," she said. "We have some traveling to do today."

Sam looked around at the snow-covered landscape one more time, then followed her to the stairs.

They found Nicole with Skitter's nephew in the meeting room in which they had agreed to assemble. Sam had collected the gear and supplies they would use and stored them there the night before. Sam's mother had a look on her face that indicated she was concentrating on something. He knew it meant she was communicating with the younger hapaki. Skitter lounged nearby.

"Sam," she said, turning to him. "I want you to meet Max." She motioned to the smaller of the two hapaki.

"Mom, I've already met him. Don't you remember?"

Nicole rolled her eyes. "I know, silly. I want to introduce him to you by his name. He didn't have one before, as you recall."

"Oh, right. Sorry." Sam sent greetings to Max, calling him by name. He got a polite response, colored with happiness at his new name. "Max?" Sam asked his mother.

"Yes. Max is rather…intense. He's what we'd call an over-achiever on Telani. Everything he does, he does to the maximum. It just seemed to fit. I explained it to him and he likes it. He likes what it represents."

Sam smiled at his mother. "Sounds like a great name to me."

The younger hapaki and Nicole had been inseparable since they had returned to Whitehall. Sam caught snippets of their conversations—at least, Max's side of it—and they seemed to be understanding each other better and better all the time. His smile grew wider at the thought. He hadn't seen his mother so involved in anything in years. It was nice.

Good morning, Sam, Skitter sent.

Good morning, Skitter, Sam returned.

I have met your cat, Skitter sent. *His name is Stoker?*

Yes, Sam sent back, smiling at the thought of the two meeting. *How did it go?*

I like him. We can't communicate, but he narrows his eyes at me and rubs against me, so I think that may mean we are friends.

Yes, Sam sent, *that means you are friends.*

I have met the baby cats, too, Skitter added. There was some emotion there Sam didn't fully recognize. It was similar to affection, but a different kind than he had felt from Skitter before. It was almost like parental pride.

And what do you think of them? Sam asked, trying to keep from laughing at the pictures forming in his mind of Skitter being swarmed by kittens.

I love them, Skitter said without hesitation. *I played with them for more than an hour this morning. Molly doesn't mind. She seems to enjoy the break. They are very…energetic.*

Yes, they are. Sam smiled outwardly as well as through his sending. It was great that his friend got along with the cats. They were the only housecats in Gythe, but that would change when they really started reproducing. It was nice to see that they would be welcomed by at least some of the natives.

Will we be leaving soon? Skitter sent, changing the subject but keeping the underlying affection for the kittens and their older counterparts. *I'm excited to meet hapaki from another community.*

We will eat breakfast and then I will teleport us all to just outside your community. We will start from there.

Eat? Max interrupted. *Did someone say "eat?"*

Sam laughed, both in his sendings and out loud. "Okay, everyone," he said, sending the same thing, "let's eat a big breakfast and then we'll get started. We'll be covering a lot of miles today."

They moved to one of the small dining halls just down the corridor, talking excitedly about two hapaki communities meeting for the first time in the memory of Skitter's folk. Max was anxious, too, to see some of the unknown territory in the world, as his uncle had done. When they were finished, the humans donned the packs Sam had gathered for them.

"Sam," Nicole said. "You're going to teleport us there, aren't you? Why do we need gear?"

"Well, yes and no," Sam said. "In order to teleport to a location, I have to know the vibratory signature there. I don't know the area where the community is, so I can only bring us to the closest location that I know intimately. That would be the site of my old house, where you met Skitter the other day. Once we get there, we'll have to travel just like anyone else. The packs have all the stuff we'll need, including food, some basic tools, and some lengths of rope. You should always carry rope." He winked at her.

"Oh," she responded. "I guess I'm being a bit spoiled, huh? I just expected you to snap your fingers and we'd be there. Sorry."

He laughed. "No worries. The more places I learn, the easier it will be to travel instantly. I just don't know many yet, that's all. Okay, everyone follow me. I have a surprise."

He led them down to one of the stables, all the while fending off the questions that bombarded him. When he brought them through to one of the stalls, he stopped.

"Mom, let me present you with your companion for this trip. Meet Chipper." He opened the stall door and led out a very large bird outfitted with a harness and reins and with a saddle strapped tightly to its torso. "Chipper, Mom."

Nicole's eyes grew wide. "Is that an ostrich?" she asked.

Sam handed the reins to her. "Not quite. Chipper is a manu bird. They are larger and stronger than ostriches. And smarter, by a bit anyway. He is well trained and all you'll have to do is lightly move the reins to the side you want him to turn and he'll go that way. It takes much less skill than riding a horse because manu are pretty easygoing. Their personalities, and their extensive training, make it relatively simple to travel with them. They won't fight you."

Nicole went close to the bird, looking into its big brown eye. She reached a hand out tentatively.

The bird looked at her, not moving.

She slowly moved her hand to the bird's head and started to stroke it. The bird made a sort of cooing sound. She looked at Sam questioningly.

"He seems to like that," Sam said. "Do you want to try to ride him around the yard for a bit before we leave?"

Nicole kept petting the bird's head. "What do you think, Chipper," she said to him, "do you want to run a little?" The bird cooed and blinked at her.

She was easily able to swing up onto the saddle. She started him walking by making a clucking sound and squeezing with her legs, at Sam's direction. Soon, she was walking and then trotting the bird around the small yard in front of the stable. When she was ready to stop, she tugged gently back on both reins as Sam had told her to do and the bird came to a stop. She dismounted.

"That was easy," she said as she got back down onto her own feet, "and fun. I think we'll be good friends, Chipper." She stroked the bird's head.

"I had a litter strapped to the back of the saddle, as you can see. It's like the one Skitter used when I was here last time. I figured Max could ride with you. Is that okay?"

"That's perfect," his mother said, eyes dancing excitedly. "But, where are your birds?"

"Nalia and I will be riding our rakkeben. You remember me telling you about the rakkeben, right?"

"The big intelligent wolves?" his mother asked. "Yes, I remember. I can't wait to see them."

Sam laughed. His mother loved animals. All animals. "We'll call them when we get to where my old house is located. I have Skitter's litter right here so he can ride along with me. Just like old times."

"Are we ready to go then?" Nalia asked. "It would be good to get started so we have more daylight in which to travel."

"True," Sam agreed. "Okay, everyone gather around. This will only take a couple of minutes." He sent the same thing to the hapaki, wondering at the same time why he and his mother couldn't communicate when he could send thoughts to two hapaki at a time. He's have to ask Dr. Walt about it.

Sam sat in a section of the yard underneath an awning so that it was free of snow. He quickly entered the *khulim* and was focusing on the vibratory signature of his old house. A moment later, he had created an envelope of *rohw* around his party and changed their vibrations to match his destination. He felt his reality lurch and when he opened his eyes, he was again in the familiar clearing he had left a little more than a week before.

He had no sooner stood and dusted off his pants than he felt Max panic. The little hapaki was frantic, crying out and then suddenly becoming silent and freezing. Sam wasn't sure what was happening at first, but then he saw some foliage move toward the edge of the clearing. He understood.

Don't panic, Max, he sent, *it's okay*.

"Mom, don't freak out or anything, okay? The rakkeben are here. Somehow."

"What?" Nicole asked, but didn't need an answer. A large white-furred animal was entering the clearing. When it had emerged completely from the surrounding vegetation, it was plain to all there what it was.

The rakkeben were large wolves. Very large wolves. This particular rakkeban stood almost as tall as Sam. She was completely white, unlike the other wolf entering the meadow behind her. That one was a light gray color.

Sam swept a hand out toward the approaching wolves. "Mom, let me introduce Shonyb, my friend and companion during my first trip here. Behind her is Cleave, Nalia's bond-mate."

"Oh, Sam, they're absolutely beautiful!" his mother said. "Do you think she would let me pet her?"

Sam thought he covered his surprise well. "I, uh, well, maybe. Let's go see."

Before they could take a step, though, a blur of reddish brown zipped past them toward the rakkeben. Skitter bounded up, skidding to a stop just in front of Shonyb. He reached his tiny paws up to the rakkeban, who lowered her head, and gave her his best hapaki hug. It was almost comical to see the hapaki try to reach around the massive shaggy head. The wolf's tongue darted out, licking Skitter's face, plastering the fur along the side of his scalp. Sam could hear the hapaki laughing in his mind.

"Um, they're kind of friends," Sam said to his mother. "I probably didn't mention that when I told you the stories about my time here."

When the humans drew near the wolves, Shonyb dipped her head respectfully. Sam did likewise, then went up to the big rakkeban and hugged her head much like Skitter had. She licked his face, too, but not quite so wetly. Soon, Sam had introduced his mother to Shonyb and the wolf's head got another hug. Nalia was reacquainting herself with her own rakkeban, hugging him and petting his furry head.

Then, Sam remembered Max. *Max, are you all right?* Sam sent.

Fine.

Come on. Let me introduce you to Shonyb and Cleave.

No. Rakkeben eat hapaki, Max sent back.

Skitter? Max sent. *Can you explain it to him, make him feel better?*

The two hapaki discussed it and Max finally agreed to move. He was still cautious around the wolves and wouldn't go too close to them, but Sam knew he would grow accustomed to them. Eventually.

"Sam," Nicole said while alternating between stroking Shonyb's head and Chipper's head, "I have a couple of questions."

"Okay, shoot."

"First, why isn't Chipper freaked out about the rakkeben?"

"Oh, that one is easy," Sam said. "Part of the manu bird's training is to cooperate with rakkeben. It is pretty likely that they will travel with them or at least encounter them, so the birds are acclimated as they are grown and trained."

"Okay," Nicole said. "The other question is: how did the rakkeben know we'd be here today? Are they close enough to have sensed us and then came here?"

Nalia answered for Sam. "Communication with

rakkeben is not understood completely. They seem to be able to read minds or feelings in some way, but can't communicate to others like the hapaki can. They share a special sensitivity with their bond-mate, but no one has been able to explain anything more than that. Dr. Walt has tried. Repeatedly. It drives him to distraction that he cannot figure it out."

"I can understand that," Nicole said. "Well, I'm just glad they have that sense. Now we can get started without delay."

15

Sam marveled at how much his sensitivity to the *rohw* had changed while he was in his own world. He had to work harder to even sense the energy on Telani, so it was like he was swimming through molasses. To do it, he had to develop his "muscles" just to get by. Now, back in Gythe, where the *rohw* was abundant and strong, he felt energized, more powerful than ever before.

He could easily sense the ley lines stretched out before him. He did so without having to enter the *khulim*. Even now, as he fitted the framework of Skitter's resting place onto Shonyb, he could tell which way he needed to go. It was almost intoxicating. Was this how Rindu and the other Zouyim felt all the time?

It didn't take long for them to get started. Skitter climbed into his litter and Sam onto Shonyb's back in front of it. Nalia mounted Cleave. Nicole and Max got into their respective places. Sam turned Shonyb north and they started their journey. Their destination was northwest, but they'd have to take a meandering course because of the thick forest.

The forest was heavy and travel was not fast, but Sam

enjoyed it. He missed traveling like this, with the rakkeben and his friends. The forest was alive with birds, squirrels, and other small animals. The smell of the vegetation and the loamy scent of the forest floor made Sam smile. There were trees in Telani, but he hadn't seen anything there to compare with Gythe.

After several hours of travel, the party halted in a meadow to eat lunch.

"Well, Mom," Sam said, "what do you think so far?"

She smiled at him. "I love this place. It's gorgeous and the air is so clean, it feels like I am more energetic. Traveling by manu bird is nice, too, but I'm starting to get saddle sore. I'm not used to riding like this." She rubbed her back side and winced.

Sam laughed. "Yeah, I'm sorry about that. There's really nothing to be done. All I can say is that you'll probably get used to it. We'll take it easy the first few days to let you acclimate. I don't want to be a pain in the butt."

"Very funny." She mock-scowled at him, but couldn't hold back the smile that burst through.

"How are you and Max getting along?" Nalia asked Nicole. "Is communication getting easier?"

"Oh yes. The first week or so it was tough. We had to go slowly and couldn't really form complete sentences. In the last few days, it's much smoother. I can understand more of the feelings and senses he sends to me and I think he understands better how to hear complete thoughts from me. We're becoming good friends."

"That is good," Nalia said. "There will be many more hapaki to talk to when we get to the other community. You will be needed as a translator."

Nicole frowned. "I need to become better at speaking Kasmali first. That language is not going so well. I need a lot more practice."

"I will speak to you only in Kasmali during this trip, then, to help. If you must use English to make yourself understood then do so, but we should try to use only the language of Gythe. I'm sure Sam will do the same. We will force you to learn."

"I guess that's the best way to do it," Nicole admitted, her shoulders slumping.

Nalia smiled at her reaction. "It will not be that bad. You will learn more quickly. You will see. It is as when Sam was learning. Rindu and I forced him to speak our language. He whined and complained like a child who is not allowed sweets, but he learned quickly and he can now speak almost as an adult." She looked out of the corner of her eye at Sam, who was sitting nearby rubbing Shonyb's ears.

"I heard that," he said. Both women chuckled.

They traveled until the sun was down past the trees andced the forest they were passing through was getting darker. It would be fully night in another hour or so and Sam halted them in a convenient clearing.

Sam removed the litter from Shonyb's back and the two rakkeben were allowed to go out and hunt for their dinner. Nicole removed Chipper's saddle and fed him the food they had brought for him. With those chores done, the humans sat on convenient logs and the hapaki made themselves comfortable in the undergrowth.

"I have a surprise for everyone," he said. "Just let me meditate here for a few minutes and I'll show you." He went off to a flat grassy area, sat in the familiar cross-legged position, closed his eyes, and began to breathe deeply. Soon, he was in the *khulim*.

Just shy of half an hour later, he opened his eyes, just as the rakkeben were returning. *Game must be plentiful here. It didn't take the wolves long at all to eat.* Sam felt a shudder in his mind, coming from either Skitter or Max, at the thought of the wolves running down and eating another living creature. It was probably Max.

"Okay," Sam said. "Here's our surprise. I have just learned this area, the unique vibration of this location. Now, we can teleport back to Whitehall and spend the night in our own beds. In the morning, when we're ready to set off again, I can teleport us back and we can start traveling from here."

The others nodded. They had to have known about this or he would have gotten more questions about why they hadn't brought tents or more food. He knew they were just humoring him to make him feel good about his cleverness. He appreciated it.

Everyone gathered around him as he sat again and concentrated. Within a few minutes, the familiar disconnected feeling grabbed hold of them and they were suddenly back in the yard in front of the stables where they had started that morning.

"I believe we are here in time for dinner. Shall we?" He handed Chipper's reins to a stable boy and nodded to Shonyb, who understood and ran off to spend the night in one of the parks on the fortress grounds. Cleave followed her lead. Everyone else made their way into the keep, first to their rooms to drop off their gear, and then to the dining hall where they knew Rindu and Dr. Walt would be.

The party had a nice meal in one of the dining halls, chatting amongst themselves and with Dr. Walt and Rindu about their travels that day. They all turned in early, sleeping in their own chambers, and all were up and in the yard near the stables before the sun came up.

"You know," Nicole said to Sam, "traveling this way is not so bad. We can be home each night, eat a nice meal, and sleep in our own beds. It's even easier than camping back home."

Sam smiled. He liked it, too, but it almost felt like cheating to him compared to his travels when he was here last. "I'm glad you like it. It does make it easier to stay nights here in the fortress."

Sam prepared himself, relaxing and connecting with the vibratory signature of the location where they stopped the day before. Soon, he had them transported to the forest clearing they had just vacated not a dozen hours before.

As the group traveled, they settled into an easy rhythm. They would go through the forests and the few clear areas during the day, at a pace that was an easy stroll for the rakkeben and the manu. They would take several breaks during the day to rest and to eat. It was as if they were out for an enjoyable ride. There was no pressure, no stress, and the landscape through which they traveled was beautiful.

Each evening, as it was beginning to get dark, Sam called them to a halt and he would memorize the area. Then he would teleport them all back to the fortress and they would eat, clean up, and sleep in their own beds. The next morning, they would do it all again.

On the fifth day they came to the area where Sam knew the city of Barstow was in Telani. Looking out over the forest, he had to remind himself of this fact. "Mom, we're in Barstow."

"What?"

"Where we are, right now, it's where Barstow is in our world. Exactly where we're standing."

Nicole scanned the endless forest that stretched out in all directions. "It's a little different than in our world, don't you think?" She winked at him.

"I'd say," Sam said. "Barstow is desert in Telani. It's hard to believe. Anyway, we should be close, so keep an eye out."

He sent to Skitter and Max, *We are here. Do you sense or hear any other hapaki?*

No, Skitter answered. *It is very quiet.*

Well, keep an ear out, or a mind out, whichever is appropriate, Sam sent back.

We'll let you know if we find something. The rakkeben are probably scaring them.

Sam realized that Skitter was most likely correct. He talked softly with Shonyb for a few minutes and the wolves headed back the way they had come to hunt for food. It was only mid-morning, but the rakkeben seemed content to go off on their own. Sam had stressed that the food must not be hapaki. *That ought to help*, Sam thought.

The party continued to move around in the area, looking for signs of the hapaki community. Sam could feel the anxiety and anticipation in Skitter and Max. He saw it, too, in his mother and Nalia, by the way their eyes were wide and how they were scanning the forest floor intently, hardly blinking. Nalia's beautiful face was so focused, it almost made him laugh. When in combat, every inch of her was relaxed and fluid. Right now, she swung her head from side to side mechanically, stiffly. She was excited to make contact as well, even if she couldn't actually communicate with the creatures.

Sam gaped at the forest around him. It was thicker than most of the other forest he had traveled through when he was here last. Of course, he had been traveling on roads and paths then. This area seemed not even to have animal trails in it. He noticed oak mixed in with juniper, cypress, and several types of pine. Beneath the trees, the tangled underbrush made it difficult to move, even with some of it dead for the season. At least, it was difficult for the humans. The hapaki were right at home, slithering through the vegetation as if swimming through water.

The first indication that there was something wrong came when Nalia, up ahead of the rest of them, broke into a large area where all the foliage had been trampled down. It looked like someone had thrown a party in the area. Sam estimated that it would have taken hundreds of people to do this kind of damage. There were even signs that some of the tree branches and larger plants had been cut. Sections were lying on the ground with neat slices where they had been separated from the main plant or tree.

They all stood there, looking around. None of them one knew what to make of it.

"What do you think happened?" Nalia asked. "Is it related to the hapaki or just a coincidence?"

"The chances that it's a coincidence aren't good, I

think," Sam answered. "I still can't sense any hapaki around, so maybe the community is not here, but farther away."

Sam saw that the damage extended off to the east. There was a wide path as if a large group had been traveling. It similarly extended to the northwest. Sam could tell from the way the vegetation was crushed that whoever came through this area was going east, not the other way around.

"Which way should we go?" he asked, while sending the question to Skitter as well. They had been traveling northeast, so the choice was basically whether they would go left, back from where the group of people had come, or right, following whoever it was that made all the damage.

"I think we should go left," his mother said, "toward where they came from."

Sam looked at her, knowing that surprise was painted all over his face.

"What?" she said. "Didn't you think I'd notice the direction in which the plants had been stomped down? I may not be the savior of a world, but I've read my fair share of fiction and seen an episode or two of Man Vs. Wild. I'm not that much of a city girl."

"You should not underestimate your mother like that, Sam," Nalia chimed in. "She is very clever. I have found this to be true."

"I'm sorry," Sam said. "I just didn't expect it, that's all. I know you're smart." Why did it feel so hot all of a sudden? "Anyway, I agree with you. Let's try to backtrack on their path."

They did so, walking through the middle of the devastated forest. It looked strange with the trees standing up out of the crushed and mutilated undergrowth. The trees themselves had not escaped unscathed, though. Their bark was scraped, their exposed roots scuffed, and there were sections that even had their bark peeled for a few inches.

In one area where it was obvious the group of people had stopped to rest, Sam was able to pick out more pronounced damage. Some trees had names carved in them. A small pile of wood shavings indicated that someone had whittled while resting here. The bodies of several squirrels and birds lay around the area, all with the holes of the arrows that ended their lives. Several fire pits, really only small divots dug in the soil, contained doused bits of half-burned wood and ash. Sam shook his head. *At least they didn't burn the forest down.* As he scanned the faces of the others, he saw that they were as disgusted as he was.

An hour later, just as Sam was going to suggest they turn around and head east, he saw something he couldn't really understand. There was a very large hole in the ground in front of him. He had strayed off toward the side of the path of devastation, so, as yet, the others hadn't seen it. He just stood there staring.

It looked as if someone had dug a trench in the forest floor. It appeared to start at one location where there was a four-foot hole. From there, it wandered in a crooked path like a miniature river-carved canyon, stretching out for five feet or so and then branching, going on, and branching again. It almost seemed like someone had dug up a large burrow.

Feelings of incredulity, sorrow, and then fear flooded his mind. He turned his attention to his right and saw Skitter motionless, having also noticed the trench. *No, no!* the feelings came. *Who would do this? How could they possibly—*

Skitter, Sam sent to his friend. *What's wrong? What are you talking about?* As he was sending it, he saw that Nalia and his mother had stopped and were looking over at them. The look on his mother's face was a mix between the intense expression she had when communicating with the hapaki and one of deep sorrow.

Don't you see, Sam? Skitter sent. *This is a hapaki den. It has been dug up. We have found what is left of the community.*

16

Sam's legs felt like overcooked noodles. He knelt down at the end of the trench before they collapsed on their own. He tried to suck in a full breath, but failed. *Why would someone do this?* he sent to Skitter. *What's the purpose?* His friend was silent, sending only feelings of horror.

He could see now, within the trench, that the original tunnels were of a size that would accommodate the hapaki he'd seen. There were also bits of flat stone and some shiny smooth material that seemed to be concentrated in just a few places.

Solar tubes, Skitter sent, along with images of long tunnels going down into the ground, lined with quartz and other shiny rock, allowing sunlight to make its way into some of the deeper chambers in the den. Sam knew the images he was looking at were from Skitter's own den, but he got the sense that all hapaki used similar designs.

Sam heard his mother crying. He looked over to see her on her knees, with her head in her hands, tears in her eyes. "Mom?" he said.

She looked at him, eyes red and puffy. "Don't you see, Sam? This wasn't an accident. It wasn't an isolated occurrence." She pointed further up the path where other series of trenches were evident. "Someone purposely attacked this community."

Sam realized she was right. All of the sets of dug-up tunnels looked like the one in front of him. The people hadn't seen one and decided to dig. They made an effort to destroy the entire community's dens.

"They specifically targeted the community," his mother continued. "Why would anyone do that? The hapaki are the most peaceful creatures I've ever heard of. Why?"

He had no answer for her.

"Let's look around and see if there are any hapaki left. They could have missed some. Skitter, Max, do you sense any others here?" His last sentence was accompanied by a sending to the hapaki.

We don't sense anyone, but we will try harder, Skitter sent back as he shuffled toward the bulk of the destroyed dens.

As they headed off, Sam looked over to Nalia, who had remained silent throughout the exchange. She was scanning the damaged dens, a murderous look on her face. She sensed his gaze and her head snapped up. Her eyes flashed in the afternoon sun and the rage on her face made Sam want to step back.

"Nal?" he said.

"The hapaki are peaceful," she said in firm, tight words. "From your translations, I know they can be arrogant, but in their own way, they are as honorable a race as any I have seen. They do not harm others and only want to live their lives. The monsters who performed this deed deserve death."

Sam stood silent, shocked at the intensity of her feelings.

"We must find out who did this, Sam." She looked him in the eyes, her own blue-green orbs afire. "We must find them and we must dispense justice."

Then the rage left her as she spotted Skitter frantically scrambling amidst the trenches that used to be the homes of his cousins. Her head dipped and she sighed. "And we must try to find the captured hapaki and rescue them."

Sam's head snapped up. *That's right, there are no bodies. They must have been carried away.* He smacked his forehead with his palm. How could he have missed that detail?

He went to her and wrapped his arms around her. "We will. We definitely will."

A sudden sending from Skitter broke into his thoughts. *We found a survivor!* The hapaki sent to him. *We found one of our brethren alive.*

Sam and Nalia rushed to where Skitter was, fifty feet away. Nicole, picking up on the sending, was right behind them. When they got to him, he was standing in front of a patch of heavy vegetation at the edge of the flattened section of the forest. Sam could see some of the leaves trembling and could pick up on faint sendings of terror. He tried to send soothing thoughts of his own, but they only made the feelings emanating from the bushes worse, so he stopped.

The hapaki is terrified of you, Skitter sent. *She has seen creatures that look like you rip her community-members out of their homes and drag them off. She thinks they are going to eat them later.*

She? Sam sent back. *Hapaki have no gender. Why do you call her "she?"*

Whereas I have some qualities that you associate with being a "he," she has more that would be associated with being a "she" in your race, Skitter explained. *It's complicated and not important right now.*

"What can I do to help?" Sam said aloud for the humans, as he sent it to Skitter.

The best thing is to go back for a distance and let me talk to her. I'll let you know when I can get through to her.

Do you want me to try to send thoughts to her? Sam asked.

No. It will only make her frantic. She thinks you will eat her.

"Okay," Sam said. "Mom, Nalia, let's go over there," he pointed back toward where they were before, "so Skitter can calm her down."

It took over an hour for Skitter to coax the other hapaki out of her hiding place. Then, when the rakkeben returned, it took another hour and a half for her to emerge once again. Sam took the time to learn the vibratory signature of the place, knowing that the frightened hapaki would not submit to traveling on the path the humans had made.

She was smaller than Skitter, close to the size of Max. Her fur was a deep chocolate color. Other than that, she looked like they did. Sam had thought that maybe with all the decades or even hundreds of years the different communities had been separated, they would have changed until they didn't resemble each other so closely.

As soon as they could get the surviving hapaki to sit still and Skitter was able to explain to her that they would travel, Sam sat on the trampled forest floor, attained the *khulim*, and transported them to the location of Sam's old house.

I will take her to my community, Skitter sent to Sam. *It will take some time to explain the situation to them, but she will be welcome to stay with us. She will cause quite a stir, the first stranger in as long as any hapaki can remember. She will be fine.*

Skitter allowed his sending to go to Nicole, too, so she heard it the same time Sam did, and Sam related what the hapaki said to Nalia. He would really have to learn to control where his sendings went like that, communicating with only one hapaki if he wanted to. It could be useful, he thought.

The humans settled down to wait as the three hapaki—Max would not be left out—went to Skitter's home.

"Why do you think someone would attack a hapaki community?" Sam's mother asked.

"I've been wondering about that, too," Sam responded. "I have no idea. It seems an awful lot of trouble to go through to get specimens for a zoo or a collection. If they even have such things here."

"They do not, in general," Nalia said, "though there are

rich men who may collect animals to show off to their friends. I do not think that was the case here."

"Neither do I," said Sam. "I don't know why, but I have a feeling it's much worse."

When Skitter and Max returned almost four hours later, it was already dark. The moon was almost full, so Sam spotted the hapaki scuttling across the clearing before they even sent that they were back.

"How is she doing?" Sam said it aloud as he sent it to Skitter.

She is frightened, confused, and is telling all the community that men are coming to destroy and eat them all. Skitter's sadness came through in his sending. *I told everyone that not all humans are bad. They have heard the stories from my adventure when you were here last, Sam. Hopefully they will continue to remember them.*

Is there any information that might help us to know who did it?

No. All humans look the same to her. She was out foraging when the people showed up. She hid far enough away from the community so that she wasn't seen. They had some kind of animal that could track the hapaki to their dens so they could start to dig them up. She doesn't know why they attacked the community.

Sam shook his head. "Well, everyone, we need to go back to Whitehall. It's too dark for us to travel even if I teleported us back to the path. We'll have to start tomorrow morning. We should be able to catch them. We're traveling mounted and they're obviously on foot. I didn't see any evidence of mounts. We'll catch them."

He sat in the grass in the clearing and soon they were back at Whitehall. When they arrived, Dr. Walt was waiting for them in front of the stables.

"Please come with me," he said. His hair was even more flyaway than normal and he looked flustered. "Lahim Chode has had a viewing, and it involves that destroyed hapaki community."

17

Sam stared at Dr. Walt, at a loss for words. Nalia asked the question Sam wanted to ask. "When did he have this vision? Why did he not tell us?"

"He just had it a few hours ago. After he told me, I came down here to wait for you. You normally come back earlier in the day than this. I was beginning to worry."

Sam shook off his confusion. "Let's go. I want to hear what he has to say."

They bade goodnight to the rakkeben and to the hapaki and headed toward the keep.

Sam, Skitter sent, *I would like to come with you, to hear what this man has to say.*

Of course, Sam sent back. *Come on.*

The four humans and the hapaki—Max decided to go to a den he had made in one of the parks—were at the door to Lahim Chode's room twenty minutes later. When they knocked, he called to them to come in.

Chode was sitting up in bed, looking stronger than he was before. He had shaved and looked healthier. When they came in, he stopped writing in the book on his lap. "So, you saw what was once the hapaki community?" he asked.

"We did," Sam answered. "Did you see the same thing?"

Lahim Chode looked down to Skitter, who was hunched at Sam's feet. "I'm sorry about your people. If I would have had this vision a week ago, maybe we could have done something."

"Lahim," Dr. Walt said, "please tell them what you told me earlier."

The man blinked and then nodded. "Of course."

"Earlier today, while I was meditating, trying to find information useful to you, something to help in our efforts, I saw what could only have been several days ago in the area where you found the destroyed community.

"You have to understand that my talents are not precise. It's not like reading a book or looking at a picture. I get glimpses, unformed images, sometimes sound. Most often, I am unable to determine where or when the viewing occurs. In the matrix, viewers are able to see across both space and time, so it is difficult to decipher what is being viewed.

"In any case, I saw a man of some authority interacting with one of his underlings. The minion called the man Baron Tingai and referred to his experiments. Tingai directed the man to use some type of creature to hunt down the hapaki he knew were in the area. The viewing jumped to another time, when Tingai's forces were digging up and chasing down the hapaki, one at a time. They were captured, put in cages, and carried off.

"The last viewing was of another time and place, I think. Tingai was in some sort of stone structure, speaking with a woman. He was deferential to her, explaining that if he could just get more specimens, he could do many things that would help her in her efforts. She nodded, giving him permission. It was the same woman as in my earlier vision about the artifacts. Ayim Rasaad. That is all I saw and heard."

Sam leaned hard against the wall of the chamber. "I still don't understand how you see what you do, but I guess I have to believe you see something. There's no way you could have guessed that the hapaki community was destroyed."

Everyone in the room was silent. Sam could hear Dr. Walt breathing, could hear Skitter's claws lightly scratching the rough floor as he fidgeted.

I don't understand how he knew about it, Skitter sent to Sam. *Can you explain it?*

I don't get it myself, Sam answered. *How can we use his talent to help us if we can't figure out if he's right or wrong each time he tells us something?*

"Skitter doesn't understand, either," Sam said. "Is there any way you can explain it so that we understand how you do what you do?"

"Maybe if I tell you about how I learned to use the talent I possess, it may help you understand," Chode said. "Would you like to hear the tale?"

"I would," Sam said. Turning to the others, he continued, "but if any of you don't want to stay to hear, we can meet up later to decide what we'll do."

They all decided to stay.

*****

Lahim Chode looked out over the people gathered in front of him. He had never told his story to anyone. He wasn't sure why he offered to do so now. Maybe he was just desperate for them to believe him, wanting them to accept him as helpful. He wanted to aid them, desired to be seen as an asset in their endeavors. It would be good to get it off his chest anyway. Why not? He began.

"I was born into a family of farmers. We were simple folk, just barely making a living working long hours in the fields. One year, I accompanied my parents and my brother to go see a local seer. He was a kindly man who would trade tellings for produce or hand-made goods. My parents wanted to know what crop they should plant to have the best yield.

"As my parents were dealing with the seer, he kept looking over toward me and my older brother. When his business with my parents was concluded, he called me over to him. Trembling, not knowing what he planned to do to me, I did as I was told and came closer. My parents, looks of confusion on their faces, just watched.

"After looking me up and down, making me feel like he was looking into my very soul, he spoke. To my parents. 'Your son has a natural talent with viewing. I could teach him to develop it. He might be talented enough to be a seer himself one day.'

"I was amazed. Me, a seer? I had talent that he could help me develop? Visions of being important and having lots of money swam in my head. I begged my parents to let me learn.

"My parents were skeptical, but agreed to allow me to spend some time with the seer, learning to develop my natural talent, as long as it did not interfere with my work in the fields. So it was that I began my tutelage in remote viewing.

"The first thing I learned was that 'viewer' was the appropriate term. I had to work hard to become an impartial observer. It is interesting how much everyone, even a child, makes judgments on things in their lives. Having an interest in the outcome can skew the results of a viewing, making it inaccurate.

"After I became proficient at impartial observation, the seer taught me how to search for specific viewings. Now, when I say 'specific' I do not mean what you may think. There is no way, for example, to look for a particular person and to always see that person. The way in which the viewer looks, using certain boundaries as he goes into a meditative trance, helps to increase the chance to find something related to what you are looking for, but only by a small amount. The simple fact is that a viewer sees what the matrix allows him to see, and that is all.

"Speaking of the matrix, the seer taught me about that in the beginning of my education. You see, all space and time are one big field, or matrix. A skilled viewer can navigate through the matrix, seeing things that are removed by distance as well as time. So, when there is a viewing, it can literally be anywhere and at any time, whether here on Gythe now or in another world in the past or future. The trick is figuring out the when and the where.

"I studied with the seer for six years. When I was fifteen, I decided I was skilled enough to set out on my own. The seer didn't bother arguing. He had known for years the exact day I would leave. He had only one thing to say to me. 'Lahim, try to use your power to help others, not selfishly keeping it to yourself.' The first thing I did was hire myself out to the richest man I could find.

"My life became a dream for a young man. I started by proving myself with small viewings, gradually getting to bigger ones. In the meantime, my sponsors kept me in fine clothes with access to parties and other well-off people. I had achieved the life I had always dreamed of, never thinking of what my teacher had told me.

"When the Gray Man was told about my talent, he had me abducted and brought to the Gray Fortress. At first, he discussed my talent, asking me general questions about how it worked. I gave him the answers I prepared over the years when others asked about it. He had me do a few small viewings for him and asked me to explain the process in great detail. He wanted to try his hand at it himself.

"When he was unable to find the answers he wanted, he began to torture me, believing I had withheld information from him. I had, of course, but I yielded everything in the first torture session. But he didn't believe me.

"The thing about remote viewing is that it takes quite a long time to learn to do effectively. That is, it usually does. For those with a talent for it, it comes much more quickly. The Gray Man did not have a talent for it. When he had tortured me until I was close to death and still didn't get the answers he wanted, he stuffed me in the dungeon to die and forgot about me.

"Luckily, you defeated him and I was freed."

Lahim took a drink of water from the cup on his nightstand. "While I was being tortured and later was in the dungeon waiting to die, one thought kept going through my head. It was what my teacher had said to me. I failed in using my power on behalf of others. I felt like I was receiving a fitting punishment. All the good I could have done and I squandered my talent for money and fame.

"I promised myself that if I survived, I would do my best to use my talents for the good of Gythe, on behalf of all the people," he nodded to Skitter, "and creatures, who needed my help."

He looked at Sam. "I may not be able to make you understand how my talent works, but I can prove to you that I can be of help. You'll see. I won't stop trying until we have created a better Gythe."

Sam nodded solemnly. He raised his eyes to meet Lahim's own. "I understand. I'm still confused about how your talent works, but that's okay. Welcome to the new government of Gythe. Now, let's figure out what we're going to do about our new problem."

18

"Are you sure you're okay with this, Mom?" Sam asked her again.

Nicole looked at her son. He was a man, an important one. She had heard little bits of conversation around the keep. She even understood a few words of it. She'd been working hard at learning Kasmali. She understood things like "hero," "savior," and "protector." These people had great faith in her son. She guessed she shouldn't still see him as her little boy.

She really couldn't help it. She was his mother. To her, he would always be the cute little boy filled with wonder and hope for the future. She could sometimes see his chubby little toddler face superimposed with his man's face. His rugged, handsome man's face. It made her heart ache to remember those times. And now he was concerned about her. Their roles had switched.

"Yes, sweetie," she said, going over to him and giving him a hug. "It's necessary, Sam. The other hapaki community must be warned, must be protected."

"I know," he said, "but do *you* have to go? I'm worried about you. What if there is another force there to destroy that community, too?"

"Aw, honey," she squeezed him harder. "I'll be fine. Dr. Walt is sending a group of twenty of the soldiers from the new army he's building. The captain is highly recommended by Dr. Walt himself, and Danaba Kemp. I'll be all right. Just a quick trip to warn the community and invite them to take part in the new government and we'll be back in a jiffy."

He squirmed and made a silly whining noise, just like he used to when he was a child.

"Besides," she said to him, "if I don't go do this, then I will have to accompany you. I will not be left here without doing something useful. You can choose. I can go on this ambassadorial mission to the hapaki or I can go with you."

He pouted some more. "You know that what we're doing is very dangerous. There is a one hundred percent chance that you will see battle if you come with me. I don't want you involved in that."

"I do know, which is why I am going to the hapaki." She released him and took his face in her hands, looking into his eyes, "I'll be fine. The hapaki need to be warned and you and I are the only humans who can communicate with them. Without me, this mission won't work. You know it's true. You can't protect me all the time. Nor should you."

"Okay, okay, I get it. I just worry, you know." His eyes raised to meet hers. "Please be careful. I don't want to think about losing you again like when I was trapped in Gythe last time."

"I'll be very careful and do whatever the captain tells me." She kissed him on the mouth. "I love you. You be careful yourself. I don't want to think about losing you either. I'll see you back here in the fortress when I get back. Okay?"

"Okay."

He hugged her tight, lifting her off her feet for a second. She laughed and slapped his shoulder. "Don't get too big for your britches, mister hero. You know that I brought you into this world and only I can take you out. Don't mess with mom."

His mood finally broke and he laughed the laugh she loved so much. It was his child's laugh, but deeper. He released her and she started to leave the room. Just before going through the door, she turned to him again. "You watch out for Nalia, too. If either one of you gets hurt, I'll have some strong words for the other. Keep that in mind."

"I definitely will. Stay safe, mom. I love you. I'll meet you back here in a few weeks."

She headed toward the meeting room in which she was supposed to meet the rest of her party. She hoped she had hidden her nervous feelings about the trip. She was scared, but didn't want him to know that. He had enough to worry about. This wasn't some story or play. They could all die.

With a last look over her shoulder at the open doorway, she started counting the minutes until they were both back home safe.

*****

Sam was on his way to the stables to meet the others when Dr. Walt caught him in the corridor. "Sam, I would like to talk to you for just a moment, if you can spare it," he said.

"Sure, Dr. Walt," Sam answered, "but it has to be quick. We're leaving in a few minutes."

"I understand." The older man looked at Sam seriously. "That is what I wanted to talk about. What are your plans?"

"I plan on catching up to the forces that took the hapaki away and rescuing the members of the community."

"Of course, of course," Dr. Walt said. "What I meant was, what are your longer-term plans? What will you do after you rescue the hapaki?"

"I'm not really sure. At this point, rescuing them and stopping the people who perpetrated this crime are all I'm thinking about. I don't see a need to think further than that for right now. Why are you asking? Is there something else going on?"

Dr. Walt sighed. "You are very astute, Sam. Yes, there are other matters to be addressed. Word has spread to some of the leaders and diplomats here to help set up the new government. They are concerned about this Ayim Rasaad and more concerned that there is a force out there attacking whole communities, even if they are 'just hapaki.' They want to know what we will do about it. They want to know if *you* will do something about it."

"Me?" Sam asked, surprised by the turn in the conversation. "Why do they think I will do something about it?"

"You are the 'Savior of Gythe,' Sam."

"I'm the what?" Sam looked carefully at Dr. Walt to see if he was joking. His face was as serious as Sam had ever seen it.

"That's what they're calling you, the Savior of Gythe, or sometimes just the Hero of Gythe. They expect that you will handle this new crisis as well as you did the last."

Sam scoffed. "That's ridiculous on so many levels. Listen, I have to get going. The others are waiting for me. When I get back tonight, we can discuss this further, okay?"

"Of course. I'm sorry to trouble you with this. Please think on what I have said, though, about long-term plans. We can discuss it tonight. Be careful out there. We're dealing with a dangerous foe."

"Don't I know it?"

Sam made his way down to the stables a handful of minutes later. The others who were with him when he found the destroyed community were all there. Rindu was also there, his rakkeban loping around in the yard, expending nervous energy.

"Master Rindu," Sam said, "are you joining us?"

"Yes, Sam. I thought it would be good to do so. Also, we still have much to do in the way of training for you, so I believe it would be advantageous to be able to talk while we travel, in addition to training in the evenings when we return each day. There is still so much for you to learn."

Sam felt his ears grow hot. He hadn't even thought of asking Rindu. "That sounds great. I'm sorry—"

"Think nothing of it, Sam," Rindu said. "I know there is much on your mind or you would have thought to ask me. Do not be embarrassed."

"Okay, thank you. It really will be nice to have you along. It'll almost be like old times." He saw Rindu's mouth twitch slightly into his approximation of a smile.

The party gathered around Sam as he prepared to teleport them to the destroyed hapaki community. Within minutes, he was ready and matched their vibrations to their destination. Then they were there again, looking out over the devastated homes of the hapaki.

Feelings of sorrow and anger came into Sam's mind from Skitter. They weren't necessary to sour his mood, though. He had enough of those feelings of his own. He gritted his teeth and stood. "Okay, let's go find the ones who did this and rescue their prisoners."

Everyone nodded and set about mounting their rakkeben, but no one said a thing. They set off at a moderate pace, going toward the east. There were kidnappers to catch.

The group pushed hard all day long, taking a few short breaks to eat and to allow their mounts to move around unencumbered. By the time it was fully dark out, Rindu brought his rakkeben up next to Shonyb.

"Sam, we must stop."

Sam felt irritation at first, but then realized that Rindu was right. He had been pushing the pace all day, trying to gain as much ground on their prey as possible, without thought of anything else. Everyone was tired, the mounts most of all.

"We must not push too hard," Rindu said. "It is as the story from your world about the turtle and the rabbit. The turtle achieved his goal because he stored up his food for the winter while the rabbit ran too fast and was eaten by the wolf."

Sam looked at Rindu, at a loss for what to say. Instead of saying anything, he started laughing, more heartily than the situation deserved. He guessed he was tired, too, and forced it down to a chuckle after a few seconds. Rindu's face registered surprise, in the barely-noticeable way that was pure Rindu.

"I'm sorry," he told the Zouy. "It's just that you mixed up three different stories there. Maybe it's a language thing. Anyway, I understand what you are saying. We'll stop for the night and let the rakkeben rest. We aren't going to catch them in one day."

Sam learned the area where they stopped and transported all of them back to Whitehall.

After dinner, Sam found himself again in Lahim Chode's chambers. Dr. Walt, Nalia, and Rindu were there with him

"Have you viewed anything further about our foe?" Sam asked. "What was her name again?"

"Ayim Rasaad," Lahim Chode answered, "and no, I haven't been able to find out anything else about her. I have seen a glimpse of where I think one of the artifacts may be, though all I saw was red rock."

"Lahim Chode," Rindu said, "do you know about the individual items? Do you know what they do, why they are so sought after?"

"I'm afraid not, Master Rindu. As I explained before, it is difficult to direct exactly where or when I see. I'm sorry."

Rindu nodded. "It is all right. You cannot be blamed for the limitations on your talents. It is said, 'The fool believes he can do anything, but the wise man recognizes his limits.'"

"If I may," Dr. Walt broke in, "I have found some information that may be useful. I have been searching the records since Lahim mentioned the artifacts three weeks ago. It's amazing how much information the Gray Man, I mean Grayson, had gathered. There are so many books, scrolls, and fragments that I could read all day for years and never get around to all of them. In fact, just in the main library—"

"Dr. Walt," Nalia interrupted, "please remain on the point of the discussion."

"Oh, yes, yes, sorry." The old man looked sheepish. "As I was saying, I have been trying to find information on the artifacts he mentioned and I believe I have found something of use. It was in a partial book that is very old. It was, in fact, just a copy of something even more ancient, perhaps on the storage plaques deep in one of the lower libraries. Those plaques appear to be some type of media on which things were recorded, but the technology is something I've never seen—"

Nalia cleared her throat.

"Yes," Dr. Walt's face burned crimson in between his whiskers and his unkempt hair. "Anyway, here is what I have found. It appears to be a poem or part of a song about our artifacts.

> Of ancient lore has come to be
> A tale of totems, numbered three
> When gathered hence can make a whole
> A master mage to take control
> And then the supreme power be
>
> Booming, rumbling, crushing meter
> Orum's sound in wartime theater
> Rushes forth to crush the ramparts
> Causing fear in all viewer's hearts
> Breaking flesh and stone and cedar

> The toll of Azgo clear and true
> Allows the master to pursue
> Another place to be transferred
> From whence the crystal chime is heard
> To the desired place anew
>
> Bruqil is the key to stealing
> Other places' paths revealing
> Through its clear and sacred calling
> Doors to other worlds unbarring
> Veils to dif'rent homes unpeeling
>
> Gathered three to one and using
> Nat'ral energy abusing
> Three in one the power beckons
> Use for good as user reckons
> Power for the mage's choosing

"So, you see," Dr. Walt continued, "the three artifacts seem to be very powerful. This bit of text predates even the technological age on Gythe. These artifacts must be ancient indeed."

"But," Sam said, "that really doesn't give us much to go on. What exactly does each item do? Where are they found? How are they used? We just don't have enough information."

"Yes, I agree," Dr. Walt said, head dipping in defeat. "I will keep looking. Maybe I'll find more information. We have a few days yet before you catch the force that captured the hapaki, even running yourself ragged each day like you did today. They have a large head start on you."

"I guess you're right, Dr. Walt," Sam admitted. "I'm exhausted, and the rakkeben are probably feeling it even more so. I want to catch them quickly, but I suppose it's better to pace ourselves. I don't like spending the nights here in the fortress when we could be chasing them down at night, but we will."

Rindu spoke up. "Sam, we must be patient and work within the limits of our—and the rakkeben's—abilities. If we push too hard, travel too quickly, we may injure ourselves or our mounts. Or we may run headlong into the force without sufficient preparation. It is difficult, I know, to rest when the matter seems urgent, but that is the path we must take. It is the *wireh*."

Sam didn't like it at all, but he saw the sense in what the Zouy was saying. "I will try to be more patient," he said.

"And while Dr. Walt is trying to find information in his way," Lahim Chode added, "I will try to find some in mine. We will determine what to do next, Sam. Trust that we will."

Sam forced a smile and hoped it looked genuine. "Thank you, Lahim. That eases my mind. I am still anxious to catch the hapaki-nappers, but I won't worry about what to do after we catch them. Not just yet."

He looked at Nalia, who smiled and nodded firmly. Rindu stood there, looking as if he was content to wait in his relaxed stance for the next week. Dr. Walt was softly muttering to himself, working through something in his head.

"Okay, I think I'm going to bed. We have to be up and on the trail as the sun comes up tomorrow. I don't want to lose any daylight. I'll see everyone tomorrow morning. At an hour before sunrise. Goodnight."

They all left Lahim Chode's crowded chambers and went their separate ways. Nalia kissed Sam and rubbed his neck for a moment before splitting off. Soon, he was alone in the corridor near his room, thinking about what he had heard and what he needed to do. He would worry about artifacts and villains later. For now, he needed to concentrate on the hapaki. He must rescue them. That was his primary concern.

19

Nicole Sharp looked to the west and sighed. It had only been nine days since she left Whitehall, since she left Sam, but it felt like much longer. She could hardly believe that it has been barely over a month since she had come to this new world. She thought she had probably experienced more new things during that time than she had in any five years back on Telani. Maybe any ten.

Where her gaze fell looked to be solid forest, as if the green could stretch to the other side of the world, though since she wasn't on high ground, it could just have easily ended a mile from where she was. It was beautiful, but scary too. They would be traveling into that dense green world. And hopefully coming back out again.

"Are you well, Nicole," Chisin Ling asked her in the hybrid Kasmali-English they had developed. The captain of the guard unit escorting her had learned as much English as she herself had Kasmali. The soldier seemed to have a facility with language Nicole wished she had.

"I'm fine," she said, only half-truthfully. "A little homesick, a little anxious, and maybe a little queasy from the boat ride."

Chisin laughed. "I understand. Some do not prefer travel by boat."

They had taken a boat from Wethaven—she still thought of the place as Seattle, but she needed to get used to their name for places and things here—across the water to the northeastern edge of what would be the Olympic Peninsula in her world. The water was choppy and she had gotten a little nauseous from the motion.

Nicole eyed her friend—yes, she did see her as her friend, though they hadn't known each other for long—and laughed along with her. Chisin Ling was a massive woman, the biggest woman Nicole had ever seen. Not fat. No. She was perfectly proportioned, but just big. When she first saw the captain, from a distance, Nicole thought the woman athletic and almost slender, with maybe a little more muscle than she was used to seeing on a woman. When she came close, though, Nicole had realized Chisin was well over six and a half feet tall and probably outweighed most of the men in the guard unit, with not an ounce of fat on her.

Her long black hair was tied behind her to keep it out of the way. Her face, narrow and long, had high cheekbones and full lips that always seemed ready to smile. Or smirk. Her thin brown eyes seemed to catch everything. Nicole didn't think she was either pretty or ugly, though what that meant to someone from Gythe, with their peculiar notion of beauty, she didn't know. She thought that maybe Chisin was just plain and pleasant-looking on both worlds.

There weren't really uniforms for the new government's troops yet, but they could do worse than to pattern them after Chisin Ling's attire. She wore snug britches and tunic, large pockets sewn throughout where plating could be slipped in, turning normal tactical gear into battle armor in a surprisingly short time. Her boots, also with pockets for armor plating, extended nearly all the way up her calf and laced ingeniously on the side so that the plate pockets were not obstructed. The finishing touches on her uniform were the two swords she used—both heavier than Nicole could have used with both hands on one—in scabbards strapped to her back, their hilts jutting up above each shoulder. Nicole had seen her practice with those and if anyone could protect her from dangers on the road, she knew it was Chisin Ling.

Nicole looked around again, feeling her stomach lurch when her eyes rested on the water. The twenty guards—seven women and thirteen men—who were her protection were still unloading the boat.

"What's the plan?" she asked.

"Well," Chisin said, "it's not quite winter yet, but we can probalby expect some snow along the way. That will make things slower. The interior of this area is very mountainous and travel will be difficult, not only because of the weather but also because of the heavy forest. I'm thinking we should skirt around most of the mountainous areas and hug the coast, going around until we get to the eastern side. Then we can head inland. Of course, it's your decision. I am just here to protect you."

"I agree with you," Nicole said. "About our route. I do not agree with you about being just a guard, though. I want your help and guidance. I've only been in this world for a handfull of weeks, so please, don't ever hesitate to tell me what you think. I know Danaba Kemp said that I'm in charge, but that doesn't mean I don't want your opinion."

Chisin Ling smiled at her. No, maybe more than just plain. That smile made the woman pretty. At least, to her it did. Nicole wondered if that meant it made her uglier to people from Gythe. It was all very confusing.

"You have yourself a deal," the warrior said."I better get things all settled for travel. We have a long way to go."

What am I doing here? Nicole thought. *I'm way out of my league. I have no clue what I'm supposed to do.*

That's easy, Max sent into her mind, *you do whatever I say.*

The sending was tinged with humor, though there was

something else there, too. Anxiety maybe? She really had to have a talk with Sam about the communication with the hapaki. How could she keep her stray thoughts from being broadcast to any of the telepathic creatures who might be closeby? It wasn't a problem with Max—he was her friend—but when they were visiting a whole community? That could be embarrassing.

I heard all that, Max sent. Nicole laughed, both in sending to Max and out loud.

I'm nervous about this whole thing, Max. I've only been in this world for a few weeks and now I'm off on a mission that I am not sure I can handle.

Feelings of sympathy leaked into her mind from the hapaki. *I know. It is new for all of us. We will do fine. After all, I'm here to protect you and tell you what to do.*

Feelings of affection welled within her for the little hapaki. They had become good friends, much like Sam and Skitter had. Truth be told, it did make her feel better that he was along, and not just because it would better their chances that the hapaki community would communicate with them if they saw one of their kind. She knew that Max would do his best to help her in any way he could.

Sam had described the peculiar honor and loyalty of the hapaki. Well, of Skitter. He hadn't had any dealings with other hapaki. She could see now, after contact with Max, that it was not simply something Skitter had developed. It was a hapaki trait. Yes, Max would be there for her, just as she knew she'd be there for him if things got difficult. A spike of emotion pulled her out of her thoughts. It felt like excitement.

Max? she sent

I just realized something. She could feel the smile in his sending. *I am probably the first hapaki ever to go across a large expanse of water in a boat. We are not known as a sea-faring people, after all.* It was interesting to Nicole that Max was able to pull thoughts from her mind, using phrases that he otherwise never would have used. Like "sea-faring." Sam had told her that even the concept of words was foreign to the creatures. They saw no reason for labels when they could communicate mind to mind, expressing feelings and sending vivid pictures that articulated their thoughts more fully than words ever could. She found that while he became more comfortable with words, she became better suited to sending thoughts and feelings directly. It was amazing.

She wondered if Sam had described it all to Dr. Walt. He would probably want to write a book on it.

Max continued. *I don't think that even the great traveler Skitter has done such a thing. I will be famous, a renowned explorer!*

Max, Nicole sent, *what do you think about what we're trying to do? About trying to find a hapaki community that only Lahim Chode knows about, one that is in rugged, isolated terrain?*

The hapaki's excitement turned to anxiety. *To be honest*, he sent, *I am a little apprehensive. It's a big world and we will be traveling a long way, relying only on the vision of one man and on our friends for protection. What if there are pantors or rakkeben—not the friendly kind that Sam has but the kind that only want to eat hapaki—or something else that we don't even know about? It makes me nervous.*

Me too, Nicole sent back.

They sat there together, looking out over the landscape, silent. Nicole could feel the moisture laden air blowing in from the water. She normally liked sea spray, but it was chilly and she didn't appreciate it right then. After a few minutes, she realized that it wasn't the spray she was feeling. There were droplets falling on her.

"Oh no," she said, and cursed under her breath as the heavens opened up and rain started falling in earnest. She pulled up her cloak and drew it tight around her.

Chisin and her soldiers had finished loading the supplies onto the manu birds and were leading them toward where Nicole and Max were.

"We need to find some kind of shelter, or make it," Chisin Ling said. She pointed toward the trees a stone's throw away. "Over there. Come on."

Nicole stumbled after her, the uneven ground trying to snatch her foot and trip her with each step. By the time she got into the trees, the rain was falling in sheets. She was impressed that the cloak she wore did not soak through in the first few seconds. It seemed to have some sort of water-proofing on it. Sam was right, cloaks were very nice. Especially in the rain.

It was so cold, she wondered why it wasn't snowing instead of raining. Even if she could stay dry, she felt as if she would freeze to death in no time if they didn't get shelter. She was surprised that before she even finished the thought, she no longer felt the rain striking her. Looking up, she saw that three of the soldiers had spread a tarp over her and were securing it to surrounding tree branches. She hadn't even noticed them working.

"Thank you," she said and they nodded their heads in acknowledgement.

Within ten minutes, there was a fire glowing in front of her—somehow the soldiers had found deadwood that was not soaked through—and warmth suffused her body, enough so that she took her cloak off. That she hung on a branch under the tarp. She watched it as the water dripped off the ouside and onto the ground.

"I'm not sure what the weather is like in the area," Chisin Ling said, sitting down next to her. "We only know what the geography is because of Dr. Walt and some old maps. I've never talked to anyone who lived here or has been here."

"I know a little," Nicole said. "I visited here once, on my world. It's called the Olympic Peninsula. As we discussed, there are mountains in the center, with Mount Olympus—I don't know what the mountain is called here—dominating. They have what they call a 'rain shadow' on the western side of the mountains, so there is much more rainfall there than here. It doesn't snow as much along the coast as in the interior, either, but it still does snow occasionally. The forest is thick on my world, but I'm sure it is heavier here. I think that's about all I know."

Chisin considered. "That information will be helpful." She looked out from the tarp at the sky. "I don't know how long this will last, but I do know that we will have to do some traveling in the rain, even in snow, if we want to finish by Qiyat."

Nicole nodded. She knew that Qiyat was the summer season, just as she knew that they were in Teshyrat, the fall, right then. The captain was exaggerating. At least she hoped the woman was. "I figured as much. We'll keep as dry as we can, and hopefully we won't freeze to death."

The women and the hapaki stared out at the rain as the soldiers bustled about to prepare their meal. *What have I gotten myself into*, Nicole thought. She knew it wouldn't be the last time she asked herself that.

20

The days seemed to stretch on for much longer than the clock could account for. Sam scanned the endless path of tamped-down vegetation as they traveled. At least they didn't have to waste time finding trail signs or tracking their prey. If it wasn't for them trying to prevent running the rakkeben to exhaustion, they could easily follow the trail during the night, even with a partial moon. He thought of using manu birds so they could keep traveling each day after the rakkeben were tired, but it was too late. All the birds had been taken with the group going to the other hapaki community. The group with his mother. It made him feel anxious that they were limited in how far they could go each day.

Rindu had apparently noticed how tense Sam was. He spent a good portion of each day training Sam and trying to refine his skills. Nalia helped, too. When they took breaks to allow the rakkeben to rest or to eat, she would spar with him, working him hard so he could expend some of the nervous energy he had. Rindu would work with Sam on using the *rohw* for defense against another *rohw*-user. He was glad of his friends. Even if only for a handful of minutes at a time, they distracted him and calmed him.

"Sam," Rindu said at midmorning as they were moving down the path, "I must speak to you of an important part of your training that you are missing."

"Of course, Master Rindu." he responded.

"What is your understanding of the *rohw*?"

"The *rohw*? What is…what is my understanding of it?" Sam was confused. "I thought we were well past that, Master Rindu. You know what my understanding of it is."

"I do," the Zouy answered, "but humor me. What is your understanding of the universal energy?"

Sam thought for a moment, wondering what the monk was wanting to hear. "The *rohw* is the force, vibrational in nature, that infuses all life in the world. It is all around us and all through us. To use it, I have only to channel and control it, using the energy within myself and also the energy surrounding me."

"Good," the master said. "But how do you use it? How do you control it and gather it?"

"I…uh… come into harmony with it and then redirect and use it according to what I desire to do."

"Yes, that is correct. In order to use the *rohw*, one must be in harmony with his surroundings, must be part of all things. The more 'one' all things are, the more powerful the *rohw*. Do you understand?"

"Yes," Sam answered. "Is there something I'm missing? We covered these basic lessons long ago."

Rindu looked into Sam's eyes. "Ah, but did we?"

"Didn't we?"

"Perhaps we touched upon the subject, but we did not cover it fully." The Zouy looked pensive for a moment, the continued. "I would tell you a story when we take our next break. It will, perhaps, illustrate that of which I speak."

Sam wasn't sure if he was up to listening to another story from Rindu's childhood. He knew the monk liked to use stories to illustrate his point, but at times they seemed so obscure he could barely follow them. He was pretty sure the master was making the story up as he waited for the next break. Oh, well. At least it would distract him for a few minutes.

When they stopped for the rakkeben's next break, Sam sat on a fallen tree across from Rindu, who was sitting on a lichen-covered rock. Nalia sat down next to Sam and Skitter curled up at his feet.

What are we doing? Skitter sent to him.

Sam sent back his answer, *Rindu is going to tell me a story to try to teach me something.*

Will it be a good one, or one he makes up on the spot? the hapaki sent, along with a feeling of humor. He was well familiar with Rindu's tales and sayings.

I don't know, Sam sent back. *Let's wait and see.*

Rindu looked to Sam and nodded, then began. "There was once an old, wise hapaki."

I like this story already, Skitter sent to Sam.

Sh! Don't interrupt, Sam sent back.

"This hapaki, being very old and very wise, saw it as his duty to teach the younger generations. To do that, he would test the youngsters in matters of skill and intelligence. His contests always promised grand rewards and the other hapaki in his large community looked forward to them.

"One year, the prize was a fair-sized pile of onekai, the favorite food of hapaki."

He's right about that, Skitter sent, *there is nothing better than onekai. Not even granola bars.*

Be quiet! Sam insisted with his thoughts. *Don't make me block you out.*

A sending of feelings of embarrassment and apology filtered through to Sam's mind from the hapaki.

"To get the prize, all the winning hapaki had to do was to reach it. Somehow, the old hapaki had put it within plain sight, on a pedestal of unclimbable rock in the middle of a deep pond.

"The pond was surrounded by many tall trees, and hanging from the trees were vines in all different lengths and thicknesses. However, none of the vines could reach the top of the pedestal.

"Throughout the day, the younger hapaki threw themselves at the obstacle. Some tried to swim to the rock and then climb it. None succeeded. Some tried to swing on the vines to reach the prize, but they ended up splashing in the pond. Some clever hapaki even swung on the vines, going back and forth like a pendulum and then jumping to try to reach the pedestal. All failed.

"The old hapaki noticed one of the smallest hapaki, a youngster only fifteen years of age. She sat and contemplated, watching the others and working through ideas in her head. After all the other hapaki were worn out from their endeavors, ready to quit, she selected two other young hapaki and conversed with them for a few minutes.

"The three discussed something at length. At one time or another while they spoke, each of them looked up toward the pedestal, to the vines and trees above, and over to the wise old hapaki. When they had reached some sort of agreement, they went up one of the trees as a group. All the other hapaki stopped and watched them.

"With some signal, all three of the youngsters snatched a vine. All of the ropy appendages attached to the same slender tree, very near the top. They jumped off their branches, swinging in unison. Back and forth, back and forth, they swung together and began to pick up speed, going higher and higher each time.

"As they swung, much to the other competitors' surprise, the tree itself began to flex. Still they continued to swing, in perfect synchronicity, gliding through that air as one, bending the tree more and more. At a signal from their leader, all three, timing themselves perfectly, leapt from the vines. They landed almost on top of one another, directly in the center of the high pedestal.

"The other hapaki looked at them in amazement. The

old hapaki looked at them with pride. The three themselves hadn't noticed, of course. They were too busy eating their onekai, and discussing how they would divide the leftovers."

Rindu stopped speaking and looked at Sam.

Sam looked back at Rindu.

Skitter was silent for a few seconds. Then he sent, *Is that it? What does it mean?*

I'm not really sure. Let me think.

The seconds stretched on, seeming to be minutes. Rindu's expressionless face stiffened. A slight line appeared in his forehead. "Do you not understand what the hapaki learned that day?" he asked.

"That teamwork is important?" Sam guessed. From the deepening of the crease on Rindu's forehead, he decided that it was the wrong answer.

"Harmony, Sam. Harmony. Teamwork would not have been enough to flex the tree. All three had to be in perfect synchronization with each other for it to work. They needed to be in harmony. They needed to be one."

"Okay, I can see that," Sam said, looking over at Nalia for help. "but I don't understand why it's so important. I know that your story is just an illustration and the onekai is a metaphor, but I already know that I need to be in harmony with the *rohw*."

"Yes, Sam," the Zouy said. "You know. But do you really *know*? To know something intellectually does not mean you truly have intimate knowledge of it."

"But Master Rindu, I have been working in harmony with the *rohw*. I have been training and practicing to become one with the energy all around me. What am I doing wrong?"

"Sam, it is not so much that what you are doing is wrong, but you are not doing enough that is right. You must go further, refine your knowledge and your power. When you say you are in harmony with the *rohw*, you are not entirely correct. When you have attained the level where you cannot determine where you end and the *rohw* or your fellow energy-users begin, you will understand. It is only at that point where you will truly be in harmony. You will have achieved true oneness."

"But how will I get there?" Sam asked. "What can I do to make it happen?"

"Ah, that is the question of importance. You must find your own path. Each person is different. As it is said, 'At the end of the road, looking back, the way is clear, but the road ahead is misty and unfocused.'"

He just made that one up, huh? Skitter sent to Sam. Sam didn't respond.

"I have a suggestion, though," Rindu continued. "Try to understand other things and other people. Really understand. Without understanding, oneness is impossible. You must become the other, stepping outside of yourself and sharing feeling and experience with that to which you would be in harmony. Do you understand?"

"Yes," Sam said, "I think I do. I'll try during my meditation."

"Good. But remember, 'Do or do not. There is no try.'"

"Did you just quote Yoda?" Sam asked, chuckling.

"I did," Rindu said proudly. "Was he a great scholar among your histories? His words were some that I have translated into Kasmali from one of the books you gave me."

"Uh, yeah. I guess all things considered, he was a wise figure in our histories."

"I thought so. His words have the ring of truth."

21

Zouyim master Torim Jet marveled at the immense structure in front of him. He had heard of the Gray Fortress—now called Whitehall—of course, but the reality was far more impressive than his imaginings were. The place was massive.

He had traveled north and was staying in an area around Wolf's Run when he had first heard of the Gray Man's defeat. His heart had rejoiced when he heard that Rindu had been victorious. He immediately started traveling toward the fortress, proceeding carefully and warily. It was only when he was in Patchel's Folly that he heard that the name of the fortress had changed to Whitehall and somehow, with someone using *rohw* powers he had never heard of, the stone of all the structures had been turned white.

Almost more surprising than even all of this was what he had found while traveling through the Dead Zone on the way to his destination. He had just left Patchel's Folly a day or so before and he had two or three days of travel until he would be within sight of the fortress.

The monk had seen glimpses of the riati already on his

way through the Dead Zone. The creatures were rumored to have been leftovers from the time of the Great War. Humanoid in appearance, they were completely hairless with ash-colored skin that blended in with the landscape of the Dead Zone perfectly. Small and sinewy, they were disgusting creatures that ate anything, alive or dead. They were cowardly, though, and would not attack unless they were sure they would not be injured or killed. Because of this trait, they often ate carrion instead of live prey. The riati would not attack groups, but Torim Jet was wary that they may misjudge him as easy prey because he was alone.

The riati he had seen were far enough away that they did not bother him. So far, he had seen three groups of them, with six to eight of the creatures each. The Zouyim master did not relish doing battle with them. Rumors said they were strong and fast and most likely carried disease. Still, he was confident they could not overwhelm him. He would keep an eye out, but he would not be concerned overmuch.

On his second day out of Patchel's Folly, Jet saw a large group of the creatures encircling something, obviously intending to kill it, if it was not already dead. Because the group was directly in the path he was taking, he decided he would investigate. Perhaps he could lend assistance. The group consisted of at least twelve riati.

When he arrived at the location of the creatures, he could not believe his eyes. The gangly monsters were circling around a single figure, none having noticed him yet. In the center of the constantly moving ring, he saw something that could not be, something out of a dream. He blinked his eyes twice, three times, and shook his head. The image remained.

There, amidst the foul creatures, was a small woman in off-white robes, same-colored trousers flashing in the dim light, with sandals laced up her calves in a criss-crossed pattern. Her pixie face was framed in short, fine, blond—almost silver—hair. She turned counter to the direction of the circle, holding her weapon at the ready. The weapon consisted of three stout sticks, just over two feet long, connected in a string by two sections of chain. The triple staff. Torim Jet knew this weapon, and its wielder, well.

Not hesitating, he ran as swiftly and quietly as the wind and then launched himself at the nearest riati. He delivered a flying kick to the neck of one of the aggressors while slicing the throat of another with his straight sword as he passed. He landed next to the woman and flicked the blood from his blade.

"Palusa Filk," he said. "It is my great pleasure and honor to see you again. I would fight alongside you, if it would seem appropriate to you."

Her white teeth flashed in a beautiful smile. "Master Jet, it would be my honor to destroy these creatures with your help."

And then they set about doing just that.

The riati soon decided they were not willing to pay the price of this combat. Three more were dead before the main group had even attacked. When the remainder broke formation, some running away and some attacking and trying to eat their dying comrades, another two were killed. Within a minute, the seven that were dead or dying were lying alone on the cracked soil, the others fleeing for their lives.

Torim Jet flicked his sword and wiped the blood from it with a rag he took from his travel pouch. He put the sword back into the scabbard at his waist with a smooth motion. Then he turned to the other Zouyim monk and saluted her, his hands held in front of his chest with the right curled into a fist cradled inside the left. "Indeed it is good to see you, Palusa Filk."

She saluted him and bowed. Then, impulsively, she rushed to him and enfolded him in a crushing hug. "Master Jet, I have missed you. I did not know if anyone else had survived."

He hugged her back and, after a moment, extricated

himself. "I, too, was unaware of any other surviving Zouyim. Any other than Rindu, of course."

"Master Rindu is still alive?" she asked excitedly. "How do you know?"

"I saw him not two months past. He it was that defeated the Gray Man. At least, it was his party that did so. Rindu, Nalia, and their new companion, Sam. That last one is very strong in the *rohw*, and comes from another world. The world from which the Gray Man came."

"Nalia as well? That is very good. Then the Sapsyra yet live. The news lifts my heart. Perhaps there is a chance yet to re-establish the protectors of Gythe. That is why I was going to Whitehall. I have heard they are creating a new government and I desire to be part of it."

Torim Jet looked at her. It had been over eight years since he had seen her and she was obviously older, but she seemed not to have aged. Perhaps her face held a more serious cast, but she was still the pretty, young-faced disciple he had helped train when the Zouyim temple was still whole.

"That is my desire as well," he said. "May we travel together? I would enjoy the conversation and the company. We both have stories to tell, I believe."

"I would be truly honored, Master. It would be appropriate for two of the three remaining Zouyim to enter Whitehall together. Perhaps we will even find others who yet live."

*****

Palusa Filk and Torim Jet made it to the corridor cut through the forest surrounding Whitehall. As they entered the wide roadway, their heads swiveled from side to side, studying the thick vegetation on either side.

"I have never seen a forest like this," Palusa Filk said. "It is so pale, almost as if the color has been leached from the very leaves."

"Yes," Torim Jet said vaguely. He seemed to be preoccupied with trying to peer into the thick undergrowth. "I had heard of this place. It is called the Undead Forest. It surrounds the fortress for miles all the way around. It is sickly, malformed, a result of the Great War and the energies released during the conflicts. This corridor is the only easy path through the foliage."

Palusa Filk looked ahead, up the roadway. It was very wide, perhaps twenty-five or thirty feet across, and was fairly straight. From where they were, she could see the winding road in the distance, making its lazy way up the plateau on which Whitehall sat. All of the cliffs surrounding the fortress were sheer and unclimbable, from the looks of them. At this one location only there was a path, rising from the ground level up the two hundred feet to the walls perched atop the cliffs.

The road was a series of switchbacks, raised in the manner of aqueducts in some of the large cities of Gythe. The entire thing had a look of supreme attention to detail and a timelessness that defied belief.

"The fortress is more than two thousand years old," Jet said, scanning the path, the cliffs, and the walls above it all. "Perhaps much more than that. The legend says that it was created with a power unknown in our time, even exceeding the power of technology that came later and eventually destroyed almost all life on Gythe. And still it stands, a bastion in the storm that is our world. I have very much desired to see the structures themselves, since I heard the legends as a boy. It is good that Whitehall is now under the control of honorable men instead of the Arzbedim or the Gray Man."

Palusa Filk nodded as she looked up, and up, and up, until she could see the keep rising above the walls. It was all impossibly high. "It is amazing," was all she could think to say.

Torim Jet's eyes twinkled and for a moment. It seemed as if the last eight years of tragedy had not happened. It was to her like they were simply discussing some mystery, some aspect of life that was part of her training at the Zouyim temple. Just like old times.

The old master blinked and then his guarded, careful expression was back, making Palusa Filk sigh. "Shall we make our way to the seat of the new government of Gythe, then?" he offered.

"Definitely," she said with a smile as they continued on.

The corridor through the forest ended with a flat, empty stretch of land that appeared to ring Whitehall completely. They made their way across and up the path, which started at ground level and quickly rose to a height of nearly twenty feet from the slope of the hill. The stones of the path were impressive, all fitting together cleverly to create a surface that was almost completely smooth. When looking at it from a distance, she hadn't realized it was as wide as it was, almost as wide as the corridor through the Undead Forest.

Up they went, making the climb with little trouble. The switchbacks were designed to maintain a gentle, consistent grade. Palusa appreciated the engineering and effort required to do such a thing.

She felt something emanating from the path, a warm sort of glow. "Master Jet, are the paving stones infused with some kind of power?" she asked.

"I believe they are," he said, "though it is of an unfamiliar variety. I do sense something, but cannot decide what it is." He stopped and put his hand to the rock at his feet. "Fascinating."

They continued on their way and soon were crossing the drawbridge—which was down—and going through the massive portcullis into the gatehouse.

"Ho there," a voice called from just inside the tunnel in the gatehouse, "what is your business at Whitehall?"

Two men in boiled leather armor, one carrying a shield and the other with a crossbow cradled loosely in his arms, came up to them. Their swords were sheathed and Palusa Filk noted their easy manner. *They are not expecting trouble,* she thought. *This is just routine for them.*

One of the men—the one with the shield—stepped ahead of the other. "It's an honor to welcome not one, but two Zouyim monks to Whitehall. Your like hasn't been seen in many years. My name is Martin Steeves. May I have the privilege of escorting you to our leader?"

Torim Jet bowed to the men. "It is a pleasure to meet you, Martin Steeves. I am Torim Jet and this is Palusa Filk. We would appreciate your guidance greatly. Would you know if Rindu Zose is present? We would very much like to see him."

"I'm sorry, but Master Rindu isn't in the keep. I believe he'll be back tonight. In the meantime, I'll take you to Dr. Walt."

"Thank you. I have met Dr. Walt. It will be good to speak with him again."

Martin said a few words to the other guard and then turned to the monks. "Please, follow me."

22

The two Zouyim and Martin Steeves set off through the tunnel, passing through a massive set of metal-bound wooden doors and under another open portcullis. Before reaching the next portcullis, they turned and used a side door that led to an open area. Torim Jet whispered to Palusa Filk that this area was called the bailey, or sometimes just the courtyard.

As they traveled, Palusa followed the guard mindlessly. She focused her attention on the grand scale of the place. Everything was so big, it was hard to believe. She stared up at the thick stone block making up the walls of the keep and tried to imagine it all being constructed. She couldn't. Even knowing how to use the *rohw* to lighten massive blocks so they could be moved, it was beyond her understanding how such structures could be built.

The white walls glared in the sunlight, dominating her vision wherever she looked. How had the color been changed from gray to white? For that matter, how had it been changed from the black of the Arzbedim to the gray color when the Gray Man occupied it? Was it the use of the *rohw* or something else?

Palusa Filk thought she saw a stand of trees around one edge of the keep and wondered if it was natural or a cultivated park. The entire place was so massive, it boggled the mind. She had to explore it.

As the three made their way to the main building of the keep, she shivered when she saw the arrow slits in the walls and remembered the story of how the Sapsyra had come to attack the Gray Man. She could not help but to flick her eyes back to the holes in the wall that were specifically made for shooting arrows at people who were exactly where she was now.

Soon, they were through a door and into the interior of the keep. Many turns and what seemed to be miles of walking through hallways later, they had stopped at a set of large double doors. Martin Steeves knocked on the doors and a strong, but obviously older, voice rang out. "Come in."

The guardsman opened the door and stepped aside, allowing the monks to enter the room. Palusa Filk's eyes widened when she saw what the room contained. It was some sort of library, with hundreds of books and scrolls on shelves, on tables, or arranged within wooden frames. She had never seen so much written material. Even the library that had been at the Zouyim temple could not compare.

She looked over and saw Torim Jet with his mouth open, eyes scanning the room, a hungry look on his face. She knew he was feeling the same things she was.

"Ah, Torim Jet," said a tall, stooped man with messy white hair. "It's good to see you again. I'm glad you are safe and that you made it here. We can definitely use your help."

"Dr. Walt," Master Jet said, "it is good to see you again as well." The master bowed and saluted the taller man. "Please let me introduce my sister Zouy, Palusa Filk. I just found out not many days past that she was still alive. Palusa Filk, this is Dr. Walt, scholar and traveling companion of Brother Rindu."

"It's a pleasure to meet you, Palusa Filk," the man said to her. It was then that she noticed the other man in the room. She had been so preoccupied with looking at the books and scrolls, she hadn't noticed him.

"This," Dr. Walt said, "is my friend Danaba Kemp, here to help us from his…uh…abode in the south."

The other man nodded companionably to the two monks, a big smile playing on his face. He was compact, shorter than the other two in the room, but built solidly. His brown eyes met hers and he removed the triangular hat from his head and bowed. His clothing, of obvious quality, provided him room for movement yet still looked comfortable and snug. The green color of his ensemble looked to be functional in camouflaging him in the forest as well. The sword strapped to his back and the dueling dagger that hung from his belt looked to be of good quality and as if they had seen heavy use.

"Greetings!" Danaba Kemp said. "It is my pleasure indeed to meet yet two more Zouyim monks. After so many years without any report of those of your order, it's nice to know that Master Rindu is not the only one left. Please, sit. No need for us to be formal. I myself have just arrived and was discussing matters with Dr. Walt. Things that may interest you."

Dr. Walt looked embarrassed. "Oh, my," he said. "Forgive me. Your arrival has made me forget my manners. Would you like something to drink? Dinner will be served in an hour or so, but I can send for some bread and cheese to tide us over until then."

"Thank you," Torim Jet told him, "but there is no need for that. Some water would be appreciated. We can wait until later to eat." He looked toward Palusa. She nodded.

"Splendid," Dr. Walt said, motioning toward the chairs at a nearby table. All four sat. "Martin, thank you. Could you please send a steward in on your way back to your post? We must have rooms prepared for our guests." The guard nodded, smiled at the monks, and left.

Palusa Filk had taken the opportunity to scan the bookshelves again. She noticed Torim Jet doing the same thing.

Dr. Walt noticed their searching eyes. "Feel free to read here whenever you like," he said. "This is just one library, and not even the largest one. I like to use this room for a meeting hall since I am here quite often doing research and because there is plenty of space. Are you as fond of reading histories as I am?"

"I have never seen so fine a collection," Torim Jet said as Palusa was nodding emphatically. "I am honored that you would allow me to read here."

"Not at all, not at all. Those of us who appreciate knowledge are all brothers, as far as I'm concerned." He looked to Palusa. "And sisters, of course."

He cleared his throat. "Danaba here has accepted the position of Head of Forces for the new government. We'll have to create some high-sounding title for him, of course, but for now we can just call him General Kemp."

"No, not that," the other man said, chuckling. "Just Danaba is fine for me. I need no new titles."

"He has graciously agreed to build our army for the new government," Dr. Walt said.

"A monumental task," Kemp said, "one for which I expect to be paid handsomely." He laughed again, clapping Dr. Walt on the back.

"So, Master Jet," Dr. Walt said, "tell us about what you have been up to since we saw you last. And your story, too, Palusa Filk. We want to hear all about it."

The four passed the time in discussion until they were informed that dinner was ready. The two monks were shown their rooms so they could put their belongings in them before cleaning up and sitting down at one of the dining halls. The discussions lasted late into the night, each person sharing stories of daring deeds and danger, the others enthusiastically listening and asking questions.

Palusa Filk felt a comraderie she hadn't felt in many years. It made her hopeful for the future.

"Oh, I must show you the scroll I mentioned," Dr. Walt said to the monks as they left the dining hall. "Let's swing by the library and I'll show it to you. I often sleep in a little cot there because I have so much research to do lately and I have brought some of the most interesting books and scrolls from other libraries there for further study. It's on the way to your rooms, so it won't take any longer for you to get settled in."

"That would be most kind of you," Torim Jet said. "It has been much too long since I was able to read before bed. The library at the temple was destroyed along with everything else."

Danaba Kemp was engaged in conversation with Palusa Filk, asking about how life was in the Zouyim Temple. The two dutifully followed the other two men as they headed toward the library. When they came to the door, Dr. Walt reached for the handle and was stopped by Torim Jet's hand holding him back.

"A moment please, Dr. Walt," Jet said. He closed his eyes briefly and a look of concentration crossed his face. Palusa Filk and Danaba Kemp stopped talking and watched him.

Torim Jet opened his eyes. "Please step back and stand at the other side of the hall," he said to Dr. Walt. "There is someone in that room, someone with ill intent, I believe."

As he said it, Palusa Filk noticed that the room was dark, with no light spilling out from the space beneath the door. The braziers in the library were lit when they had left earlier.

Dr. Walt moved against the wall on the opposite side of the corridor. Torim Jet looked at the other Zouy and at Danaba Kemp and nodded. Kemp drew his sword slowly with his left hand and his dueling dagger with his right. He nodded back at the Master.

When Torim Jet threw open the door, Palusa Filk saw

him generate a pulse of *rohw* and throw it out toward where he knew the braziers to be. Three of them instantly flared to life and the room was flooded with light. Just in front of them, on the left side of the room, a figure was revealed by the firelight. It moved, more quickly than anything should have been able to move, disappearing behind one of the bookshelves.

It was a man, or at least shaped like a man. Tall, thin, and sinuous, it was completely naked except for a small patch of clothing tightly bound around its crotch area. Palusa assumed that meant the it was a "he." His head, bigger than it should have been for his skinny body, had overlarge eyes, the pupils of which had filled almost the entire orbs before the light shrank them into pinpricks. As they contracted, a semi-clear cover flipped down over them as if to protect them. He had flowed away from them on his flexible limbs, sharp nails on his feet clicking on the stone floor.

Torim Jet rushed into the room, followed closely by Danaba Kemp and Palusa herself. When the three were inside, Master Jet closed the door behind them, to the obvious astonishment of Dr. Walt, if the exclamations he made were any indication.

"Do not let it leave the room," Torim Jet said as he started toward where the creature had gone.

The two monks and Danaba Kemp circled around the bookshelf behind which the creature went. They moved slowly, carefully, watching intently in all directions so it would not escape. As they surrounded the shelf, Torim Jet snapped his head toward the other side of the room.

"Over there," he said, moving with blinding speed toward the opposite wall.

He arrived there one step ahead of Palusa Filk, who was in turn one step ahead of Kemp. She saw a blur of movement and Torim Jet was parrying blows and delivering some of his own.

At least, he was trying to do so. The person or

whatever this thing was had the flexibility of a snake. He moved and weaved and avoided the master's strikes as if the monk were standing still. The intruder, in turn, struck out with his sharp fingernails, so long they looked like claws.

Torim Jet was not so easy to strike, however. He defended and attacked, defended and attacked. The two seemed at a stalemate. Palusa Filk, deciding she would tip the balance, rushed in with strikes of her own and found the stranger impossible to hit.

With attacks from both sides, though, Torim Jet was finally able to land a strike. His open-handed blow caught the sinuous opponent in the abdomen, causing him to huff as he was propelled backward toward the wall.

Amazingly, he twisted mid-motion, scrambled toward a window that was half-opened, and dove out into the night.

The three rushed to the window and looked out. There were a few ledges and several balconies on this side of the keep, but they could not see any sign of the intruder. He—it—was gone.

The three combatants looked at each other, out through the window into the night, and then back at one another. Danaba Kemp shrugged and pulled the window closed, locking it and tugging to make sure it was shut fast. Palusa wondered at the mechanism that allowed the window to open and close. She had never seen such a device.

"Master Jet," she said, "what was that thing?"

"I do not know," he said, "but it is clear he was here to capture or kill Dr. Walt. It is only providence that caused us to be here to foil the attack."

The three were silent. A knocking on the door rang out. "I say," they heard in a muffled voice, "is it all right for me to come in now? Has the danger passed?"

Danaba Kemp sheathed his sword and dagger and opened the door. "Come on in, Dr. Walt. The assassin has fled."

The old man's eyes grew wide. "Assassin? Dear me, why would you think it was an assassin?"

"It's the only thing that fits," Danaba Kemp answered. "He was waiting for you in the room in which you are accustomed to sleep or study until late in the night. With the way he fought, he was obviously a skilled combatant. He didn't even use weapons, just his sharp nails. They looked like an animal's claws. Still, he fought us to a standstill."

"But why would an assassin be after me?" Dr. Walt asked. "I'm nobody important."

"Oh," Torim Jet said, "but you are. You are gathering together the leaders from many places in Gythe. You are organizing them and attempting to create a united government. There are those who would like to stop that from happening."

"I see." Dr. Walt's face lost its color. "I'm an old man, too old for an adventure like this. What can we do?"

Danaba Kemp answered. "I have brought some of my Red Fangs with me." Dr. Walt's bushy eyebrows shot up. "Not the ones who were bandits at heart. Honorable men who had no other way to survive but to resort to banditry, like me. Anyway, there are several who are very competent and with whom I'd entrust my life. I will create from them a special detail to act as your bodyguards. As my first act as commander of the new government's forces, I order you to be under guard every minute until we can come up with something better."

Dr. Walt's gaze dropped to the ground. He sighed. "I suppose that's best. I have lived much of my life in Gythe running and hiding from agents of the Gray Man. I guess having a bodyguard won't be too much more of an inconvenience."

Danaba Kemp slapped the older man on the back. "That's the spirit. Torim, Palusa, are you able to stay with Dr. Walt while I gather a few of the guards? It shouldn't take long, but we don't know where the assassin went, so

I'd rather be careful."

"Of course," Torim Jet said. "We will stay here. It will be pleasant to look at some of the books and scrolls and I am sure we have much to discuss."

"Good, good," Kemp said. "I'll be back with the guards as soon as I can. Thank you." He left at a jog.

Dr. Walt turned to Torim Jet, who had a pensive look on his face. "Torim, what did the assassin look like? Was he or she wearing a uniform or anything else that may help us with identification?"

"No," Master Jet said. "In fact, he was wearing nothing but some cloth wrapped around his waist and crotch area. Otherwise, he was bare."

"Bare," the doctor said. "It's cold out there. Why would an assassin be moving around with no clothes?"

"I do not believe the assassin was human," Torim Jet said calmly. "I do now know what else he could be, but I do not think he was entirely human. He reminds me of the riati, humanoid but not quite human."

Dr. Walt's eyes narrowed. "Please describe this assassin to me."

Palusa Filk answered. "He was very tall, perhaps close to seven feet, very skinny, with no hair visible anywhere on his body. His head was larger than it should have been for a human and his eyes were even bigger still. They seemed perfectly adapted for seeing in almost total darkness, if the response of his pupils are any indication. I saw a protective layer flip down onto his eyes when the light flared. It looked to be able to shield his sight from the sudden flash, preventing him from being blinded.

"He moved like a serpent. He was very fast and very difficult to hit. At first, I thought I could see his bones through his skin, but realized when I was closer that what I saw were the actual strings of muscle."

"And his flesh felt like leather when I struck him," Torim Jet added.

"Most remarkable," Dr. Walt said. "I believe I may

know what we're dealing with here. It may take me some time to find the correct book, but it should be in this room. Something I read a few weeks ago. Skimmed, really. I was looking for information about the origin of this fortress and got sidetracked by a history that had been rewritten from one of the scrolls to book form. The topic was fascinating, delving into the time before the Great War and then discussing the war effort itself. I had planned on reading it more thoroughly, but…"

Dr. Walt trailed off. Palusa Filk saw Torim Jet's eyes glazing over and she realized hers probably had been doing the same.

"Anyway, I'll try to find it. Make yourselves comfortable and read anything you'd like." He went off to look for the book he mentioned as the Zouyim wandered the shelves looking for something to read.

Almost half an hour later, Dr. Walt exclaimed, "Aha, here it is." He held up an ancient book, then lowered it again and gently set it on the table in front of him.

"Listen to this," he said:

"Three weapons there were, created by men of science. The riati, the rabadur, and the bhorgabir. When it was clear that hostilities would not be alleviated, each side struggled to destroy the other in the most expedient matter. Experiments using men and animals were conducted and mutated life began to be used.

"The riati were the first, and least of the three. Stronger and faster than a man, they were nevertheless found to be unacceptable because of their cowardice.

"Learning from their mistakes, the scientists created the rabadur. Larger than men, grown with four arms and skin like armor plating, these creatures were used as shock troops or front-line soldiers in great battles.

"Finally were the bhorgabir created. The bhor were made from humans, mutated and bred to be the perfect assassin. Strong, limber, and very intelligent, they were sent after the leaders of the opposing side. Many fell in the events leading to the culmination of the war in which the powerful mass weapons were unleashed.

"I believe that the creature you saw was a bhorgabir, or bhor for short," Dr. Walt continued. "It seems one may have survived the Great War. He would have to be hundreds of years old, though. Nothing in this book says anything of them living so long."

"Perhaps many of them survived and continued to breed," Torim Jet said. "I am not sure if I like better the idea of a centuries-old assassin or a colony of assassins."

"I like neither," Dr. Walt said. Palusa Filk agreed wholeheartedly.

23

Sam was exhausted. They had been traveling hard for several days now. He was so anxious about catching the force that destroyed the hapaki community, had such a strong feeling they were just about to catch them that he had convinced the others not to go back to Whitehall. Instead, they slept a few hours and then were up again, pushing on, going ever forward. It was obvious that he had misjudged the situation.

"Sam," Nalia said softly, "we must allow the rakkeben to rest. Whether we stop here or go back to Whitehall, they must rest. We do not have enough food to stay another night away from the fortress. We must reprovision."

Sam rubbed his eyes. They felt like they were filled with sand. "I know. I was so sure we were close."

She moved a stray wisp of hair from his face and kissed him, a quick peck. "I know. You are perhaps over-anxious. We will catch them, but we must make sure we are in condition to do battle when we do."

It wasn't anything he hadn't told himself several times a day since they started. He could still feel the anger burning in him at what this Baron Tingai had done to the hapaki. Continued to do to the hapaki, for all he knew.

Sam looked at the others in his small party. Rindu, Nalia, and Skitter were all sitting and watching him as the last rays of the filtered sunlight reached their way through the foliage. They had not complained, not once, though he could see they were as tired as he was.

The rakkeben were lying on the ground, resting. They understood his urgency and Shonyb kept the others moving, but he had been pushing them too hard. He saw that now. "I'm sorry, everyone," he said to no one in particular. "Let's go back to Whitehall, have a nice meal, and get a full night's sleep. You're right, it'll do us no good to catch up to the kidnappers if we're too exhausted to fight them. Just stay where you are while I learn this place. We'll be back home in a few minutes."

When they returned, Sam whispered to Shonyb, "I'm sorry for pushing so hard. Go and rest. We'll take it easier from now on, okay?" The big wolf looked into his eyes, made a humming noise, and licked his face. Then, turning, she headed toward one of the bigger parks, the one the rakkeben favored for sleeping.

Skitter headed off to the temporary den he had made in another of the parks. *I understand why you were so anxious, Sam*, he sent. *Thank you for caring so much about my people.* A strong feeling of affection came through into Sam's mind. He formed a small smile as he saw his friend leave.

Hand in hand with Nalia, Sam accompanied Rindu into the keep. They would eat a quick dinner and then he would fall into bed. When they got to the dining hall, though, he found an unexpected gift.

"Brother Torim," Sam heard Rindu say, "and sister Palusa. Glad is my heart to see both of you."

Sam felt Nalia's grip tighten as a small, silver-haired woman in Zouyim robes launched herself at Rindu, wrapping him in her arms and hugging him. He looked to Nalia and saw her face expectant, her mouth compressed in what could only be nervous tension, her eyes focused on the ground.

The woman—Palusa, Rindu called her?—released the older Zouy and looked toward Nalia. Her eyes grew wide and she rushed to the Sapsyr, drawing her into a hug that looked to be even more bone-crushing than the first. "Nalia? It is you, is it not? I almost did not recognize you without your mask."

Sam felt Nalia's hand relax and then she let go of his to wrap her arms around the Zouy. Her eyes squeezed shut as she held the other woman.

Nalia opened her eyes as their embrace ended and she smiled, causing warmth to rush through Sam. "Palusa Filk," Nalia said, "this is Sam Sharp. He—"

"I know of Sam Sharp," Palusa Filk said. She saluted him formally and bowed low, "the Hero of Gythe. I have heard much about your exploits. It is my honor to meet you."

Sam felt as if his face was on fire. "It's a pleasure to meet you, Palusa Filk. Please, though, none of that stuff about being a hero. Mine was the least part of what happened. The Zouyim and the Sapsyra are the real heroes of Gythe. I'm honored to meet you, and to see you again, Torim Jet." He smiled at the older Zouy.

Nalia hugged Torim Jet and frantic conversation ensued, Nalia speaking quickly with Palusa Filk, Torim Jet and Rindu conversing with each other, and Sam chatting with Dr. Walt.

"What are the guards for?" Sam asked the doctor, pointing toward the five men surrounding Dr. Walt.

"Oh, an assassin tried to kill me last night. Danaba decided it would be good to have me guarded around the clock."

"Danaba? Danaba Kemp? He's here, too?" Sam asked, excited.

"You bet your little booties, he is," Danaba's voice preceded the man. "How are you Sam? Or should I say

Hero of Gythe?" He laughed his booming laugh.

Sam turned and saw Kemp, wincing. "Please, don't start everyone saying that. Please."

The shorter man patted Sam on the shoulder. "Oh, I'm just teasing you. I won't actually call you that. After all, it was only because of me that you were able to kill that bastard."

The room became quiet. Nalia looked toward Sam, gauging his reaction. Sam sighed.

"He was my uncle, Danaba," was all he said.

For the first time Sam had ever seen, Danaba Kemp was actually speechless.

"I...uh...I didn't know," Danaba said softly. "I'm sorry."

"It's okay. You couldn't have known. I didn't know, either. He had been tortured and driven almost insane. At the end, he came back to me, if only for a moment. He took his own life, his conscience not allowing him to continue living. I like to remember him as he was, not as the thing he became." He paused for a moment. "On the other hand, you can call Shordan Drees six kinds of bastard if you want. I won't mind that at all."

Danaba laughed and slapped Sam's shoulder again. "That I will, Sam. That I will."

*****

Nalia patted Cleave's shaggy head. Sam had transported himself, Rindu, her, Skitter, and the three rakkeben to the location they left the evening before. They had stayed in the dining hall conversing with Danaba Kemp, Torim Jet, and Palusa Filk for an hour or so longer than she had planned, begging their pardon to leave so she could get some sleep. She felt adequate this morning, still slightly tired but much better than the previous day. It was amazing what a full night of sleep could do for a body. Almost a full night's sleep.

The small party headed east on the trampled path the large force had made, just like the previous days. She wondered when they would reach the people who had destroyed the hapaki community. Would it be today? Anxious feelings to engage them in combat rushed through her, causing her hands to tighten as if holding her shrapezi. The hapaki were an honorable people, even if not human. She shared Sam's anger at what happened, but did not show it like he did. With a lifetime of controlling her emotions, it was to be expected that she did not show them as readily.

She looked to Sam. He was conversing with her father softly before starting out. His gestures, his facial expressions, so familiar to her after all this time, still held her attention and fascinated her. She could watch him for hours, never getting tired of doing so. Her mother used to stare at her father when he was talking. Was she thinking or feeling the same thing Nalia did in those times? She wished she could ask her mother about it, and about so many other things.

Nalia shook her head, not wanting her thoughts to go down that path. Sam and her father were finishing their conversation. He looked at her and smiled. Her heart felt as if was floating upward. She smiled back at him and saw him take a deep breath. She loved it that she affected him so. What had she ever done without him?

Sam and Rindu mounted their rakkeben. Skitter was already in place in his litter on Shoynb's back. She took the hint and mounted Cleave. As they headed out for another day of tedious travel, she wondered what the end of the chase would look like. Would the three of them be enough to defeat such a large force?

Long odds were nothing new to any of them. Even Sam, who had less experience than she and her father did, had been tested when they were in Gythe the last time. His skill had only increased while in Telani. She did not worry about him as much as before. Still, how large an army could the three of them battle? Perhaps they would find out soon.

In the early afternoon, the small party crested a hill and a view of a valley leapt to meet them. The path of devastation wound its way down onto the valley floor and went through what looked to be a village. It surprised Nalia because she had seen no roads or anything else that would indicate that there were dwellings near, especially not a large grouping of them. She could see no less than twenty structures nestled amongst the trees.

The three looked at each other, then alternated between looking at the buildings, the surrounding area, and each other.

"I think we need to be careful," Sam said. He spoke softly to Shonyb. "The rakkeben don't seem to sense anything dangerous, but I'd rather be sure."

Nalia and Rindu just nodded.

The party set off down into the valley at a slow walk, their heads swiveling as they went. They made it to the level of the village without mishap. With their new vantage point, the details of the buildings, closer now, could be picked out. All of the ones visible were made of rough-hewn wood, log cabin style. They were generally squarish, but there were two of them that were long rectangles, low to the ground. Nalia could only count three that had more than one floor. Many had obvious fire damage and more than half the doors seemed to have been broken, as if being kicked in.

"Oh no," Sam said as he scanned the scene. "It's like with the hapaki dens except that it was probably easier to kick doors in and take the occupants than to dig up an entire community. Let's see if we can find any survivors." He leaned over and took Nalia's hand and squeezed it. "Be careful."

She chuckled at that. "I will," she said, smiling at him.

They dismounted and headed toward the center of the village. When they had only taken two steps, all three rakkeben suddenly started growling, their hackles rising. Their heads turned toward the same area, just off to the left. An answering growl, much deeper, sounded from that direction.

"I wouldn't move if I were you," a man's voice said from the trees. "Put your weapons down."

24

Nalia realized that she had drawn her shrapezi. Sam was holding *Ahimiro* in a guard position as well. Rindu was standing there, as if the rakkeben and whatever creature that was in the forest were not growling.

"I won't tell you again," the man said, "put your weapons down or we'll loose the arrows we have pointed at you."

Rindu looked at Nalia and then at Sam. His face showed no emotion. He knew as well as she that unless there was a large force in the trees—something that wasn't possible because the rakkeben would have sensed or smelled them—they could not shoot enough arrows at them to prevent them from dodging them all.

"Who are you?" Rindu said in the direction of the voice.

There was a whispered exchange that seemed like arguing, but Nalia could not hear it clearly with the animal growls. There was a pause.

"We live in this village," the voice said. "Who are you?"

"We are following the force that made this path," Rindu said. "They attacked a community of friends and we plan to rescue the captives. We mean you no harm. We are simply passing through and wanted to help any survivors here. We will be on our way."

There was another pause. The growling in the trees lessened slightly. There was another whispered conversation.

"What other community? There are no other towns or villages for two hundred miles."

"It was a hapaki community," Sam said, "more than a hundred miles to the west. Their dens were dug up and the hapaki taken captive. Listen, we don't have time for this. If you don't want our help, we're leaving. I'm sure you recognize that one of my companions is a Zouyim monk and the other is a Sapsyr. You would be mistaken to think you could survive attacking us, even with the beast you have. We will leave now."

With that, he turned his back and began walking around the village, keeping to the edge of the path. Shonyb growled once more, sniffed, and followed him.

Nalia looked at Rindu. He shrugged slightly, put his hand on his rakkeben, and followed Sam. With one more look toward where the voice was, she turned and did the same.

"Wait!" a different voice said, a woman's this time. "Wait. Maybe we can help each other."

The bushes parted and a young woman stepped out, dressed all in green with a bow in her hand and the fletching of more than two dozen arrows poking up over her right shoulder. A man with an exasperated look on his face followed her, also carrying a bow, his other hand on the fur of the largest bear Nalia had ever seen.

The man lifted his hand from the bear and grabbed the woman's wrist, trying to pull her back. She shook his hand off and took three more steps toward the party. The man eyed the three of them warily and the bear growled low in its throat at them.

The two people were obviously related. They shared

the same angular features and the same wavy hair, hers a bit closer to auburn and his redder. Whereas he was large and muscular, she was muscled but toned instead of bulky. He looked like he was as strong as an ox and she looked as supple and quick as a viper. They both had green eyes, hers shining bright in the afternoon light and his paler.

They both wore garb that made Nalia think they were hunters. Snug leather pants, green sleeveless tunics, and high boots that looked to be functional for traveling through the forest without being heard. The way they held those bows—which were exquisitely made—she knew they were skilled with them. The weapons almost seemed part of them.

The bear, on the other hand, Nalia could not figure out. It was as large as the rakkeben, probably outweighing them by several hundred pounds. It stood there on four paws, alternately sniffing at her and growling.

"We're sorry for the rude welcome," the woman said. "But we just returned from a hunting trip and found our village destroyed, all the survivors carried off. We were just checking for anyone left when you showed up. Despite my brother's blustering, we do know of the Zouyim and the Sapsyra, the protectors of Gythe. It has been years since anyone has really seen them."

She stopped then, and shook her head. "I'm sorry, but I'm showing bad manners. I am Inoria Dinn, and this," she patted the man's arm, "is my brother Emerius. Oh, and that's Oro. He's our friend."

Nalia saw Emerius watching her intently. She ignored him. "I am Nalia Wroun. This is my father Rindu Zose and our companion is named Sam Sharp."

"Sam Sharp?" Emerius said. "*The* Sam Sharp, Hero of Gythe? The one all the traders are talking about?"

Nalia saw Sam flush. "Yes, that is he."

"Funny, I thought you'd be older," Emerius said, and then turned to Nalia.. "You must be the pair that we have heard all the stories about. The Lone Zouy and the

Faceless Sapsyr. But all the stories say that you always wear a mask, that you never take it off."

"I have taken it off now," she said.

Inoria sensed her tension. "Em, mind your manners. We're in the presence of legends." Turning to them, she continued. "It's an honor to meet all of you. Maybe we can go to our house and see if any of the furniture has survived. It's just over there. We can tell you what we know and, like I said before, maybe we can help each other."

"That sounds like a good idea," Sam said. "Is Oro going to have problems with the rakkeben?"

"No," Inoria said happily. "He's really very gentle, unless he thinks we're in danger. Then, um, he's not very gentle at all."

Just then, Skitter poked his head up from the litter strapped to Shonyb, trying to get a better look. Inoria's eyes grew wide. "Oh my. Is that a hapaki? A real hapaki? I've never actually seen one before, just heard about them in old stories."

Sam smiled and put his hand on Skitter's head. "This is Skitter. He's an old friend. He is the true Hero of Gythe. Maybe I can tell you about it some time."

Inoria kept her eyes locked on Skitter and said, "I'd love to hear it. Come on, we'll see if there is any tea that wasn't stolen or destroyed."

They went toward a small house on the outskirts of the village. Inoria went to the kitchen and searched for tea while Emerius paced anxiously. Oro remained in front of the house, occupying himself with pawing at a log lying there.

"In, we don't have time for this. We need to get going. Every second we waste is another second they take Ancha further away."

"I think they'll be able to help, Em," she said to him. "Let's just discuss it for a few minutes and then we can leave."

She returned with a tray on which sat cups and a tea kettle. She poured a cup for each of them, then sat down in one of the empty chairs.

"The truth is," Inoria Dinn said, "we could use your help. Oh, stop scowling at me, Em. You know we're out of our league here. The force that destroyed the village is too much for just the two of us."

Her brother continued to scowl, but said nothing.

"As I was saying," she continued, "we could use your help. This village, called Blackwood, has been the home of our family for as long as anyone can remember. It's like everyone here is family. In reality, some are family. Our brother, Ancha, was here, staying with our aunt while we went on an extended hunting trip. We didn't find his body, which means he must have been taken captive. We have to rescue him."

"It sounds like we have the same goal," Sam said. "It makes sense to join forces. Like you said, we can help each other."

"Em?" Inoria said. "What do you say?"

"I say that we can handle it," Emerius said, "but I suppose having more people couldn't hurt, especially if it comes to battle. The Zouy and the Sapsyr can take care of themselves, but what about you, junior? Can you use that toothpick of yours?"

Sam smiled. Nalia could read in that smile that he had known people like Emerius. "I can use it well enough to keep from hitting myself. Usually." He winked.

The big man's face registered confusion for a split second, and then he smirked. "We'll see."

"I think we should get going," Sam said. "I don't want to waste time that could be spent chasing Tingai down. There's no telling what he may do to the captives. What does he do, use them as slave labor or something?"

Nalia watched as Inoria and Emerius glanced at each other. They obviously had heard the name before. "No, Sam," Inoria finally said, "he uses them for experiments.

He tries to mutate them into creatures he can use for battle."

*****

The party started out immediately, Sam and his friends mounting their rakkeben and their two new additions both riding on the back of the bear Oro.

"What's in the sack?" Sam asked Inoria. He knew Emerius wouldn't answer him if he had asked the man.

"A little of this and a little of that," she said, smiling. "There are some tools in there and some materials used to make things. Em and I tinker."

"Tinker?" Sam said.

"Yes," she answered. "We can make things that may help us in our quest."

"Things like explosives?" Sam asked.

The woman looked surprised, her bright green eyes going wide. She stared into his gray eyes. "How did you know?"

Sam shrugged. "Just a lucky guess. I'm not from Gythe. I came here from another place, called Telani. We have things such as explosives there. They are common."

"I have heard of Telani, but thought it was a legend. Will you tell me more about it? How did you come to be here?"

As they rode, Sam explained. "I came here by accident. I was meditating and tried experimenting with controlling the vibrations of my body. Without really knowing what I was doing, I found myself here in Gythe.

"Once here, I couldn't get back to my own world, no matter how hard I tried. I met Skitter here and then soon after that I met Rindu, Nalia, and another friend, Dr. Walt. They agreed to help me try to get back home, but even all of us together couldn't figure out how to do it.

"When it all came down to it, the only thing we could do was to try to get the information from the Gray Man.

Do you know of him, of the Gray Man?"

Inoria nodded. "I have heard of him. He was very powerful, powerful enough to destroy the Zouyim and the Sapsyra both."

"Yes, that's him, though I am glad to report that he did not destroy either group completely, as the presence of Rindu and Nalia will attest. So, we started on a journey to the Gray Fortress to try to get the secret from him. In the meantime, Rindu trained me in the *rohw*, the vibrational energy of the universe—"

"I know about the *rohw*," she said. "As a child, I heard many tales about the Zouyim and their magical power."

"Oh, okay. Anyway, Rindu trained me in the use of the *rohw* and Nalia trained me in combat. And, of course, they all, including Dr. Walt, taught me how to speak, read, and write Kasmali and Old Kasmali, even a little Ancient Kasmali.

"I won't bore you with the details. Needless to say, we made it to the Gray Fortress, battled with the Gray Man's forces, and came face to face with him.

"In the end, it was Skitter here who saved us all and allowed us to survive. He was able to bring out memories from the Gray Man, revealing his past to him, a past he had forgotten. When he realized who he was, what had happened to him, and what he had done, he couldn't live with it all. He killed himself after bequeathing the fortress and all that was in it to me."

"To you," Emerius interrupted. "Why would he do that?"

"Well," Sam said, "it turns out that he was my uncle. He had been transported from my world to Gythe against his will and was tortured by the Arzbedim—do you know them?—and eventually he got powerful enough to break out and destroy his captors. In the end, he remembered who he was, and who I was."

"Wait," Inoria said. "I heard some rumors that he was killed. That was you? Is that why they're calling you the

Hero of Gythe?"

"Aw, not that again," Sam said. "I hate that name. Like I said, Skitter was the real hero. People somehow believe that I did it all.

"Anyway, that's my story. In the world from which I come, there are marvelous inventions. There are weapons that can shoot faster than a bow and with more force. One man could kill hundreds using what we call a gun."

"You have never seen me or my sister shoot a bow," Emerius said. "If you did, you wouldn't brag about your 'gun.'"

"I," Inoria said, glowering at her brother, "would like to hear more about Telani. It sounds exciting."

"It can be," Sam said. "But Gythe is exciting, too. They're exciting in different ways. How about you, Inoria? What is your story, yours and Emerius's? The life of a hunter is exciting."

"Maybe," she said. "I suppose that anything we're not used to is exciting. Okay, you told me your story, so I'll tell you ours. Unless, that is, you want to tell it, Em."

Her brother just looked at her as they bounced along on the back of their bear.

"Yeah, I didn't think so." Inoria laughed, a high tinkling giggle that was genuine and made Sam smile. He liked this woman. It was interesting to him how different she was from her brother.

"Emerius and I are not just brother and sister. We are twins. You may not be able to tell because we seem so different, but we actually were born only a few minutes apart. We came into the world together and we've been together ever since."

She patted her brother's arm, which was encircling her as he rode behind her on Oro.

"Our father was a skilled hunter, but his greater ability was in thinking, creating. He always told us that before the Great War, there were people who imagined wonderful new things and then actually brought them to reality. He said that these special people were called 'inventors.' He said that he was an inventor. I know that it is true.

"He was always making new things and improving old ones. He taught us, as soon as we could walk and talk, to think, always think. There would be times when, in a hunt or in battle, we would have to act without thought, but thinking and training our minds and bodies before that happened was the way to succeed.

"He taught us the bow and the long knife. He taught us to make traps and snares. He taught us to think like our prey. He taught us to make machines and explosives and poisons. Though we have only two books in the entire village—no, *had* two books; they were both destroyed in the fire—we are able to read and write.

"The point is, our father taught us the skills we need to survive, and to allow the village to thrive. When our brother Ancha was born, it was expected that he would learn all those things, too.

"Five years ago, our parents died of a sickness that swept through the village. A third of the people in Blackwood contracted it, weakened rapidly for several days, and then died. All who showed the symptoms were dead within a week. We don't know why some were afflicted and others not. It went through the village, pruning parts of families, and then disappeared again just as quickly. We were left without our parents, responsible for raising Ancha ourselves.

"We have done the best we can, teaching him the things that our father taught us. We made a small bow for him and long knives that are of a size he can use. Within a few years, he will be going with us on hunting expeditions to help feed the village. Our father would have wanted it that way."

She dropped her gaze and paused. When she raised her eyes again to meet Sam's they glowed like green fire. "We must get him back. We have lost too much. He has lost too much. I will put an arrow into Tingai's heart myself and snatch our little brother from his grip."

Sam nodded. "I understand exactly how you feel. We'll catch up to Tingai and we'll rescue his prisoners. All his prisoners. Then you can have your brother back and the hapaki will be free to live their lives. We'll stop that monster."

"Yes, I think we will. Thank you, Sam."

They were quiet for a moment, both swaying on their respective mounts, the sound of heavy bear footfalls drowning out the sounds of the soft, padded feet of the rakkeben.

"Inoria," Sam said. "How did you come to be friends with a giant bear?"

She laughed again. "Oh, that. It's simple enough. We were out on a hunting trip and came upon a mother bear that had been crushed by a tree. There was a storm the day before with lightning and extremely strong winds. The tree had been struck by lightning and toppled, falling onto the bear. Her baby was there crying, confused and hungry.

"It took several hours, but we were able to coax him to us with some food and he finally allowed us to touch him. Another few hours and we were petting him, making him feel more comfortable. We discussed it and decided that the little guy would die if we didn't take him in, so we did. We didn't realize how large he would grow. Did we buddy?" She patted the neck of the bear.

"He's totally devoted to us, another member of our family. He eats a lot, but he comes in handy, too. Especially when it's cold." She ruffled the bear's fur and he cocked his head, looking like he was enjoying it.

When they stopped for a break, Nalia came up to Sam to show him something. "Sam, look at this," she said. She showed him a large splotch on the back of her hand that appeared to be inflamed and allergic.

"Nal, what happened? What is that?"

"I do not know. I felt a stinging as I was passing through some bushes and then my hand began to turn red like this."

Inoria came up to her. "May I see that?" she asked. Nalia held her hand out to the other woman.

"Did you brush a plant that had jagged leaves and seemed hairy?"

"I saw bushes such as that nearby, yes," Nalia said.

"I thought so," Inoria said. "Wait here for a moment." She rushed off the path into the forest. When she returned a few minutes later, she was carrying something cupped in her hands.

Sam peered into her palms and saw some long, curled leaves in one hand and some pieces of succulent leaves in the other, their fleshy surface shiny and reflecting light. She set them down on a rock.

"This is yellow dockweed," Inoria said. "We need to crush it up like this." She crushed the leaves in her fingers. "Now, let me put it on your hand." Nalia silently put her hand out and let the woman put the crushed leaves on the reddening skin.

After a few minutes, Inoria took out a clean cloth from one of her pockets and wiped it across Nalia's hand, wiping off the crushed leaves she had put there. "That should have neutralized the nettle's poison and this will remove the little hairs that inject the poison into your skin. Now, all we have left," she squeezed the succulent leaves until a clear gel dripped from them, "is to put the sap of the stonecrop on the skin." She wiped the gel liberally onto Nalia's hand. It already seemed that the redness was lessening.

"That feels much better," Nalia said. "Thank you."

Sam was inspecting the leaves Inoria had brought, both the thin, curly ones and the succulent ones. "Inoria, how did you know to do that?"

"It's just one of the things I know about. Em is better with machines and traps, I'm better with herbs and poisons. It comes in handy."

"Yes, I can see that it does," he said. "I've always been

interested in medicinal herbs. I'll have to try to remember these."

The party started off again, Nalia's hand barely showing that it had been red and swollen just a few minutes before.

As night approached, Sam called the party to a halt.

"Why are we stopping?" Emerius asked. "The road is easy to find, even in darkness."

"We don't want to push the rakkeben too much. We've been traveling hard for days. We need to let them rest."

"Don't you understand that—"

"Em, they're right," Inoria cut in. "We do the same thing when traveling long distances and riding Oro. It's not fair to the wolves to push them harder."

"I know," Emerius said, "but they have Ancha. We have to catch them."

"We will. We know where they're going."

"Wait," Sam said. "You know where they're headed?"

"Yes," Inoria said. "Tingai has a stronghold less than fifty miles from here. It's called Agago."

"Do you know a shortcut, a faster way to get there?"

"No," Emerius said. "The fastest route is the one his forces have taken. There was a path there before it was widened by the size of Tingai's troops. We just have to go faster and not take as many breaks."

"We have to let the rakkeben rest and we need to sleep. We've already been on this chase for seven days. We have to make sure we're in a condition to fight when we finally do catch them."

Emerius looked at Sam, appearing as if he was going to say something, but just turned and walked away. Sam looked at Inoria. She gave a slight shrug and put her hands up at her sides.

Sam settled into his normal position for meditation and reached the *khulim* quickly. He heard Emerius questioning Nalia and Rindu about what he was doing, but he blocked it out and concentrated on learning the place. After a dozen minutes, he had learned the unique vibrations of the location and he came out from his half-trance.

Rindu and Nalia had explained to the twins what he was doing and what they were going to do, teleporting back to Whitehall. They were still arguing about it.

"We're not leaving here and going hundreds of miles away by some magic," Emerius was saying. "We have an army to catch and captives to rescue."

It sounded to Sam as if the same arguments had been made several times and the same objections followed. When everything settled down, it was clear that the party would be split for the night. The twins would camp in their current location and the rest would go back to the fortress. With a shrug, Sam gathered Rindu, Nalia, Skitter, and the rakkeben to him and teleported them all away from the twins and the forest.

25

The party had settled into a rhythm of sorts, Nicole thought. It had been nine days since they had stepped off the boat to start the overland travel on the Olympic peninsula. It was called Syburowq here, but she still thought of it by the Telani name.

She had been sore every day, not used to hard travel. Hiking, for her, had always been a sort of light exercise, something that allowed her to get out into the open air and experience nature. She had not hiked strenuous trails, or long ones for that matter. She had thought that her yoga and pilates had kept her in shape. After the first full day of hiking, she realized that her legs were not as strong as she had believed.

She thanked her lucky stars that Sam had taken her to buy some nice hiking boots several months ago. Without them, she would be unable to walk for all the blisters. If she had to walk these distances over rough terrain in the flat boots all the others wore, she's have died. Her legs, from her feet all the way up to her waist, throbbed by the end of the day. Her butt had been so sore—from climbing up sharp inclines, Chisin told her—she was hardly able to sit down. She was better now than the first few days, but it was still difficult. All that, and they estimated that they were only traveling ten or twelve miles a day. Hopefully they'd speed up as her fitness increased. She knew she was holding the rest of them back.

The manu birds they brought were used mainly to carry supplies. They had ridden them at times, but with the heavy forest they were traveling through, they walked more than they rode. Nicole still couldn't get over how thick the vegetation was.

They had been hugging the coast to avoid the mountainous areas. There was also the benefit that they couldn't get completely lost as long as they knew where the water was. It would make the trip longer, but the benefit outweighed the extra time, even if they were racing the winter. They were at the end of the month called Tolit, just a few days from winter, called Sutow here in Gythe. This was probably the worst time of year they could have done this. They had no choice, though. Events were playing out as they would and everyone had to do their part. She just wished her part didn't make her so sore.

"How are you?" Chisin asked. "Are you getting used to the travel yet? It is rugged terrain, more so for someone not used to long distances."

"I'm fine," Nicole said, and realized that she meant it. "Each day is a little easier. I think I'm becoming more accustomed to the hard travel. I will be much fitter by the time we're done with our mission."

The captain laughed. "Yes, I am sure you will. More so even than your son, who is taking it easy and sleeping in his bed every night after traveling on roads."

"Don't remind me. I think I'll slap his head the next time I see him just because of it, even if it was my choice to do this."

One of the soldiers stepped up to Chisin and saluted. "Captain, one of the men saw smoke ahead. It looks to be on the beach several miles to the west."

"I see. Send Hant Marr to investigate," she told him. "And call a halt for everyone else. There are only a few hours of daylight left, so we can set up camp while we wait for him to report what he finds." He saluted again and went to find the man.

"That's right in our path and I don't want to be surprised," she told Nicole. "We can swing wide if necessary, but I'd rather hug the coast as we move. The way is easier there."

Nicole nodded. She dropped her pack and sighed. Another day of travel done. "I'll help make the fire and dinner tonight," she said. "I feel bad that you all are working but I'm not pulling my weight. No—" she held her hands up toward the captain, "—I know you're going to argue, but it's only fair. I want to help. Don't make me order you to let me do so."

"Okay, Nicole," she chuckled. "I will sit back and rest while you slave over a cook fire. Just don't tell Danaba or we'll both be in trouble, I think."

It was nearly dark by the time Hant Marr came back. He was a small, thin man with close shorn brown hair and an odd way of tilting his head at anyone speaking to him. His unblinking dark eyes locked onto the person addressing him, mainainting unblinking eye contact for longer than seemed natural. When Nicole had first met him, the staring made her uncomfortable, but she soon realized that it was just what he did. He paid attention to every little detail, always focused on the matter at hand.

He was a good man, she came to find, the father of two young boys. He had moved his family to Whitehall recently, his wife getting a job as a servant in the keep when he came to join the new government's forces. At times, he would tell of his sons during meals around the fire. Nicole liked how he talked about them. It reminded her of Sam when he was a boy.

"It was a large camp fire," he reported. "Whoever made it left it to burn itself out. It was on the beach, so there was no chance of it catching the trees on fire. There were scrapes nearby, the tracks of two boats being dragged up on the sand. Footprints, too, but they overlapped so much it was hard to tell how many people there were. I'd guess nearly twenty. I scouted the area but found no one."

"Maybe they were traveling around the peninsula, hugging the coast, and they stopped for a rest," Nicole offered.

"That's my assessment, too," Marr said.

"Maybe," the captain said. "Still, double the guard tonight. I don't like it that they were so close." She turned to Nicole. "We'll have to decide if we should go a little inland to skirt the area in case they come back. I don't like things I can't explain and my gut is telling me there's more here than we see."

Nicole was woken from her sleep by an insistent sending from Max. *Nicole. Nicole! There is something going on. Can you hear it?*

She sat up and rubbed her eyes. The fire was only embers nearby and the silhouettes of the others sleeping around her were still. *What? What is it Max?* She listened, but could hear nothing but the soft popping of the embers, the breathing of her companions, and the crickets around them.

I heard something, like a large animal moving about outside of camp. Or several of them.

Do you know what it is? she sent to him.

No. Wait, that sounded like—

Nicole heard a sound then, a soft thump a dozen feet away. She pushed Chisin, who was lying less than two feet away. The captain jerked up, knife flashing out from somewhere, stopping just short of Nicole's throat. When her eyes focused, she pulled the knife away and an embarrassed expression crept onto her face.

"What—?" was all Chisin got out before there was an explosion of movement around the camp.

The captain ducked under a sword swing, rolled, and

came up while unsheathing one of her own swords which had been lying next to her. The blade came out of the scabbard in an arc, cutting into the man who had been trying to kill her. He cried out and fell to the ground, his lifeblood spilling out.

Chisin Ling was already moving toward another shape in the darkness as she called out. "Up, up, we are attacked. Up!"

The other soldiers roused and brought their weapons to bear. It was all Nicole could do to cower in her cloak and hope that no one noticed her. She watched in horror as people died around her.

Max, are you safe? Max, talk to me, she sent to the hapaki.

I'm fine, he sent. *I am huddled near the manu birds and supplies. I will be fine. We hapaki are good at hiding.*

She had no time to respond to him. A shadow had detached itself from the others and was coming toward her, the red glow from the embers reflecting in his eyes. He raised a massive sword as he came.

Looking left and right and finding combatants all around her, she did the only thing she could. She scuttled backwards like a crab, trying to put more distance between herself and that weapon. The man smiled, rotted teeth clenched, and swung downward.

Nicole rolled to the side as the sword struck the ground where she had been. Her body rammed into a fallen log, stopping her escape and trapping her just as thoroughly as if she would have been in a cage. The man turned toward her, raising his sword again. This time, she knew there would be no escape. He widened his stance and swung the sword downward once again.

Not knowing what else to do, Nicole kicked up as hard as she could. Her foot glanced off the inside of the man's leg and struck his crotch. It wouldn't stop her from being killed, but at least she would hurt him. She closed her eyes and waited for death.

It didn't' come. There was a clanging, grating sound

and the sense of movement above her. She opened her eyes in time to see Chisin Ling's sword deflecting the one that had been coming at her and then flow in a smooth arc around to strike the neck of the man. His head came cleanly off his body and the momentum of the strike caused his headless corpse to lean over and fall to the side.

The captain looked at her, scanning her to make sure she was unharmed, and then wordlessly engaged another intruder coming toward them.

Nicole was in shock for a moment, not knowing what to think or how to feel. After that, she rolled onto her hands and knees and vomited everything she had ever eaten.

26

Dr. Walt rubbed his eyes. He had been spending almost all his time in the libraries, searching for information that would help Sam and the others locate the artifacts. He hadn't seen his chambers in days, just taking short naps in the library when he physically couldn't go on. He had to find the information. It must be here. Somewhere.

He had at his disposal the largest library in the world, as far as he knew. He had thought much about it and decided that the Gray Man was probably only responsible for collecting a small part of the knowledge housed at Whitehall. Though the keep had changed owners many times over the centuries, it had always retained its wealth in the written word. He was sure of it.

The old scholar looked across the room to Torim Jet and Palusa Filk. They had kindly put themselves at his disposal, searching through the libraries and trying to find what they all so desperately sought.

"Hmm, interesting," Torim Jet said in a whisper. The heavy silence in the room allowed Dr. Walt to hear it clearly.

"Have you found something, Torim?" Dr. Walt asked.

"Not something related to our search, no. Something of interest to me, however."

Dr. Walt got up slowly, his limbs creaking. He walked over to where Torim Jet had a book open. He was flipping through the pages. The book didn't look very old.

"This," Torim Jet said, "is a book written by the great Zouyim master Chetra Dal. It is called *The Twelve Forms of the Wind*. It was required reading in the Zouyim temple for more than forty years before the temple was destroyed. I remember Master Dal. He had a large part in shaping who and what I would be as I grew older."

Dr. Walt looked at the book. "It's a book of wisdom, then?"

"Something like that," Jet answered. "Master Dal always had a very clear picture of how the universe worked, how the *rohw* interacted with everything. The title is metaphoric, of course. The book describes how the wind is symbolic of all things, of all life. After all, the word *rohw* itself means 'breath' or 'wind' in Ancient Kasmali, as well as Old Kasmali. It is a fascinating work, and each time I read it, I perceived new information I had not understood before."

"Well, then," Dr. Walt said, "you should take it. You will need to start a library when you re-establish the Zouyim temple. Let this work be your first."

Torim Jet's eyes glistened and he bowed his head. "Thank you, Dr. Walt. That is very kind of you. I have waited for more than eight years for a time when that would be possible. I can hardly believe that it is true. Often when I was hiding and running for my life I had wondered if the Zouyim would be erased from Gythe forever. It makes my heart sing that we can begin working to establish the order anew."

"Yes, I understand," Dr. Walt said. "Gythe would be a very different place without the Zouyim. I wouldn't like to see it. Know that you will have the full support of the new government and that you have the full support of Whitehall right now. Anything you need to rebuild the temple is yours."

The old monk nodded and wiped a tear from his eye. "Thank you Dr. Walt. That means much to me."

"Is it true?" Palusa Filk said. "We are really going to rebuild the temple, re-establish the order?"

"I have talked about it with Rindu from the very start," Dr. Walt said. "It has always been the plan to bring back both the Zouyim and the Sapsyra. It is one of our highest priorities. It will happen. Sam supports the idea as much as I."

Palusa Filk smiled and let loose with a little giggle. "That will be wonderful." Her face grew more serious. "For now, though, we have work to do. Sam needs our help, so we better not let him down."

They went back to searching through the library, after Torim Jet placed the book he had been given in the center of the table. As he went about his work, he glanced at it often and got a faraway look in his eyes.

An hour and a half later, Dr. Walt's tired eyes went wide. He read the passage over again that he had just read twice before. He wanted to be sure. When he finished, he took a deep breath, read the passage one more time, and then whooped, causing Torim Jet and Palusa Filk to snap their heads up. The guards standing near the door and windows jumped and had their weapons out in the blink of an eye.

"What is it?" Torim Jet asked calmly.

"I've found it. I found a reference to the artifacts."

*****

Sam, Nalia, Rindu, and Skitter arrived at Whitehall in time to meet the others for dinner. He wanted to tell them of Blackwood and of the twins they had met. And that huge bear. He was still feeling a bit subdued, not entirely comfortable with leaving his two new party members. It was strange to leave the path and sleep in a bed while they stayed behind.

"Sam," Nalia said, touching his arm and interrupting his thoughts, "do not worry about what Emerius says. We have discussed this before. It is right to allow the rakkeben to rest and it is right for us to rest. Nothing would have been gained had we stayed with Emerius and Inoria and camped there."

"I know," he said. "I just feel like we could be doing more. Obviously, Emerius agrees."

"You must not worry about what others think, Sam," Rindu said. "As it is said, 'The fool worries over what other fools believe, but the wise man knows his path and listens only to himself.'"

Sam caught himself staring at the Zouy. He saw that Nalia was as well. They both shook their heads as if to clear their thoughts.

"Thank you, Master Rindu," Sam said. "I'll try to remember that."

Did you understand that? Skitter sent to Sam.

I think I know what he was saying, yes, Sam sent back. *It was...awkwardly worded.*

The four went to the dining room and found Dr. Walt, Torim Jet, Palusa Filk, and Danaba Kemp just sitting down to eat.

"Sam!" Dr. Walt was speaking quickly and obviously excited, "I found it."

"That's great, Dr. Walt," Sam said. "Uh, found what?"

"Information on the artifacts. What else?"

"Oh. Fantastic," Sam said. "What did you find out? How did you find it? Was it one of Lahim's viewings?"

"No, no," Dr. Walt waved his hand as if shooing an insect away. "I did it the old-fashioned way. I skimmed a lot of books. Torim and Palusa helped me. We have hardly slept since you came back with news of the hapaki community. Let me tell you, it was quite a chore finding any information at all. There are so many books and scrolls and other types of records here. Three people can hardly be expected to—"

Dr. Walt seemd to notice that everyone was staring at him, glaring at him, or rolling their eyes at him. "Anyway, anyway, I found a reference to the passages I showed you the other day. It's actually commentary on what we read before."

"I won't go into the specific information right now, but the important part is this…" He lifted a book from the chair next to him and put it on the table. A piece of pale blue ribbon was inserted between the pages to mark his place.

Dr. Walt opened the book and began to read:

> It is evident that Azgo, the bell, is a tool by which the user can transport himself and an unknown number of people and things instantly to a location with which they are familiar. This effect, of course, is a minor one, shared by other artifacts, though perhaps it is more powerful in Azgo because one person can use it and there is no long ritual required to perform the transport. The true value of Azgo, however, is its ability to link with the other two artifacts to create a power like nothing Gythe has ever seen.
>
> It is likely that the bell is interred at Gromarisa, as per the ancient riddle, "How does one find its dulcet tones? Bed of bones, bed of bones!"

The scholar looked up from the book, eyes dancing. "So, you see, it's as clear as crystal."

Sam looked around. No one else was saying anything. He felt the room grow warmer. He could just hear Rindu saying, "If one asks a question, he is a fool, but if he does not, he is a fool for much longer. Or something like that." He laughed inwardly at that, but the point was still valid.

"Um, Dr. Walt," Sam said. "I don't understand what that means."

Dr. Walt's eyebrows climbed his forehead and then his eyes softened. "I'm sorry, Sam. Sometimes I forget you haven't spent a lot of time in Gythe. There is a very well-known geographical feature that is named Gromarisa. In Ancient Kasmali, 'Gromarisa' means 'bed of bones.'"

"Yeah, I got that part. I recognized the words. The name doesn't mean anything to me other than what its literal translation is, though."

"Ah," Dr. Walt said, "but it will make sense to you if I tell you in Telani terms. Gromarisa is called by another name on Earth. There, it's known as the Grand Canyon."

Sam was flabbergasted. One of the three artifacts Ayim Rasaad was looking for was hidden in the Grand Canyon. All he could come up with was, "Why?".

"Ah," Dr. Walt said, "that's the fascinating part. The reference here says that it's likely because of the unique acoustics of the area. Perhaps they strengthen it, though I'm of a mind that it's because the acoustics help to hide it, foiling attempts to use vibratory means to find it. Whoever hid the three artifacts—I haven't found any reference yet that explains who they were—they wanted to be sure the items weren't easy to find."

"But why, then," Rindu asked, "would the bell be hidden in such a popular place as Gromarisa? After all, it is rumored that before the Great War, many people flocked to see the natural wonder."

"Yeah," Sam said. "If it was anything like it is on Telani, millions of people a year would have visited it."

Dr. Walt pushed his glasses up further onto the bridge of his nose and tapped his forehead with his index finger, thinking. He suddenly looked up and pointed toward the ceiling with the finger. "Aha. I think it was hidden somewhere it could be found if it was ever needed, somewhere that doesn't change. What better place than one that has been unique for thousands of years?"

"Didn't you just contradict yourself?" Sam asked.

"Not at all, my boy. Not at all. You see, whoever hid the artifacts knew that they would eventually need to be found, that they would be needed. Still, they didn't want to make them too easy to find. If they had wanted to keep anyone from ever using them, they would have just destroyed them."

"Okay," Sam admitted. "That's logical. But where are the others. Is that the only one mentioned?"

"No," Dr. Walt said. "All three are referenced, but the commentary skips around in this book and I haven't had time to read all of the other sections yet to see if the locations are recorded. Azgo is the one we need to be concerned about right now. I'll tell you about the others when I read the rest of the book."

"But Dr. Walt," Nalia said, "how can you be sure that the bell is the first artifact Ayim Rasaad will go after?"

"You tell me, my dear," Dr. Walt said. "Why would she go after that one first? Why not go after Orum the drum, with the power to break down walls with its sound, or Bruqil the tuning fork, with the ability to combine all three artifacts together to make a powerful weapon?"

Nalia nodded. "Of course, you are correct. She would go for the artifact that would let her teleport. Sam and the Gray Man are the only ones who have ever been powerful enough to teleport without the aid of others. Except for the assassin Ix, of course, but her ability is a talent and not a use of the *rohw*. With that ability, it would be much easier for her to obtain the other two artifacts, or at least to go back to her home when she got each one. That is very clever of you, Dr. Walt."

The old man bowed his head. "Thank you. I rather thought so myself. It didn't take much of a nudge for you to figure it out. You are as clever as I am."

"It is decided, then," Rindu said. "As soon as we rescue the hapaki and the citizens of Blackwood, we will attempt to retrieve the artifact before Rasaad does."

"Blackwood?" Torim Jet asked. "What is Blackwood?"

Sam told them quickly how they had come upon the half-destroyed village and the twins. "They didn't want to come back with us. We'll meet them tomorrow morning to continue on. They seem to have useful talents."

"Emerius Dinn?" Danaba Kemp said. He had been quiet throughout the entire conversation. "Big guy, red hair, green eyes, built like he was chiseled from the raw rock of the mountain? And his sister, tall and muscular, but slenderer than him, also with reddish hair and bright green eyes?"

"Yes," Sam said, "that's them. Do you know them?"

"Not really. They came to Kempton one year for our archery contest. They outshot everyone who entered. Both of them. They can do things with arrows that shouldn't be possible, and they were just teenagers then. Yes, they will be handy in a fight. They will be handy indeed."

When Sam and the others teleported back to where they had left the twins, all they saw was the empty road.

"There's no trace of them," Sam said. "I mean, literally, there is nothing. No tracks, no camp, not even signs of that monster bear Oro. How is that possible?"

Rindu's eyes went out of focus and he looked around. "They are very good," the Zouy said. "Even using my *rohw* sight, I can see little of them, and nothing that tells of where they went. Still, it is no great mystery. They went east to find their brother. We must travel that way also. Perhaps we will meet them again."

Sam wasn't sure why, but he was disappointed. He thought the twins would be good allies. Sure, Emerius was kind of rough around the edges, but Sam saw good in him. He genuinely liked Inoria. She was more of a "people person." Sam had just met her but already he felt comfortable with her. He thought they could be good friends.

"You are disappointed," Nalia said. "It does not reflect on you, Sam. They are anxious to find their brother. We will meet them again. I am sure of it." She smiled at him and the morning sunlight seemed to grow brighter.

"Thanks, Nal," he said. "I'm sure you're right. Like you always are."

Two hours later, they turned a corner in the road and found the twins and Oro sitting in the shade, eating some type of dried meat.

"Hey, Sam," Inoria said, "and good morning to you, Master Rindu and Nalia, and Skitter. Would you like some dried venison?"

The party stopped and dismounted. There was enough of the meat to give the rakkeben some as well. The wolves snapped it up hungrily, though it was seasoned and fairly spicy.

"We scouted ahead several miles," Inoria said. "We were too anxious to wait around and wanted to get started doing something. The path is clear for at least five miles."

"That was nice of you," Sam said. "And we appreciate that you waited for us. I was disappointed when we didn't find you this morning."

"We're a team," Inoria said. "We won't abandon you and we expect that you won't abandon us."

"We definitely won't," Sam said.

"So, Sam, you said that you were trying to learn how to identify different trees and plants. Would you like me to teach you some of what I know as we travel? It may make the time pass more quickly."

"That would be fantastic," Sam said. "I'd be honored to learn anything that you could teach me."

"Are you really going to waste your time with that, In?" Emerius said. "He'll never be a tracker and he'll never learn herb lore. He's too *sophisticated* for that."

"Oh, don't listen to him, Sam," Inoria said. "He's a perpetual pessimist. Tell me, can you identify any of the trees around us?"

"Yes," Sam said, looking at Emerius. "I see some fir trees over there, and those are pine. Oh, and that tree is an oak—"

"But what kind of pine, and fir, and oak?" Inoria prodded him.

Sam scratched his head. "I'm not sure. It's hard enough

to identify the families of trees without going into the specific types. They never look the same in the wild as they do in books."

"I understand, Sam. It's a lot to learn. Here, let me show you a secret. You will look for four things: the overall shape of the tree, the leaves or needles, the fruit, and the bark. If you pay attention to those, most of the hard work is done. Here, let's look at those pine over there and I'll show you what I'm talking about."

Sam passed two hours talking with Inoria and learning of the trees they passed as well as some of the shrubs covering the forest floor. By the time they stopped to rest the mounts, his mind was filled to brimming with what he had learned. He smiled at her as she went off with Emerius to scout the area.

As they continued in their travels, Sam divided his time between learning about the surrounding plants and trees from Inoria and learning more about *wireh* from Rindu.

"You must understand, Sam," Rindu said, "the *wireh* encompasses everything the Zouyim are and stand for, but it is not just for the Zouyim. The *wireh* is the *wireh*, no matter who you are. There is but one true path and all who follow it are in harmony with the universe."

"I still don't understand exactly what the *wireh* is, though," Sam said. "For that matter, I'm not sure I know what you mean by harmony. I have felt myself in harmony with the *rohw*. Aren't the things I have been able to do proof that I was in harmony with it?"

"No," Rindu said. "Sam, you must understand that although you have experienced harmony in one sense, grasping true harmonic motion still eludes you."

The Zouy was silent for a moment as they bounced along on the backs of their rakkeben. "Do you remember when Nalia demonstrated for you the Song of Battle?"

"Of course," Sam said. "I could never forget that."

"Good. When she was singing, what did your body do?"

"It moved. It was almost like a dance. There was nothing I was doing consciously. The sound seemed to go through my body and make me move in a way that was compatible with the sound."

"Compatible?" Rindu asked. "Do you mean that the sound caused your body to move *in harmony* with the song?"

"Well," Sam said, "yes. I guess so."

"Then you have felt the harmony of which I speak. It is not a simple acting together of two things, but a true melding, so that two become one. Do you understand this?"

Sam thought for a moment. "That makes sense, but I think that's what I've been doing. When you and I meditate and you help me to channel the *rohw*, we are acting in harmony, right?"

"Yes and no," Rindu said. "We will continue to work on this. When you have achieved harmony, you will know it, and then it will become clear. For now, let us focus on the *wireh* itself, for when you understand that which cannot be understood, you will have achieved that which is unachievable."

"Um, okay," Sam said, head reeling.

27

Baron Tingai listened to Ayim Rasaad. She was intelligent, in her own way, though her mental abilities paled in comparison to his own. She was striking, though. Tall, with an athlete's form, her motions graceful and powerful at the same time. He wondered what color her hair was. She must have shaved her head daily to keep it perfectly bald with no stubble. The swirling tattoos across her scalp had a mesmerizing effect if one looked at them too closely.

Tingai found it interesting that she didn't show the effects of using dark powers as all the Arzbedim had. He wondered what was different about her that kept her looking like a normal person. A normal person with a bald head covered in tattoos, that is. And there was the matter of the power she manifested. She seemed to glow, but when seen out of the corner of one's eye, there appeared to be a penumbra, a dark halo, around her. It was eerie. He wasn't sure if it was preferable to how the Arzbedim used to appear, maggot-like with no hair whatsoever and with red-rimmed eyes.

"Your experiments are secondary, Tingai," she said.

"The number one priority is to get the artifacts. Anything that does not contribute to that is optional. Do you understand me?"

"Of course, of course," he responded. "I would never let my work interfere with the bigger picture. I would remind you, though, that my little experiments will come in handy if the new government is able to marshal forces to defy us."

"You let me worry about our adversaries. We are on the verge of obtaining the first of the artifacts. With all three, no army on Gythe will be able to stand against us."

"I understand. I will send half of my forces with your own to get the first artifact."

"You will be coming with me," Ayim Rasaad said. "After getting the artifact, I will be teleporting directly to my own fortress. You will be too far from me to be of any use if you stay here."

"But my work—" Tingai started.

"—can be carried out at Gutu while we determine where the next artifact is. This is not a discussion. Prepare yourself and your followers to depart tomorrow."

She left the room without looking back toward Tingai, as if he were of little consequence. Baron Tingai sighed. He would do as she said, of course. He was not under the misconception that they were equal partners. He served her. For now.

Tingai glanced at the mirror on the other side of the chamber. His long thin frame was hunched, as always. His black hair fell limply around his narrow, pale face. He looked into his own dark brown eyes, saw the skin beneath his eyes, how they were puffy and dark. Didn't Rasaad know that to do his best, he needed to get adequate sleep?

He supposed it was his own fault, though. He could have bypassed that village instead of attacking it and taking more captives. They were a nuisance when traveling, so he pushed hard to get back to his home at Agago. Here, the captives could be stored out of the way in the extensive cages and dungeons until he had need for them.

Tingai had planned on resting and then starting his work in earnest, but he was anxious to begin with the hapaki so he had slept little in the time he'd been back, figuring he would catch up in the next day or two. That wasn't going to happen now. He supposed that there was nothing he could do about it, so there was no use dwelling on the situation.

The scientist pondered his life for a moment. He hadn't done badly for himself. He was able to conduct his research and the experiments he loved so much and he had all the resources he could want. It was a far cry from the child who found himself fascinated by life and the ways in which it could be made to adapt.

The memories he had of being very young were fond ones. He had found from an early age that creatures were willing to do extreme things to keep from dying. He studied this phenomenon carefully, catching and torturing insects and small animals and observing the actions they took to prevent their deaths. The interest soon grew into an obsession, with him spending as much of his time as he could in his studies. There were secrets there, waiting to be found. He was sure of it, and he was sure he wanted to discover all of them.

One day, he discovered a strange, mutated creature in the ruins not too far from where he lived. He thought it may have been a squirrel once, or at least one of its ancestors was. When he was finished inflicting pain and wounds on the creature and it had finally died, young Tingai started to question how it had come to be. Did someone create this creature or was is somehow left over from the time of the Great War, mutated creatures reproducing in an endless line to the one he had found? He decided to investigate.

After hours of picking through the rubble, he was ready to give up. As he was turning to leave, he saw the tracks of a small animal surrounding what looked like an animal burrow. The odd thing, though, was that the top of the burrow was made of some type of metal.

Tingai looked into the hole but couldn't see anything. Not being able to think of anything else, he started digging with his hands. He was soon bleeding and found a tree branch lying on the ground nearby. The boy used it to dig and loosen the soil around the hole. He kept up for hours, finally opening the hole enough so he could enter, but did he dare?

It was dark inside and he wasn't sure how deep it went. What if it was very deep? What if he fell and hurt himself and couldn't climb back out? He dug more and removed the dirt while he thought. In the end, the decision was made for him. As he dug one more stroke with the stick, he heard it strike something hard. A rock? It didn't sound like a rock.

He plunged the stick into the soil again and heard a metallic clank. His energy renewed, he quickly cleared the dirt from the source of the sound and found a long metal strip. Another fifteen minutes and he realized that the metal he had hit was one step in a set of stairs. He was able to clear part of another step in that amount of time. He was suddenly reassured that he would be able to get out of the hole if he went in because even if the steps were covered, there would be a mound of dirt he could climb up. He had decided; he was going down.

The young Tingai carefully crawled down the hole he had made, but didn't get far. The dirt had accumulated over the centuries since the Great War and there was only a small opening. With no other choice, he spent the rest of the day digging. By the time the sun was going down, he was covered from head to toe in dirt, had bleeding hands, and had nothing else to show for his effort. Still, he was onto something, he knew he was. He would come back the next day and work on it some more. And this time, he would have the proper tools.

The next morning, he was up so early that his parents

were not even awake when he left. They had chores for him to do, but he was able to sneak out without them seeing him. He would be in trouble when he came home, but that would be a minor inconvenience. They had tried punishing him before but it never worked.

With sticks and his striker to make torches, and a shovel and spade to dig with, he headed back to the ruins, determined to make progress. He worked all day, stopping only to eat the snacks he had brought, and by the end he had made a hole big enough for him to go through that descended more than ten feet underground. While digging, he had cleared the steps so that he could use them to easily go up and down with his shovel filled with dirt.

Still, he hadn't found anything other than the stairs. He made a torch and waved it around, looking for anything interesting, but he only saw a small hole, about the size a badger would make, going down into whatever this place used to be. Too soon, the sun was going down again and he had to go back home. He left his tools hidden nearby so he wouldn't have to carry them back the next day.

His parents yelled and blustered, but when it came down to it, they just impotently warned him to straighten up. They had his brothers and sisters to deal with, so they left him to his own devices.

Every day, Tingai went back to the hole he was gradually making bigger and bigger. It was amazing to him that the hole could go down so far. He daydreamed about what he would find when he finally reached the end. He hoped it would be something worthwhile.

Finally, five days after he had first brought the shovel, he plunged it into the dirt and it pushed through into empty air. Excited, he hurriedly dug the hole bigger, enough so he could crawl through. He took his torch from where he had thrust it into the dirt and squeezed through the opening he had made. What he saw made his eyes grow double in size.

He slid down the pile of dirt and found himself in a

large room with many counters with sets of drawers in front of them. They weren't just square wooden boxes that slid in and out of a hole like the furniture he was familiar with. They were actually set on some kind of metal strip that made them open and close smoothly, with little effort. They were filled with objects he had never seen before.

On the tops of the benches were cages made of wire and glass, and many containers with liquid. One had been cracked, apparently from a piece of the ceiling that had dropped on it. From the crack was leaking some kind of thick yellow-brown liquid. Little footprints went through the puddle and out across the floor, toward the opening to the surface.

Tingai smiled. This liquid was responsible for the mutation in that creature he had found. Knowing better than to touch the liquid himself, he looked around the rest of the room. There were enough complex objects, liquids, and powders here to keep him busy for years in trying to figure out what they did. First he would clean up the dirt and then he would start experimenting. This was even better than he could have imagined.

After cleaning the room up, Tingai was able to rig up a door to keep his laboratory—he had decided that was what this room used to be—secret. He found, too, that there were two other rooms attached to the laboratory. There had been more, but the others were victims of collapses and he didn't think he'd ever be able to get the dirt and rubble cleared.

Young Tingai spent all of his time in his new laboratory. He found some records in one of the other rooms that detailed the work that they did there. While most of it was completely foreign to him, he was able to pick out small details. With that information and endless experimentation first with insects and then with animals, he was soon able to cause changes in his subjects.

The devices in the lab didn't work because there was no power source, but as he studied them he was able to utilize some of the basic concepts and make his own devices that helped with his work. He also taught himself how to distill out some of the active chemicals from local herbs. He knew the substances in the laboratory wouldn't last forever, so he worked hard to find new ways of causing the changes he wanted to make.

As he learned, Tingai mutated larger and larger animals. Rodents, squirrels, wild dogs, even some of the local monkeys, were all used to refine his art. When he chanced upon a stranger who was passing through the area and weak from a fever, he knew the situation for what it was. He kept the man in one of the larger cages and fed him, nursing him back to health, though keeping him sedated from his own concoction of herbal drugs. When he was healthy again, Tingai began treatments on him.

In the end, the man died, though not before providing valuable information on how a person could be changed into something more. He was anxious to find his next subject.

One of Tingai's mutant monkeys escaped while he was trying to clean its cage. He thought the creature a loss until several people showed up at his hideout with its body. One of those people was Ayim Rasaad. She questioned him about the creature and when Tingai explained his work and showed her some examples, she told him that if he worked for her, he would be assured all the subjects he would ever need. She didn't have to ask him twice, once she had agreed to one small condition.

"I want to be called 'Baron Tingai,'" he said. He had heard of an important man once, in a story his parents had told him. The man had a title, he was called a "baron." Tingai was going to be just as important as any man in a story, and he liked the ring of the title with his name. Rasaad answered him satisfactorily. "Of course, Baron Tingai."

All in all, it had been a good arrangement. He had increased his skill a hundredfold and had successfully mutated many different types of creatures. He was working now on trying to combine talents of different creatures into one superior mutation. When he finally figured out the supreme mixture, he could create an army of them, which is really what Ayim Rasaad had sponsored him for to begin with. Yes, things could be worse. Once he got some sleep and made this trip with her, he would be able to continue with his work. He was on the verge of something great, he could feel it.

28

It wasn't long until the party started seeing signs that they would soon reach the home of the man who attacked the hapaki village.

"The road is wider, more frequently used here," Sam said. "Does that mean we're close to this Agago place?"

"Yes," Inoria answered. We'll reach it before the end of the day. We should probably start thinking about what we'll do when we get there."

What will we do when we get there? Sam thought. *How big is their army? How tall are their walls?*

Skitter sent reassuring thoughts to Sam's mind, trying to let his friend know he was there with him and that he trusted that Sam would come up with something. He was, after all, Skitter sent, almost as smart as a hapaki.

Rindu spoke up, "Have you seen the stronghold here before? Do you know its configuration?"

"No," Emerius answered. "We haven't had need before to get too close to it. We knew its location and stayed far enough away so as not to arouse suspicion."

"I see," Rindu said. "Then perhaps the first thing we should do is scout the area. Nalia is adept at moving unseen and unheard, but—"

"We'll do it," Inoria said. "None of you can move as invisibly as we do in the forest."

"Continue on the road for another two hours and then stop," Emerius said. "We will scout ahead and come back for you. Then we can design a plan to breach Agago and reclaim the captives."

*****

Emerius looked at his sister. "What do you think, In?" he said.

"I like them."

"Of course you do" Emerius said. "They're people, and not from our village. I mean, what do you think about this whole thing, about joining forces with them? I think you and I will do just fine getting into the fortress ourselves and then freeing the prisoners. We don't really need them."

"I think we do," she answered. "Besides, they have their own captives to free. We can't take that away from them."

"I guess you're right. I just don't like having to rely on others. It's always been just you and me, at least since Mother and Father died."

"I know," Inoria said, squeezing his shoulder, "but times are changing so maybe that should, too. You know, your hero Suka Templar would help them and accept their help."

"Yeah, yeah, I know," he said. "Fine, we'll come back for them. Are you satisfied?"

"Yes, thank you."

The twins had left Oro in an area alongside the road. The big bear was happy to curl up his great bulk and take a nap, waiting for the others to arrive. He was much too large and cumbersome to move quietly through the trees.

Inoria and Emerius flitted through the shadows as if

they were made of darkness. They left no trail and made no sound. So silently did they move that at one point, Emerius put his hand on a doe that was standing, sniffing the air for danger. The deer started and bounded away.

They soon came to where the road widened and found a cleared area around a set of high walls. Agago. They watched the walls, tried to get a sense of any weaknesses. They were stone, of course, and appeared to be well-built. Twenty-five feet high, they were not the mammoth size Emerius had heard some fortresses and castles had, but climbing them would not be an easy task, either. The gates, heavy wood in multiple layers with bronze banding, looked secure.

There were a few guards walking about on the tops of the walls, their figures appearing and disappearing as they passed by the crenellations. Emerius counted only four in total, though he expected there were at least that many walking on the other sides of the battlements as well. Still, it seemed like a small number to him. But what did he know about maintaining security at a fortress? He was a hunter and woodsman.

"The walls seem to be solid, though the blocks don't fit that tightly so we can probably climb them, if necessary," Inoria said.

"Maybe. Let's look around on the other sides. There might be a door or something else that provides easier passage."

They stayed in the forest, deep enough so that they couldn't be seen from the walls, and circled the entire fortress. Even moving silently and carefully, it only took an hour and a half to travel the perimeter.

They found that there was another gate, almost directly across from the first, which opened onto another road. That road seemed to have had use within the last few days. A large force had come through the gate onto it and moved on toward the east.

"How many do you think are in the fortress?" Inoria

asked.

"I don't know," Emerius answered, still looking at the jumbled mass of tracks from the cover of nearby foliage. "It looks to me as if at least two hundred left, though. With the size of the fortress, I wouldn't think there were any more than that left. Come on, I think we have the information we need. Let's get back to the others. I want to crack this nut soon and get our people back."

Inoria smiled as they made their way back through the trees to where they would meet the rest of their party.

*****

Sam sat on a fallen tree, eyeing the huge bear sleeping nearby. The rakkeben were resting a dozen feet away. They looked toward Oro occasionally, especially when some dream or another caused the animal to make a noise. At times, he emitted a grunt or a growl.

The bear's head suddenly lifted, his eyes scanning the clearing quickly and then locking on one location in the trees. The rakkeben, too, lifted their heads to look in the same direction, just as Emerius and Inoria made their way into the open. Sam realized that the slight breeze was coming from where the twins were. That was probably the only reason even their bear noticed them. If they had been staking prey, they would have come from downwind.

"Well?" Sam said. "What's the situation?"

Emerius smirked. "No problem. We can get inside. We can do it either the slow, quiet way or we can do it the loud and quick way."

"Stealth would be better," Nalia said. "We would not want to battle all the forces in the fortress at once."

"Don't pay attention to him," Inoria said. "He's just being goofy, trying to pretend he's a hero. We'll do it the smart way."

"Let's move toward the fortress," Emerius said. "We found a perfect place to wait for dark. It's close to the walls, but not so close anyone will find us."

As they mounted up and moved, the twins explained the configuration of the walls and the buildings.

"We're not sure how many people are still behind the walls," Inoria said. "It looks like at least half of them left within the last few days. Hopefully the captives are still here."

"And Tingai," Emerius said. "I want to see his face as I put several arrows into him. In non-lethal places, of course. I want to be able to make him suffer before he dies."

Sam looked at Emerius out of the corner of his eye. He thought he probably agreed, but it sounded so—he didn't know—villainous.

One thing is for sure, Skitter sent. *That man needs to be stopped. Hapaki don't believe in killing in general, but in this case, I think it is necessary. The suffering part is not, though. Killing him quickly will stop him from ever attacking innocents again.*

You're right, Sam sent back. *Emerius is just angry at the death Tingai has already caused and the uncertainty that he will get his brother and his friends back. Humans sometimes engage in vengeance to ease their emotional suffering.*

Skitter paused to think about it. *I know. I've seen it in your memories and in your emotions. It's not logical, though. There is nothing gained by torturing or causing injury. Maybe humans will figure that out eventually and then they'll be happy like the hapaki.*

I hope so, Sam sent. *I really do.*

"How will we enter the fortress?" Rindu asked. "What part do we play?"

Emerius answered, "In and I will go over the walls. They are easily climbable. Once we get to the top, we'll take care of any of the sentries along the walls. Then we'll open the gate and allow the rest of you to come in. Simple."

Rindu nodded. Sam remembered how Rindu had scaled the walls of the Gray Fortress and chuckled. These walls were like building blocks compared to that.

"Something funny?" Emerius scowled.

"No, not really" Sam said. "I was just thinking of another time we had to scale some walls. It sounds like a simple enough plan to me. Let's wait until three hours after full dark."

"Is this your operation or mine?" Emerius said, getting agitated.

"It is *ours*," Rindu interrupted. "We should not fight amongst ourselves. There are plenty of enemies behind those walls for all of us. Remember our purpose here. We must rescue the captives, both human and hapaki."

"And kill Tingai," Emerius added. "Slowly."

*****

Three hours after full dark, Emerius and Inoria gave the others instructions to move to the edge of the trees and watch the gate. Before heading toward the wall, Emerius knelt and spoke softly to Oro. The bear sat on his haunches and waited patiently.

"Tell the rakkeben to stay here with Oro. I don't want them jumping in the way when the arrows start to fly," Emerius told Sam.

Sam looked like he would argue, but then seemed to realize that what he was told was practical, so he whispered to his wolf. The other two did the same and the rakkeben moved to an area near Oro. The hapaki seemed content to stay on the perch strapped to Sam's rakkeban.

Emerius made the hand signal indicating that he would go first and that Inoria should watch and cover him. He hardly needed to do so. They had been working together for years, hunting, tracking, even participating in the odd battle now and then. Always together. They had a set of complex hand signals that they had devised and had started to teach Ancha, but they really didn't need to use them with each other. They each knew what the other was thinking, reacting to it before any signals were even traded.

He saw the slight tilt of her head and knew she had already started scanning for guards, her bow out with an arrow nocked.

The walls really weren't hard to climb at all. They obviously weren't made to prevent skilled climbers from ascending the wall and infiltrating the fortress. They were the kind of brute force methods Tingai used. Militarily, it seemed that he was rather simple. His strategy: throw soldiers at a problem until it was gone. At least, that's what he had heard from the occasional trader.

Using the large spaces where the blocks of the wall met imperfectly, Emerius made his way up, slowly and silently. He hugged the wall, placing the toes of his soft boots into the crevices as he reached one hand up to find a handhold in another of the cracks. Then, he straightened one of his legs while raising the other to a higher foothold and pulling up with one arm. His other hand then stretched for a higher hold. In this smooth, methodical way, he ate up the distance and was carefully poking his head through one of the crenels at the top in no time.

He looked to the left, to the right, saw nothing, and, with a powerful pull, launched himself up so that his feet cleared the top of the battlement and swung inward to land softly on the walkway.

Emerius looked down to Inoria. He could hardly see her standing stone still in the midst of the bushes. If he didn't know exactly where she was and didn't have such excellent night vision, he would never have been able to pick her out. He nodded to her and she nodded back. Taking the bow off his back, he nocked an arrow in an effortless motion, and began to scan the area in earnest for signs of guards. Inoria moved swiftly to the wall and began her climb.

Emerius noticed a small movement out of the corner of his eye. He looked down quickly to see that Inoria was only halfway up the wall, exposed and vulnerable. Looking back at the location where he saw the movement, he couldn't make out any specific shape.

"Remember," his father had told him, "whether you are stalking or being stalked, the key to success is understanding more than your opponent. In the dark, people and animals notice things in this order: movement, shape, color. If you have trouble focusing on something that is not moving, look through the side of your eye. The parts inside that make good night vision are thicker on the sides. The parts that see color better will not help."

Emerius tilted his head and looked from the side of his eye. There, he saw it now. It was a guard who had moved into a shadowy spot to take a drink from a small flask he held. He was close enough to see In when she topped the wall. He would have to be eliminated.

The hunter slowly drew back his nocked arrow, doing so in such a manner that the movement didn't capture the guard's attention. He sighted from the side of his eye and then, memorizing the position, turned his head to face where he knew the guard to be. He closed his eyes, pictured where the guard was, exhaled slowly while tensing his stomach muscles, and then released the bowstring, soft and smooth as butter.

The sharp twang seemed very loud to Emerius, but he hoped the sound didn't carry. He heard the arrow strike with a sort of soft thump, indicating that his aim was true and that he didn't hit bone. There was a muffled thunk and a soft clink of the man falling and his flask joining him on the stone of the walkway.

Inoria made it to the top of the wall and pulled herself up easily, swinging her legs over the battlement and onto the walkway. "What was that?" She signed to him.

"There was a guard sneaking away for a drink," he signed back. "It was his last."

She nodded, and they headed toward the stairs to the ground level. They were just on the other side of the downed guard. As they passed him, Emerius reached down to retrieve his arrow. As he thought, it entered the man's head through his right eye, a perfect shot. He put his foot on the guard's face and yanked his arrow, being sure to grip the shaft and not damage his fletching. He wiped it on the dead soldier's clothes and nocked it for further use.

"Nice shot," Inoria signed. "Side of the eye shot?"

"Yep," he said, not able to keep the pride out of his voice as he answered her verbally with a soft whisper.

Inoria shook her head and helped him tie a rope to the guard and lower the body to the ground outside the wall so it wouldn't be found. They wrapped the rope in such a way that once the corpse was down, one of them could let go of their side of it and the other could tug, rolling the body over and unwinding the rope from around him. Either of them could do this themselves, but it was easier with two. They didn't want the bodies found by another patrol that could set the alarm. Simply throwing it over the wall would make too much noise.

As they approached the stairs, Inoria signed that she would clear their half of the battlements and he could clear the area down below. He nodded and made his way silently down the stairs. Before he even got to the ground level, he heard an arrow being launched by his sister's bow and another of the guards falling to the walkway.

The stairs he was using were exposed, built into the wall itself, so he looked around carefully as he descended. He was a quarter of the way around the wall from the gate, but because the guards moved about on patrol, they had to clear at least half the perimeter of the walls.

When it was all said and done, there were nine bodies that had to be lowered outside the wall or hidden on the ground level inside the wall. Only twice were there pairs. Taking out two within a fraction of a second in the dark took skill and focus. A missed shot could cause a guard to be injured instead of instantly killed and then the alarm would be sounded. As it was, though, all the twins' shots were perfect and there were no problems.

They stood at the gate. Emerius signed to Inoria, "Get ready. If this gate squeals or makes other loud noises, we are going to have some company."

"Ready," she signed back.

Emerius lifted the heavy crossbar and slowly set it off to the side. He made no noise doing so. Then, he tensed his torso and bunched his shoulders, lifting up slightly on the gate as he tried to swing it in, knowing that if there was less weight on the hinges, the sound would be lessened.

The door wouldn't budge.

Inoria looked at him questioningly.

Emerius scratched his head. What was happening? He prepared himself to try again. He got into a low, powerful stance, feet wide and flat on the ground, legs flexed. He grabbed the crossbar brace and lifted and heaved again.

Nothing.

Inoria, still scanning for guards, tapped him on his shoulder with her bow. When he looked over, she pointed to a section in the center between the two halves of the door. There was a heavy hook-and-eye latch there. The hook was firmly set within the loop attached to the other door.

He rolled his eyes as Inoria silently chuckled. Reaching to the latch, he lifted up on it and separated the hook from the eye. He once again lifted up on the gate and pulled inward. This time, the gate swung easily, and silently. He opened it only a few feet and waited.

Within seconds, the others came through, the monk and the Sapsyr making no noise, and Sam making about as much noise as a drunk squirrel rustling through dead leaves. He winced at the sound. Someone needed to teach that boy how to move silently.

The party, all together now, moved toward the main building.

29

Emerius watched the others as they moved toward the central part of the fortress. The Zouy and the woman were really very good when it came to moving silently. He couldn't hear Nalia at all and Rindu had only made one sound, so slight that he wasn't even sure it was the older man. He was looking forward to seeing how they fought. There were lots of stories about the Zouyim and the Sapsyra. Their skill was legendary. But were the legends true? He'd soon see.

There was a blur of motion and before Emerius could even react, Rindu had crossed ten feet and struck a guard coming around the corner so precisely that the man fell into the monk's arms, unconscious but not dead. How was it possible for someone to move that fast?

Rindu looked at him and whispered, "Only the fool, the madman, or one truly evil kills when it is unnecessary." Emerius didn't answer him.

They continued on with no further contact with guards and soon they were standing at one of the side doors to the main building. It was locked.

"This is the biggest building," Emerius whispered.

"They will have captives in here. We have to get in. Quietly."

"I've been playing around with something," Sam said. "ever since my first trip to Gythe. Let me try."

Emerius just looked at him.

"Allow him to try," Rindu said. "I believe he can do what is needed."

Emerius stepped out of his way, doubtful.

Sam stepped up to the door and tugged on it. Emerius frowned and looked at Rindu, a question plain on his face. Rindu shrugged.

"Just checking," Sam said. "You never know."

The boy—he didn't know why he called him that; he was at least a couple of years older than Emerius—stood in front of the door and closed his eyes. He took a few deep breaths and then held his hand out toward the door. He wiggled his fingers for a moment, as if feeling something and then he flexed them and turned his hand slightly. There was a click and the door came toward them just an inch. It was enough to show that the door was unlocked.

Sam smiled and Nalia patted his arm affectionately. Emerius didn't really know what to say, so he said nothing and pushed past their celebration to open the door and peer inside.

The rest of the party followed him as he found his way through the corridor. If they were lucky, they wouldn't see anyone until they got to where the captives were. He was assuming the cages and cells were in the lower floors, so the next order of business was to find stairs.

Emerius was beginning to worry. It was too quiet. He didn't want to get into a pitched battle, but they should have encountered people by now, if not guards or soldiers then at least others who would be wandering the stronghold. What was going on here?

Just as he was finishing that thought, they came around a corner and ran into six soldiers who looked as if they had just finished their shift. In the split second it took everyone else to register what was happening, Rindu had incapacitated four of them and Nalia had knocked out the other two.

Their methods were different, Emerius noticed, Rindu striking precisely to make the soldiers lose consciousness and Nalia using strong strikes to knock them out conventionally, with hits to the jaw or solar plexus. What they had in common was that they were as fast as lightning. Emerius and Inoria were as fast as a striking viper with their bows, and close to that fast with their long knives, but they hadn't even had time to unsheathe their blades. Maybe there was something to the legends after all.

Even Sam had reacted faster than them. He had his staff, somehow broken into two sticks, at a guard position and he was looking down the hall from where the soldiers came. He shook his head. No others. Emerius was shocked when he saw Sam put the sticks together, end to end, and they melted together to form the staff again.

The group moved on.

"I don't feel comfortable with just knocking the guards out," Emerius complained to Rindu. "What if they wake up and sound the alarm or attack us as we're trying to leave?"

"They will not," the Zouy said. "This infiltration is different than when we attacked the Gray Fortress. We will rescue the captives and leave quickly. When Sam, Nalia, and I went after the Gray Man, we did not know how long we would be in the fortress. Regrettably, our only option was to kill, or risk being trapped or killed ourselves. Here, we have the luxury of not ending lives. Yet. Do not worry, Emerius Dinn. If our skills are pressed, we will take lives rather than to be defeated. For now, though, we must follow a higher path."

Emerius looked to Sam. "Does he always talk like that?"

"Always. Just wait until he wants to tell you a story."

Sam winked.

The party slunk through the corridors and went down several sets of stairs they had found. Soon, they were in a hall with doors spaced regularly on either side. They had smaller hatches built into them at about head level and at the floor.

"Cells," Sam said.

"Yes," Emerius said. "In?"

Inoria went to the first door and opened the cover on the hole at head height as the others moved ahead and watched for guards. She shook her head, went to the next, and looked into it as well. Nothing. So it went, the party watching in front of and behind Inoria as she peered into the cells. They were all empty.

When they got to the end of the hall, everyone stopped. There was one door left, the one directly in front of them.

They all looked at each other. Emerius saw his sister set her jaw and shift her eyes to the door. Whatever was behind it, he hoped it held the answers they were looking for.

"There is no one immediately on the other side of the door," Rindu said. "I feel no vibrations of the living there, unless the room is very large and the occupants are at the far end."

Swallowing hard, Emerius put his hand on the handle and opened the door slowly, ducking low in case the monk was wrong and someone was aiming an arrow at him. He looked for a long time, scanning the large chamber, taking in all the details as he slowly stood up, then pushed the door open and let the others see, not surprised at the shocked look on their faces. He knew he wore a similar expression.

The chamber had to be thirty feet on either side. There were braziers set regularly throughout the room, as well as torches on sconces mounted to the wall. There were six tables with restraints set in them, straps empty in all but one. Wooden cabinets lined two walls, doors closed tight. In between there were shorter tables, wicked-looking implements adorning their surfaces. There were jars of liquid, as well as tubing that had the appearance of the blood vessels of animals. Altogether, it was a gruesome and disturbing sight, but these paled in comparison to the others there, the things that acted like magnets, drawing the eyes.

The table that was not empty held what seemed once to have been a human. The figure was stripped bare and lying on its back. Whatever kind of creature it was now, it was male. The skin on the figure was off-colored, a sort of sickly gray-green. Emerius wasn't sure if the hue was the result of death or not. It was almost completely bald, which he was sure was not the result of death. The right leg of the thing on the table, in contrast with the rest of the body, was covered with a thick tangle of hair. The hair started and ended abruptly, in a straight line, as if it had been painted on.

The limbs on the creature were abnormally long. They looked sinewy and strong, but the proportions were all wrong for a human. The spine seemed to be misshaped, also, curving with exaggerated lines that could be seen even in its horizontal position. The toes and fingers came to sharp points, like spikes. It didn't move, not even to breathe.

Maybe even more disturbing was what was on the floor at regular intervals near the tables. There were small piles consisting of several bodies each. They seemed to be at various stages of some type of metamorphosis. They were not all human, or what could conceivably have come from humans. Some were smaller, most still with their fur even if their form was not as they were when the work on them had started. They were hapaki.

"What in the name of all that is good has happened here?" Sam said.

"This is what Baron Tingai does," Emerius answered.

"This is the work he does with the subjects he captures. I guess it doesn't always come out like he plans it."

Inoria, frozen up until that moment, came alive. She started searching frantically, inspecting each pile for something. Emerius knew what that something was.

"I don't see Ancha here," she said after making a full inspection. The rest of the party had moved little during the time. "That could be good news. Tingai hasn't tried to work his evil on our brother yet. There is still time."

Sam looked at Inoria with liquid eyes, but whether it was because of her dilemma or because of the hapaki lying there in piles, Emerius couldn't be sure. He turned his gaze to Emerius and the hunter saw those steel gray eyes harden.

"I think I agree with you, Emerius," he said in a way that made the man feel a chill. "I think a quick death may just be too good for Tingai. Let's catch him and discuss it."

"Sam," Rindu said softly. "Do not think foul thoughts. It is true that Tingai must be stopped, but vengeance is not the proper attitude. As it is said, 'The task must be done, but pleasure in dark deeds injures the soul.'"

"It is also said," Sam said, "'The piper deserves his pay.'"

"But, too, it is said that 'He who seeks vengeance must dig two graves.'"

"What about 'Revenge is an act of passion; vengeance of justice.'" Sam countered.

"Is that what you speak of, Sam?" Rindu asked. "Justice? Or are you in fact speaking of revenge?"

Sam glared at the floor for a moment. Then, he took two deep breaths. As he exhaled the second breath, his shoulders slumped and his body relaxed, tension leaving him. He bowed his head to Rindu.

"You're right, Master Rindu. Still, he must be stopped. This can never be allowed to happen again."

"We will stop him," Rindu said. "but we must do so in harmony with the universal *rohw* or we will become as that with which we battle. We must follow the *wireh* in all things."

"That's great," Emerius said. "However, all this talk doesn't get us any closer to rescuing the remaining villagers and hapaki. We need to get moving."

"Agreed," Nalia said. "It is urgent that we catch Tingai before he has time to perform more of his torture and mutation on the remaining captives. Let us go quickly."

They turned to leave and Emerius realized their error. They had been so shocked by what they found, they had not been aware that a force of what looked like two dozen soldiers had assembled at the end of the corridor, the front line of which had arrows pointed at them. Only the fact that they were still setting up their ranks had kept them from firing projectiles into the party's backs.

30

"Take cover!" Sam said and found himself not retreating into the room, but heading toward the soldiers. He had just enough time to wonder what had caused him to do that on instinct before it was too late. Eight of the archers loosed arrows.

Without thought, Sam broke *Ahimiro* into the two halves and twirled them quickly, deflecting arrows coming at him. He was able to evade two other arrows, noticing that Nalia and Rindu were on either side of him, dodging or deflecting arrows coming at them. Rindu snatched one of the arrows from the air, dropped his right shoulder, rolled under two more arrows, and came up launching his captured arrow back at one of the archers. The man dropped to the ground, out of the battle and the realm of the living, feathered shaft jutting out of one eye.

As one of the archers directly in front of Sam looked him in the eye and moved his bow to aim at Sam's head, he wondered if he would be able to dodge the projectile from such a close range. The question didn't need to be answered, though, because a blur streaked past Sam's shoulder and impaled the man in the throat. Another arrow whizzed by on his other side and struck a different archer. The twins were providing backup.

Sam found himself just a few feet in front of the first row of soldiers. He saw in his peripheral vision that Nalia was to the left of him and Rindu to the right. All three struck at the same time. They were too close now for the archers to use their bows, but some were still falling from arrows shot by Inoria and Emerius.

Sam waded in, striking left, right, and center with his sticks. He deflected a sword strike so that the blade bit into the arm of one of the swordsman's fellows. A strong jab to the eyes with the end of his stick and the sword was dropped in favor of covering the bloody eye socket. Sam moved on.

He turned to evade a thrust from another blade and saw Rindu parrying a hand holding a long knife, deflecting a mace with his right foot, and striking a third attacker with the other hand. The strike was with an open palm that glowed as the Zouy fortified it with a *rohw* burst, causing the unfortunate opponent to receive a shattered elbow for his trouble.

Nalia, too, was wreaking havoc. She was using her shrapezi, but with obvious restraint. Instead of the death-dealing he had seen in previous conflicts, she was inflicting cuts that, while serious, would not kill the assailant unless allowed to bleed freely for some time. She cut through weapons like they were made of paper, but the control with which she attacked incapacitated but did not kill.

Before Sam knew it, the last few soldiers were defeated. Rindu delivered a precise strike to the upper part of a man's chest, causing him to fold up and drop. He was sure that the man had just been knocked out, not killed.

Sam stood there, scanning the corridor for more soldiers, but there were none.

"Are you out of your mind?" Emerius yelled as he strode toward them. "Going *toward* a line of archers? What in seven hells made you go *toward* them?"

Sam shrugged. "I don't know. Before I knew what was happening, I was halfway there. It was too late to turn back."

Emerius looked him over carefully, then raised his eyes to meet Sam's. "You…you weren't hit? You didn't take an arrow anywhere? How is that possible?"

"Just lucky, I guess."

Emerius shook his head and scowled. Then, abruptly, he burst out in raucous laughter. "Just lucky. Hmm. I guess."

"Guys," Inoria said, "I hate to break up a bonding moment, but we better get out of here. There are probably more where they came from."

"Agreed," said Rindu. "It is time to leave."

They made their way up the stairs and toward the gate. As they were crossing the courtyard, Sam heard what sounded like many feet moving quickly across stone. He looked toward one of the smaller buildings just in time to see a large group of figures coming at them from a hundred feet away. Something about them didn't look quite right, but in the darkness, he couldn't see them well.

As they got closer, he realized why their silhouettes seemed to be awkward. These weren't people, they were some of Tingai's creatures. The successes. They must have been housed in one of the other buildings.

As he scanned them, he was appalled. There were a few that looked like the dead, mutated human strapped to the table in the lower level, but there were others, even more grotesque. Some were taller, some shorter, some bulky and some that were so thin he swore the bodies moved in ways contrary to how human joints and bones worked. There were even a few that were small like a human child or a hapaki. Sam guessed it was the latter because of the splotchy fur that adhered to them. Some of the creatures howled or hissed as they came at the party.

Rindu's voice rang out. "These creatures are no longer our friends. They are something else entirely. Do not be taken in by the form that is close to human or hapaki. They are attainted and their energy is dark. I can see it. They must be destroyed."

Sam looked at the creatures coming toward them. They seemed to have no fear, no caution. They were mindlessly charging, obviously wanting to rip the party to shreds. He held his sticks at the ready, saddened that it would come to this, doing battle to the death with those who should have been their friends. Some of whom *were* their friends.

Emerius and Inoria had already started firing arrows into individual attackers. For most, it didn't seem as if the arrows did much damage. Some of the creatures reached over and pulled them out, or snapped the shafts, leaving the tips in their bodies. Others didn't pay attention to them at all but kept running toward the party. One or two were struck in a vital area, such as through the eye, and they stumbled and fell, only to be trampled by the others. It made Sam sick to see it.

When the charging throng was almost to them, Sam, Nalia, and Rindu spread out. They needed room to fight. Sam was slightly behind the other two, so more attackers went for them, but four were rushing him, intent on ripping him apart. Three of them were humanoid and one was formerly hapaki.

The trio of mutated humans were of different forms. One was tall and completely hairless, with sinewy limbs and flexible movements. There was one that was thick—that was the best way to describe it—and seemed to be very dense and heavy. The third looked like a mix between a human and some kind of dog. Honestly, that one looked to Sam like a werewolf from all the old horror movies. The hapaki was a little larger than Skitter, with a permanent scowl on its face and overlarge teeth and claws. It was spitting and hissing like a mad raccoon as it came toward him, looking like it was ready to jump on him.

They all reached Sam at the same time, the tall one striking with its long claws before the others. Sam moved to the side and struck the thing's forearm with his stick. The sound it made was the same as clacking two hardwood poles together. The deflection caused the creature to stumble past him and Sam took the opportunity to crack his weapon on the back of its bald head, with a sound like a wooden mallet hitting a concrete block.

As the first creature stumbled past and rolled to keep from falling on its face, the thick creature attacked, moving relatively slowly, but inexorably, forward. Sam stepped to the right to evade the creature's swing and was almost raked by the werewolf's claws. He was able to pivot and turn just enough to evade the claws as he saw the hapaki creature in mid-air coming right at him.

Not thinking, acting on the training he had been doing for the last year and a half, Sam continued his pivot and let his knees collapse, twisting his body clockwise and ending up in a classic twist stance, legs tangled around each other but keeping the body stable, as the hapaki narrowly missed his head and flew past him. Sam knew he couldn't play the defense game for much longer or they would get him. He wasn't sure if their claws or bite were poison, but at the very least they looked filthy and able to cause a nasty infection. He didn't want to be struck.

Untwisting his body by rotating counter-clockwise, he spun quickly and threw out his sticks, catching the thick creature on the ear with a crack and striking the thin one in the neck with a sickening crunch. The thick assailant seemed to be dazed for a moment, so Sam went after the hapaki creature, which had landed and was turning to go at him again. Sam batted its claws away, swung his foot in front of him in an arc, then forcefully brought it down in an ax kick. His heel contacted the creature on the top of the head and there was a breaking sound as its skull was subjected to a force greater than it could take. The mutated hapaki twitched once and then was still, but Sam hardly noticed because the werewolf had joined the fray.

It came at him with a fury that was unbelievable. It swiped quickly with its claws, snapped with its teeth and bounded around Sam, trying to find an opening in his guard. It was all Sam could do to strike the thing's arms to keep its claws away from him. He saw in his peripheral vision that the thick creature was shaking its head and starting to look at him and the thin creature was doing some motion that looked like it was winding up for a strike.

Sam emptied his mind and felt the song of battle more fully. Instantly he knew what to do. The next time the werewolf swung at him, he ducked under the swipe and moved to his left, striking as hard as he could with his stick on the creature's ribs. He heard them crack just before it howled in fury and pain. Sam was already moving on to the thin creature, though, striking upward with both sticks and connecting with its jaw as it was striking at him. So powerful was the double strike that its jaws clacked shut, cutting part of its tongue off in its teeth and shattering the lower jawbone.

While the thin creature was reeling, Sam twisted, did an aerial cartwheel to gain momentum and landed to translate all his force into a double-downward strike to the head of the thick creature. The porzul wood, as hard as steel, vibrated in Sam's hands so violently that he almost lost his grip. It had the intended effect, though, crushing the skull of the mutation. The creature dropped.

As he spun away from that strike, Sam saw the werewolf turn to swipe at him again. He ducked, then straightened both knees to thrust his body upwards while swinging the sticks diagonally upward, contacting the crotch of the creature with so much force it was lifted off the ground. It howled again and Sam took the opportunity to crush its windpipe with one of his sticks as he rotated to lend force to the strike. The furry beast collapsed with strange gurgling sounds, trying to breathe but unable.

The only creature of the four that was still standing was

the thin creature with the broken jaw. It was coming at him to attack again. Sam saw an opening and thrust once of his sticks straight forward, projecting his *rohw* as he did so. The strike, and the energy he sent through it, went into the creature's chest, found the heart that had once been human, and burst it, ending the threat.

Sam looked around and saw that Nalia and Rindu were just finishing up the last few creatures. She made quick work of them with her shrapezi, lopping off limbs or heads, but Rindu seemed to be moving around his attackers as if they were standing still. He would strike in several locations, causing brief flashes of *rohw* to be visible to Sam, and then the mutation would drop. Sam was pretty sure they were dead when they fell. Inoria and Emerius were just coming up to them, having run out of targets to shoot at.

"I think we should leave now," Inoria said. "We still have Tingai to catch and I don't really want to fight any more of these things. It's kind of creepy. They may have been my friends or family."

Everyone agreed and the party ran through the gate through which they had come, toward the waiting rakkeben and Oro. They reached the beasts, mounted, and headed around the fortress to the road going east. They still had to catch Tingai.

There was no pursuit.

31

A shadow slipped through the soldiers. Whether they were sleeping or wide awake, chatting with their friends or scanning the area because they felt uneasy, none saw the moving patch of darkness. At least, those who did wouldn't recognize it or be able to describe it.

Vahi smiled a wicked smile. These humans were so limited. He could have slit the throat of any one of them and just disappeared, no chance of being caught. He was born to do it, quite literally.

He was one of the bhorgabir, the race of genetically created assassins, the most potent living weapons created at that time. Or at any time, really. All of the unnecessary parts were distilled out and what was left was superbly adapted to the purpose for which they were made.

The bhor thought about how his ancestors had been created from raw human genetic material, how they had been engineered. They were completely hairless, for one thing. Historians had speculated this trait was added for the simple reason that hair could get in the way and distract. Anything that could affect focus on the mission was undesirable.

They were also made to be strong and flexible. In fact, they were three to five times as strong as humans, and faster. Their skin had the consistency of leather and was resistant to all but the sharpest blades. Even sharp blades were less effective than their enemies would hope, since in addition to their thick skin, the bhor healed much faster than humans. Vahi looked at the humans he evaded so effortlessly with derision. His was a superior race, even if they were relatives, in a way.

Whether by design or as a side benefit, the bhor retained their human genitals and ability to reproduce. The small number of the assassins that survived the war reproduced and a community consisting solely of the bhorgabir was begun. Because their reproduction rate was not high, however, the community was still small, numbering just above two dozen.

The young bhor were trained in the arts of assassination as they matured. They received the same training and were expected to perform in the same manner as the bhorgabir that were first created during the war. Because of this, when a bhor as old as Vahi, twenty years, was contracted to eliminate a target, he was just doing what he and all of his ancestors had trained to do for hundreds of years.

He sometimes jokingly referred to it as a "family business." It seemed incongruous to some that a mutation, a creature that lived only to kill, would even have a sense of humor. But the bhor came from human stock, were extremely intelligent, and tended toward a dark view of the world. What better soil for the root of humor to grow?

Vahi made it to the largest tent in the camp, through rings of guards that looked progressively like they knew their business and were skilled at their jobs. He finally stopped just in front of the tent, stepping out of the shadow he was using as cover. The two guards at the door of the tent hardly flinched. They were good, these two. Of course, they had seen him do the same thing several other times, so they were not as surprised as they could have been.

"Is she in?" Vahi said in his low, hoarse whisper.

"Yessir," one of the guards said. "Tingai is in there with her."

Vahi hissed through his teeth and headed into the tent.

As he made it through the foyer of the tent—who ever heard of a tent needing an entryway?—he caught his reflection in a mirror. His bald, pointed face stared back at him. He wore no clothes other than a kind of breechcloth that covered his private area. His thin, pale body moved with a purpose, muscles shifting visibly under his thick skin. He didn't need clothes. Temperature didn't affect him and clothing got in the way of his free movement. The little clothing he wore kept his private parts from being vulnerable to being grasped.

He opened the flap to the main chamber of the tent and scanned the room out of habit. Tingai, pale, greasy-haired, and stooped, stood next to Ayim Rasaad at a map table. It struck Vahi as odd that Rasaad looked so young to be in charge of so many men, to be an up-and-coming ruler. Then again, he was only twenty and he was the leader of his community of bhorgabir, so maybe it was not so odd.

Rasaad, nearly a foot shorter than Vahi himself, was still tall for a woman. The tattoos swirling about on her bald head almost seemed to move in the shifting brazier light. He supposed if he were human, he would find her attractive, with defined features in her face and a perfect physical form, attesting that her power was not limited to the mental energies she possessed. But he wasn't, and the darkness that seemed to surround her at all times would be too strange in an intimate situation. He preferred darkness, but this was something else. He couldn't define it, but it was too peculiar, too dangerous. He chuckled inwardly. Too dangerous for the most dangerous creatures on Gythe. That was saying something.

He stepped up to the two, eyeing Tingai with disgust and turning to address Rasaad. Tingai's little jump when

Vahi was suddenly next to him made the bhor smile.

"Did you kill Dr. Walt?" Rasaad asked.

"No."

"No?" she looked into Vahi's eyes, no mean feat for a human. "Nothing else? Just no?"

"No, I didn't kill him," Vahi said.

"That has been established," Rasaad said. "Please enlighten me as to why he is still alive."

"It was an error in my judgment," Vahi said, noticing Tingai smiling at him. The moron obviously thought Vahi would be uncomfortable with the situation. He was wrong. "I spent a few days tracking the man, learning his habits. I wanted to make sure I was not noticed, that he was found dead and they would not know you were actively working against them.

"The night I had chosen to carry out the deed, he was up late, conversing with some long-lost friends who had arrived. I waited in the library it was his custom to study in and, most nights, sleep in. When he finally arrived, one of his companions sensed me."

Ayim Rasaad's forehead crinkled. It was a strange sight. Her eyebrows climbed her bald pate. "You were…sensed?"

"Yes. I waited until a time that Rindu Zose was not in the fortress because I wasn't sure if he could detect me. He was gone, so my plan seemed to be progressing accordingly. Unfortunately, the two long-lost friends were also Zouyim. One, an older man, probably a master, sensed me."

"And…?" Rasaad was starting to get irritated, he could tell.

"We did battle, but with two Zouyim and a skilled warrior who is the acting leader of the forces of the new government, it was advantageous for me to escape. I may have been able to defeat all of them, but I think not."

"So, you failed," Tingai said, eyes bright in his revel.

"I was not able to complete the mission at that time.

Dr. Walt is now guarded at all times. I thought it best to ask you if the mission parameters have changed. They know I was there, but they do not know my connection to you. I can return and finish the job. I didn't see the delay as significant."

Tingai's smile started to lessen as he realized that Vahi was not ashamed of his "failure."

Rasaad looked pensive for a moment. "I think not," she said. "Let the old man play his games for now. There is something more important I want you to do. You chose correctly in coming back. Let me explain to you what I need."

Vahi nodded slightly. Tingai's mouth had turned into a thin line. The bhor decided to make it worse for the man.

"Don't you have corpses to play with, undertaker?" Vahi said to Tingai. "The grownups have things to discuss."

Baron Tingai opened his mouth to retort, but Rasaad lifted her hand. "Tingai, we're done. You don't need to stay for this. We'll discuss your current work later."

The man bowed his head, turned on his heels, and shuffled off, casting a baleful glare at Vahi as he did so. Vahi's opinion of the man's lack of common sense was reinforced. Trying to challenge a bhorgabir in any way wasn't wise. Some bhor would have killed the man by now, just because he needed it. The scientist was lucky that Vahi didn't normally kill unless it contributed to a mission's success. Or if the mission itself was to kill, which was normally the case. He turned his attention back to Ayim Rasaad as Tingai left.

"Here is what you are going to use your formidable skills to accomplish…" Rasaad began, and Tingai left Vahi's thoughts altogether.

32

Sam watched Emerius reading signs in the trail. He wondered what the man was looking for. It was obvious that the bulk of Tingai's forces went this way. There were no other roads and it would be evident if that many people had gone through the thick forest lining the roadway. What information could the hunter glean from a hard-packed dirt road?

"Are you listening to me, Sam?" Rindu said.

"What? Oh, I'm sorry Master Rindu. My mind was wandering. What were we talking about?"

"Would you like to go and ask Emerius what he is looking for? I know that you are curious. Perhaps when you have satisfied your thirst for knowing, you will be able to pay attention to the lesson at hand."

"No," Sam said. "I'm sorry. Please, let's continue."

"Very well," Rindu said. "Have you seen a flock of birds in flight, Sam?"

"Yes."

"And have you noticed anything interesting about the way they act?"

"Act?" Sam asked. "I'm not sure what you mean."

Rindu looked at him blankly. "Do you see anything out of the ordinary in the way they fly compared to when they fly alone?"

"They fly in formation, in a kind of V shape," Sam said, holding out two fingers pointing upward. "Is that what you mean?"

"Yes, that is correct. They fly according to a certain pattern. Within that pattern, they act as one. It is beautiful to behold a large group of birds flying in such a way, almost as if they were of one mind, of one body."

"Drafting," Sam said.

"Pardon me?" Rindu responded.

"Drafting. The birds, when they fly in a V formation like that, do it to allow the first bird, the one at the point, to set the pace and to do most of the work in cutting through the air. The ones behind are taking advantage of his draft, so it's easier for them to fly. On my world, people ride in machines that are powered by their legs, called bicycles. They ride in formations much like the birds. One rider will do the work at the front and then they rotate out so another can take up the work. They continue to do this so that, as a whole, less effort is expended to cut through the wind."

"That is fascinating, Sam," Rindu said, "and I thank you for sharing this information with me. But you are missing my point."

Sam was disappointed with himself. "Oh, sorry."

"The point I was trying to make is that the birds, although not as intelligent as humans, still act in harmony and unity, by instinct alone. This is the *rohw* at work. Do you understand?"

"Yes, I think I do."

"Good. Take heed of the birds and other animals. Much can be learned thus. Animals often act in harmony with the *rohw*, not because they are masters at vibrational energy, but because it is embedded within them to do so. They think not, so their thoughts do not distract them from acting rightly."

"I'll try, Master Rindu. Thank you."

"Be more like an instinctual animal, Sam. Find the energy of all things and act in harmony with them and you will be successful."

Sam thought about it for a moment. Rindu was silent, watching him.

"Master Rindu," Sam said, "why do I have so much trouble with this harmonics thing? I feel like I understand it and that I'm applying what you're teaching me, but you keep telling me I'm not acting in a harmonious way. I don't understand what I'm doing wrong."

"It is not that you are doing anything wrong," Rindu said. "I am just trying to teach you to go beyond your current understanding and skill, so you may become more than what you are. I believe that you are having trouble because you have learned many things, have had some success, and you have trained for more than a year while you were gone in Telani, away from me.

"These things are good and I am proud of your accomplishments. However, there comes a time in training during which a student…"

Rindu looked thoughtful for a moment, and then spoke again, "Rather than tell you, I think it would be advantageous for me to relate the idea in a story, so that you may draw your own conclusions and learn the lesson for yourself."

"Okay," Sam said, settling into a comfortable position.

"There was once a baby ahu bird, newly hatched. From the start, the tiny creature, as well as his parents and all the neighboring birds, thought him to be rather clever and skillful. The tiny bundle of soft baby feathers studied the world intently with intelligent eyes, taking in all the information he could. He often tilted his head to the side while looking at things, obviously figuring out the world and all that was within it.

"As expected, the bird learned quickly and grew out of

his baby feathers in a remarkably short time. He began to experiment with his wings, flapping them, stopping to think, and then flapping them in a slightly different manner. He had watched his parents and the other birds take to the skies and he was determined to do so himself.

"The baby bird became obsessed with flying. He spent his days watching the other birds, noticing how they flapped their wings, what their tail feathers did, and the little adjustments they all made with their bodies during takeoff, flight, and landing. All the while, he practiced with his own wings, becoming accustomed to moving them in the manner he chose. He dreamed of flying, knowing that if he could only take flight, he would be an adult, a master of his own destiny.

"As the days went on, the little ahu bird got closer and closer to actually flying. He flapped and flapped, running to gain speed, and on several hops, he seemed to be airborne for longer than a jump would account for. Still, he did not fly. He redoubled his efforts, determined.

"Then, one day, after trying to take off for perhaps the thousandth time, or maybe the ten thousandth, he stayed aloft for several seconds. That was it! He had flown. There was no doubt. Now all he had to do was to practice more and get stronger and he could fly for greater distances and longer times.

"Within two more days, he was able to fly for long stretches. He was jubilant, knowing that he had conquered life and was an adult now, master of all he could see. He hopped into the air and started flying in circles around his family's home. As he passed by a particularly thick patch of grass, a young pantor leapt out and snatched the ahu bird from the air, eating him in one bite."

Rindu sat silent, watching Sam for his reaction. Sam just sat there, dumbfounded.

"Close your mouth, Sam," Rindu said. "Do you not know that if you sit with your mouth open like that a beetle may fly into it?"

"You…he…the baby…the pantor ate him," Sam finally got out. "That's a horrible story. Why would you tell me something like that?"

"As with all the stories I tell you, it has a lesson. You must think and find the value in it. Do you understand nothing of the tale?"

"I don't know," Sam said. "Is it something about arrogance? The bird thought quite a bit of himself, though I hardly think it was worth him dying over."

"No," Rindu said. "It was not about arrogance. It was about the ahu's nature, but also about human nature." He lifted an eyebrow at Sam and waited.

"He thought that he had all the world's problems solved, but then he ran into something he didn't count on?" Sam answered. He hoped Rindu didn't give him a hard time for making is sound like a question instead of stating it forcefully.

"Ah, yes," Rindu said while holding one finger up, "that is much closer to the lesson. You see, Sam, it is not an uncommon thing for humans, or for birds apparently,"—the Zouy chuckled at that—"for the attainment of one goal to crowd out thoughts that there are many other goals out there.

"It is typical for one who trains hard and attains a certain level of skill to think himself as a master, as an 'adult.' We very often see this in disciples when they have become skilled. They seem to convince themselves that they have learned all that they must and from then on they will simply need to practice to progress. They are wrong. When one attains a high level of skill, it is not the end of learning, but the beginning. Do you understand what I am saying?"

Sam looked at the ground. "Yes. I've fallen into the 'new black belt' frame of mind."

"The what?" Rindu said, his voice betraying his confusion.

"Oh," Sam said, "it's a reference to how people learn

martial arts in my world. Many schools indicate how far a student has progressed by awarding them belts of different colors. As they go through the ranks, the belt they wear changes color. A student eventually earns a black belt, the highest belt rank for most schools.

"There is a common problem with new black belts. They become arrogant and think they know more than they do, that they are more skilled than they truly are. Any master will tell you that a student's learning and training doesn't end when he gets a black belt. It's then that it really begins."

Sam raised his eyes to meet Rindu's. "So, I guess I've been acting like an arrogant new black belt because I'm on some kind of high from the battles I've managed to survive and all the training I've had with you and Nalia. I'm sorry."

"Do not be sorry, Sam," Rindu said as he patted his shoulder. "You are not nearly so insufferable as many disciples become. However, it has been holding you back from seeing that true power and true skill comes not from isolating oneself from others, but from acting in unity with them. Once you understand that you are more powerful as a part of a whole than as a whole unto yourself, you will be on the path of learning."

"On the *wireh*?" Sam asked.

"The *wireh* includes the path of learning, but the two are not the same thing. Let us work on understanding harmonious action with others and it will help us move toward understanding and applying the *wireh*. Does this sound reasonable to you?"

"Definitely," Sam said. "Thank you, Master Rindu. I guess maybe there were times when I thought I knew more than I actually did. I'm glad I have you around to tell me that I still know little. You and Nalia."

"It is our job and happy privilege to aid and train you, Sam. You are capable of much more than you know. We will show you how to reach your potential, or at least set you on the correct path so you can find it yourself. Come, it is time to continue our journey. Emerius looks as if he has discovered something important. Let us go ask him about it."

The Zouy turned toward the hunter and Sam followed, thinking about an ahu bird and a man and wondering what would jump out of the grass to eat him.

33

Emerius paused in his reading of the prints on the roadway to look at Sam and Rindu. What were they doing over there? It looked like the Zouy was telling a story, moving his hands in descriptive gestures. Didn't they understand the urgency of what they were doing? Every moment they did not catch up to Tingai's forces would be one more moment he could be conducting his experiments on his captives.

He understood the need to pace the rakkeben. Even Oro was getting tired. Still, they should be doing more. *He* should be doing more.

Inoria had gone off into the trees looking to replenish some of her herbs. The wolves and Oro had eaten and were resting for a few minutes before heading out again. Emerius looked toward the other two in time to see them heading for him. Where were Nalia and the hapaki?

"Have you found something?" Rindu asked.

"Yes," Emerius said. "I found several sets of prints mixed in with the others that may be of interest. There are some hapaki prints and there is a set of prints that I believe belong to my brother. They have him walking along with the troops. That's good news. It means he is not so injured that he can't walk by himself. I would like to catch up to them before that condition changes."

"I agree," Rindu said. "As soon as the others return, we will be off. The rakkeben could use more rest, but we must move while there is still daylight to do so."

Soon, Nalia came from one direction while Skitter bounded out of the foliage from another. The Sapsyr looked as if she had washed off, while the hapaki was carrying some onekai he had found somewhere. Inoria arrived a few minutes later, arms full of herbs. They mounted the rakkeben and Oro and headed out.

An hour later, they came across the first of the outriders.

Emerius had been scouting ahead and saw three men ranging on either side of the path, looking for game while searching for anyone who may have been following the main force. He saw them long before they would have seen him, so he was able to swing wide and go back toward the others.

"There are men looking for anyone following Tingai's forces," Emerius told them as he returned. "We have a choice. Either we hide and hope they don't see any sign of us following them, or we eliminate them to make sure they don't report our presence. We don't have long to decide."

All the others looked at Sam.

"Well?" Emerius said, impatient. "Decide."

"What are the chances they will miss seeing us and the evidence that we were here?" Sam asked.

"Not very good. We haven't been hiding our trail. If they are half as competent as they seem, they'll see someone was here and they'll start looking. At least one will probably head back to report it while the other two track us."

Sam seemed to hesitate. He bit his bottom lip and looked toward Rindu and Nalia. He opened his mouth, probably to ask them what they thought, but then he closed it again. He thought for another moment before he spoke. "I don't believe in ambushing people and killing them," he said. "Let's try to hide and hope they don't see our tracks mixed in with all the others on the road."

Emerius gritted his teeth. This boy had an overdeveloped sense of honor and fairness. It would get him killed. "Fine. Inoria, keep your bow handy. If they break for it back toward the main force, put an arrow in them. Stop them at all costs."

Inoria nodded and nocked an arrow.

They split up and found hiding places far enough away so as not to be in the immediate area, but close enough to observe the men. Ten minutes later, Emerius saw them, one by one, moving through the trees beside the road. They were very good They hardly made a sound. He watched their eyes from his vantage point, saw how they scanned the area methodically. He found himself holding his breath as he waited in the space between two rock formations.

Suddenly, one of the men snapped his head up. Emerius swore that the man actually sniffed the air as if catching a scent. He started looking around, scanning, searching. His head swiveled and then went back to where it had just looked. A shrill bird whistle came from his mouth and Emerius saw the other two spread out and start heading back toward where they had come from. The man had spotted one of the party, or their tracks.

Cursing under his breath, Emerius drew an arrow to his cheek, exhaled, calculated mentally where the closest man would be by the time the arrow reached him, and let loose. A twang and a zipping sound broke the silence and one of the men dropped out of sight. The fall was noiseless. Less than a second later, there was a flash of movement and the man who had whistled seemed to sprout an arrow out of the front of his face, angled as it came through the base of the skull from behind.

The third man was running through the trees in a

zigzag pattern, trying to foil Emerius's aim. Nevertheless, the hunter let fly with another arrow. The man tripped just as the shaft was about to strike and the arrow went through his shoulder instead of his neck. Emerius was already hopping out of his hiding place, drawing an arrow from the quiver on his back, nocking it, and shooting as he jumped over a log in front of him. This one took the man in the left eye as he was searching for where the arrow had come from.

When they checked, all three men were dead, as Emerius knew they would be. He knew his business well enough to know when he had delivered a killing shot. So did Inoria. They looked for possessions that may aid them in their quest, but found nothing but their weapons. The quality of their arrows weren't nearly what he Emerius was used to—he and In made their own—but they took them anyway. They left the bodies to the forest. Sam wasn't happy about having to kill all three of them, but he finally agreed that they had done their best and had done the only thing they could.

Over the course of the next few days, Emerius and Inoria made a game of hunting Tingai's outriders. The terrain became mountainous and even more wild, which Emerius loved. He felt at home in wild places such as this.

Emerius looked over at his sister. They were, as normal, out in front of the rest of their party, scouting and searching for trackers.

"That Sam," he said to her, "has no stomach for what needs to be done. He's okay in a fight, but he's too hesitant to take a life when it's necessary."

"I don't know, Em," Inoria said. "I think he's made of tougher stuff than you give him credit for." She thought for a moment, her face going pensive as she took a bite of the dried meat in her hand. "Still, he does have a certain innocence. It makes me wonder if we're just jaded and have lost sight of who we truly are."

"What is that supposed to mean?" he felt something

stir in his belly. He didn't know why he felt so defensive.

"Just that maybe we're a little too quick to kill, a little too slow to look for other ways." She patted his forearm. "I don't know. It just all makes me think that there may be other options sometimes, other means for succeeding without killing everything in sight."

"Yeah, yeah," he huffed. "Are you ready?"

She stood and dusted off her pants. "Yep. Let's get moving. We only have a couple of hours of daylight left."

Each evening, Sam, Nalia, Rindu, and Skitter transported back to Whitehall. Sam always offered to have the twins come with them, but Emerius always "stubbornly" refused—that was how Inoria described it. "We'll just stay here and camp," he would tell them.

He had to admit that he was curious to feel the sensation of teleporting to another location more than a thousand miles away, just as he was curious to see this Whitehall he had heard so much about. He couldn't bring himself to agree, though. Maybe after they rescued the captives he'd go. Maybe then. Ancha would like to see the fortress, he reckoned.

"There's no doubt," he told Sam and the others on the seventh day since they had infiltrated Agago, "Tingai is headed for Gromarisa."

The land had flattened out again, but the trees had become even thicker. In the afternoon of the day before, they had made their way up a high hill and were able to see through the trees. In front of them, maybe twenty miles away, they saw the land drop off. Magnificent, obviously water-carved, formations poked through a massive scar that stretched on as far as they could see. They all just stood there, taking it in. It was the most spectacular thing Emerius had ever seen

"It's the Grand Canyon," Sam said under his breath. Of course it was grand, Emerius thought. It was silly for the boy to even say it.

Now, with a whole day of travel ahead of them,

Emerius thought that they would probably reach the canyon itself. Then they would have to try to catch Tingai. He wasn't sure what the scientist was going there for—Sam hadn't really been clear about that—but he knew he didn't want to wait until Tingai met up with his boss. What was her name? Rashad or something?

"Let's go," he said impatiently. "We need to catch them before they go down into the canyon."

There were no arguments. Everyone was probably feeling the same as he was: tired of the chase and excited to finally be at the end of it. The odd mix of anxiety and fatigue gave things a dream-like quality, making it seem almost unreal.

As they started off, it began to snow.

34

"Are you sure you're all right?" Chisin Ling asked Nicole as she handed her some tea.

"Yes, I am. Thank you. And thank you for saving me. I thought I was dead."

"I'm sorry it was so close. I should have been guarding you the whole time, not trying to engage the intruders like that."

"You saved me," Nicole said. "That's all that matters to me."

She looked around at the shambles that had been their camp. It would be daylight soon and she would be able to see better, but they had built the fire up so that it was very bright, allowing her to see more than she felt she wanted to. All told, six of the soldiers had been killed, four men and two women. There had been over twenty of the attackers, though they would probably never know the exact number because some had escaped. They were the same men who had made the fire Marr had scouted earlier, she was sure.

The only reason their losses weren't greater was that the soldiers were more experienced. They had been trained and were simply better warriors compared to the bandits. Pirates, she should probably call them, since they traveled by boat. Of those left in Nicole's party, probably half of them were injured. Thankfully, none of the injuries were life-threatening, though traveling through the forest with no medicine or modern technology might make them so.

"The fire was a ruse," Marr said, limping up toward where Nicole was talking to the captain. "They used it to lure me there and then tracked me back here. It's my fault that we were attacked. I'm sorry, Captain."

"Hant Marr," Chisin snapped. "Don't act like one of your children. It was not your fault. I don't want to hear another word. Is that clear?"

"Yes ma'am," Marr said, snapping to attention.

"Good. Do you have a total for me yet?"

"Twenty-two dead, Captain. I think there were probably five or six more that escaped. Do you want us to hunt them down?"

Chisin Ling pondered the question for a moment and then shook her head. "No. They won't bother us again. We'll have to try to find their boats when it's light out. We may be able to use them to reduce our travel time. See to it."

"Yes, ma'am," Hant Marr said again. He saluted, fist to heart, turned, and walked off, favoring his left leg.

As it turned out, they found only one of the boats. The survivors had taken the other one and apparently didn't have enough men to take both. The party found the burned-out husk of the second boat, useless for anything other than using the pieces to make charcoal drawings on rocks. It looked as if they would be continuing their trek on land.

The day after the attack was a partial travel day. The captain wanted to take it easy to see what toll the soldiers' injuries would take. As Nicole sat resting with three full hours of daylight still left, Chisin Ling came to her holding some sort of leather parcel. When she got to Nicole, she held it out for her.

"What's that?" Nicole asked.

"Something that may be useful in the future."

Nicole took the object from the captain. It was a rolled-up piece of leather with a leather thong attached to it and tied around it. She untied and unrolled it to see its contents. Five knives were strapped to the hide, all exquisitely made, each in a custom-fitted leather sheath. They were oddly shaped, all one piece without a hilt or a conventional handle, and made of something other than metal. Taking one out of the sheath, she saw that the blade of each was a long triangle, sharp at both edges, with a point so narrow it looked like it would break with any use.

"Be careful," Chisin said to her, "they are very sharp."

"What are these for?" Nicole asked.

"Last night made me think," Chisin said. "You should have a way of defending yourself in case you need it again. If I would have been just a little slower, you'd be dead."

"I'm not a violent person, Chisin," Nicole said. "I don't know how to use these."

"I know, not yet. I will teach you, though, if you want me to. They are throwing knives, which is why they are shaped like that. They're perfectly balanced for throwing and made of ceramic glass. They look fragile, but are almost unbreakable, much more durable than the metal knives that are so common. Well, all but fine steel knives, but those are too expensive for me to have ever even seen, let alone have."

Nicole turned the blade over in her hand. It caught the afternoon sunlight and split it. She slashed at a nearby branch with it and the twig, as thick as her little finger, separated neatly in two. The captain wasn't kidding; the thing was sharp.

"I don't really know," Nicole said. "I'm not sure if I could ever kill a person."

"Could you hurt one," Chisin Ling asked, "if you were in danger?"

"I...I suppose so."

"Then take them, let me show you how to use them, practice with them. The better you get, the more able you will be to just hurt or discourage someone from hurting you without killing them. It would make me feel better if you had a way to defend yourself if necessary. Consider it a favor to me."

"Okay," Nicole finally said after a pause. "I'll try it out and see how it goes."

"Good. Thank you. They can be used as throwing knives or they can be fought with as any other blades. I'll show you how to do both."

The captain went over the basics with the blades and set up a target for Nicole, showing her the proper way to throw. Within an hour, she was sticking them into the target.

Are you going to join the army now, too? Max sent to her, the thought tinged with humor.

No, she sent, more seriously. *The captain is right, though. I need to be able to defend myself. I don't want to be a burden if we get attacked again. Someone else could risk their life for me and I'd hate it if they got killed trying to protect me.*

I understand, Max sent back. *Maybe you should learn to hide like the hapaki do.* The sending had the sense of him shaking his head. *But no, you are too big to hide well. It's a good thing for you to learn to fight. Maybe you'll have to save me one day.* The humor was back, but there was a serious note beneath it.

Over the next several days, it rained off and on, but not like the sustained deluge they experienced on the first day on the peninsula. It seemed to Nicole that it was cold enough for snow, but other than finding frost and iced-over puddles some mornings, they didn't see any sign it was winter. She guessed that the ocean air kept the temperature more moderate than inland.

When they finally reached what could only have been the rainforest they were looking for—as evidenced by the lusher growth than they had seen and the presence of more moss streaming from the trees—Nicole sighed in relief. It was time for them to move inland.

"At least there's one good thing about the season," Nicole said to Chisin Ling as they were traveling. "There aren't any bugs to worry about."

"True," the captain said. "I hate bugs."

"Do you think we'll really find them," Nicole asked. "The hapaki, I mean. This whole journey is based on the word that Lahim Chode saw a viewing of them. Does that make you nervous?"

"Nervous? No. As for if we'll find it, I can only say that if it is here, we'll find it. If not, then my job is still to protect you and make sure you return to Whitehall unharmed. I'm a simple soldier. I leave the worrying about such things to others."

Nicole smiled at that. It *was* nice sometimes just to do what one was told and not have to worry about other things. "I think it's here. I'm not sure why, but I do. If I was hapaki, I think I would like to make my home here."

It's okay here, I guess, Max sent, *but it's not as good as my home. I have hardly seen any onekai here at all. What kind of place is that for a hapaki?*

Will you be able to help us find the community? she sent to him. *Can you sense them?*

I'm afraid not. I will be able to hear them when we're close, but I would have to be within a hundred feet or so. It is more likely that they will see us. Maybe they will approach us if they see me.

It took another three days to find what they were looking for. It was mid-morning of the twenty-ninth day since they had left Whitehall.

Nicole! Max sent. *Do you see?* Look at all the onekai here. It's more than I can eat in a week.

Looking around, Nicole thought that it was probably more than the little creature could eat in a month, but she didn't say so. It was strange to find a patch of the vegetables in the middle of the forest like this. She was under the impression that it grew sparsely, with only a few plants in one place. It almost had the look of—

There are hapaki near. Max's sending took her by surprise. She heard murmurrings in her mind, as if they were memories of voices. She tried to "listen" to them more carefully, closing her eyes so she wasn't distracted. The sendings were not words, precisely, just feelings and images, but she got the sense of them because of all her communication with Max over the last several weeks.

…are big and awkward, a voice came.

…will probably try to eat us, another echoed.

There is one of us with them… a third sounded in her mind.

..is unfamiliar. Where is his community?

Nicole sent thoughts in greeting, a feeling of safety and respect, introducing herself and Max. The other sendings stopped abruptly. The silence stretched on for what seemed like hours.

Did they hear you? Max asked. *They are too far for me to even hear them clearly. I could never send thoughts that far, even with a close family member.*

As if in answer to his question, a sending came into Nicole's mind. It was clearer than before, so at least one of the hapaki had moved closer. *Who are you?* it asked.

"Chisin," Nicole whispered. "Make sure everyone stays still. I don't want to scare the hapaki. They're nearby. I'm communicating with them."

"Understood," the captain said, and passed along the word.

I am Nicole Sharp, she sent. *I am from far away, looking for the hapaki community here.*

Hapaki? the voice repeated.

Of course, Nicole thought. That was the name humans gave the telepathic creatures. They had no name, no label for themselves. She quickly amended her sending to images of the hapaki themselves, of Skitter and Max. The feelings of confusion disappeared.

Why are you looking for us? the same hapaki sent. *What do you want?*

There are important things happening in the world, she answered. *Those who are doing great things want you to participate. Your people are part of this world and deserve to be heard.*

There were no other sendings. Nicole had the sense that the hapaki were probably discussing things among themselves.

What do you think? she sent to Max.

I don't know. I think they are deciding amongst themselves. We will just have to wait.

A few minutes later, another hapaki sent thoughts to Nicole. *You have with you one of our people, but not from our community.*

I do, she replied.

Send him to us but remain where you are. We wish to communicate with him alone.

Max did as they directed, bounding off toward the east. With nothing else to do, Nicole sat on a nearby fallen tree to wait. The soldiers took that as a cue to sit down themselves. Chisin Ling came and sat down next to her and they waited together.

It was half an hour before she saw Max scuttling through the undergrowth back toward her.

They will meet with you, he sent. *Only you. Come with me. I will show you where to go.*

Nicole took a deep breath and stood. "I'll be back," she said to the captain, and followed her hapaki friend. This was what she had come all this way for. She hoped she didn't blow it.

35

Nalia had been watching the twins, not quite sure of them or their agenda. Inoria was likeable enough, but Emerius was self-centered and arrogant. She thought maybe the brother and sister were just concerned for their younger sibling, but there was something she did not like about the man. She would continue to watch him carefully.

As they finally set out for the canyon, she could almost taste the closeness of the men they were hunting. The snow would hinder the larger group more than their small party. It would also make it easier to follow where they went, without having to take time to actually track them. This was all good.

She rubbed at Cleave's ears as they rode. With how heavy the forest was in this area, she was glad they were using the path that had been created by Tingai's forces. It made for a much faster pace, which is what they needed.

What was Tingai doing? It was fortuitous how their two main concerns came together as one. She did not like the thought of abandoning the captives to look for Rasaad, but also did not want to allow the woman to get the artifacts while they chased Tingai. If they were fortunate, the party would catch up to Tingai, rescue the captives, destroy his forces, and then move on to stop Rasaad from getting the artifact, all in one motion.

The party reached the edge of the chasm. Again, Nalia was thankful for the snow. Without it, they would have had a hard time finding the path going down into the canyon itself. As it was, it took several minutes to figure out exactly where to find the path down.

"Damn," Sam said. "We must have completely misjudged the distance. I thought we'd catch them before the went in."

At the same time, Emerius said, "How do they always stay ahead of us? We should have caught them by now."

The two men looked at each other, glaring at first. Then Sam's face lightened and he almost looked like he would smile. Almost. He turned away, scanning the maw before them. "There they are," he said, pointing near the bottom of the canyon. Nalia looked and saw a thin line of people reaching the floor and gathering with all the others who had already come off the trail. "It will take us half the day to get down there."

"It will take half a day from when we start," Rindu said. "If we start now, we will arrive at the bottom ten minutes before we would have gotten there if we leave ten minutes from now. It is said, 'procrastination steals your time.'"

"I think the saying is 'procrastination is a thief of time,'" Sam said, "but I guess that's close enough. You're right, of course. We should get moving."

Nalia looked down the trail, icy and treacherous. It was clear how it wound and curved because the slushy snow from the multitudes of feet stood out in stark contrast with the brilliant white of the untrampled snow.

Sam stepped onto the trail first, looking as if he were scanning it as far as he could see. He paused as he looked at the people assembling at the bottom of the trail. "I don't think they'll see us unless they're looking for us. It's a long way and we are only a few. I also don't think we need to rope ourselves together. The snow isn't that deep and it's not too icy, as long as we get down before the sun sets."

The others nodded, preparing themselves for the long descent. The rakkeben and Oro stood patiently, seeming to understand that now was the time for caution, not haste. Skitter was looking at Sam and Sam had that expression on his face, the one he got when he communicated with the hapaki mind-to-mind.

Nodding, Sam started off, using *Ahimiro* as a walking stick. Nalia noticed that he had transformed the tip of the staff into a point, the better to provide traction in the muddy, slushy surface of the trail. She wondered when he had learned that.

*****

Baron Tingai watched the last of the soldiers empty off the trail. He estimated that between his own forces and Rasaad's, there were at least two thousand fighters, several dozen support people, and his thirty-seven remaining captives, hapaki and human. The hapaki had proved to be too stubborn for them to be allowed to walk, so they were carried in cages or sacks. The humans, though, were tethered to each other and forced to march along with the main body of the army.

Thirty-seven. He would need more than that. Rasaad had told him that she had several dozen new subjects in her dungeons at her fortress, Gutu. Once he got there, he could start again on his experiments. He still had not found the perfect mix of attributes he was looking for.

Tingai looked over toward Ayim Rasaad. The colors of the tattoos covering her bald head shone in the sunlight; reds, blues, and yellows. The designs were unrecognizable to him. Maybe they were symbols of power or some type of arcane language that he didn't understand. He wouldn't ask her, of course. She didn't like personal questions and he had found in his experience that nothing was so personal as tattoos.

She didn't seem to notice any of the people around her. Her eyes, unfocused, moved from side to side, as if looking for something hidden far away. What was she searching for? He decided his best course of action was to sit and wait for her to finish whatever it was she was doing. When she wanted them to move again, she would say so.

The area in front of the trail was bare for some reason. Maybe it was all the countless feet that had trampled the dirt there over the centuries. Not everyone fit in the roughly circular hundred-foot patch of dirt. Some were forced to wait in the trees that stretched from wall to wall in the canyon. Tingai knew there was a mighty river hiding within the green. He had seen it as they made their way down the trail. He hoped they didn't have to cross it.

Ayim Rasaad's head snapped up and she looked off into the trees. Her gaze seemed as if it was locked onto something and as if she was memorizing the path there. Then she looked at him. Her too-young, placid face was unmoving for a moment. "I know where we must go."

She headed into the foliage without looking back, expecting to be followed. Her captains started barking orders, rousing the soldiers and getting them moving. Tingai gave the sign to his own commander, raising his index finger and moving it in a circle. Immediately, his forces were also up and ready to go. Tingai himself hurried to catch up to Rasaad, glancing at his handlers to make sure they were preparing the captives for traveling also.

Within a handful of steps, the thick vegetation swallowed up the sunlight and turned day to night. The sun would set early in this place. Could Ayim Rasaad find her way in the dark?

Even above the racket from all the people around, Tingai heard other sounds, especially as he got closer to where Rasaad was up ahead of the mass of the soldiers. Birds, and small animals rustling around in the underbrush. He would occasionally hear a sound as if something larger was just out of sight, moving around.

He wasn't really the traveling type, preferring to stay in his lab, doing work by firelight and lamplight. Wild animals were good for exactly one thing: to be used as experiments for him to improve his craft. It was so dirty, so chaotic, so…wild out here. He just wanted to go back to his laboratory.

Tingai made his way up to Rasaad, stumbling over roots and scraping himself on branches. The scientist barked his shin once on a protruding root that felt as if it was made of stone. He cursed under his breath, not wanting to break the eerie silence that contrasted so strongly with the noise a dozen feet behind him. The trees seemed to soak up the sound.

"We are close to the artifact," Ayim Rasaad said to him. "I can feel it. It is unlike anything else I have ever sensed. It must be mine."

"Is it safe in here?" Tingai said. "I mean, are there wild animals and such that could attack us?"

She looked at him coldly, her eyes boring into his own. Finally, after a long time, she spoke. "You have nothing to worry about. At least, not until we get to the artifact."

"What do you mean? Why do we have to worry when we get to where it is?"

"Would you have hidden an artifact of great power in a secret location without protecting it in some way?" she asked him. "Would you not have put in place traps or puzzles or other such things?"

Tingai pondered that for a moment. "I guess you're right. I wouldn't leave it unprotected. What do you expect?"

"I do not know. I will try to sense it before we reach it, but we are dealing with a power that is older than anything we are familiar with. Who knows what those who hid the artifacts were capable of?"

Progress through the foliage became slower as the vegetation became progressively thicker. The bulk of the forces kept the distance between Rasaad, Tingai, and the few special guards that she kept near her at all times. Truthfully, he didn't know why the guards were there. She was deadly enough by herself. Maybe they kept watch when she slept. He wouldn't think of crossing her even if she was in deep sleep. The woman scared him.

As they continued, the light became dimmer with each moment. Finally, with the disappearance of the one thin sliver of light that was left, the forest grew completely dark. The moon was nowhere Tingai could see through the trees. He didn't realize that Ayim Rasaad had stopped until he ran into her back. She spun, striking him with her shoulder and throwing him back from her. The strength in that one movement almost made him leave his feet.

"Will we set up camp and wait for daylight?" he asked.

"No."

"How will we find the artifact or the protective measures if we can't see?" he said.

"I will find it." She said. "We have torches. We can light them. I can also generate light of my own. In any case, my sensing of its power is not affected by light. Searching in the darkness may actually prove to be easier because there will be no distraction from what I see."

Baron Tingai felt his stomach drop. He had hoped she would allow them to stop and continue when the sun came up again.

"How many of your outriders and scouts did you lose in the last week?" she asked him.

"Nine," he answered.

"And that means nothing to you? It does not concern you?" In the weak light of a torch one of the soldiers had lit, he saw her silhouette facing him.

"I've been wondering what happened to them, but my soldiers tell me that losing men like that is normal. Wild animals and such."

He got the sense that she was staring at him incredulously. "You are a smart man. You cannot be that ignorant."

He felt himself flush and anger wriggled in his midsection. "What?"

"Your men are simply telling you that so that you don't get upset at them," she said. "You really are not familiar with travel in the wild at all, are you?"

He gritted his teeth "I'm not an outside person. I spend my time inside, in my lab."

"I see," she said. "Well, let me tell you that men don't just disappear like that. Especially trained trackers. There is someone following us. They are killing your men to prevent them from reporting to us."

"But…who would be foolish enough to do that?" he said.

"I don't know for sure, but I have suspicions," she said. "In any case, I am not interested in being attacked as we make camp and try to sleep. We need to finish this and get the artifact before those complications can arise."

"Why don't we send a large force to find the followers and take care of them?" he asked.

More torches had been lit, so he could see her shake her head at him. "Because they will just evade them. It is better not to play this game. I have sent Vahi to find them. We will leave it to him and we will do our part. In a few minutes, we will continue."

When they did continue, it was with Ayim Rasaad out in front as before. Tingai kept back. She insisted on searching for the artifact's hiding place without any light. He couldn't move two steps without tripping over a root or getting snagged on a twig or branch. He stayed safely in the midst of the torchlight among her guards. They kept the circle of the yellow glow so that it just showed Rasaad's shape beyond it, but didn't affect her focus. They followed her this way for hours.

The woman seemed to go in circles, though honestly Tingai couldn't tell if the trees all around him were the same trees or different ones that looked exactly the same.

His world seemed to consist of the small sphere of torchlight in front of him. He just wanted to go back to his lab, to his familiar surroundings. This was not the place for him.

Rasaad moved on, and all the rest followed her. Tingai and her guards were less than twenty feet from her. The bulk of the army was back more than a hundred feet from them, staying out of the way in case their leader changed direction suddenly. The torches for the group Tingai was in were easy enough to spot in the darkness, even through the trees, so the bulk of the force would not lose them.

There were twelve of the biggest, meanest-looking soldiers Tingai had ever seen surrounding him. Three of them were women. He thought at first that there was only one woman until the other two spoke and he took a closer look. Yes, definitely scary. These were the personal bodyguard for Rasaad. She could probably have destroyed all of them in the blink of an eye, but their job was to make sure she didn't actually have to fight. As far as he knew, they had never been tested. One would have to be mad to attack someone such as her.

Suddenly, Ayim Rasaad stopped walking. She seemed to be casting around for something, like an animal that had caught a scent. She called for a torch. As one of her guards brought it to her, Tingai followed the man. In the flickering torchlight, he saw the ruddy color of a massive stone formation in front of them. It looked the same as every other water-carved shape he'd seen when it was daylight. Rasaad took the torch from the man who had brought it to her and began to wave it in front of the rock. She walked first to the left for several feet, and then she turned and walked to the right.

Nodding her head, she waved the torch at the rock as high as she could reach and then squatted down and put it right next to the boulder, very near the ground. Still, her eyes were jumping about, looking for something that Tingai thought probably wasn't there.

She handed the torch back to the man and told him to step back a few feet. As the circle of light receded, he could see her close her eyes and breathe in a regular, deep pattern. She put her hands out and moved them mere inches from the surface of the stone. It reminded Tingai of the charlatans who used divining rods to find water. Her hands twitched as they moved, as if feeling some unknown vibration.

Her hand abruptly stopped. She took two more deep breaths. Then she mimed pushing something very heavy.

Tingai wasn't sure if he saw a slight glow or not. It could have been a trick of the light, but he thought he saw something flicker. As he watched, a man-sized hole in the rock materialized. Rasaad slumped as if she had just dropped a heavy weight from her back. Tingai stepped away from the hole, not sure what to make of it. That was what saved his life.

There was a blur of movement and the guard who was standing next to him, holding the torch, just disappeared. Warm liquid splashed Tingai's face and, from the metallic taste of the drops that hit his mouth, he knew immediately that it was blood.

Ayim Rasaad had been fast enough to jump out of the way, her superhuman reflexes developed over years of training saving her life. Tingai knew that he had just gotten lucky. He stumbled behind a tree and then watched in terror as he saw events unfold.

The thing that had killed the first guard so quickly was going through the others as well. The brief moment it had taken it to destroy him allowed the others to draw their weapons. Some had a torch in one hand and a weapon in the other, but most of them dropped their torches so they could fight with two hands. Two of them had clear enough minds to wedge the torches into rocks so there was enough light to fight.

Whatever creature was attacking them, it was about one and a half times the size of a man, and humanoid. It didn't appear to be wearing any clothing and its skin seemed strange. When it stopped for a fraction of a second to determine which of the men to attack, Baron Tingai saw that it had rough skin, the same color and consistency of the rock in the canyon. When one of the guards delivered a strong overhand strike toward the attacker and it blocked it with its forearm, breaking the sword, Tingai realized that it was actually *made* of stone.

There were eight guards left and, with how quickly the rock creature was killing them, Tingai knew that he and all the remaining guards would be dead before the main force could even get to them. He hoped that the thing didn't know where he was, or that he was unimportant enough that it didn't attack him.

In a blink, there were only three guards left. How was it killing them at such a rate? His question was answered as the monster moved—more quickly than Tingai could even see in the dim light—and literally tore one of the guards in half with its hands, not bothering to try to block or parry the strike from the mace that was the guard's last act in this life.

The golem turned and looked right at Tingai. Its blank face showed no expression, didn't even have a mouth. The holes in the creature's head didn't seem to have eyes in it, but they were pointing at Tingai and he knew that it saw him. It started moving toward him, ready to lunge.

As it readied itself to spring, Tingai noticed movement to the side. Ayim Rasaad was standing there, hands outstretched, a look of concentration on her face. She made a cutting movement with her right hand and the creature moved as it had been struck. Turning its head toward her, it charged the new threat.

36

By the time Sam and the others got to the bottom of the path, it was completely dark. They stood there, looking for signs of their prey. The light of the partial moon allowed them to see the cleared area at the bottom of the trail, but not much else.

"I don't see any lights," Sam whispered, worried about Rasaad's scouts. "Do you think they kept moving or do you think they camped somewhere close?"

"With how thick these trees are, you wouldn't see any light unless they were right in front of us," Emerius said. "Stay here a minute. Inoria?"

The man's sister nodded. She patted Oro on the head, said something that made the bear sit back on his haunches and relax, and she followed Emerius into the trees, scrutinizing the ground for signs.

Nalia came over to Sam and put her arm around him, putting her head on his shoulder. "Are you well, Sam?" she said.

He kissed the top of her head. "I am now." He grinned and hugged her. "I wish we could just go and fight them. This chasing but never catching is driving me crazy."

"Yes," she said. "It is frustrating. I am sure the twins will find out where they are and then we can make a decision."

"Yeah," he said, "you're right. I just don't like doing nothing as they are getting further from us. I know they're probably not able to do much in the way of experiments with the captives while they move, but they're also getting closer to the artifact."

Do you think any of the hapaki still live? Skitter sent to Sam. He had come up and curled up near Sam's feet.

I hope so, my friend, Sam sent back as he and Nalia sat on a rock outcropping. *It's horrible that such a peaceful people were attacked and carried away like that. We'll do all we can to get them back, I promise you.*

I know you will, Sam. You are a good friend to me and to the hapaki. You have shown it time and again.

Sam absently patted Skitter's head and scratched his ears, anxious to move on with things.

Time seemed to stretch. The rakkeben had gone off to the edge of the clearing and were lying down. Oro was still sitting where he was when Inoria patted him. Rindu was about twenty feet from Sam, Nalia, and Skitter, in a seated meditation position, unmoving and seemingly unbreathing.

Rindu's eyes opened. He tilted his head toward the trees to one side of the clearing. Less than a minute later, Emerius and his sister appeared like wraiths, materializing from the trees, making no sounds that Sam could hear. They walked over to Sam and Nalia. Rindu got up and came toward them as well.

"They're not camped anywhere close," Emerius said. "Their trail is easy enough to follow. With how many people they have, they have trampled the vegetation so badly, we could follow them just by feel if necessary."

Everyone was silent for a moment, as if waiting for something. Waiting for Sam to make a decision. He wasn't sure how it happened, but he had apparently become their leader. Even Emerius was waiting to hear what he would say.

"They're making a push for the artifact," Sam said. "Rasaad probably knows where it's at and they're so close she doesn't want to wait until morning."

"She can sense it," Rindu put in.

"What?" Sam said.

"She can sense the artifact," the Zouy repeated. "In my meditation, I tried to do so, but was unable. However, when I shifted my thinking, searching not for something I could sense but for something I could *not* sense, I found a strange feeling. It is as if there was a hole in the *rohw* somewhere, the absence of anything where there should be flows of vibrational energy."

Sam found himself speechless for a moment. "You literally sensed nothing? And by sensing nothing, you are saying you sensed something?"

"That is correct," Rindu said.

"Father," Nalia said, "please do not play games at this time. Can you explain it more clearly to us?"

Rindu fixed Nalia with that blank expression he wore so well. "It is as if the wind could be seen as a colored smoke. It flows, it swirls, it moves around and engulfs all. If the wind encounters an obstacle, perhaps a very large rock, it flows around it, not occupying that space, because the space is already occupied. In this case, the *rohw* is flowing around something that does not appear to be there, as if the wind swirled around an invisible rock. We could see the absence of the colored smoke, the wind, and know that something is there, even if we cannot see it with our eyes."

"So," Sam said, "you're saying that the artifact is hiding itself? It's not putting out *rohw* energy but is somehow camouflaged?"

"That is correct."

"But," Sam said, "how is that possible? Wouldn't the camouflage have to be done with the *rohw*? And if it was, then you could see the energy being used to actually create the invisibility, right?"

"The artifact does not use the *rohw*," Rindu said. "Or, it does not use it in any form I have ever encountered. It is something I would very much like to study. It is a power I have never encountered."

"Wow," Sam said. "Anyway, if you can sense the 'hole' in the *rohw*, then we can go straight to it, right? You can lead us there, maybe even soon enough to beat Rasaad?"

"It is very weak," Rindu said. "I expect it will get stronger as we get closer to the actual artifact, but following the trail would probably be more efficient for now. I would have to stop and devote full concentration in meditation every few minutes, which would slow us down. I believe Ayim Rasaad can sense what I can, so following her would be the fastest way to proceed."

Sam ran his fingers through his hair. "Okay, then it's settled. Let's get moving. If she isn't going to wait until morning, we can't either. Hopefully she'll have been slowed down by trying to find it and by other obstacles and we can catch her before she puts her hands on the bell."

Sam lit the tip of *Ahimiro* to light the way. They followed the trail for hours. It seemed to wander in circles, but Sam couldn't really tell because after the first fifteen minutes he had lost his sense of direction. Even when he used the trick Rindu taught him, using the ley lines to figure out which way he was going, it didn't help. The path didn't follow the lines so he still couldn't tell where he was.

"This forest goes on forever," he said when Nalia asked him how he was doing.

"Do not exaggerate, Sam," she said. "You know full well that it only fills the canyon. If we walk in one direction long enough, we will hit the canyon wall, or the Zirquay River."

"It just an expre—" he started but then saw her mischievous smile. "Okay, very funny." He pretended to pout.

Nalia smiled at him and walked on ahead.

As was the case since the twins had joined them, Emerius and Inoria scouted ahead, circling back occasionally to speak with the others. They didn't use torches, but somehow moved about in the total darkness. Skitter was riding on the litter strapped to Shonyb and the rakkeben and Oro were ranging out to the sides, doing whatever they felt like, coming back to check on the humans from time to time. They moved well through the heavy foliage, as well as the humans were moving through the trampled path.

Rindu seemed preoccupied to Sam. When he asked the Zouy why, Rindu said that he was concentrating on the strange hole in the *rohw*. He could sense it better as they got closer. He still had to concentrate on it, but he could do it while moving now instead of needing to stop and meditate to feel it as before. He was making sure the path was going toward the artifact.

An hour before dawn, Rindu suddenly stopped. "It has changed," he said. "Something about the hole in the *rohw* has changed. I am afraid that Ayim Rasaad may have reached Azgo, the bell artifact."

"Are you sure?" Sam asked.

"No," the Zouy answered. "I cannot be certain. Something is different, but I cannot confirm that it involves Ayim Rasaad. I believe that it does, however."

"Let's find out," Sam said.

They followed the trail as quickly as they could. All the while, in the back of Sam's mind, he weighed the chance of them being surprised by Rasaad's forces in an ambush because they were so preoccupied with speed. Gone for the moment were thoughts of the captives. If the ex-Arzbed got the bell, she would be more powerful than before. Tingai would carry on with his experiments as soon as they left this place. They had to catch her.

The party rushed frantically through the forest, but they didn't seem to make any progress. To Sam, it seemed like one of those dreams in which he was running from some danger and he moved in slow motion, not going forward, even tripping and falling occasionally. He tried to dispel the negative thoughts from his head, but they persisted.

The light of the new day lit the tiny patches of sky Sam could occasionally see through the tree boughs. Soon, light filtered in so that they could see better within the tunnel-like confines of the forest. Sam allowed the light to fade from his staff's tip.

As sunlight diffused through the leaves, Sam finally saw clearly the devastation the ones they were following had wrought on the vegetation. There must have been thousands of people trampling the underbrush for them to have done that much damage. Sam shook his head. He knew the forest would recuperate; it was just underbrush after all, and not the trees themselves. Still, it was sad to see all the broken plants, the green-brown pulp that was the only thing left of the grasses, ferns, and vines.

They caught up to the twins an hour later. They were sitting on a rock, waiting for the rest of them to catch up. "Just through there," Emerius said, pointing between groups of trees that had grown very close together.

Sam looked from Emerius to Inoria. "Is it bad?" he asked them.

"Take a look," Emerius answered. "See for yourself."

Sam took a breath and threaded his way through the trees. As he did so, he stepped on something. It didn't feel like the forest floor, the spongy, loamy layer made from decaying plant matter and rich soil. It was firmer, but not like wood or a rock. He lifted his foot and looked at it. It was a human hand, separated at the wrist. The jagged edge made it look like it had been torn from the arm, not cut off. He looked back to the others, trying to keep his face from showing that he wanted to be sick.

He stepped around the hand and into a partial clearing. The trees were thinner here and on the far side was a large rock face. Through the slanting beams of sunlight filtering in from above, Sam saw what looked like a battleground. There was blood—more brown than red now because it was hours old—splashed about. There were the bodies of at least ten people, maybe a few more, some whole but most not. The snow had stopped sometime during the night, so the bloody slush and corpses were easily seen. It looked like something had torn them apart.

That something was still there, lying in the blood of its enemies in front of the rock. It was man-shaped, made entirely of red sandstone, the same as the rock formations around them. It was bigger than a man, too. And it had no head. That puzzled Sam for a moment, until he saw red gravel scattered near the body of the thing.

Sam thought maybe he was in shock and that's why he was concentrating on the details of the scene rather than the fact that several people lay dead before him. If that was the case, then he would take advantage of it and try to think logically while he still could. Once his emotions at seeing all that death kicked in, he wasn't sure how well he'd be able to think.

Emerius had come up behind him. "A helluva thing, huh?" the big man said to him.

"Yeah," Sam was able to say. "This creature must have attacked them. I don't see Rasaad, so she's probably the one who blew its head apart."

Emerius nodded.

"So where is she?" Sam asked. "And where is the bell?"

Emerius stood silent, watching him. He was evaluating Sam.

Sam looked to the rock face. There was a hole in it approximately the same size as a doorway in a house. He picked his way toward it, being careful not to step on bodies, or parts of them. When he got there, he looked in, but couldn't see how far into the rock the hole went. He concentrated for a moment and caused light to flare up on the end of *Ahimiro* again. He poked it into the hole.

The cavity went back no more than twenty feet. It was some kind of hollow that had been bored into the rock. The cuts were smooth. They hadn't been done with chisels and picks. It must have been done with some kind of power or tool that Sam was unfamiliar with.

Holding *Ahimiro* up ahead of him, he walked into the chamber carved in the rock. Near the back wall, there was a simple pedestal that appeared to be actually formed from the stone floor, as if the chamber was carved around it and it was left intact. On top of it was a perfect depression in the shape of a bell.

"She got it," Sam sighed.

"Yes," Rindu said from right next to Sam.

Sam jumped in surprise. He hadn't known that Rindu was there.

"Then where did she go?" Nalia said from the other side of Sam, causing him to start again.

"I didn't see any tracks leading away," Emerius said from just behind Sam.

"Maybe she just disappeared by magic," Inoria said. She was standing next to Emerius.

"You know," Sam said, "I wish you four would make more noise. You startle the wits out of me sneaking around like that!"

The question they brought up was valid, though. Where did Rasaad, Tingai, and their forces gone? "Ahh," he said, smacking his forehead with his palm. "Duh. Azgo, the bell, and its power to teleport. Rasaad must have used it to teleport them all somewhere else."

"Oh, no," Inoria said. "Does that mean they teleported directly to where the second artifact is? We'll never catch them if they did."

"No, I don't think so," Sam said. "I'm betting that Azgo has the same limitations as my teleportation. In order to travel somewhere, the user has to know the destination. If Rasaad hasn't been there before, she'll have to travel there the old-fashioned way, on foot or mount."

"That's good, at least," Inoria said.

"So then," Emerius said. "What do we do now? I'm still more concerned about my brother than about some stupid artifacts. Are you going to help us save the captives or are you going to go haring off to be some kind of hero and try to save the world?"

"We still have the same goal, Emerius Dinn," Nalia said. "Baron Tingai and Ayim Rasaad are together, so preventing them from getting the next artifact and saving the captives are the same thing. We can continue to work together."

"Yeah, I guess," Emerius grumbled.

"Okay," Sam said. "I think we should go back to Whitehall and regroup. Maybe Dr. Walt has come up with more information for us to help us decide where we need to go next."

He turned to Emerius and Inoria. "Will you come with us? Staying here and trying to find them on foot is not really an option. They teleported away. We have to do the same to catch them. What do you say?"

Inoria stepped forward. "I think we should go with them, Em. It's the only way we'll ever find Ancha. Besides, we've been through a lot with these folks. They're our friends now."

"We don't need any more friends," Emerius said. "But we'll go with them. They seem to be our only hope in rescuing Ancha and the rest of the villagers."

"Good," Sam said. "It's settled then. Give me a few minutes to memorize this location, just in case we need to come back here later, and then we'll go."

Within a few minutes, Sam was ready to leave. The whole party gathered around him and he teleported them all to the area in front of the stables at Whitehall.

Sam had one of the servants set up rooms for the twins. Oro was allowed to go find a corner of his own in one of the parks, after Inoria assured Sam that he would not kill everything in sight. Skitter sent something to Sam about checking on "the babies"—the kittens, Sam knew—and left them. The rest ate a quick breakfast and slept until the afternoon, tired from hunting Rasaad through the night.

When they gathered for an early dinner, Dr. Walt, Danaba Kemp, and the two Zouyim were there also. Emerius rolled his eyes at the thought of more Zouyim, but Inoria seemed to hit it off right away with Palusa Filk.

"I'm afraid I haven't come across any more information that will be helpful to you, Sam," Dr. Walt said. "It is indeed a dilemma, with Rasaad now able to teleport. Maybe Lahim Chode will know something about where you should go. He sent me a message earlier today asking me to visit him this evening. I don't think it's urgent, but if you would like to go with me, you can ask him what you will."

"Yes," Sam said, "I think I'll do that. Any information right now would be helpful."

"Who is this Lahim Chode?" Emerius asked.

"He's a seer," Dr. Walt answered. "He has tipped us off with good information before."

"You people and your magic," he spat. "Give me a hunter's instincts and a good bow any day."

"Em!" Inoria said. "Be polite. We're guests here."

"I'm going to see Oro," Emerius said. "You know how nervous he gets when he's in new surroundings." He got up and left the dining hall.

"I'm sorry for my brother," Inoria said. "He's tied up in knots about our younger brother. Please forgive him."

Dr. Walt smiled at Inoria. "Of course, my dear, of course. We quite understand. No offense taken."

After dinner, Sam accompanied Dr. Walt to Lahim Chode's chambers. Rindu, Nalia, Inoria, and Danaba Kemp came as well.

"I wonder if Lahim will be able to tell us where to go next," Sam said, hoping someone would give him some hope.

The silence that was his answer was both ominous and depressing.

37

"Come in," Lahim Chode said in answer to the knock at his door.

Chode watched as Dr. Walt, Sam, Nalia, Rindu, Danaba Kemp, and some woman he had never seen before—she was dressed like some kind of hunter—filed into his chamber. He was glad to see that Sam and the others had returned safely from another day of trying to catch up to Rasaad. The teleportation thing was useful, he had to admit. Travel all day, come back home at night in the blink of the eye so that they didn't have to carry food or tents. It was remarkable.

Sam smiled at Chode. "Lahim, you are looking even better than last time I saw you. How are you feeling?"

"I'm feeling well, Sam," Chode answered, "thank you. I think I will be able to move around soon. It has been too long since I've been able to walk on my own. I'm looking forward to it."

"That's great," Sam said. The skepticism Sam had shown previously seemed to have disappeared with their last conversation. That was good. Besides the fact that Sam was the "Hero of Gythe," Lahim genuinely liked him.

"How is the search for Rasaad and Tingai going," Lahim asked Sam. "Have you almost caught up to her?"

Sam's head dropped and he sighed. "No. She got to the first artifact ahead of us. She used it to teleport away. We're at a loss about what to do."

"I'm sorry. I didn't have a viewing of that. I have seen some things that I think are important, though. I have seen that an army is being built, soldiers being gathered. It has one purpose: to attack Whitehall and destroy every last vestige of the new government."

"What?" Dr. Walt exclaimed. "Why would anyone do that? I don't understand. Who is building this army?"

"I'm not sure," Lahim said, "but who could it be but Ayim Rasaad? She has sent an assassin to kill you, Dr. Walt, trying to stall out the formation of the new government that way. Even if she does get all three artifacts, she still has to deal with a coalition of local governors. For that, she'll need an army. Yes, I'm sure it's her, though I didn't see her specifically. I did, however, see her speaking to that assassin—she called him Vahi. She seemed to be giving him a special mission, but I could not hear it clearly. We must be wary of him as well."

"Hold on there, mister," Danaba Kemp said. "I need some details. What kind of army are you talking about? How many soldiers, and what kind? Infantry, mounted, pikes, archers, crossbows, what?"

"I only saw flashes of the army itself, Danaba. It looks to be thousands strong, maybe five thousand. Much of it is made up of mutated creatures, monsters of different shapes and sizes. All I know is that it will be marching here."

"Five thousand?" Danaba Kemp said. "And made up of mutated creatures? There's no way we can match those numbers."

"Now, now, Danaba," Dr. Walt said. "We don't have to match their numbers. We have walls and cliffs, after all."

"Yes," Sam said, "but if Rasaad gets all three artifacts, she may be able to tear our walls down. We may have to fight."

"I better get to work," Danaba said. "I have to increase our numbers as soon as possible. There is recruitment, training, provisioning, and we'll need weapons. Excuse me, but I need to go meet with my captains. I need to get started right away." He left the room in a hurry.

"I'm sorry to give you such bad news," Lahim said. "I thought it best to tell you as soon as possible."

The seer looked at the grim faces around him. He had become used to that during his life, people being sad around him. It was an art, telling others about tragedies that would occur without having them blame him.

"There is one other thing," he said. "I believe it could be helpful."

"What is it?" Dr Walt asked.

"I believe I know where Ayim Rasaad's home is, where she may have gone after she got the first artifact."

"Really?" Sam said. "That's great. We can go there and stop the army from being built, and prevent her from going to get the next artifact."

It was Lahim's turn to wear a sad face. "I'm afraid not, Sam. While it is true you might be able to find Rasaad there, her fortress is not the place I saw the army being built. That is being done somewhere far north of her home. I haven't been able to pinpoint the location of the army, but I can tell you where Gutu, Ayim Rasaad's home base, is. I'll keep trying to find out where the army is headquartered."

Sam looked as if his hopes had been crushed again. "Oh. Well, if you can give us the location of Gutu, that will be a start anyway. I'm sure that's where Rasaad, Tingai, and all the captives teleported."

"I'll try my hardest to get the other information to you before you've reached Gutu," Lahim said.

He leaned toward his nightstand and picked up a crude

map he had drawn. "Here is where Gutu is. It's more than five hundred miles from the destroyed hapaki community, to the south. I think that's the closest place you can teleport to. Or, at least, it's the shortest route that doesn't involve going through many more mountain ranges than necessary."

"That's a long way," Sam said.

"That's where Rasaad is," Lahim answered. "I'm sorry, Sam. I just view things. I don't make them happen."

"It's okay," he responded, forcing a smile. "There's nothing that can be done about it. We should probably get started as soon as possible." Sam looked to his friends, each one nodding or saying verbally the he or she would go. "That is, unless you have found the location of the other artifacts, Dr. Walt."

"I am afraid not, Sam," Dr. Walt said sadly. "I read the entire book from where we got the location of the Azgo and though there is information on the powers of the other two artifacts and some of the history of them, there is not a clue as to where they are hidden. I'm sorry."

"We'll go, too," Inoria said. "Emerius will grumble about it, but it's the only way to get to where Ancha is. I'll go talk to him."

"It looks like we're going to be traveling again," Sam said. "I'll meet everyone in the morning, at the same location where we have been teleporting to and from. I have something I need to do tonight. Nalia, Rindu, can you help me?"

"Of course," Rindu said.

Nalia nodded.

"I'll come and talk to you later, Dr. Walt," Sam said as he turned toward the door. "Lahim, thank you for your help. Please let us know if you find any other information." He left with the others.

Dr. Walt remained for a moment. "Lahim," he said, "how are you doing?"

"I'm doing much better," he answered. "I feel stronger

every day."

"Okay," Dr. Walt said. "Just don't push too hard in trying to get more information. Your body is not healed completely yet. Don't have a relapse. Do what you can, but don't work so hard that you weaken yourself."

"I won't," Lahim lied. "I want to get more information than I have, but I'll be careful. Don't worry about me." He smiled a small smile and Dr. Walt seemed to believe it sincere.

"Very good," the old scholar said. "Well, then, have a good night. I will talk with you soon."

"Goodnight, Dr. Walt. Thank you again for nursing me back to health and all else you have done for me. I really do appreciate it."

Dr. Walt waved as he left the room. Lahim Chode looked around his small chamber and sighed. He would have to double his efforts to find more helpful information. It was possible that he could be the difference between success and failure. People underestimated the value of knowledge, but not him. He knew its power as he knew that he was the only one who could get what they needed. He had better get to work. There was not a moment to waste.

*****

Rindu and Nalia sat in Sam's room as he tried to explain what he was going to do.

Rindu eyed him critically. "I am not sure what you are proposing is honorable."

"Master Rindu," Sam said, "they're going to attack us with thousands of soldiers. We don't even have an army. What I'm talking about doing will just even the odds a bit, no more."

"It is taking unfair advantage of your unique situation, the powers you possess," Rindu countered.

"It seems to me," Sam said, "that it's just using what

power I possess. Is it unfair for one of the Zouyim to enter combat with a normal soldier, someone who doesn't have the benefit of using the *rohw*, or of having trained his whole life to fight?"

"That is different," Rindu said. "The power the Zouyim have over the *rohw* is within them. You are talking about using your power to obtain external things that can be used to unfairly turn the advantage to us. That is not honorable."

"But it's not honorable to send assassins or to gather an army to attack a lesser force. They're not being honorable."

"I know it is difficult," Rindu said, "but such is the burden for one who must walk the true path, the *wireh*, the path of honor."

Sam felt his mouth form a frown. "I have to do something." His eyes dropped. Then, as a thought occurred to him, he raised his eyes and snapped his fingers. "I have it. How about I just get things that will protect us. Not offensive weapons, but defensive items. Would that be honorable?"

"It is unseemly to split hairs in such a way, Sam," Rindu said, "but it would not be strictly dishonorable to obtain items that are meant for defense."

"Yes." Sam pumped his fist in the air, but, noticing Rindu's expression, stopped. "I could get some body armor, riot shields, other things that are strictly defensive. That could help us. I know it could."

Sam looked to Nalia. "Will you help me? Will you aid me in traveling back to Telani to gather some gear and then come right back here?"

Nalia stepped over and kissed him. "You know I will go wherever you do. I have seen many things in your world that could aid us in our struggle. I will help you. You must remember, however, that time is not constant between the two worlds. We may have been gone from Telani for a few minutes or several years. Also, we may only be there for a day but years may pass here. What if, by trying to help, we miss the conflict altogether?"

"Oh," Sam sighed. "I didn't really think about that. I still think the risk is worth what we could accomplish. If Rasaad's army gets through to us, we're finished."

"I understand," Nalia said. "It is your choice. I will help you if you want to go to Telani."

Sam hugged her and then looked at Rindu. "I have to try to do something, Master Rindu."

"I understand," the Zouy said. "I will not condemn you. You must do what you think to be the honorable thing. I will wait as you transport. Perhaps you will return in a few minutes."

"Thank you," Sam said.

Sam sat down on the thick rug sprawling across his floor. Nalia joined him and matched the cross-legged posture he was in. Soon, they were both breathing slowly and deeply, both were attaining the *khulim*.

Sam felt the familiar sensations of the unique vibratory signature of his room. He let the vibrations flow through him and he became one with them. He saw Nalia there in his mind's eye, sitting right in front of him as she was in real life. In his mind, she opened her eyes and looked at him, her eyes bright green in the strange light swirling around them. He felt his heart flutter, as it normally did when she trained those beautiful eyes on him. She smiled at him and he smiled back.

The sequence was familiar to him now. He would give control over to Nalia once he had sensed the tunnel opening to Telani. Then, she would lead him there. It was a revelation when he found that all he had ever needed to return home was to trust someone enough to give control over completely to her. Once that was clear, their traveling to and from Gythe had been relatively easy. He waited for the tunnel in the midst of the swirling lights to appear.

It didn't.

He focused more intensely on the vibration of his

world, of Telani.

Still nothing.

Puzzled, he tried changing little things. He adjusted his vibrations a little this way and that, but that didn't help. He tried giving over control of everything to Nalia, thinking maybe he had left one small part of him that he didn't surrender. That didn't help either.

He tried for what seemed to be hours to no avail. Finally frustrated, he left the *khulim* and turned his mind back on the waking world. He took a deep breath with his body. It felt like the first breath his physical form had taken in a very long time. He opened his eyes slowly, the dim brazier light hurting them with its brightness.

When he was able to see clearly, he was looking right into Nalia's eyes. Not her eyes in his mind, but in truth. His heart fluttered again. They were back to their normal blue/green color, but they were just as amazing as they were in his mind.

"What happened?" Rindu asked.

Sam had forgotten the Zouy was there. He turned to look at the master. "I don't know. I tried to go, but I couldn't. Maybe I'm just tired or I didn't give it enough time."

"You have been in the *khulim* for more than three hours, Sam," Rindu said.

Sam was shocked. It had seemed a long time, but he didn't actually think it *had* been a long time in reality.

"It felt the same as it did before," Nalia said, "except that it felt like something was keeping the tunnel from opening. It was easy when we came back to Gythe, even easier than when we went to Telani together the first time."

"I don't understand it," Sam said.

"Perhaps it is the *rohw* telling you that what you had planned is not of the *wireh*," Rindu said. "Perhaps it is telling you to address Gythe's problems with that which is already in Gythe."

Sam scratched his head. "Maybe. It just doesn't make any sense."

He got up and stretched his legs, which were stiff from sitting motionless for so long. "I'm going to go and talk to Dr. Walt. Maybe he has some ideas."

"We will come with you," Rindu said. "We will see if he agrees with me in this."

Fifteen minutes later, the three were in front of Dr. Walt in his library.

"And you felt no connection at all to Telani?" Dr. Walt asked.

"None," Sam said. "It was different than before when I just didn't know how to do it. It was like something was blocking me from finding the particular vibratory signature I was looking for. It was like what I was trying to find didn't exist."

"Oh, dear," Dr. Walt said. "I was afraid of this. Do you remember how you told me that it was much easier to get back to Gythe than it had been to get to Telani after the last time you were here? And how you thought it was just that you had increased in your ability to use the *rohw*? Do you remember how you told me that the *rohw* was much less powerful in Telani when you went back?"

"Yes, I remember all of that." Sam started to get a sinking feeling in his belly.

"Well," Dr. Walt said. "I have been thinking about those things and I have a theory."

"A theory about the *rohw*?" Rindu asked. "Does it involve taking the honorable path?"

"No," Dr. Walt answered, wearing a puzzled look, "not exactly. I believe that technology affects the *rohw*. Whether it's because the energies used by technology, magnetic fields and microwaves and such, are increased and interfere with the *rohw* or if it is simply because less people use and nurture the *rohw* when technology is present, I don't know. Either way, I believe the more technology is present, the weaker the universal *rohw*. I believe the *rohw* on

Telani is simply not strong enough any longer to sustain a doorway from our world.

"From the few records I've seen about the subject here, it looks as if *rohw*-users were rare during the time of Gythe's high technology. It wouldn't surprise me if there were similar problems with the energy being weaker during that time as well."

"So," Sam said, "you're saying that there is no getting back to Telani because the *rohw* is too weak there? How is that possible? I just came from there."

"Yes, Sam," Rindu said. "You came *from* there. Going back to Telani has always given you difficulties. Perhaps what Dr. Walt says is correct. I believe that the *rohw* could be affected thusly by science."

"That would mean I'm here for good, then," Sam said. "It's not a big deal because I had already decided to stay, but it means we won't have the ability to get things from Telani that could help us in our quest. Or in our defense."

"I'm afraid so, my boy," Dr. Walt said. "if what I believe is correct. Feel free to try it out. I could be wrong, but I've been thinking about it since you returned and it fits into what I had already been hypothesizing."

"It is okay, Sam," Nalia said, patting his arm. "We will be victorious without things from Telani. We are not defenseless."

"I know, Nal." Sam felt as if the energy had been sucked out of him. "It seemed like it would make things better, give us an edge. Maybe we'll just have to do things the old-fashioned way. Let's get some sleep. We need to head out in the morning. There are still villains to catch."

38

Everyone met in one of the dining halls before the sun was up. They ate quietly, all of them either still sleepy or not in the mood for conversation. After their meal, they all made their way to the area in front of the stables they had been using as a teleport point.

"Everyone gather close," Sam said. There were five humans—Sam, Rindu, Nalia, Emerius, and Inoria—as well as three rakkeben, Skitter, and Oro the bear. They made quite a sight preparing to disappear like they were. The party traveled light, with only snacks, minor provisions, and their weapons. Sam sat in his normal cross-legged posture, went almost instantly into the *khulim*, and had teleported them all within a few minutes.

They appeared just outside the ruined hapaki community. Sam had almost forgotten how devastated the area looked, with dens half dug up and the vegetation trampled everywhere. He got a lump in his throat when he saw it again. It became worse when he felt Skitter's sorrow leak into his mind. *We'll find them, Skitter, and we'll rescue the hapaki that are left and punish those who did this.*

I know, Sam, Skitter sent back, *but that won't bring back the dead hapaki or rebuild their ruined dens.*

Sam shook his head sadly and mounted Shonyb to begin the day's travel.

They were to travel south and east, hugging the base of the mountain range that would be to their left as they moved. Rindu told Sam that he would ensure that they traveled in the correct direction, but that his help would not be needed. If they stayed to the flatter lands—flatter compared to the mountains, anyway—they would be going the right way.

An hour into their trip, Sam looked off toward where they were heading. The land was fairly flat and the trees were not as thick as those they passed through in Gromarisa, so he could see ahead for several miles when they were on top of one of the small hills they had to climb. It looked to be a slow, constant grind to where they were going. He just wished they could speed it up somehow.

They took occasional breaks to allow the rakkeben and Oro to rest. The humans needed the breaks anyway. Mile after mile of monotonous travel sapped the energy and made the mind complacent. They didn't have the twins scout ahead because there was no reason to believe there were any forces nearby that needed to be detected. The pace they kept was so fast that in order for anyone to scout effectively, they would need several mounts or risk killing one.

With the trees thinner and spread out more, it was easy to keep a fast pace. They didn't need a path or trail but could travel in the direction they needed to go without being slowed so much by the forest.

"What tree is that, Sam?" Inoria asked as they stopped in a clearing for a break. She was pointing to a fifty-foot tree that still had green cloaking it, despite the winter season.

"It's a pine." He slumped his shoulders and waited.

"What kind of pine, Sam?" she mock-scolded him.

"Um, knobcone?"

"Very good. Why did you guess that particular tree?"

Sam thought for a moment. "The needles are in groups of three and the cones look to be about four inches and they are tightly bound. There is no drop of resin at the base of the needles, either. So, unless I don't remember correctly, all those things point to knobcone pine."

Inoria smiled at him and winked one of her bright green eyes. "Yes. You are a very good student."

He felt his face heat and turned to look at the tree again. "You are a good teacher. Thank you for showing me all this."

In response, she quizzed him on other trees. It was more difficult to identify those that had lost their leaves, but he was able to narrow the choices down and guessed correctly more often than he guessed wrong. Soon, they were on their way again.

Sam felt good about the progress they made the first day. In fact, he felt so good about it that they continued to travel for a while after it became dark. Finally, he decided that it was risky to travel at that speed in the dark, even though he thought the moon provided enough light to see by. He didn't want to have one of the rakkeben or Oro break a leg or get injured in some way because they wanted to push on for an extra hour or two. Besides, they all needed rest, so they stopped and Sam learned the area where they had halted. He teleported them back to Whitehall where they could eat and rest for the night, starting off early the next morning.

On the fourth day of travel, they reached a heavily forested area. They could see it from several miles off before they reached it. Sam was wondering which way they should go. Should they try to skirt it or simply go straight through it? As he was wondering, Emerius spoke.

"We should go to the left," he said. "We can ride around the edge of the trees at the base of the foothills. It will be easier travel that way."

Inoria looked at him, but didn't say anything. Sam looked toward Rindu and Nalia, but neither of them seemed to disagree. With a shrug, Sam followed their lead, heading toward the foothills to the east.

Emerius was correct. The trees thinned at the foothills and they were almost able to keep their pace the same as it had been all day.

The party topped an elevated section of the land and started down into what looked like a shallow bowl. There were very few trees, only some long grasses. When they reached the bottom and started across the meadow, Rindu shouted, "Down!"

Sam, not knowing what was happening, nevertheless dove off Shonyb to the soft ground. Two arrows passed through the space he had just vacated.

He looked around, but with the grass so high, he was unable to see any of his friends. He would just have to hope they weren't hit. The arrows were too fast for him to determine from where they had come, so he didn't know where his attackers were. It probably didn't matter. They had obviously been waiting for the party to arrive, and it seemed that they were surrounded on at least three sides. How were they going to get out of this?

Sam heard a rustling in the grass and separated *Ahimiro* into two sticks, ready to do battle. It was just Shonyb, crawling toward him. He was amazed again at the intelligence of the big wolf.

"Are you okay?" he asked her, running his hands over her fur to see if he could find any wounds. There were none. The archers, seemingly very skilled, had targeted him, not the rakkeben. Shonyb whined softly at him.

"I know," he said. "Just stay here. We'll figure something out."

Then Sam thought of something. He ran his hands over Shonyb's back, not wanting to lift his head above the grass to see. When he found what he was looking for, he gasped. Skitter's litter was empty. What had happened to the hapaki?

Skitter, Sam yelled in his mind. *Skitter, are you all right?*

A touch on Sam's shoulder made him jump, almost causing him to rise up above the level of the grass, revealing himself. It was Nalia.

"I'm getting good and tired of being startled by all you ninjas," he said, trying to regain his breath.

"I am not a ninja, Sam. I am a Sapsyr. That is much better." She winked at him.

Sam. Sam, are you there? Skitter sent.

Skitter, are you hurt? Sam sent back. *Are you okay?*

I'm fine, the hapaki sent. *The ground is soft, so when I fell off Shonyb as she rolled to the ground, I was only bumped and bruised a little.*

Where are you? Sam sent.

Here, I will show you what I am seeing, the hapaki sent back.

An image filled Sam's mind. It was a viewpoint low to the ground, nestled within the grasses. Through the blades, Sam could see four people, three men and a woman. One of the men had a crossbow and the others had bows. They were scanning the grasses, obviously trying to find Sam and the others.

One of the men was speaking, but since Skitter couldn't understand the words, it was gibberish to Sam. He would have to tell Dr. Walt about that. It would send the scholar off into his own world thinking about it. Skitter could use Sam's mind to understand people talking but Sam couldn't understand human speech coming through Skitter's mind.

What are you doing? Sam sent. *It's dangerous to be there. Get out of there.*

It's fine, Sam, Skitter sent. *If I move, they may see me. It will be best for me to stay where I'm at and spy on them for you.* Sam saw the viewpoint shift, Skitter swinging his head and looking to the left and to the right. Almost out of sight, there were people to both sides.

Sam quickly told Nalia what Skitter was seeing. If there

were four in front and others within sight of the hapaki, how many must there be all together? It didn't look good for their escape. At least, not without injury or death.

Not for the first time, Sam wished he could communicate with his other friends like he did with Skitter. Mind-to-mind communication definitely had its advantages.

"Have you seen any of the others?" Sam asked Nalia.

"No, just you. Stay here for a moment. I will be back."

She crawled through the grasses, barely disturbing them and somehow not making any sound. Even crawling, Nalia was graceful. He found himself inspecting her as she moved. She really was perfectly formed. He could watch her all day.

Sam shook his head to clear the thoughts of how much he liked to look at her. It was not the time to think of such things. When he heard Skitter's chuckling in his head, he felt his face go warm. He watched as she disappeared from his sight and turned his attention back to what Skitter was seeing.

The man who seemed to be the leader of the four, maybe the leader of the entire group, looked agitated. He was whisper-yelling to the others. Sam thought he could hear it from where he sat, but it was too soft for him to understand what was being said. The man glared at one of the others, obviously not happy with how things had turned out. He turned toward the meadow again, scanning it.

"There is no escape," the man yelled. "Stand up and surrender and we will take you captive. There's no need for you all to die here." As he said it, he motioned for the others to ready their bows. He drew a finger across his throat. There would be no taking of captives here, Sam knew.

The man waited, yelled again, and waited some more. He was becoming more and more agitated. Sam imagined he didn't want to be the one to tell Ayim Rasaad that he had not completed his mission.

Sam saw the man in Skitter's vision as he said something to the woman who was with him. She moved out of sight. Less than a minute later, she returned, carrying three lit torches. Skitter turned to face the other people on the periphery of his vision and saw that they, likewise, had torches in their hands.

Another touch on his shoulder made Sam clench his teeth to keep from yelping. He turned quickly, his breaths short and quick.

"Sam, you really must relax," Nalia said. "You are too excitable." Her small smile was the only thing that kept him from slapping her. In a playful way. Well, trying to slap her. He knew he would never be able to actually land a blow. Not that he wanted to, anyway. He loved her. He shook his head again. Why was he arguing with himself at a time like this?

"We have trouble," Sam whispered to her. "They're about to catch the whole meadow on fire. The grass is mostly green, but I think maybe there's enough dead grass in here for the fire to spread."

"My father was correct, then," she said. "He was wondering why they had not tried to burn us out yet. I am not sure where the twins are, but my father is just over there." She pointed to a location south of them. "He said he will try to reach the edge and eliminate some of the archers."

Skitter, Sam sent, *can you find a way out of the meadow, between two of the groups of people? If they start burning the grass with you so close to them, you won't survive.*

I have already found a place to slip through them, the hapaki sent back. *I will try to move slowly outside their ring. Wish me luck.*

Good luck, Sam sent. *Be careful.*

Of course. You too. I'll see you after you take care of these scary men. There was a bit of humor in the last sending.

Sam hoped they could get out of this one, as the hapaki

thought they could.

While he was thinking, the images from Skitter's mind suddenly stopped.

39

Sam gasped.

Skitter! Sam sent. *Are you all right?*

Yes, Skitter replied. *Sorry, I should have warned you. It takes concentration to send images to you. I need to pay attention to trying to slip around the humans.*

Oh, okay. Sam took a deep breath. *Let me know when you're safe.*

Yessir, Skitter sent. Sam thought that maybe the hapaki had spent too much time in Sam's memories. He seemed more and more human all the time. He let a hint of a smile creep onto his face.

"Be ready, Sam," Nalia said. "We must be prepared to move when the time is right. Caught between arrows and fire, there will be no second chance to do it correctly."

"I understand," he said. He felt like a whole bucket of worms had been dumped into his belly.

He reached over and squeezed her arm, looking into those beautiful eyes of hers. She leaned toward him, kissed him quickly, and said, "Do not die, Sam. We have much living yet to do. Together."

"Together," he agreed, and suddenly felt as if he could

do anything, would do anything, to make that a reality.

The entire world seemed to be holding its breath. There was no sound but the soft rustling of the grass in the breeze, no sight but Nalia and their grassy prison. He could smell the greenness of their surroundings, the smell of fresh air and grass that had been trampled and broken, so much like the smell of freshly cut lawn he remembered so well.

Then, he smelled smoke. Whether it was from the torches or from the grass burning, he didn't know. He looked at Nalia in alarm, but she didn't seem to be worried. To fight the panic, he remembered Rindu's lessons. He closed his eyes, breathed deeply, and calmed his heart.

He pictured himself in the center of his own vision. Around him, he spread his aura, his energy, in a wide circle. He had done this before. He would sense anything that intruded into his space. Including flames. He felt better knowing that there were none close to him. Yet.

Sam thought he heard some kind of commotion to the south, but couldn't be sure. His ears seemed to be searching for things, picking up on sounds and then trying to interpret them. He would have to wait until something more definite happened, until he could clearly see or hear danger.

I'm safely outside the ring of people, Skitter sent to Sam. *I'll show you what I'm seeing.*

Images rushed into Sam's head of the same people Skitter showed him before. They still had not put the torches to the grass. They were apparently waiting for the others surrounding the meadow to get into position.

There was a squishing sound and then something falling to the grass. At first Sam wasn't sure if he had heard it correctly, but he quickly realized that it was something Skitter had heard with his better-than-human ears. There was no doubt about it, Rindu or the others were on the move.

"Almost now," Nalia said. "We will move in just a moment." She was looking to the south, as if the grass wasn't there to block her view.

Sudden shouts broke out and Sam watched through Skitter's eyes as the men and women in his view dipped the torches to the grass. The brown blades caught fire immediately, and the green weren't too far behind. Before long, there would be a firestorm heading toward them.

"Come quickly," Nalia said to him, tugging on his arm. "We must go this way."

She headed off toward the south, in a crouch-run. Shonyb and Cleave crawled on their bellies after them. Sam hoped that she knew where she was going. He also hoped the twins had made it out of what would soon be a furnace.

They broke into a tamped-down section of the grass. It appeared to be the edge of the meadow, but it was still sheltered from sight by the long grass. In the middle of the small clearing were two bodies, both bleeding from holes in their necks. Rindu's throwing spikes.

Sam saw motion at the edge of the grass and turned to see Rindu moving toward them in a crouch.

"This way," he said. "There are still many archers out there, so continue to stay low."

Sam and Nalia followed him. The smell of burned brush was getting stronger and there was a thick layer of smoke forming from the wet grass being burned. The smoke would help hide them. If it didn't kill them first.

They passed three more bodies as they followed Rindu. They were almost to the trees bordering the meadow. All they had to do was to get into the cover of the trees and they could escape. There was no way their attackers could outrun the rakkeben once they were able to mount.

"Where are the twins?" Sam asked. "Did you see them?"

Rindu shook his head.

"We can't just leave them here," Sam said. "What if

they're hurt? What if they get trapped in the fire? We have to help them."

"Shh," Rindu said. "Yes, Sam, I know. We will not leave them. But we must circle around and defeat the archers who are waiting to kill us as we flee. Only then can we search for Emerius and Inoria effectively."

The monk was right, Sam knew. He looked to the trees and then back at the burning grass. The twins wouldn't have come for him if the situation was reversed, he thought. At least, Emerius wouldn't. Maybe Inoria would. He supposed it didn't make a difference. The situation was not different. They needed his help and he would give it. Clenching his teeth, he crouch-ran into the trees and then stopped.

With all the smoke, it was difficult to see, but he thought he saw movement off to his left. He nodded to Nalia and Rindu and started moving in that direction. Nalia came with him, but Rindu pointed to himself and then off to the right. He would go and take care of the attackers in that direction.

The smoke ended abruptly, surprising Sam. Fortunately, his appearance thirty feet away surprised the three archers as well. While they froze for a fraction of a second, trying to understand what was happening, Sam was already in action, running at a full sprint toward them, throwing the stick in his right hand at the woman who was drawing her bow back to shoot an arrow at him.

His stick hit her square in the face. Even above the other sounds, he heard her nose break. She fell backward, the arrow spinning off above Sam's head. Another woman, this one with a crossbow, had regained her senses and shot a bolt at Sam. Too committed in his run to dodge, he used his *rohw* to sense where it would be and swing his remaining stick at it. He was happy to hear the thunk of his weapon striking the shaft and causing it to go wide. He was vaguely aware of the man with a bow shooting at Nalia on his left and her deflecting his arrow with one of her shrapezi so that it passed harmlessly to her side.

Then they were on the three attackers. Sam didn't stop, but launched himself into a flying kick as the woman with the crossbow was trying to crank back the handle to load another quarrel. He struck her square in the chest, knocking her from her feet and causing the crossbow to fly out of her hands. He dropped his shoulder, rolled to pick up the stick he had thrown without stopping, and came to his feet as the woman he had just kicked was trying to regain hers. One solid strike on the back of her head and she crumpled into a heap. Sam didn't use full force for fear of killing her, which wasn't necessary.

The man Nalia had gone after was able to draw a sword and had tried to attack the Sapsyr. He was on the ground, bleeding from several nasty cuts, including one that had taken his hand off at the wrist. Nalia held her shrapezi at the ready, looking around for other opponents.

Sam found the woman with the broken nose lying in the grass, blood pouring from her face. Tears were streaming from her eyes as the blood came from her ruined nose. She looked to be trying to see through the red liquid, but couldn't. Sam tried to apply the *rohw* strike to the base of her skull like Rindu did, but it didn't work for him. Nalia stepped up calmly and punched the woman—softly, Sam thought—on the temple. She collapsed. Nalia rolled her to her side, with her head facing down.

Sam looked at her.

"There is no use killing this one," she said. "This way, she will not choke on her blood."

They found three more groups of attackers before they started to see bodies with arrows in them. That was a good sign; the twins had survived, or at least one of them had.

A few minutes later they saw Emerius bent over one of the attackers, reclaiming his arrows from the body. The fire had burned the grass quickly but then started to fizzle out when it got to the trees, which were too green to catch fire. The ferns and other green foliage under the trees weren't catching fire, either. It seemed that the danger of being burned alive was lessening.

Inoria came up from behind Emerius, waving. Oro lumbered behind her. "Are you okay?" she asked them as she came up to the body at their feet so she could remove her arrow. It had gone through the attacker's right eye.

"We're fine," Sam said. "Have you seen Rindu? He's finishing up the last of the people who ambushed us, I think."

"No," Emerius said. "We saw some bodies that were probably his handiwork, but we haven't seen him."

Sam noticed that Emerius had a strip of cloth tied around his left arm. It was soaked with blood. "Are you injured?" Sam asked him.

"Just a minor cut," Emerius said. "He winged me. I got the bastard, though."

"Em pushed me out of the way of an arrow coming at me but wasn't able to get out of the way himself," Inoria said. "He saved my life." She turned to him. "What does that make, six times you've saved my life to only four times I saved yours. I'm getting behind."

Emerius grinned at her through gritted teeth. "You'll just have to try harder, sis."

Rindu came jogging up to the others, looking as if he had just been wandering the meadow, out on a stroll. "Are we all accounted for?" he asked.

"No," Sam said. "There's still—"

I'm here, Skitter sent. *Right behind you.*

Sam looked back and saw the hapaki bounding through the grass toward them. "Oh. Yes, that's all of us. Quite the adventure, eh?"

The party moved out of the burned area, heading south and east again. They traveled for another hour, just to get far enough away so that they weren't smelling smoke anymore. Sam learned the area and they went back to Whitehall early, needing to wash and to tend to Emerius's wound. It was only two hours until sundown in any case, so they wouldn't be losing too much travel time.

*****

Dr. Walt sat heavily into a cushioned chair in his library, looking over at Torim Jet and Palusa Filk.

"These meetings are getting harder and harder to get through," he said. "We don't have much more than a dozen delegates and it's already impossible to get an idea across. It makes me understand why dictators just take power."

"You do not mean that, Dr. Walt," Torim Jet said. "It is difficult, true, but it will be worth the work when the new government is formed and operating."

"Yes, you're right, of course," the old scholar said. "It's just frustrating trying to design a government from the ground up. It makes me respect the group of men who created the country I come from much more. In fact, I am using what they did as a model for the structure we are trying to set up."

"I was glad to see that it was nearly unanimous when deciding if resources will be allocated to rebuild the Zouyim temple," Palusa Filk said. "It is good to know that the Zouyim are still respected."

"Yes, there is that," Dr. Walt said. "If only we could get them to agree to our other proposals as easily."

Torim Jet patted the scholar's shoulder as he walked toward the door. "Do not worry. Things will become easier, more organized. The beginning is always the hardest part. You will see."

"Thank you, Torim. And thank both of you for joining me in the meeting. It's always nice to have someone else to take some of the focus off me when people start to argue."

"It is our honor to help," Torim said. "Individual local governments would often ask the Zouyim for counsel in matters of governance. Perhaps we will have some small part in the structure you will set up for Gythe."

"You definitely will, whether it is a permanent seat on the ruling council or in some other capacity." Dr. Walt rubbed his eyes and sighed. "I will see you in the dining hall in a couple of hours. I have a few things to look up."

The two Zouyim left, passing between the guards that shadowed Dr. Walt's steps every moment of the day. He hardly noticed them anymore. He hoped Sam and the others could clear up this mess with Ayim Rasaad and he could get the new government up and running so he could fade into the background again. He dearly missed being able to spend his time researching the subjects that were near to his heart.

Sighing again, he picked up the book he had last been skimming. He had an hour or two to try to find more information for Sam before going to eat. He would make use of every minute.

40

Nicole followed Max into the depths of the rainforest. She was nervous on so many levels. Most unreasonable was the feeling that she was stepping into danger. That was ridiculous. She had come to know Max, to trust him. Why would he lead her into a trap? For his own racial pride, choosing his people over the strange human? She thrust the thought from her mind. She knew the hapaki to be honorable and fair. They would never do something like that. Max would never do something like that. She hoped she wasn't broadcasting those thoughts. That made her even more nervous.

More than anything else, though, she felt like she was about to make a first impression that was of utmost importance to this community, the hapaki in general, and probably to all of Gythe. The task was hers to succeed in, or fail at miserably. That didn't do a lot for her nerves. She already felt pterodactyls active in her stomach. The feeling was much too big for butterflies.

It will be fine, Max sent to her along with feelings of comfort. *I already explained who you are and what your mission is. They just want to hear it from you. Relax.*

I'm trying, Nicole sent back, *but everyone back at Whitehall is relying on me. Sam is relying on me.*

It will be fine.

She realized her friend had slowed and was stopping. She didn't see anything different about this section of forest compared to where she was before, but it felt different. That was it, she felt comfortable and welcome. It was the community's emotions being sent into her mind. It felt wonderful, as if she had come home after a long trip.

Max, a sending came, awkward as if using the label was something unfamiliar, *has told us of you humans.* That last word seemed to give the sender even more trouble, as if he—or she—had difficulty pronouncing it. She remembered that both she and Max had to become accustomed to communicating. She had learned to send her feelings, but she wasn't as proficient as she should have been to speak with hapaki who didn't understand the humans' differing form of communication. Well, she had to work with what she had.

Nicole was not sure if she was supposed to answer. She remained silent.

The voice sent again. *We would like for you to tell us of your people, of your task. We would like to know about you, as well.*

Nicole took a deep breath to steady her nerves. *To tell you about myself, and my task, I must tell you of another. Of my son, and of his friend Skitter, the first hapaki in memory to communicate with a human…*

For some reason, Nicole sensed a small feeling of contradiction about what she had just said, but she tried not to let it shake her and continued on.

The communication was slow and at times difficult, due mostly to the hapaki getting accustomed to the unfamiliar concepts of words, labels, even gender. They muddled through, however, and when three hours had passed—Nicole guessed it had been that long from how far the sun had traveled—she finished all that she had planned to say. She was exhausted, but no longer nervous.

The feelings filtering in from the hapaki were cordial, if not friendly, as well as polite and respectful. Even more importantly, as she was communicating with them, a number of the furry creatures had stepped out into the open, many coming from openings to dens she had not seen until the movements caught her eye.

She remembered the hapaki community she had seen to the far South, the one that had been destroyed and the hapaki taken away. A lump formed in her throat

Are you well? a hapaki voice came into her mind, one she had not heard before. It must have felt the spike in her sadness.

She swallowed and sent her thoughts back, *I have not told you everything that has happened. We tried to contact another community before yours.* She told them the story, sending images of the hapaki dens torn up and the solar tubes destroyed and was not surprised by the feelings of horror coming back toward her.

We have heard enough, the original hapaki sent. She got the sense that it was the eldest, the most respected hapaki, that was sending thoughts to her. Max had told her that the communities did not have leaders but cooperated with each other to make decisions. Still, the older and wiser hapaki were respected and their opinions given more weight. *Of course we will take part in the government*—that word was sent with difficulty, also—*that is being set up. How could we withhold our vast intelligence from the lesser creatures of Gythe? One of us will go with you as our representative. Is this acceptable to you?*

Nicole smiled, both outwardly and in her sendings. *It is. That would be wonderful. Thank you. We will leave to return to Whitehall at once.*

A small hapaki, smaller than Max ambled up to Nicole and looked up at her. Its coloring was different than the three hapaki she had seen before today, different than the others present. In all honesty, Nicole thought it looked a lot like a skunk, with black fur and a white pattern reminiscent of the odorous mephitids. The only difference was the white banding on the black tail.

Its large amber eyes looked up at her and a voice came into her head. *I will be going with you.* It was the same voice that asked if she was well earlier.

Nicole looked into her eyes—for some reason, this hapaki's sendings fairly screamed femininity, though hapaki were neither male nor female—and sent, *It is my honor to have you accompany me.*

I would like a name—she had less difficulty with labels than the elder had—*too. Like Max got a human name.*

Yes, of course, Nicole sent.

I enjoyed your story of the Hero of Gythe. I want to be called Sam Sharp.

Nicole froze. She wasn't sure how to answer that. She didn't want to insult any of the hapaki, but she could see many problems with the little creature taking her son's name. *Ummm…*she sent.

Is there something wrong? the hapaki sent back. *Is there a problem with using that name?*

*I…that is…*Nicole tried to sort out her words as she sent them to the hapaki. *It's just that the name is used by my son. It will cause confusion if there are two with the same name, especially with how much interaction you will have with others in the government.*

Yes, she said. *I could see that there could be a problem. That is one of the reasons our way is best. With these labels, there is confusion. Still, I like the name for myself. Maybe your son can change his name?*

Nicole looked at Max, who had remained silent since they arrived. He looked at her significantly, but offered no assistance.

I know, Nicole sent. *How about we call you Sammy? It is the name you like, but twice the size. In some eyes, that would make you greater even than my son.*

Sammy, the hapaki tried the name out. *Yes, I think I like that name. I will keep it. Please call me Sammy from now on.*

Thank you, Nicole. I think we will be good friends.
Me too.

The party spent another four days near the hapaki community. The soldiers scouted, repaired tarps and weapons, and generally rested up. Nicole spent much of the time speaking with the hapaki, individually or in small groups. There were twenty-seven of the creatures, ranging from a youngster of five years to an amazing one hundred thirty-three years old for the eldest. He was the one she spent the most time with, telling him of humans and her world and listening as he told her of the history of his race, as passed down from elders who preceded him.

Nicole was fascinated. The hapaki had not always been as they were, according to the stories. Tales from the distant past told of their coming to Gythe.

We do not know where we came from, the elder said. *It was too long ago and the details have been lost. The stories all agree that at one point in time, a human—a man—befriended us. He was somehow able to speak to us, as the hapaki speak, mind-to-mind. With him as a guide, we lived near and cooperated with other humans. Our intellect and powers of reason helped humans to become superior to what they were before meeting us.*

When the humans created great weapons with which to kill each other, my people fled to the forests and to other places to hide. We do not fight. It is barbaric and meaningless. When the weapons created flashes of light and loud noises, destroying the dens of men, we watched sadly from our remote places. Some died because of the poisons the weapons leaked across the world, but some survived. The hapaki decided they would isolate themselves and never be involved with the fighting amongst the humans. So we have been for all this time, many generations. It has been so long that many do not even believe humans exist.

But your story of what happened to the other community you visited shows us that we cannot hide forever. Maybe with our guidance and our example of peacefulness, things will not be so bad this time. We now have not one but two humans who can speak with us. Perhaps there are more. It may be that this time, the hapaki way will win out and Gythe will be at peace for all time.

Nicole nodded, sending feelings of agreement to the aged creature in front of her. *I hope that, too. I'll definitely do everything I can to make sure it happens. So will Sam.*

I know, the elder said. *That is why Sammy will go with you. I have seen your memories and heard your thoughts. We see that you respect us and will look out for our interests.*

Nicole sighed. *I'm afraid it is time to start back toward the fortress. Thank you for speaking with me, and for trusting me to help Sammy speak on your behalf to the government leaders. We will return or send word as soon as we can.*

The elder put his little paw on Nicole's leg as she got up. *I am glad to have met you, Nicole. I would very much like to meet and speak with Sam and Skitter one day. I hope I will live long enough to do so.*

I will make it a priority. Sam will love talking to you.

As she gathered up the others, Nicole looked out over the forest hiding the dens of the hapaki. She was more determined than ever to make sure the new government acted in the interest of the creatures. All she needed to do was to get back to the fortress alive and convince everyone that what she said was actually from the hapaki and that she wasn't making it up on her own. Suddenly, the thought of pirates attacking in the night didn't seem such a trial.

41

The party had dragged themselves from the teleport point up to their rooms, earning strange looks from all those they passed. Sam knew that they probably looked as if they had been pulled through a keyhole. Backwards.

"Sam," Dr. Walt said as he spotted them in the halls, sniffing, "why do you smell like smoke? Was there trouble?"

Sam nodded numbly and gave Dr. Walt the barest of summaries of their day. "If you don't mind, Dr. Walt," Sam said, "I'd really like to take a bath and get into some clean clothes. Maybe we can talk more about it at dinner."

"Oh, of course, of course," Dr. Walt responded. "I'm sorry to be so rude. Yes, by all means, clean up. I will talk with you later. I'm glad that you are uninjured. I was heading to the dining hall now, but I will wait another hour so we can eat together. There is more research I can do in the meantime."

Dinner was, as always, a time for everyone to catch up on what the others were doing. Dr. Walt had not found anything important to report, though he summarized the meeting earlier that day with the delegates of the new government. Sam gave a slightly more detailed account of the day he had. Danaba Kemp complained that he was not building the army nearly fast enough to suit him. It was nice, Sam thought, to have these informal meetings over their meal. The subjects were serious, but the entire thing made him think of a family getting together to eat. He just wished his mother was there with them.

The next morning, everyone was subdued as they gathered together just before sunrise to head out for another day of traveling. Everyone, that is, except Rindu, who seemed perpetually to be the same stoic, reserved monk. Sam had to smile inwardly at that, though he couldn't quite manage an external smile. He could always count on Rindu to be constant.

The first days after their ambush were uneventful. They continued onward to the southeast, through ever more verdant territory. It was a mindless sort of travel, out on the trail before the sun came up, a few breaks during the day, and then going back to Whitehall at night. Inoria continued to teach Sam about herbs and her hunting and tracking trades. The subjects fascinated Sam.

The day dawned on the twentieth day of their journey to Rasaad's fortress. The terrain was getting mountainous again, and the trees were thick. There were oak, walnut, even some elm trees. Inoria pointed them out as they traveled, drilling Sam on the ways to identify each.

"You know," Sam said to Inoria, "it's kind of a shame."

"What's that?"

"That I don't really have a reason to use the things you are teaching me about hunting and survival. With my teleportation abilities, there is really no need for me to know it, other than that I love learning about it."

Inoria considered for a moment. "I see your point. The herblore is still useful, though. As for the other information, maybe it will be more important than you think. We can never know what we will need, so the best thing is to prepare for any eventuality. My father always used to tell us that."

"I can see the wisdom in that. I've always believed in learning everything I can. I can't thank you enough for teaching me all this. Thank you."

"You're welcome, Sam. It's nice to have a good student like you."

She paused for a moment, thoughtful. "It should be less than a week now to the fortress," she said, "according to what Lahim has told us. It's killing me that we've been traveling this whole time while Tingai could have been continuing his experiments."

"I know what you mean," Sam said. "Unfortunately, this is as fast as we can go. At least, it's as fast as we can go without hurting the rakkeben and Oro. We're doing all we can."

"I know, Sam," she said. "I'm just anxious. It's a long time to leave my little brother in the hands of that monster."

*****

The party wound their way into heavier forest, the lighting dim. It was cold out of the direct sunlight and Nalia felt the prickles of goose bumps on her skin. The winters were very cold at Marybador, but it had been so long since she had lived there, she was afraid she had grown weak.

She looked over at Sam, who seemed to be having more trouble with the cold than her. He was breathing on his hands—even though he was wearing gloves he had brought from Telani—and letting his breath bounce back on his face to warm it. He was wearing one of those snug caps on his head, a "beanie," that he said kept his head and ears warm. Perhaps she should wear the one he had given her. Her ears did feel cold right now.

Cleave suddenly stopped and pricked his ears up. Nalia saw Shonyb and Zumra, Rindu's rakkeben, do the same.

Zumra was humming softly in the way he did when on alert. Nalia patted her rakkeban's head. "What is it, Cleave?" she asked. "Is there something ahead?"

An ear-splitting shriek rushed through the forest, startling birds from the trees. Nalia saw a family of squirrels make their way to the safety of their den.

"What was that?" Sam asked, looking around for the source of the sound. He had *Ahimiro* at the ready, held out in front of him in a guard position. Nalia was proud of him for that. A year and a half ago, he may have panicked in such a situation, but now he was ready for danger.

"It came from that way," Inoria said, pointing off to the southeast, the direction they had been heading. She had her bow out, and was pulling an arrow from her quiver. Emerius already had one nocked.

Rindu merely patted Zumra's head and turned those intense eyes of his toward the sound. "Let us go investigate. Be wary of your surroundings. Things may not be what they seem."

They dismounted to walk toward the sound, which had continued in a long, keening scream of something in pain. Skitter remained on his perch, strapped tightly to Shonyb. Sam had that blank look on his face, the one he wore when speaking to the hapaki mind-to-mind.

As they moved, they spread out, watching not only the area from where the sound was coming, but also all around them. They were wary since the ambush two weeks before and were determined not to be trapped again.

The sound became louder as there were less trees between them and the source. Nalia looked at Sam to her right, Rindu to her left, and the twins barely visible further out, one on each side. The rakkeben and Oro were behind them, arrayed in what looked to be defensive positions, ensuring they were not being herded into another trap.

Nalia made it through the last of the trees separating them from the sound and she finally saw what was making the noise. In between two large oak trees, something was thrashing and screaming. It seemed that it had one of its limbs caught in a vicious-looking trap made of metal with teeth that had snapped shut. The creature was bleeding and trying to pry open the jaws of the trap. It was not having any success.

At first, Nalia thought that it was a person, but looking more closely, she saw that though it was humanoid, there were things that were different about it. It had no hair, but instead had some type of scales covering its body, as if it was a snake in the form of a man. Its face, still recognizable, had a large, bulbous nose and big ears, making it look incongruous. Even from twenty feet, Nalia could see the blue of its eyes shining in fear and pain.

"Fren?" Inoria said. "Fren Tussel? Is that you?"

The creature stopped screaming for a moment and looked to Inoria. A look of sadness flickered across its face and then disappeared. It started screaming and thrashing again, trying to get to her. Nalia had no doubt it would tear its own leg off to get to Inoria to rip her limb from limb.

The twang of a bow sounded much too loudly in the forest air. Nalia projected her senses, expecting a missile to be coming at her. But it was not directed toward the party. The screaming abruptly ended and Nalia saw that the point of an arrow had sprouted from the back of creature's head, having come all the way through from the front. Emerius stood on the other side of what was once human, bow hanging from his limp hand, a look of sorrow and disgust on his face.

"Oh, Em," Inoria said. "I know it was necessary, but I'm sorry it had to be you."

They all moved slowly toward the creature's corpse, the body of what was once a villager of Blackwood. Wary still, they scanned the surroundings, looking for traps and trip wires. There were none.

When they reached the body, they all looked at each other and then at the mutated thing that had finally found peace.

"He was one of the people from your village?" Sam asked.

"Yes," was all Inoria said. She was kneeling alongside the fallen monster, using some kind of tool she carried to pry open the trap, releasing its leg.

"I'm sorry," Sam said.

There was silence.

After a moment, Emerius spoke, "Death is better than to live like that, half man, half lizard. He would have thanked me for it. Fren was always doing things for others. He was one of the kindest men I have ever known. To turn him into this…this…monster! I have special plans for Tingai. He will not die so quickly as my friend here. There will be no friends to end his suffering too soon." He turned to Oro, checking his paws, obviously just so he would have something to keep him busy.

Nalia lowered her gaze to the ground. Images of her sisters, all so vital and beautiful, passed in front of her vision. She saw them as they were killed, one by one or several at a time, whittled down in front of her when they attacked the Gray Man and his forces. The memories made her suck in a sharp breath and clench her fists. Watching them die was bad enough; it would have been worse if she had been required to do it herself. She wanted to say something to make the twins feel better, but could not think of what she could say. Instead, she remained silent.

"Be on your guard," Rindu said. "There is something coming." Nalia noticed the rakkeben bristling just as Rindu spoke.

Then Nalia sensed it, too. There were a number of "somethings" coming at them, very fast. Mere seconds later, the sound of the plants around them being trampled by many feet filled the air. She drew her shrapezi and readied herself. She saw Sam ready *Ahimiro* as well. The twins gave each other a look and then turned outward, drawing arrows from their quivers.

They didn't have to wait long.

At least two dozen creatures of all shapes and sizes were descending upon them. Some ran on two legs, some on four, but they all had one thing in common: in their eyes was a bloodlust Nalia had seen before. It was the same hungry look the riati mutants had given her when she was injured and trying to make her way home from the Gray Fortress all those years ago. Nothing short of death would stop these creatures.

Nalia sought her center and calmed herself, taking in a deep breath. The song of battle was strong and she found her body responding to it, increasing her blood flow, dilating her eyes, putting a keener edge on her fighting skills. When the first of the mutant creatures reached her, she was ready.

Bowstrings twanged and creatures screamed as arrows pierced them. There were four in the forefront that came for her: three human-sized and one hapaki-sized. The larger of the creatures looked like mixtures of men and animals. Two of them had fur all over their bodies and ran on all fours while the other ran upright and seemed to have small feathers on different parts of its form. The smaller creature, still looking like a hapaki but slightly larger, had exaggerated claws and teeth that appeared to be very sharp.

The furry creatures leapt before the others could make it to her. She ducked, allowing one of them to pass harmlessly over her, but the other she deflected with her shrapezi, redirecting its force away from her while slicing at the creature's front paws. It yowled as it landed and then its right leg collapsed from the injury she had inflicted. Its face plowed into the forest floor and it tumbled into a heap, tripping up two more creatures that were going toward Sam.

The bird-human and hapaki reached her as she spun toward them. The smaller slashed at her with its claws and the larger struck out with blinding speed with its talons, much like a striking snake. Nalia evaded the hapaki's claws and parried the other's hands with her blades, thinking the razor edges of the shrapezi would do some damage in addition to keeping them from her. She was wrong.

When her blades struck the bird creature's arms, there was a ringing sound like steel striking bone or rock. It didn't seem to do any damage to the creature's arms or hands; it just kept striking at her. She slipped to the left, moving under a strike and to the side of the other hand. It found a target in a branch near Nalia's head and there was a ripping, breaking sound as a chunk of the wood exploded outward. She knew she didn't want to get hit by one of those strikes.

Nalia spun around a tree and faced her opponents again. The furry creatures had rejoined the fray, though the one with the damaged front legs did not look to be too dangerous a foe. She knew she had to end this soon or she would be overwhelmed. Even now, other creatures were arriving.

She feinted toward the bird creature, then stepped back quickly, just in time for its renewed strikes to connect with the unharmed furry creature. It screamed as the hand of its fellow tore a chunk from its side. Pivoting while dodging the hapaki creature's claws, she brought both shrapezi down as hard as she could onto one of her feathered foe's arms. The vibrations felt like she had struck stone, but the razor edge of the fine steel cut through the arm and separated its hand.

Taking advantage of the distraction, Nalia squatted as she spun, throwing out the blades of her swords, slicing a furrow in the bird creature's belly with one sword, then deepening it with the other, causing its entrails to spill out. As she came up from the spin and blocked the hapaki's claws, she could feel her hands vibrate from the contact with the toughened skin.

The two furry creatures were coming at her again, but the toughest opponent was bleeding its life out a few feet away, so now she could focus on them. One leaped at her while the other, the one with injured legs, tried to bite her with a face that was too human for comfort. She sliced the leaper open with the spikes on both shrapezi as it came toward her. Then, spinning, she delivered a double downward strike with her blades, angling them diagonally from each side and causing the other mutant's head to fall from its twitching body.

She turned and saw the hapaki in mid-air coming at her. Rotating, she connected with a spin kick to intercept and launch the creature several feet. It hit a tree and started sliding down the trunk. Before it could do anything else, she impaled it with both hooks and ripped outward, almost tearing its body completely apart.

Nalia looked over at Sam, who was fighting with three human-shaped mutants. He seemed to be doing well, so she left him to it. There was a mass of creatures surrounding the twins, too many for them to shoot at once. She headed there to help.

She didn't encounter any more of the tough-skinned bird mutants, though she did fight two humanoid creatures with scales like an alligator. Still, she had things well under control by the time Sam came up next to her to help with the remaining foes. When she looked over at her father, she could barely see him for the bodies of mutant creatures around him. She frowned. *Sure, I had the misfortune to go against "stone skin," causing me to win less battles.* She recognized the thought as petty and competitive as soon as it entered her mind and she immediately regretted it.

When all the attackers were finally dead, they counted the bodies. There were thirty-two. Thirty-two villagers and hapaki who had been changed into mutant creatures. It made Nalia's blood burn like fire.

The twins and Skitter were walking among the dead. Inoria was crying and Emerius had a look of anger on his face. Skitter seemed to be wandering aimlessly, stopping to look at what once was a hapaki of the destroyed community. She saw the little creature look up to Sam, his face twisted in sorrow and confusion.

Sam, on the other hand, wore none of these expressions. He was staring toward the southeast, his eyes unfocused. His teeth were clenched and his mouth was a thin line. She had never seen him look like that. It scared her.

"Sam," she said, coming up to him and touching his arm. "Sam, are you well?"

He turned and aimed that gaze at her. His eyes were slate gray and burned from behind as if his skull was full of fire. Involuntarily, she tensed to defend herself.

His eyes lost a little bit of their intensity, softening from diamond to the finest steel, as he noticed her. Then his orbs became liquid and his gaze dropped, shoulders slumping. "Nal," he whispered, "how can we stop this? Killing is one thing but this," he pointed to the corpses lying nearby, "this is unnatural."

"I know, Sam," she said, "I know." She wrapped him in a hug and they stood there, silent, for a full minute.

Sam sniffed, then gently pulled away from her. He straightened. "Rindu," he said, "can you do something with the *rohw*, create a pit or something? At least we can bury them in a mass grave, if nothing else, to keep scavengers from picking over their bodies. Burning them in a pyre would be too dangerous in the forest."

"I can do such a thing, Sam," Rindu said sadly. "Though it would be honorable to ask Skitter and the twins if they would object. There are different customs involving death on Gythe and I would not wish to insult theirs."

"Of course," Sam said. "Thank you."

He walked away from Nalia and questioned the twins. Nalia saw Emerius nod once and Inoria burst into tears while nodding her head vigorously. She hugged Sam, thanking him.

Sam then turned to where Skitter was sitting quietly next to one of the hapaki creatures. He got the blank look on his face. A few seconds later, Sam nodded and patted the hapaki on the head, face again full of emotion.

"Okay, Rindu, if you will," Sam said, pointing to a location in between trees that seemed large enough to suffice. "We'll drag the bodies to the pit you make and try to give these creatures who used to be our friends a respectful burial."

It was hard work dragging and carrying the bodies to the pit Rindu had made, but they did it. He had vibrated a large chunk of the soil, phasing it out. Nalia wondered if that dirt was now in Telani, or somewhere else.

After all the bodies were placed in the pit, Rindu changed the vibration of the soil in a slightly different way than he had to make it go away. He phased it in slowly, a little at a time, at a height ten feet above where it had been, so that it rained down and covered the pit and the bodies.

Sam sat nearby on a fallen tree that one of the larger creatures had broken in a charge. He looked at Emerius. "Do you want to say anything?" he asked. "Most of the victims were from your village."

The big man nodded slowly and stood. The rest of them gathered at the edge of the mound of dirt. "I'm not good with words or speeches," Emerius said. "but something needs to be said. You all deserve at least that much.

"We're sorry we couldn't have been faster, that we couldn't have been better. We're sorry that we left you to the devices of that monster Tingai. For those of you from my village, I grew up with many of you and feel like you were all my family. For the hapaki, I have come to know that yours is a kind, gentle people, one that doesn't deserve this kind of end. I know that in the end, if you would have had a choice, you all would have chosen death rather than life as the monstrous creatures you were made into.

"Tingai will pay for this. Not only that, but we will make sure that he will never again be able to do this to any others. We will track him down and we will destroy him and all his research so that no other can ever rise in his place. And we will stop Ayim Rasaad, who has enabled scum like Tingai to do the horrible things they do. Rest now, and be assured that your sacrifice will not have gone unnoticed. If there are any left, even one, from Blackwood or the hapaki community, we will rescue them. We swear this to you."

Emerius dipped his head as Inoria hugged him and cried softly into his chest. Nalia saw that the big hunter had tears of his own in his eyes.

Everyone was silent for a few minutes, each wrapped up in their own thoughts. Finally, Sam spoke. "I believe there is still some daylight left today. I don't know about you," he said, looking right at Emerius, "but I for one would like to spend it getting nearer to Tingai and Rasaad so we can 'discuss' with them what happened here today."

Emerius looked at Sam, green eyes meeting slate gray. A small, wicked smile crept on to his face. "Hells yes," he said, and headed toward Oro.

42

The way he saw it, Emerius Dinn had always been strong: physically, mentally, and in every other way. He had always believed himself impervious to the emotions that others felt. After all, heroes weren't affected by such petty things as emotions, right? As he sat in his room at Whitehall, having just come back from the battle with the mutant creatures that were once his friends, he wasn't so sure.

The scar on his arm where he had been cut by that arrow in the first ambush itched. He went to scratch it but heard his mother's voice, "Em, don't scratch at your scabs or they will never heal." His hand dropped to his lap.

Growing up, Emerius had always been focused, diligent in his training. Whenever his father taught him and his sister new things, he hungrily snapped it up, knowing that only by putting his whole mind, heart, and body into it would he become great. Great like Suka Templar, his hero and idol.

In an age where there were heroes everywhere, Suka was the most distinguished. Other heroes had special powers. Some could use energy like the Zouyim, some had technology that gave them an edge, some had the gift of seeing that was so refined that they knew when and how attacks would come and so could manipulate events so that they were always victorious.

Suka Templar had none of these things. His was the power of a will so strong that he could train for days at a time without sleep and thereby refine his fighting skills to such a level that he was unbeatable. His was the power of such keen intellect that he could crack any puzzle and could be inventive on the fly. Simply stated, Suka Templar had the perfect combination of mind and body. And he used it, but not for his own gain or for some ruler who had hired him. He used all his skills and abilities on behalf of the common people. He was unblemished, incorruptible, and supreme.

Emerius remembered the first tale he heard of the ancient hero. He and his sister were only six years old. Their father had sat them down before bed to tell them a story.

"I'm going to tell you about the greatest of heroes, of Suka Templar, and how he defeated the deadly Seven of Sondria." Emerius remembered his excitement. He loved it when his father told him stories, but he especially loved stories about heroes.

"Suka Templar was born to a poor farming family and, as such, no one really expected anything more from him than that he would become a hardworking farmer, raising a family and carrying on as generations of his family had done before.

"But that could not be further from the truth, for Suka had a special gift, a talent that would make him great. Now, his talent was not all that uncommon. Others had the same gift as Suka, but with him, it was merely a catalyst to greater things.

"You see, Suka was a fast learner and had a keen mind. More importantly, though, he had a willpower that was as strong as stone, as powerful as a waterfall. Armed with this, he was able to utilize his other talents.

"He would often search for riddles and mysteries when he was a child. Once he set himself on the path to knowing a thing, he would not stop until he fully understood it. So it was the first time he picked up a bow, and a sword, and his famous throwing knives. He wanted more than just to be proficient, more than to be skilled. He wanted to know why things happened the way that they did. He wanted to know why an arrow flew straight, or why it didn't when one of the fletchings was damaged. He made a study of these things and from his study grew understanding."

Their father had looked at the twins then, to make sure they understood. He tapped his temple with his finger. "Suka's greatest weapon was his ability to think, and then to use his tremendous will to prepare for any situation.

"When he was only sixteen, Suka had already left his family's farm, having already done great deeds by this point. He was getting a reputation as a hero and wanted to go where he could do the most good. His family, supportive and proud of what he had already accomplished, said their fond goodbyes and told him that he would always have a place with them, when he grew tired of being a hero.

"As he was passing through the area known as Sondria—it was the name of a large city as well as the surrounding lands—he met a family on the road. They were bedraggled and despondent, carrying only a few ratty personal possessions.

"'We are fleeing to the South,' they told him when he asked. 'The seven roam the land and take sport in snatching our young women, and sometimes young men, for their own pleasure.'

"Suka could not believe what he was hearing. 'Are there no lords or ministers to protect common folk?' he asked the man.

"'No,' the man said sadly, 'for the seven *are* the local lords.'

"Suka's surprise was palpable, as was his anger. He swore to end this farce. 'Lords should protect the smallfolk,' he said to the man. 'I will drive them from the land.'

"The man had laughed at this sixteen-year-old boy. 'Better if you turn around and go back from where you came,' he told Suka. 'Many strong heroes have tried to defeat even one or two of the seven. Their corpses are all rotting in the sun.'

"Suka didn't answer for a moment, then he simply said, 'Keep your ears open, old man. In a week's time, listen for the tale of the end of the Seven at the hands of Suka Templar.' With that, he continued on the road, already preparing himself mentally for his next challenge.

"It was soon clear that the entire countryside was in fear of the Seven. Most people would not even talk to Suka to give him information. Those who did, normally ones who were fleeing, all said the same thing: the Seven were invincible and the only thing to do was to escape. It made a rage build in Suka's heart that he could hardly contain.

"But Suka Templar was not brash, though he was young. He paid an old peasant man a month's wages to trade cloaks with him, his fine cloak that had been a gift from wealthy man Suka had saved for the threadbare cloak of a poverty-stricken commoner. The cloak was too large for him, but that worked to his advantage, helping to conceal his clothes and weapons. Armed with this simple disguise, the young hero made his way to the city of Sondria, determined to obtain information he could use to defeat the Seven.

"'I tell ya, Flin,' a toothless, skinny beggar said to another, 'I saw it. The arrow went clean through his throat. He was gurgling and dropped to the ground. He was dead. Couldn't have survived that. Well, after the other three killed the hero, they drug the body back to their mansion. The next day, I seen him riding along with the others, like nothing had ever happened. I tell ya, it's the worst kind of magic. Them Seven can't be killed. 'Least, they can't be killed permanent-like.'

"Suka heard the exchange and began to think. He spent some time in one of the local taverns, shocked by how quiet and reserved it was. It was as if all the people were just waiting for an executioner's ax. By nightfall, he knew what he must do.

"A few years earlier, he had observed a thief at his work. Fascinated, he followed the man, watching his every movement, analyzing why he did things the way he did. When the burglar had set his hands on what he meant to steal, Suka had stopped him. He told him that for the lesson he had provided, he would let the man go, but only if he swore never to steal again. When the thief heard the name of the one he was talking to, he quickly swore his oath and was not seen in the area after that. The young hero hoped he had made good on his promise and not just moved to another location. Regardless, with a few more days of thinking and a few days of practicing, Suka had developed the skill to move quietly and to infiltrate places he was not supposed to be. Those skills served him well that night in Sondria.

"He snuck into the mansion and listened as servants spoke of a room that was forbidden to all but the Seven. He was soon outside the room, trying to see in the window, but he could not. He entered the mansion through the room just beside it and heard two men talking.

"'I'm bored with this chattel,' one said. 'I want livelier sport. The merchant's daughter, now there is a game I'd like to play.' The other man responded in a deeper voice, 'We have agreements with the merchant. His family is off-limits. Find your fun somewhere else. Go to another town, why don't you.'

"Suka listened carefully. He knew that the things about which a man speaks can be exploited as weaknesses. 'You know as well as I that it's not safe to go too far from the

Giswych. With our reputation, some hero will gather a group of men and kill me. I'll be too far from it to be brought back in time to live again. Besides, outside the circle of its influence, the magic doesn't work. I'll be almost as weak as you.' The man laughed, but the other did not. 'Very funny,' the deeper voice said.

"That was it, the information Suka Templar needed. He stealthily left the mansion grounds and took a room at a local inn. The next day, he would put his plan into action.

"In the morning, Suka was up before the sunrise. He gathered his weapons and positioned himself near the front of the mansion. He waited. A few hours later, four of the Seven rode out of the stables on their manu. From his gathering of information, Suka knew who they were and, more importantly, knew who were still in the mansion. After the four were well away, he snuck back into the home, evading any eyes that might have spotted him.

"Inside, he encountered one of the remaining three lords at the base of the grand staircase. He shot three arrows in the space of a heartbeat, but was surprised when the man dodged two completely and was only clipped by the third. The man yelled for his companions and ran at Suka.

"Thinking quickly, he fired three more arrows, but this time, he fired not at where the man was, but at where he would be. Predicting how he would dodge, the first arrow made him move to the left slightly, the second made him duck low, but the third struck him in the eye as he evaded the others. The first of the Seven was dead. At least for the time being.

"The other two came rushing down the stairs, swords in their hands. Seeing their friend with an arrow in his eye, their faces twisted into rage and they yelled, swinging wildly. Once more, Suka, remaining calm in the heart of battle, fired three arrows. The first two, again, maneuvered one of the attackers so that the third struck home, this time directly in the center of his throat. There was only one left, but he was too close for arrows now.

"Suka threw his bow at the man, who dodged it easily but was delayed enough so that Suka could throw four of his knives. This man, learning the lesson from the other two, didn't dodge in the way Suka had expected. He purposely allowed one of the knives to strike him a glancing blow so that he would not be where the other knives would get him. He was now in range to cut Suka down.

"There was not enough time to draw his sword, so instead Suka drew his two long knives and sliced in one fluid motion. The man parried one with his sword and twisted to evade the other. Then, suddenly, the man's mouth grew wide in surprise and he dropped his sword. Looking down, he saw the half foot of steel strapped to Suka's knee, covered in the man's own blood. The Seven were extraordinary fighters, with strength and speed beyond that of mortal men, but they had the same flaw as most men: they only expected what was normal. Suka had two hands, so the attacker believed he would only have to deal with two weapons. As he slid to the floor, dying, perhaps he realized his error in thinking.

"Suka Templar picked up his bow and rushed upstairs. He did not doubt that the other four knew of the deaths of their companions and would be on their way back. He must finish this before they did.

"When he got to the door he kicked precisely at the weakest point and watched as the wood splintered and fell into the room. There, sitting on a table covered in silk, was a small statue made of crystal. It was in the form of some type of flying snake, with a wise face and long fangs filling its open mouth. It was beautiful and Suka thought for a moment to take it for himself, but he fought the urge to do so. Instead, he picked it up and threw it down to the floor as hard as he could.

"As the statue shattered, a blinding light was released. It dissipated and Suka watched as the shards melted into puddles, then evaporated into smoke and disappeared.

"He was leaving the house when the other four returned. They jumped off their mounts and rushed at him, intent on killing him. Suka calmly let fly with four arrows, faster than the eye could follow, and all four men dropped dead before the door to the mansion. They had not realized that their source of power had been destroyed and that they could not move faster than an arrow any longer.

"Suka let the servants of the household spread the news of the defeat of their masters. He calmly went about collecting his arrows and knives, cleaning them on the clothing of the Seven, before strolling to the town for a drink.

"When the people of Sondria found out about the death of the Seven, they erected a statue of Suka Templar and his legend continued to grow. As word spread, those who had fled returned and Sondria became once again a thriving community."

Emerius had been so excited to hear the story. Later, his father had told him other stories about Suka Templar, and each one made Emerius dream of the time when he would finally become a hero himself. His awe and reverence for the man had only grown as Emerius did, and he had dedicated his life to being like his idol.

Looking at his reflection in the mirror in his room, the hunter admitted to himself that he had not done a good job. At every turn, he had been foiled. Heroes in stories never had to deal with pacing themselves, racing against foes who could go from one place to another in the blink of an eye. They found ways around obstacles, so why couldn't he? What would his father think of him? He hadn't even been able to save Ancha. Not yet, anyway.

He shook his head. That was what distinguished little boys with dreams from true heroes: when they were beaten down and all looked lost, they would pick themselves up and attack again. They would be victorious even though it looked like there was no way it could be so. There had to be a way. He would find it. If Suka Templar could do it, then so could he.

43

Emerius was sitting on a bench petting Oro's head when the others arrived at the teleport point.

"Em," Inoria said, "we didn't see you at breakfast. Are you all right?"

"I'm fine," he lied. "I grabbed something from the kitchen and came down to see Oro. I'm not much in the mood for people."

His sister understood. Of the two of them, she was always the one who did the talking, the negotiations. She loved people, had a heart disposed to care about others. He cared, too, but in a different way. He cared about "people," whereas she cared about each individual person. He wanted to save the world while she just wanted to help one man or woman at a time. It worked for them. She could be the talker and he could be the aloof hero. He wondered which Suka Templar was.

"We're only a few days from Rasaad's headquarters, according to Lahim Chode's information," Sam said. "Is everyone ready?"

They were, so Sam sat on the ground as he always did, breathed a lot, and then they were off, appearing right where they had left off the night before. That was something, the teleporting. Emerius had grown used to it, but if he stopped to think, he realized just how amazing it was. If they had to cover the same distance without it, it would take them much longer. They would have to stop to forage and hunt, would have to carry much more weight in supplies, which would slow them down, and they would probably be more tired. When he thought of it that way, he realized that they were probably making more progress by stopping and resting at the fortress each night than they would if they had tried to push straight through. Still, it wasn't fast enough.

As if reading his mind, Sam said, "Since we're so close, maybe we can squeeze a couple more hours of travel each day. If the rakkeben and Oro seem to be strong enough, we should probably continue to travel into the dark each night." They had come upon a road the day before, one they were sure went straight to Gutu. Travel was fast and safe—at least as far as road hazards like holes and roots were concerned—so they could easily move at night at almost the same speed as during the daytime.

Emerius felt a smile crease his face as he looked at Sam. Sam nodded, showed him a small smile of his own, and continued getting his wolf ready for the day's ride. Okay, maybe this green boy wasn't such a bad guy after all.

The next two and a half days went quickly. Emerius's mind wandered as they made their way toward Gutu, more south than east now. He thought of what they would do when they got there. The fortress would no doubt be bottled up tight, with walls and fortifications as well as soldiers to keep them out. He had some ideas, but didn't want to share them just yet.

They approached Gutu in the middle of the morning. The sky was overcast, threatening to snow. Heated up from travel, Emerius didn't even feel it. His cloak was open and flapping as Oro slowed his run to a walk and then stopped altogether.

The fortress was unlike anything Emerius had ever seen. True, he hadn't seen that many castles and fortifications, but those he did see had a sort of symmetry to them. They were built in the same basic shape as homes or other buildings, but much larger and with walls around them. Gutu was definitely not like that. It seemed all wrong, like it shouldn't even be able to hold its own weight.

The walls were the most normal thing about the whole place, but even those were strange, with edges and points at random locations. The buildings looked like they had grown out of the ground like some kind of large thorn bush, all prickly and pointy. Emerius was familiar with building and design. After all, his father trained him in engineering and science. Probably because of that, it looked all the more shocking.

Inoria nudged him with her elbow. When he looked at her, she was blinking. "Em, are you seeing what I'm seeing? Is such a building possible?"

"I'm seeing it, sis," he said. "I don't know why anyone would build something so awkward. It's like the opposite of smoothly flowing lines."

"I think that's the point," Sam said. "The power that Rasaad uses isn't the *rohw*, which is all about harmony and flow. Maybe her power is based on jagged lines and awkward intervals."

They were all motionless, looking at the structures in front of them.

"Well," Emerius said. "We should probably scout it so we can figure out how to get in. In and I will go do that while you move off into the trees so no one on the road will be able to see you." He pointed to a section of the surrounding forest. "Go over there. We'll come get you after we take a look around. Oro, go with them."

The big bear looked up at his name and then dropped his nose to the ground, emitting a slight whining noise.

"Don't whine at me," Emerius said. "It'll only be for a

little while. You can't move quietly enough. You'll give us away." He patted the bear's head and he and Inoria went into the trees.

It felt good moving through the trees again. He had been riding Oro on roads or paths for too long, just trying to get here. He belonged right where he was, slipping through the trees without a trace. Just him and Inoria, like it had always been. He'd be glad when all of this was done and they could take Ancha back home. And the other villagers from Blackwood, too, of course. All of them. The ones who hadn't been turned into monsters. It would be a lot of work to rebuild their home, but he wasn't afraid of hard work.

They neared the edge of the trees and got a closer look at the walls. They were probably only thirty feet tall and it seemed that there were plenty of handholds to be had. Taking a closer look, though, Emerius changed his mind. The walls looked to be made from a hard, black type of crystal. Obsidian? If it was, climbing would be more difficult than it appeared. With the sharp angles, obsidian could slice skin easily. Gloves may work, but they would also compromise dexterity. He'd have to think about it.

Along the top of the walls, there seemed to be a walkway on which guards could move. Judging from how much of the bodies he saw of those moving about, the pointed tops of the wall probably protruded four feet or so above the walkway. As Emerius watched and timed the guards, he saw that there was a definite rotation. If someone could get up to the wall, climb it, and get over it within a minute and forty seconds, they may be successful in infiltrating the fortress. That was asking a lot.

There didn't seem to be any doors along the base of the walls, other than the main gate. It was a typical feature of walls and Emerius wasn't surprised. He did wonder if there were hidden doors, but he wasn't going to risk being seen now to go looking for them.

He and Inoria studied the walls, gates, and the roving

guards for a few minutes more and then quietly slipped back into deeper forest, toward the others.

When they arrived, Oro was sitting, head cradled in his paws, waiting patiently. "Good boy," Emerius said to him, patting his head as he passed. Sam was doing some kind of exercise with Rindu, sitting in the cross-legged position again, knees almost touching the Zouy's, who sat with the same posture. Nalia and Skitter were over by the rakkeben.

"Okay, let's go," Emerius said. "We found an area we can use to stage our attack. It's close enough to the wall so we don't have to travel far but deep enough into the trees so that we don't have to worry about being seen."

Everyone followed the twins back to the place they had found. Emerius cringed every time he heard Oro and Sam make a noise. The rakkeben moved quietly and Nalia and Rindu made no sound at all. He knew it was just his nerves. Small animals in the forest made sounds, and the guards, even if they could hear them, would think they were squirrels or a rabbit or something like that. Still, it grated on him.

No sooner had they put their gear down than they heard a commotion of something, or several somethings, rushing through the foliage. Emerius didn't like that sound. It sounded just like...

"It's more of the creatures," he said, nocking an arrow and raising his bow. "Here we go again."

He was right. Bushes were trampled and their attackers were soon visible. It was a mixture of different creatures, like before. The one thing that was the same was the hungry, hateful look in the eyes of the monsters attacking them.

Emerius set about killing as many as he could. He had determined, from his other encounters with the mutated creatures, that the only sure way to kill them was to put an arrow in their eye. No matter the armor plating or other defenses each particular creature might have, their eyes were vulnerable. Though the mutants had different forms, their bodies twisted beyond what nature would normally allow, they all still had brains that regulated their functions. Putting an arrow into the brain—through the eye—worked every time.

It was a good thing he could hit an acorn from a hundred feet. He pretended that was what he was doing. He was shooting acorns, not killing those who used to be his neighbors.

Emerius was pulling arrows from his quiver, nocking them, drawing them to his cheek, and loosing them at a rate of three or four a second. At this pace, he would empty his quiver before he ran out of foes and have to fight these monsters with his long knives. He hoped they ran out of mutants before he ran out of arrows.

There was a break in the flood of creatures coming toward him and he took the opportunity to quickly look around. Inoria was five feet away, her quiver half empty but not looking to be in any distress. Rindu and Nalia were cutting through their attackers with a cool efficiency even Emerius found chilling. Sam, on the other hand, was being tested. There were no less than seven slavering creatures coming at him at once. He was doing a good job fending them off, but one mistake would end him.

Emerius whistled shrilly and Inoria's head snapped to her brother. He jerked his own head toward Sam while he nocked an arrow. A second later, four arrows were flying and in another second, half of Sam's attackers had dropped to the ground, dead. Sam looked over at the twins, nodded his thanks, and proceeded to whittle down the remaining opponents.

In the meantime, another rush of the creatures had noticed the twins. Emerius shrugged his shoulders. Fourteen arrows left, by the weight of his quiver. He had to make them count. He settled back into the calm he always maintained when shooting and carried on with business.

The battle was winding down. There were bodies of

mutants lying all around them, choking the spaces between the trees. The rush had stopped; it seemed as if they had taken care of the bulk of the force being sent against them. Emerius shot his last arrow into what looked to be a mixture between a person and a pantor. The projectile struck exactly where it was needed, in the creature's eye, but it was—literally—mindlessly still charging at him. He drew his long knives, blades as long as his forearms, sidestepped the creature's lunge, and tore its throat out as it passed. The monster slid to a halt, trying desperately to rise again, but failing.

Then, a small, red-haired creature came charging at him. It was very fast, running and bounding off trees and the bodies of its fellows. Emerius planted his feet, held his blood-stained knives in front of him, and prepared to defend himself.

He heard the twang of a bowstring and the creature twisted in mid-air, in the middle of a jump, rolled, righted itself, and came on again, arrow protruding from its shoulder. There were two more of the distinct bow sounds, almost at the same time, and the attacker moved, narrowly dodging one arrow, only to be struck by a perfectly-aimed shot into its eye. It slid, coming to rest at Emerius's feet.

"Just like Suka Templar and the Seven," Inoria laughed. She came up to him, no other mutated creature around them. The others were finishing off the last of their attackers.

Emerius looked down at the creature Inoria had just killed. It was smaller than most of the others, not quite man-sized, but bigger than a hapaki. It was hard to tell with the way it was elongated, no doubt because of the influence of animal parts. Its slight build and red hair was different than the other mutants they faced.

Inoria kneeled and turned its head so that she could see its face more clearly, see the eye that didn't have an arrow jutting out of it.

She gasped.

"Ancha?" she cried. "Ancha?"

The creature blinked at her and she watched as the remaining intact eye focused on her. Its mouth twitched into what could have been pain or an attempt at a smile, and then the light went out of its eye and it went still.

"ANCHA!" Inoria screamed. "He told me you would be kept safe, that he would give you back to us. Oh, Ancha."

She jumped to her feet and ran toward the walls of the fortress, where figures had gathered on the battlements to watch what they could see of the battle. Emerius was too shocked to respond until she had already cleared half the distance. She was screaming unintelligibly.

Emerius and the others watched in horror as Inoria ran straight at the walls. She had three arrows left, which she drew and fired as she was running, killing three of the bystanders where they stood. Within seconds, an answering hail of arrows flew down, many of them striking her. She slowed, dropped to one knee, and started crawling toward the wall.

"Help me," Emerius shouted to the others. He ran toward his sister, snatching arrows from bodies as he went. By the time he reached the clearing before the walls, he had five in his hand.

"I'll get her," Sam said, right next to him—Emerius hadn't even heard him keeping pace with him—"you keep them busy."

Sam rushed into the clearing, using his staff to swat away the few arrows that came at him. Emerius watched the archers on the walls and killed them as they were beginning to shoot. It was enough to allow Sam to put Inoria over his shoulders and run back to the cover of the trees. Nalia and Rindu had made it to Sam, also, and were catching or destroying any arrows Emerius failed to prevent being fired.

Back in the trees, out of bowshot of those on the walls,

Sam set Inoria down on the loamy ground. She had eight arrows in her, many of them in vital locations. There was no way she would survive.

"I'm sorry Em," she said, trying to breathe but mostly failing. "It was the only way…the only way to protect Ancha." She closed her eyes in pain, trying to maintain consciousness.

"In," Emerius said, tears carving hot streaks down his cheeks, "what are you talking about. What did you do?"

"I made a deal with that bhor, Vahi. The leader of the mutant assassins." She pulled out a small object and handed it to him. "All I had to do was carry this, so they could tell where we were. He promised…Ancha would be safe. He…promised…they would just track us to avoid us. I'm…sorry. I should…should…have known…he'd betray…"

"Oh, In," her brother said. "We'll talk about it when you're better. Save your strength. We'll fix you up. Then we'll talk about it." He looked to the others. They were not making any move to help, to remove the arrows, to do anything.

"Em," Inoria panted. "don't…flee."

"What? No, In, I won't. What are you talking about?"

"Be…Suka…" she whispered, barely audible. Her head slumped and she lay still.

"No," Emerius said. "No! In, don't leave me. In, please. I'm no good without you. I need you. You are the good one, you're the hero. Please…" He hugged her to himself and whimpered.

44

"I think we can chance cutting some distance from our travel on the way back," Chisin Ling told Nicole. "On the way here, we had to make sure to find the location of the hapaki community. On the way back, we only have to be concerned with not getting lost as we go east. When we reach the water, we'll have gotten to the edge of the peninsula. If we skirt the mountains, right at their base, we should make better time."

Nicole considered what the warrior was saying. "There will be worse weather on this side of the mountains, maybe even snow."

"I'd rather have a little snow than a lot of rain."

"There's that," Nicole said. "It would be nice to get back sooner. It's been thirty-nine days since we left. Anything could have happened while we were gone." She closed her eyes and rubbed her temples. "Okay, let's do it. If the weather or terrain get rough, though, we head north until we hit the coast and then go the long way around."

"Agreed." The captain went to check on the men, who were just finishing up loading the supplies onto the manu birds. They had used the time while she was talking to the hapaki wisely, ranging out in the forest away from the community to hunt for deer and rabbit and forage for wild onions, edible roots, and herbs. They had enough food for at least a week, even if they didn't hunt again.

The rain had come, off and on, but there were no large storms. The air was on the edge of making the precipitation snow, Nicole thought, and it even hailed at times, but hunkered down underneath the tarps and tents they had set up, it wasn't that bad. Now that they would be moving, they may have to get used to traveling in wet clothes again. Well, there was nothing for it. The sooner they got started, the sooner they'd get back to the fortress.

The party settled back into a comfortable traveling pace. The rest had done Nicole some good. She was refreshed and content with getting through the heavy forest as they plodded along. She couldn't really tell if the soldiers were in better moods because they always looked the same: content with doing their assigned tasks.

Another thing Nicole had been able to do as they were immobile was to practice with her knives. She could now throw them well, striking her target with every throw, if is was within twenty feet. She also felt better about fighting with the blades, though she was still nervous about going up against a sword because of the superior reach of the longer weapon. She continued to practice at least a little each evening, throwing as well as sparring with Chisin Ling or some of the other soldiers using dummy weapons.

The first two days they traveled virtually the same path as when they had come, but on the third day, they were able to follow the edge of the rising land and head northeast instead of due north. Looking at the map they had brought—Nicole wasn't sure how accurate it was but they had made notations on their way to the community—it looked as if they could be able to cut a fair distance off the trip. The weather had cooperated with them so far and she was optimistic about making good time.

They found a nice valley that ran east to west and

traveled in it for two more days until they came to a beautiful lake that stretched farther than Nicole could see along it. She marked it on the map, guessing at its size. They set up camp on the western edge and ate their meal. As Nicole lay on her bedroll just outside the tarp that had been set up, she marveled at the stars.

"It's hard to believe that there are that many stars," she said to Chisin Ling, who had come to sit on a log nearby. "I'd been camping on my world, but even so, there never seemed like there were this many. Near the cities, you could hardly see any because of all the lights around."

"That would be something to see," the captain said, "so many lights that you cannot see the stars. I can't imagine such a thing."

Nicole laughed. She was awestruck by the beauty of the stars and her friend only thought of marvels of technology she hadn't ever seen. They had talked about many things during their travels. Chisin had told her what it was like where she grew up and Nicole had done the same. The woman was interested in all the stories of technology and science and especially how it was used in warfare. She was, after all, a soldier, so it was to be expected.

She would sit in rapt attention for hours as Nicole told her of modern military technology and of armies, navies, and air forces—people, actually flying in the sky in wagons!—and the captain asked many questions, some of which Nicole had no idea how to answer. "Ask Sam or Dr. Walt," Nicole would tell her. "They know more about those things than I do." Chisin assured her that she would ask.

As normal, the hapaki were near Nicole, listening to the two humans talk through her mind, but they were uncharacteristically quiet. She thought that maybe they were communicating to each other without allowing her to hear. She still meant to ask Sam how to do that.

The next day, they made it to the far end of the lake. They ended the day's travel early so they could stay near the water for another day. Some of the soldiers speared fish or caught them with makeshift poles and hooks they had fashioned from the bones of some of the game they killed. Stomach full and happy that it had not rained all day, Nicole went to sleep, mentally calculating how long it would take them to get back to Whitehall.

When the party started packing up to move out again in the chilly dawn air, one of the sentries whistled the alarm. Nicole froze in the middle of rolling up her bedroll and looked around. All of the soldiers had weapons in their hands, as if they had magically appeared there. Chisin Ling had both her swords out and was running toward the sound. Nicole followed her, though not as quickly.

All those in motion skidded to a halt on the damp forest floor when they got to the sentry. The woman stood there, arms raised, sword on the ground beside her. Around her were no less than twenty people, the strangest people Nicole had ever seen. Half of them had bows in their hand and arrows nocked. Some had them drawn, ready to loose. There was movement further into the trees. No, Nicole thought, not twenty. There had to be at least two or three times that number.

"Drop your weapons," Chisin shouted to her soldiers. "Stand down. We can't survive this if it comes to a fight." They all did as their captain commanded.

Nicole raised her hands—she hadn't even drawn her knives yet—and looked more carefully at the people surrounding them. They all seemed to share the same features, wide faces and flat noses, dark eyes and dark hair. They wore what looked like leather clothing, their outer garments made of the skins of wolf, rabbit, and fox, maybe a badger or beaver thrown in occasionally.

One of the strangers, a large man with hair pulled back into a braid that extended almost to his waist, started speaking at them in an accusatory fashion, harsh and demanding.

Nicole didn't understand a word of it.

"Did you understand any of that?" she asked the captain.

"Not a bit."

"Uh-oh," Nicole said. "That'll make things tougher." Addressing the man, she spoke loudly in Kasmali. "I'm afraid I don't understand you. Can you understand me?"

The man loked confused, then angry. He spoke again, spittle flying from his mouth as he raised his voice, as if speaking more loudly would make her understand. Nicole was afraid things were escalating.

A woman stepped up to the man and whispered something to him. Irritated at first that he was being interrupted, his whole demeanor changed when he recognized who it was that was speaking to him. He kept eye contact with her and ducked his head in respect as he listened to what she was saying. Finally, he nodded and moved back a step.

"You…" the woman said. Her face, sharing features will all the others around her, looked toward Nicole, chin raised and eyes drilling into hers. The way she said the word was strange, with an accent Nicole had never heard. It took her a moment to realize it was actually a word she understood. Either that, or it was a coincidence that it sounded like Kasmali. "…trespass here. Our land." She *was* speaking Kasmali, or at least a dialect of it. Her mouth worked as she spoke, as if unfamiliar with the sounds she was making.

"We're sorry," Nicole said. "We are traveling back to our place. We did not know this was yours. We will not stay. Just passing through." The woman was watching her mouth as she spoke, concentrating on the words. Nicole decided she needed to speak more slowly. "Do…you…understand?"

The woman nodded. "Understand. You trespass. Trespass mean death." Some of the strangers around them raised their bows or the spears they carried. One or two had swords of crude bronze, and Nicole saw them gripping the hilts more tightly.

"We…mean…no…harm. Want…to…leave. Peaceful."

"No leave," she said. "Steal food, take children, hurt. No. You die. It is law."

Chisin Ling tensed. It was obvious that the soldier was going to go for the swords that were on the ground at her feet. Either that, or something stupid like shielding Nicole from the arrows with her own body. Nicole's mind searched frantically for a solution. The others, more coming from the forest all the time, must have numbered more than fifty by this time. There was no way they would survive if it came to battle.

Nicole? Max's voice came into her mind. *What's going on? Is everything alright?*

The hapaki had gone out foraging for roots earlier, as was their habit. She could tell from the strength of the sending that they were coming closer. *No, Max, Sammy. Stay away. We're in danger. We may not get out of this alive. Don't show yourselves.*

But it was too late. The two came out of a section of undergrowth behind her, shuffling with their distinctive gait. When they realized that there were many more people there than they had expected, both of the creatures did what the hapaki always did when threatened. They froze where they were.

Sudden movement made Nicole flinch, expecting to feel an arrow—or many arrows—piercing her. Instead, what she saw made her mouth drop open.

All the strangers, every last one of them, had dropped to their knees, faces almost to the ground, hands outstretched as in worship.

Nicole looked at Chisin and then around at the soldiers. They looked as shocked as her. When the captain's eyes shifted to the weapons at her feet, Nicole whispered, "No." Even distracted, there were too many to fight.

"Quinshin," the woman who had spoken earlier said,

and the others repeated it.

"Quinshin, Quinshin, Quinshin." They chanted it softly, all of them remaining prostrate.

"What's going on?" Chisin Ling asked.

"I'm not sure," Nicole said, "but I think they're worshiping the hapaki."

"Oh."

Max, Nicole sent. *Please come over here and let me pick you up.*

The hapaki didn't move.

Max. Please.

I'm...I can't move, he said, as close to a whisper as Nicole had ever heard a sending be.

She exhaled. *You have to, or we may all be killed. If I step to you to pick you up, I'll be dead before I even reach you. I know it. Try. Please.*

The hapaki, sendings full of fear, radiated his resolve. Slowly, as if forgetting how to do so, he moved. The strangers stopped their chanting and looked toward him from their prostrate positions. He finally went into motion and stepped toward her. When he was at her feet, she reached down and picked him up, holding him to her chest.

The fur-clad people all let forth sounds of astonishment.

"Quinshin," she said to the woman who was ten feet in front her, still bowing down. "Quinshin...is...my... friend." She pet Max along his head and back and received grudging thoughts of pleasure from him. "Friend. Travel...through...here...for...them."

The woman looked toward the man that had spoken earlier, a question in her eyes. His eyebrows raised and he said something in that harsh tongue of theirs. She nodded.

"You friend of Quinshin, friend to Kechaala." She looked to the man, who shouted in their guttural language. The others began to stand up, slowly, still bowing their heads to the hapaki.

"We…can…go?" Nicole asked the woman.

"Yes. Go." With a final bow to the hapaki, she slipped into the trees. Others were doing so as well. Soon, there was only the man left, apparently their leader. He looked at her significantly, bowed his head toward the hapaki, and followed his people back into the trees. The forest became quiet again except for the heavy breathing of some of the soldiers. And Nicole.

Can you put me down now? Max sent. *And can you explain what that was all about? I think maybe you owe me a big favor.*

45

Rindu watched the big hunter Emerius as he grieved for his sister, talking to her corpse and smoothing the hair from her face. They would have to give him some time. He had just lost all the remaining members of his family. That was a heavy burden to bear. He did not know if the man would survive it. Rindu had seen people crack under such stress, even Zouyim. He thought of Torim Jet and the madness that came upon him when the temple was destroyed and all his brothers and sisters were killed. Yes, they would need to give him some time. Perhaps not as much as he would need, but some.

Sam was sitting with Nalia, speaking softly. He still had tears in his eyes as well. Rindu walked the few feet to the pair.

"It was stupid for her to think that she could trust the mutant assassin," Sam said, "but I don't think it was malicious. She was heartbroken over her brother and reached out for whatever she could find to protect him."

"Yes," Nalia said. "I do not believe she ever meant us harm."

"I just wish she would have confided in us, or in her

brother. This," he pointed toward the twins, Emerius still talking to his sister in hushed tones, "might have been prevented. I guess we know now how they were able to ambush us, how they knew where we were each step of the way."

"It is so," Rindu said. "I am curious about the object Inoria had, if it works with *rohw* or by another means. I cannot detect it, so perhaps it does not use *rohw*. It may be possible to use it in reverse. If the bhor utilized it to track us, could we use it to track him?"

"Chances are, it'll just tell us he's on the other side of those walls," Sam said.

"Perhaps."

An hour later, Emerius came over to where they were. "Rindu," he said quietly, "can you make another grave? I'd like to lay In and Ancha to rest. They deserve that much."

"Of course," Rindu said, getting up from the log on which he was sitting. "Choose a location and we will help you."

Emerius chose an open space away from the battle location, one with ferns and a patch of moss that was thriving—despite the cold weather—between two white birch trees. Those trees were her favorite. As Rindu was phasing out the soil, the hunter went and retrieved his sister's body. He wanted to move both corpses himself, so Sam and Nalia stood back, watching silently.

The bodies were gently laid to rest and Rindu covered them. He was able to place the moss and ferns back in place on top of the dirt. He hoped the plants would not die from the shock. He liked to think this beautiful, peaceful space would continue to be so.

Emerius said some things over the grave, doing so softly that no one else could hear. The Zouy, the Sapsyr, the hapaki, and Sam moved a dozen feet away to allow the big man to have his privacy.

"We should give the rest of the mutated people and hapaki a similar burial," Sam said, eyeing Emerius as he was on his knees still quietly talking to the grave.

"Yes, Sam," Rindu said. "I think you are correct."

Rindu excavated a large pit and the three humans busied themselves in dragging mutant corpses into it. It took another hour and a half to put them all in the grave, and then Rindu covered them up. The volume of all the bodies made the dirt pile up into a large mound. The Zouy knew that the body did not feel anything after death, but he hoped that honor was fulfilled in their simple act of respect.

"I wonder why they haven't attacked us while we've been grieving," Sam said. "There has to be a reason. They have been cruel and heartless every step of the way, so why leave us alone now, unless they're out of mutants to send at us and they don't have the numbers to leave the walls?"

"I think you are correct, " Nalia said. "but if you are, that means that Rasaad and Tingai are perhaps not in the fortress. We must get inside to find out."

"I think I can help you there," Emerius said, approaching them. His voice was rough and hoarse. "I have the beginnings of a plan."

Rindu looked at the hunter. His green eyes—puffy and lined with red—were glowing in the afternoon sun. He saw pain there, but more as well. He saw a deadly promise, a commitment to repayment. He saw revenge.

"Come, sit with us, Emerius Dinn," Rindu said, "and we will discuss it."

They sat and talked through his plan until darkness had overcome the forest, Oro at Emerius's feet, whimpering.

Rindu watched as Emerius constructed the device he was working on. He had unpacked several items from his backpack, along with powders wrapped into cloth bundles and a few small vials of liquid. Sam was next to him, asking questions.

"Will that do the trick, do you think?" Sam asked him. "Is there enough there? How did you learn how to do this? Did your father teach you? How did he learn?"

Emerius leveled a cold glare at Sam.

"Oh, sorry," Sam said and sat back. "I'll just watch quietly."

Emerius mixed some of the powders into a cup. He stirred them with his finger, then inserted some long, thin strips of metal into the powder, burying them at the bottom of the cup. Taking one of the vials, he poured it over the powders. Finally, he placed the lid on the cup, the strips of metal protruding out of the top.

"Does everyone know what you are to do?" Emerius said.

They all answered that they did. Even Skitter nodded his head.

"Okay, then let's get this done and over with."

Emerius handed the cup to Skitter. The hapaki took it gently in both of his paws, no doubt wary because of Sam's explanation of what it was for. Walking on his hind legs in his awkward, rolling gait, Skitter went toward the wall.

Rindu looked at the others. Nalia had her shrapezi out and ready. Sam had *Ahimiro* out, in staff form. He held *Sunedal* loosely in his own hands. Emerius had the arrows he had retrieved from the bodies earlier, before they were buried. His quiver was full and Inoria's was lying at his feet, nearly full. Oro and the rakkeben were alert and standing nearby.

Skitter made it to the wall without being seen. He put his bundle down precisely where Sam had instructed him and lifted the small seed pod Emerius had given him, full of others of his powders and a thin-walled vial of some liquid. Skitter tapped the pod firmly against the wall, breaking the vial. The pod emitted a weak glow as the liquid saturated the powders. He then put it in between the thin strips of metal coming out of the top of the cup, one side of the seed pod touching one strip while the opposite side touched the other. There was a small flash, indicating that the device was working correctly.

Skitter ran for all he was worth, all four legs pumping as he tried to get as far away from the device as possible. One of the men standing on the wall saw the hapaki and pointed, but had no time to do anything else. Five seconds after Skitter had activated the device, there was a flash, followed by a loud boom, and a chunk of the wall simply was no longer there. The man had been shaken off the wall, falling thirty feet to the ground. Emerius put an arrow in him just to make sure he was dead.

The big hunter was the first to run at the hole in the wall, watching the battlements above him for any sign of sentries. He saw one and put an arrow into him as well.

Less than fifteen minutes later, the entire party was in the main hall at Gutu. As it turned out, there were less than thirty soldiers still at the fortress; all the others were with Ayim Rasaad or Baron Tingai. The mutants and the walls had been thought to be sufficient protection from attackers.

"I will ask you nicely just one time," Emerius said to the fortress steward, brandishing one of his long knives. The ceramic glass blade glinted wickedly in the torch light. "Where is your master?"

"Please, sir," the man begged. "I'm just a servant, not a soldier. Ayim Rasaad has gone to the north. I don't know where. The Baron has gone north, too, but he left in a different direction, more northeast. I don't believe they are going to the same place. They both left more than two weeks ago."

"What do you know of the monsters Tingai has made?" Emerius asked

"Nothing, sir," the steward said. "I only know they were here and that there were three minders for them. They let the creatures out yesterday for some reason, but they haven't come back."

"Nor will they." Emerius looked at him coldly. "Get your possessions and leave this place. Find a new master to work for."

"Yes sir," the steward said, bowing, "thank you, sir." He left the room at a run.

"Do you think he was telling the truth?" Emerius asked no one in particular.

"Yes," Sam answered. "He's just a servant, as he said. You can't fake that kind of fear."

"We are still left with a problem," Nalia said. "We can follow Rasaad, but will be no better off than we have been previously. Unless we can catch up to her, or get ahead of her, we will not succeed."

"It is true," Rindu said, "but perhaps Dr. Walt or Lahim Chode can tell us where the next artifact is. If Sam knows a location closer to it than where Rasaad is currently, we might be able to arrive before her."

"Yeah, that's right," Sam said. "Maybe we can get lucky for a change. Let's head back to Whitehall and see what we can find."

"I won't be going with you," Emerius said softly.

"What?" Sam turned to the hunter. "Why not?"

"It's Tingai I have to catch, not Rasaad," Emerius said. "I have nothing left but to avenge my family and to keep that maniac from ever doing the same thing to other villages. I have to go after him."

"But—" Sam started.

"We understand," Rindu interrupted. "Vengeance is not the way, but it is understandable why you would choose to pursue Tingai. Be safe, Emerius Dinn. Perhaps we will see each other yet again."

Emerius nodded. He turned to Sam. "Sam, I know you don't agree with my decision, but I need to do this. Here." The big man handed Inoria's bow to him. "She was fond of you, saw you as a student. She would have wanted you to have it. Do great things with it, okay?"

Sam reverently took the bow and quiver offered to him. "I…I don't know what to say. Thank you, Emerius. I'll try to be worthy of them."

"I know you will. Come on Oro," he said to the bear,

sitting quietly nearby. "Let's see if we can catch that bastard. I'm sure he's not traveling nearly as fast as we can. Oh, and Sam, not all of those mutants we killed were from Blackwood. There were many in that last batch I didn't recognize. Tingai must have raided other villages or got people in some other way. Don't be surprised if you run into more of the monsters."

Emerius waved to the others and trotted out of the hall.

Sam stood there looking at the weapons he had just been given. He tightened his grip on the bow and looked to the others. "Okay, let's get back to Whitehall. We need to get to the second artifact before Rasaad does, and we need to do it fast so we can help Emerius with Tingai."

46

When they arrived back at Whitehall, Nalia made sure that Cleave was brushed down and given water, then she spoke quietly to the rakkeban as she checked him over for injuries. Finding none, she told him he could go hunt and went with Sam and Rindu to see Dr. Walt. Skitter went off to the den he had made in the park. Sam said the hapaki wanted a little time alone. He also mentioned some thoughts that had leaked out of the hapaki's mind as he was leaving. Sam caught the words *kittens* and *distract*.

"Sam, Nalia, Rindu," the old scholar said when they found him in his library. "You've returned. We were worried when you didn't come back last night. Is everything all right?"

"We reached Gutu," Sam said simply. "There was fighting and we lost Inoria. She had a device given to her by that assassin that tried to kill you. It let him know somehow where we were."

Sam's eyes dropped to his feet. "She was heartbroken about her little brother, desperate. She didn't do it out of malice or betrayal. She was just trying to protect her family. She…"

Dr. Walt's eyes became liquid as he looked, first to Sam, then to Nalia and her father. "Yes, Sam, I understand. It is a tragedy, to be sure, but no one can blame a sister from trying to help her brother. How did Emerius take it?"

"He was," Rindu said, "distressed." He handed Inoria's device to Dr. Walt. "After grieving, after we had buried and given our respects to the dead, he erected strong walls around himself. He is seething with cold rage. I hope he can find his way through and emerge stronger for it. He worries me."

"I see." Dr. Walt was turning the device around in his hands. It looked like a brooch for holding a cloak closed. It was made from some type of precious stone, Nalia thought, though she couldn't identify which. It was muddy brown, carved into the likeness of a beetle. "I assume you will be watching him closely to help him in his journey."

"No," Nalia said. "He went after Tingai, believing that vengeance was more important than saving all of Gythe from Ayim Rasaad."

"Nalia," Rindu said. "that is unkind. Emerius Dinn did not choose Tingai over Gythe. He merely followed his feelings to the most pressing task, as he sees it. He has a good heart, but one weighed down by sorrow. Do not judge him too harshly. Grief can cloud one's thinking, as you well know."

Nalia felt her face flush. She remembered her outbursts, her faulty reasoning when she returned, barely alive, from watching her mother and her sisters being killed by the Gray Man. "You are correct, father. Please forgive my foolish talk."

Her father put his hand on her shoulder, his eyes conveying that he understood.

"Oh," Dr. Walt said. "Well, then, I hope he is able to accomplish what he seeks. Nasty business, the mutation research that Tingai fellow engages in. May I ask, then, where Baron Tingai and Ayim Rasaad are?"

Sam cleared his throat. "That's the problem, Dr. Walt. They left Gutu going in different directions. Both north, according to the fortress steward, but different paths. Rasaad is going to the next artifact, and she has a very long head start. We were hoping you could help us. If we can teleport somewhere ahead of her, we may be able to get the artifact first, bring it back here, and stop her plans."

"Sam, I would dearly love to help, but I don't know what I can do." Dr. Walt absently turned Inoria's device over in his hand. "I know that she is probably going for Orum, the drum, but I don't know where it is. I believe she would leave Bruqil for last because it is the item that ties the others together."

"Could you figure out how that device works?" Sam pointed to it. "If we can use it in reverse, find where that assassin is, maybe he will be with Rasaad and maybe we can figure out where she's going. Then, if I know a location closer to the artifact than she is right now, we can leapfrog her."

"That is quite a lot of ifs, Sam," Dr. Walt said. "I will study this brooch and see what I can do. Perhaps we should check with Lahim. He may have had a viewing."

"That's right!" Sam exclaimed. "I had forgotten. I'll check with him now. That's a great idea." Sam started to leave, but Dr. Walt waved his hand for him to stop.

"I believe he's in the south garden, probably very close to the keep. He has been walking a bit of late, using a cane and doing so slowly, but still making it out to get some air once per day. Usually in the morning. His health is improving, albeit slowly."

"That's good news, too," Sam said. "I'll head there now. This is too important to wait for such small things as taking a bath or getting into fresh clothes." He sniffed at his shirt. "But right after talking with Lahim, then it's time for a bath and fresh clothes. Whew."

Nalia and her father went with Sam to talk to Lahim Chode. She could see from his reaction to Dr. Walt's suggestion that he was grasping at whichever idea he could find to try to learn where they would go next. She understood. She also wanted to prevent Ayim Rasaad from obtaining the artifact Orum. She fervently hoped that they would learn something of value from the man they were going to see.

The remote viewer was sitting on a wooden bench, looking out over the south park. It was peaceful, with fresh snow blanketing much of the landscape. The trees that still had their leaves or needles were weighed down by the white powder and the trackless expanse looked as if no one had ever been there before. Off to the right, a rabbit was nibbling on some vegetation it had uncovered, its tracks pursuing it and marking where it had been.

Lahim Chode had not seen them yet, as they emerged from the door to the keep. He had cut his wild hair and shaved. His gaunt face looked to have fleshed out since the last time they had seen him. He still looked frail, but not quite so much as when last they met him. He turned when Sam scuffed his boot on the path. His face lit up.

"You're back." His expression dropped and was replaced with one of sadness. "I'm sorry about Inoria, and that you weren't able to catch Rasaad in Gutu. If I'd known before, I would have told you."

"Thank you," Sam said. "You viewed what happened, then?"

"Just enough to fill in the blanks. The assassin, Vahi, contacted Inoria and gave her the brooch. Bad business, that. Do you know how frustrating it is to view things when they no longer can help? If I'd had my viewing just a few days before, things may have turned out differently." Lahim Chode put his head in his hands.

"It must be a heavy burden, this power of yours," Nalia said. The seer started as if surprised. "You must have had people your entire life blame you for not telling them their futures quickly enough to avert catastrophe. Is it not so?"

"It is," he said. "Thank you for understanding." The

seer paused for a moment. "I suppose you're here to see if I had any other viewings, something that can help."

"Yes," Sam said.

"I have been trying to get useful information, but I keep seeing the army that is being built. One of the most frustrating things about my ability is that the harder I try, the harder it is to accomplish what I want. It's like squeezing a wet cake of soap. Clench your fist too hard and it jumps out of your grasp.

"That being said, I was able to find one piece of information that may help. I saw an argument between Rasaad and Tingai. She demanded that he accompany her, but he said that their master wanted him elsewhere. I don't understand that bit of it, but that's not important right now. What is important is that Ayim Rasaad mentioned the location of the drum artifact. It was Iboghan."

"Iboghan," Sam repeated. "In Old Kasmali, that's 'heart of hell.' What does that mean?"

"I'm sorry," Lahim Chode said, "but I don't know. It could mean anything. Is it figurative, literal, some recognized name? I just don't know. Maybe Dr. Walt can help. When I get back to my room, I'll try to find more information and send for you as soon as I find out anything else."

Sam looked thoughtful and shifted his gaze to Nalia and her father. "Heart of hell. Does that name mean anything to either of you?"

"I am afraid not," Rindu said.

"No," Nalia answered.

"Okay, then. Next stop, Dr. Walt." Sam turned to Lahim Chode. "Thank you Lahim. At least it's something. We'll figure it out. Oh, and I like the haircut and shave."

The seer smiled. "Thank you, Sam. I'll look like a human again in no time. Feeling like one will take a little longer, I'm afraid, but my health is improving."

"Thank you, Lahim Chode," Nalia said as they were leaving. "May your health continue to improve."

Dr. Walt was still where they had left him, sitting in his library, poring over the books and scrolls spread out on the table in front of him.

"Dr. Walt," Sam said. "We talked with Lahim and he gave us a name. We're hoping you can help us with it."

"Yes, yes, of course," the old man said. "What is the name?"

"Iboghan."

"Iboghan? You mean, Iboghan as in 'the heart of hell?'"

Sam nodded. "That's the one. Have you heard of it?" Nalia could see the anticipation in his eyes. And hear it in his voice.

"No, I'm sorry," Dr. Walt said. Sam's eyebrows drooped and his shoulders slumped.

"It does sound familiar for some reason, though," the scholar said, putting his fist to his forehead. "Where, though? Where did I see that name? Maybe in Azel's Compendium? No, no. Chintel's Atlas of the Known World? Perhaps. If I could just—" Dr. Walt looked up and his eyes widened. Nalia was used to the old scholar getting so caught up in his internal debates that he forgot there were others there.

"Oh, sorry," Dr. Walt said. "Listen, Sam, give me a bit of time to try to find mention of this Iboghan. Without a classification system for all the records here, I find I have to rely on my memory, which, at this time, is not seeming to cooperate. When I find what I'm looking for, I will search you out. In the meantime, you can eat something and clean up, maybe rest a bit. I'll do my best."

Sam's shoulders slumped. "Okay. Thank you Dr. Walt. I'll check back with you later. Maybe I can help you look for it."

"Yes, that would be grand," Dr. Walt said toward the book he was opening, already caught up in his search for the information.

The three left the library. As they were going toward

their respective rooms, Nalia saw Torim Jet and Palusa Filk coming the other way. After fond greetings, she explained what happened the day before and asked the two Zouyim if they knew the name Lahim Chode had given them.

"It does sound familiar," Torim Jet said, "but I cannot remember any details. Perhaps we can assist Dr. Walt in finding reference to it. We have been studying in the libraries these past few weeks and may be of value to him."

"That would be very kind," Nalia said to them, bowing. "Thank you."

"It is our privilege to aid in any way we can," the old monk said. "Come, Palusa Filk, this task is more pressing than that which we were previously focused upon."

The younger Zouy waved farewell to Nalia and the others as she accompanied Torim Jet. Nalia was happy that the monks were there. Not only was it a comfort that the Zouyim order was not lost, but they would be a great help in finding the information they sought.

The day passed quickly, Nalia taking the cue from the others and napping to make up for not sleeping the day before. At dinner, Dr. Walt and the two Zouyim were not in the dining hall. Sam asked one of the servants about it and the man told him that he had brought food to the library for the three, that they hadn't wanted to take the time to leave their work.

After dinner, Sam went to the library while Nalia went out to check on the rakkeben. The wolves had gone out and found game, so they were fed and curled up in the corner of a big, unused area in the stables where they normally teleported from. She spent a little time with them, petting Cleave and the other two as well. Sam found her around midnight, his eyes bleary and unfocused from reading for hours.

"Still no luck," he said. "I'm going to get some sleep. At this point, even if I looked right at a passage about Iboghan, I may not notice. I'll go help some more in the morning."

Nalia kissed him goodnight and soon turned in herself. She was not good with Old Kasmali, so would not be any help in the search. All she could do was wait and hope the others found information. It seemed to her that much of her life consisted of waiting. She did not like it.

She saw Sam in the morning for breakfast before he went to help with the research. Rindu had gone with him. Nalia spent the morning helping Danaba Kemp with the training of some of his recruits. The ex-bandit had more than one hundred soldiers, but needed many times that. The force building against them numbered in the thousands, if Lahim Chode's viewing could be believed. She, for one, believed him.

At lunch, she was sitting in the dining hall, picking at her food—some kind of roasted fowl with baked vegetables—when Sam plopped down next to her. His eyes were tired and he seemed sluggish, but when he smiled at her, she forgot all about the bags under his eyes and smiled back. Her father was with him, too, as was Palusa Filk.

"Have you found nothing yet?" she asked them.

"Nothing," Palusa Filk answered. "There are so many books and scrolls and fragments here, something like this may take years. Dr. Walt thinks he remembers seeing the word, but cannot figure out where."

"We're close," Sam said. "I can feel it."

Nalia marveled at his constant optimism. "But Sam, how long will we wait? If we cannot find the location soon, we may be sacrificing our chance to catch her by following."

"I know," he said. "I thought of that. If we can't find it by the end of the day, we'll go back to Gutu and follow her trail. She'll be sticking to the roads as much as she can, I think, until she gets close to her destination. We shouldn't have any problems following such a large force."

The others settled in to eat. They chatted of this and

that, Nalia renewing her friendship with Palusa Filk, whom she thought was dead before she and Torim Jet showed up at Whitehall. When they were done, she went with them to the Grand Library. The search had been moved from Dr. Walt's favorite library simply because the Grand Library had more books and there was less need to move them from one room to another.

Nalia saw in Sam's demeanor that he was thinking about another time in the largest library of the keep, the time when they had fought their way there to confront the Gray Man. Sam's memories of the place were as bad as hers.

They opened the huge wooden doors to enter the room and Sam froze. Nalia looked around him and saw what he was staring at. A familiar, thin woman with black hair stood near Dr. Walt.

Ix had returned.

47

Nalia had her shrapezi out and was charging the woman before anyone else moved. She had made it halfway across the room before she realized Ix had one of her arms in the air. The other held the hand of a small girl, whose eyes were wide at Nalia coming toward her with weapons drawn.

She slid to a halt ten feet in front of the assassin, lowering her blades.

The little girl stood stone still in front of her, eyes afire. She did not cry, however.

"Bao Ling," Ix whispered, "say hello to the Sapsyr. It is polite to say hello when someone is kind enough to show you her own clan weapons."

The little girl's expression changed from fear to awe. "You are of the *Sapsyra Shin Elah*?" she said in her delicate voice. She bowed reverently. "It is my honor to meet you. I am Chen Bao Ling."

Nalia did not know what was going on, but she did know that the assassin was surrounded by no less than three Zouyim, herself, and Sam. If she attacked, she would be dispatched quickly. She put both shrapezi in one hand, saluted the little girl, and bowed. "My name is Nalia Wroun, Bao Ling. It is my honor to meet you."

Dr. Walt, who was standing nearest Ix and the little girl, let out a long breath. "Nalia, Rindu, Sam, I believe you know our guest, Ix. Please, let's all sit and perhaps she can tell you what she has just told me." He took his own advice and sat down hard on one of the benches. He looked frazzled, no doubt from being so close to getting caught between combatants again.

Nalia looked at Ix. She appeared the same as when she had last seen her. Not even five and a half feet tall, she was slender and muscular, with short black hair and the same flat features as the little girl. They both shared the eyes that tilted more sharply than most of the people Nalia had ever met, but she knew that in other areas these features were common. She had known some in Marybador. In fact, her father's side of the family had some of those traits.

The assassin was wearing the same type of garb she had when last Nalia saw her, black snug-fitting cloth that allowed movement but did not have loose folds that could be grabbed or snagged on things. She had those strange weapons attached to her hips, the ones that looked like steel circles with the fan of three blades attached to one side, opposite the cord-wrapped side. She remembered well the long blade in the center and the shorter blades to either side. She had been cut by those blades in her battle with the assassin. The woman had been one of the Gray Man's top minions, his personal killer.

Shifting her attention to Bao Ling, she saw that the little girl was staring at her. It made Nalia feel uncomfortable. Why was she looking at her like that? She almost seemed excited to see her.

"I'm sure it is a surprise to see me," Ix said. "Our parting was perhaps not on the best of terms."

"You tried to kill me and my friends," Nalia said, trying to keep her temper in check. "You are only alive because I allowed it to be so."

"Yes," Ix said, "and for that, I thank you." She gave a seated bow toward Nalia.

"I have learned much since then," Ix continued. "The honorable way you treated me made me think. I, too, once knew honor, before tragedy had leeched it from my thoughts and actions. Your sparing of my life in our last confrontation caused me to re-examine myself and my life.

"I snuck back into the fortress to retrieve my clan weapons," Ix gestured toward the blades attached to her hips, "but did not break my word and try to attack you or your friends. The ring daggers are very important to me, heirlooms of my family for hundreds of years.

"Once I had them again in my possession, I realized what I needed to do. I traveled to my homeland, the land which had been owned by my clan since the patriarch Chen Feng Dao established Zhong hundreds of years ago. When I got there, I found that corruption had rotted the very core of all life in my homeland.

"I will not bore you with details, but let me say only that the remnants of my clan were persecuted solely for bearing the name Chen. Bao Ling here watched as her parents were killed and was herself held hostage to lure me to my death. She has dreamt of being a hero from when she was able to talk and the bravery she has shown tells me it is her destiny.

"I have settled matters in my homeland, but Bao Ling is meant for greater things. I heard there were Zouyim yet alive in the land and that the temple will be rebuilt. When it has been, there will be need for disciples. I respectfully submit Chen Bao Ling as one of these disciples. It is for this that I have come back. For no other reason."

Nalia was speechless. The assassin had come back, to a place where she knew she might have been killed on sight, to give her young charge to the Zouyim? She thought frantically, trying to figure out what ploy this could be, what game she played. She could think of nothing.

Torim Jet walked to where the little girl was sitting and

knelt so he could see her eye-to-eye. "Greetings, Chen Bao Ling," he said in a kind voice. "I am Torim Jet, of the Zouyim."

Her eyes grew wide again. She scrambled off her perch and bowed deeply to the old monk, cradling her right fist in her left hand, held out before her, in a salute. Her shrill voice was tinged with awe. "It is my great honor to meet you, Master Torim Jet. Will you take me as a disciple? I am small, but I have good balance, quick movements, and I am a Chen. My family is strong with the *rohw*. Ask Auntie Ix."

"I see," the old monk said as he eyed the assassin. "I will speak with her in a moment. Do you know that the temple was destroyed and that we have no place to call our own?"

The little girl's eyes dropped to the floor and the determined line of her mouth turned downward. "I do know. I am little yet, but when I get bigger—perhaps next year—I will help to build the temple again. The Zouyim must have a place to live. Heroes must all have a place to live."

The surprise on Torim Jet's face made Nalia want to laugh. Leave it to a child to turn a conversation on its ear. She saw Master Jet look to Rindu, saw her father nod. He looked to Palusa Filk as well, as a courtesy, and she looked barely able to contain her excitement. She nodded firmly. For a wonder, Master Jet then looked to Sam, a question in his eyes. Sam looked surprised, and then regained his composure and nodded, too, smiling.

"I think," Torim Jet said, turning his attention back to Bao Ling, "we must accept you as a disciple. We must have your help if we are to combat the evil forces in the world."

Bao Ling smiled so widely it nearly split her face. She saluted Torim Jet again, then Rindu, Palusa Filk, Sam, and Nalia. Palusa Filk went to her quickly, kneeling in front of her. "We are to be sisters, you and I. Training will be hard, but I will be there if you need to talk. Welcome, sister

Chen Bao Ling."

The little girl threw her arms around Palusa Filk and hugged her. "Thank you. I will be the best disciple ever, you will see."

Nalia couldn't help but notice Torim Jet wiping a tear from his eye. Taking a breath, he squared his shoulders and faced Ix. "What is it that she said about the *rohw* being strong in your family?"

"It's true," the assassin answered. "Our great patriarch, Chen Feng Dao, had a special talent, that of teleportation. He was from a class of fighting monks on another world, Telani." Nalia saw Sam's head snap up from watching the girl to meeting Ix's eyes.

"He accidentally traveled here from that world and could not return. He found a wife and established a community far to the east of here, and called it Zhong. His strong affinity to the *rohw* was passed down through the generations, as was his ability to teleport, but the latter more rarely. I am the only one in this generation able to travel in this way.

"Our clan dwelt in peace for almost two hundred fifty years, until betrayal caused it to be all but destroyed. The Chen martial art was almost lost, but I was able to resurrect it through the ancient records I discovered along with our clan weapons, the ring daggers I now wear. My father, the clan head, was an honorable man, as was Chen Feng Dao, and our community was based on honor. That is another reason I want Bao Ling to be of the Zouyim, or of the Sapsyra," she nodded to Nalia, "because there she will grow to be honorable, an example to our people.

"I gave her the choice and she decided to be Zouyim, so she could learn combat as well as *rohw* use. It took me ten minutes to explain to her that she could not be both a Zouy and a Sapsyr. The conversation involved many tears, some from me."

"Auntie Ix," the little girl interrupted, "Sister Palusa Filk said she would take me to see the manu birds that have just arrived. May I go?"

Ix drew the girl into a hug. "You may. You are a Zouyim disciple now. You will be asking permission of the masters, not me. I will miss you, precious one. Perhaps the masters will allow me to visit you on occasion and you can show me what you are learning."

Bao Ling kissed Ix on the cheek and sniffled. "I will miss you, too. Please tell the others in the clan that I am to start my training to be a hero. They should listen well for stories about me and my heroism."

"I will do that," Ix said, not able to hide her smile.

After the little girl and Palusa Filk left, Nalia turned to Ix. "What will you do, now that your task is complete?"

"I don't know," Ix said simply. "Perhaps I will go back and help what is left of my clan. My days of assassination are done. I have regained my honor and will not let it go again."

"Maybe you can help Danaba Kemp with training soldiers in combat," Sam interjected. Nalia glared at him. Was she the only one who did not believe someone could change in such a short time?

"Yes, that may be a way I could help," Ix said. "I've heard about the new government you are trying to set up and would like to aid you."

"How about it, Dr. Walt?" Sam asked. "Do you think Danaba would let her do it? If we don't find Iboghan soon, we'll need all the skilled soldiers we can get."

"Well, Sam," Dr. Walt said, "I don't see why n—"

"Iboghan?" Ix said. "Are you going to Iboghan? Why?"

Sam's expression grew serious. "Do you know that word, Ix? Iboghan?"

"Yes, it is a great pit, a cave. It's also called the Heart of Hell."

"How do you know of it?" Dr. Walt said in a rush. "Do you know where it is?"

Ix shrugged. "I know approximately where it is. Chen Feng Dao wrote about it in the clan records. Before he found the place where Zhong would be established, he searched far and wide for a suitable location. He drew some maps of the places he visited."

"Maps?" Dr. Walt was getting even more excited. "Do you have access to these maps? Can you show them to us?"

"I could retrieve them, but there's no need. I have memorized all my clan writings. If you have a map, I'll show you where it is. It is seven or eight hundred miles southeast of Gromarisa. Do you know where that is?"

"We do," Sam said, leaving it at that.

Dr. Walt produced a map and rolled it out on the table. Ix looked at it for a moment, got her bearings, and pointed to a location.

"Of course!" Sam exclaimed. "I should have thought of that."

"What, Sam?" Dr. Walt asked, scratching his head.

"The first artifact was at the Grand Canyon. The second one is in Carlsbad Caverns."

48

Sam could have kicked himself. He should have thought of the caverns. It fit that pattern for the first artifact, Azgo. He remembered what Dr. Walt had said, that the ones who hid the artifacts would have chosen landmarks that would still be readily identifiable even hundreds or thousands of years in the future. There was no use in dwelling on it, though. They knew now where they needed to go. They just had to get there.

"I don't know any locations close enough to be of use," Sam said. "Teleporting won't help us here. We can't use it to catch Rasaad."

"What do you mean 'teleporting won't help?'" Ix said. "How do you know?"

"It is something he learned from the Gray Man," Nalia told her. "Sam can teleport."

"Oh?" Ix eyed Sam, studying him. "Interesting. Well, then, why don't you just skim ahead, overtaking whoever it is you're talking about and getting there first?"

"Skim?" Sam said. "I don't know what that means. I can only go to places I've been before, places where I have memorized the vibratory signature. I haven't done that with any locations close enough to Iboghan to make a difference."

"Your teleporting seems to work differently than mine, then," Ix said. "I can teleport to locations directly that I have been to before, but when I don't know a location, I can go there in several hops, covering many miles at a time. I call it 'skimming' or just 'jumping.'"

"You can do that?" Sam asked. "Can you teach me?"

"I don't think so, sorry," Ix said. "I do it exactly the same way I travel to a location I already know. I wouldn't know how to teach you. Besides, it's probably just something that I can do because of my inherent ability. It does come in handy, though."

Rindu had been silent, but now he spoke. "Ix, can you teleport more than just yourself? Can you transport others as well?"

"I can," she answered, "if they are touching me. I have only done so with three people at a time once before, but I believe I am limited only by how many people can physically touch me. Nalia can attest to it working, even if I don't want it to."

Sam could see Nalia tense. Ix must have been talking about when she and Nalia battled in the Gray Fortress the last time they were on Gythe. Ix had tried to teleport away and Nalia was dragged along with her.

Rindu nodded. "I thought as much. Would you be willing to help us in our endeavor? Your skills and abilities could be useful."

"Father!" Nalia said. "The last time we saw her, she was trying to kill us all. She tells us a story, brings a child, and everyone is ready to trust her with our safety? Am I the only one who still has sense?"

"Nalia," Rindu said gently, "I understand your concern. I can sense the peace and lack of ill intent within Ix. Things which were different the last time we met. She is more in harmony with the *rohw*. I trust that she will act with honor."

"But—"

"—and I see no other way to arrive at Iboghan before Ayim Rasaad," Rindu finished. "Do you? Are you willing to sacrifice our greater goal in the name of holding someone to account for their past wrongdoing? If so, why did you spare her to begin with?"

Nalia took a deep breath. She opened her mouth to speak, but then took another deep breath instead and let it out in a long, slow exhalation. "Fine. You are correct. There is no other way I can see. Perhaps it is the only way."

Sam looked to Ix. "What do you say, Ix? Would you be willing to help?"

"I will," Ix said, "if for no other reason than to make amends for my dishonorable actions before. Let me know what you would have me do and I will do my best to help."

"Great," Sam said. "I guess the first thing is to tell you what's going on. Then we can talk about how you can help."

He explained to her briefly about the three artifacts, Ayim Rasaad, Baron Tingai, the assassin Vahi—her eyebrows raised at the mention of a mutant assassin, almost as if she were interested in the rivalry—and the other things that had happened in the last several weeks. When he finished with the assault on Gutu, he stopped and looked at her.

"What we need is for you to skim for us. If we can overtake Rasaad's forces and pass them, we can get to Iboghan first, and get Orum. That will effectively stop her quest to use the artifacts because she needs all three to access their ultimate power. We'll still have the army to deal with, but it will be a major victory for our side."

"What you propose just may work," Ix said, "but how do you propose to have all the people, items, and mounts touch me so that I can carry them along when I skim? I'm not sure if you've noticed, but I am not a large person."

"Oh," Sam said, "that's the easy part. If you take just me along—"

"And me as well," Nalia added.

"If you take Nalia and me along," Sam continued, "I can learn the final location where we will stop for the day and then retrieve everyone else."

"You are larger than me, Sam, to be sure," Ix said, laughing, "but still you will find it difficult to be touching everything you need to transport."

"That's not a problem either," Sam said. "My teleporting works a little differently. I can extend it out from myself, kind of like a bubble, and teleport everything within it. The largest bubble I've made for teleporting people is about twenty feet wide, but I think I can do a larger area, if I need to."

"Really?" Ix said. "That would be useful. Our talents seem to differ in key ways. Very well, it sounds like what you propose will work. When will we leave?"

"The morning is soon enough," Sam said. "I'd rather travel in the daylight so we can see where we are. Welcome to the party, Ix."

In the morning, everyone met at a dining hall for breakfast. Dr. Walt and the Zouyim were there, too, with Bao Ling in tow. She chattered contentedly throughout breakfast, asking questions of Palusa Filk and Torim Jet. She sat next to Ix, who seemed to delight in the child and appeared to want to spend every minute she could with her before she left.

"Nalia arranged for me to be in the room next to hers," Ix said, "no doubt to make sure no one bothered me."

Sam noticed that Nalia was studying her bread a little too intensely. "That was kind of you, Nal," Sam said. He watched as her cheeks flushed red.

"It's okay, Nalia," Ix said. "I understand. You don't trust me and you'll be watching me. That's fine. I deserve it. I will prove to you that I have regained my honor and changed my ways. You'll see and then we will be good friends. Eventually." Nalia's face was carefully neutral, but Sam knew her opinion on that statement.

"Bao Ling has told me you started teaching her in your clan martial art," Palusa Filk said to Ix. "She showed me some of her movements. She shows promise. I think that what she knows will fit in nicely with the Zouyim method for combat. I would like to discuss your clan art with you sometime. It fascinates me."

Ix bowed her head to the Zouy. "I would enjoy that, Palusa Filk."

When breakfast was finished, Sam, Nalia, and Ix went to the stables. Shonyb, Cleave, and a manu bird were readied for the three.

"Why are we taking mounts?" Ix asked.

"I figure that in between skimming, we will want to scout around and get our bearings. From how you described your talent, it didn't seem like you were able to target a precise location. Between scouting and analyzing the ley lines and vortices, we should be able to keep on course, more or less. We may not need to ride, but I figure it's better to have mounts and not need them than the other way around."

"That is good reasoning," Ix said. "Are we ready, then?"

Sam and Nalia both nodded. "I'll teleport us to Gutu. We can start there, skimming the path that Ayim Rasaad's forces took. It seems like the most logical way to do it. Hold on just a minute. My teleporting is not nearly as fast as yours."

Sam sat on the ground and entered the *khulim*. Within two minutes, the three humans and their mounts appeared at the camp they had set up outside of Gutu.

"Okay," Sam said, "let's get started."

It took a few minutes to figure out the best way to ensure that there was contact between Ix and the rest of the party. Sam and Nalia simply grabbed hold of one of her arms each, but the assassin had to touch the mounts or they would be left behind. They finally settled into position with all three mounted, Ix pulling up a pant leg to expose the skin on her leg to contact the manu bird, and her grabbing a handful of rakkeben fur to complete the connection. Checking to make sure Sam and Nalia were holding her arms, she teleported them north, and they were off.

Sam noticed as they jumped that first time that it felt different than his method of traveling. With him, he felt comfortable, in control, and at peace with his surroundings. In fact, that was the whole basis of how he teleported: he became one with the vibrations of the particular place to which he would travel.

Ix's method, on the other hand, was so fast it took his breath from him. He had the sudden sensation of falling, as if the ground he was standing on instantly disappeared and he was in free fall. It was disconcerting, but kind of fun, too. He got that stomach-in-his-throat feeling like he did when on a roller coaster going down a steep decline.

They appeared in the middle of a road. Sam's stomach settled back to its normal location. "Wow!" he said. "That's much different than when I do it."

"Yes," Ix said. "Your way is much slower. I honestly don't know how you have the patience for it."

"It works for my purposes," he said. He looked around at the trees surrounding the place they were standing. "How far did we go?"

"Who knows?" Ix said with a shrug. "It's more important to me to keep from teleporting us into a tree or solid rock…or a person. My main focus is to cast my senses out ahead of us to prevent something catastrophic. I figure we will know when we get close to the ones we seek. Actual distance is irrelevant."

"It is *not* irrelevant," Nalia said. "We must know how far we travel so that we may know how long it will take to get there."

"Oh, Nalia," Ix said in a honey sweet voice, "let's not

argue. We have plenty of time to catch them."

Sam noted the nearby mountains. He would use them as landmarks for determining their course after the next hop. When he was finished looking around, he gave Ix a nod. She teleported them again.

This time, when Sam looked around, he was able to pick out a particularly large mountain he had seen at the last location. Though he couldn't estimate how far they had gone, at least he had an idea of where they were in relation to his landmark. He studied this new place as well, picking out another mountain to the north.

"The road appears to travel due north," he said, judging his direction based on where the sun sat in the sky. "It seems like the long way around to go northeast." He thought for a moment and then realized the reason. "Oh, of course. The mountains to the northeast make travel difficult. Going this way is longer, but the route is easier. I seem to recall that there are highways right along here in my world, large roads for vehicles to travel."

"That's good," Ix said. "The longer the route, the longer it will take them to get there. We'll have more time to catch and then overtake them."

They continued on, skimming to a new location, analyzing where they were, and then moving on again. Ix became more impatient with every stop they made.

"We'll never catch them if you stop and take half an hour to look around every time we get to a new location," she said.

"I'm sorry, Ix," Sam said, "but I want to make sure we're tracking them. It's been so long since they passed this way, any sign of them has been obliterated." He looked more carefully at her. "Are you feeling okay? You look kind of tired."

The assassin shook her head and rubbed her eyes. "I am a little tired. I've never teleported so many people and things before. Maybe it's more difficult for me than just skimming myself. I feel as if I have been fighting all day."

"Sam can teleport any number of people and things without it being more of a strain on him," Nalia said.

Ix just stared at the Sapsyr.

Nalia stared back.

"Now, now, come on," Sam said. "Let's not bicker. Do you want to stop for the day, Ix? We don't want you to overdo it. We have a long way to go and it's better to pace ourselves."

Ix shifted her gaze to Sam and lost the hostile expression. "I think I'm good for a couple more hops. Then we can rest a little."

"Sounds good," Sam said. "Thank you again for doing this. There's no way we'd be able to do it without your help."

Ix smirked in Nalia's direction and prepared to skim again.

After two more locations, Ix could hardly sit straight in her saddle on her manu bird. Sam finished looking around and noting the prominent landmarks and then watched her for a moment. "We're done for the day," he said. "Here, let's dismount and rest for a few minutes. I'll learn this place and then we can head back to Whitehall for some food and a good night's sleep."

"Do you not want to try to travel on the mounts for at least some further distance?" Nalia asked. "It is barely mid-afternoon."

"No. The extra time could be used to rest. If Ix can get the rest she needs, she'll make up more than a day's travel in one hop. Let's go back."

Within a few minutes, Sam had memorized the vibratory signature of the place they had stopped. It looked as most of the places they had stopped during the day, a road cut through trees with mountains off on the horizon. He knew they had traveled quite a distance, but couldn't determine how much. It was enough, he thought. With the distance Rasaad had to travel to get to the next artifact, she would be barely halfway there at this time.

There was plenty of time to catch her. Unless he had miscalculated. Forcing the thought from his head, he entered the *khulim* and teleported himself and the others back to Whitehall.

After settling in the rakkeben, Sam and the two women went to eat a late lunch. Ix walked slowly, obviously exhausted. He hadn't thought of that before. They would have to pace themselves more carefully. If Ix became too tired to skim for them, he wasn't sure they'd be able to get to the drum in time.

"I will go and rest for a bit," Ix said to them as she headed toward her room. "I'll see you at dinner time."

Sam gave her a considering look. A little rest was all she needed and she'd be as good as new. "We seem to have an entire afternoon free," he said to Nalia. "I am going to catch up on some things with Rindu, but I'd like to spar a little later, if you think you might be able to handle being beaten."

Nalia smirked at him. "Why, are you going to bring several friends to help you?" She kissed him and headed off in the other direction. "I will be ready when you are. I will visit with Palusa Filk and the girl Bao Ling. Come retrieve me when you feel you cannot stand being bruiseless any longer."

With a wave, he headed toward Rindu's room.

49

Sam found the Zouy sitting ramrod straight at his little table, doing calligraphy.

"What do those characters mean?" Sam asked, looking over the scroll on which Rindu was painting.

Rindu finished the character he was drawing and then set his brush down. "This one is 'reasoning,' this one is 'sufferance,' and this one," he pointed toward the last, "is 'curiosity.'"

"Curiosity?" Sam said, peering at it. "Really?"

Rindu rolled his eyes. "No, Sam. It was a joke. It is actually the character for 'respect.'"

"Oh," Sam said, laughing. "I see what you did there. You were poking fun at me for asking questions."

"It is said, 'One question or two are good for learning, but more than three cause tempers burning.'" He eyed Sam from the side to see his reaction.

"Is that a real saying or something you just made up again?"

"Perhaps a little of both," Rindu said, wearing a small, impish smile. At least, it was a smile for Rindu. On anyone else, it would have been only a small twitch of his mouth.

"You're in a feisty mood today, huh?" Sam asked.

"It is a good day, as all days are before our death. Why are you back so soon from your traveling?"

"We ran into a complication," Sam said. "Apparently, the more people and things Ix teleports, the more strain on her. She became exhausted from moving us around. We'll have to pace things better tomorrow."

"Why do you not just reduce the number of things she must transport?" Rindu asked.

"I thought of that, but Nalia would never agree to just me going. We could probably do without the mounts, but I'm afraid we'll need them to scout areas once we get further along. Right now, we're only seeing the road and surrounding trees. Soon, though, it won't be so easy to find our way. Maybe we can leave the rakkeben and the manu here and then I can teleport back and retrieve them if we need them."

"That sounds a reasonable compromise," Rindu said. "So, you have several hours you were not expecting. That is good. There are things we must work on. With how events have been unfolding lately, you and I have not been able to adequately address your training."

"My thought exactly," Sam said. "I'm yours for as long as you want. What shall we do?"

Rindu cleaned his brush and put it in its resting place in the cup beside the inkstone. "Come with me," the Zouy said as he headed out the door.

Sam followed the monk down corridors and turns he had never seen before. The keep was so large he still hadn't been to most of it. "Where are we going?" Sam asked.

"Be patient, my curious friend," Rindu answered, and walked on.

After more than half an hour of walking, they arrived in front of large double doors made of thick wood and bound with copper. Sam was sure he had never been here before. From their circuitous route that sloped gradually downward and the stairs they had taken, he knew they must be down very deep in the fortress. Rindu opened one of the doors and motioned for Sam to enter.

The room was dark. Sam looked at Rindu, still standing in the doorway, framed by the light of the corridor torches. The Zouy looked back at him, waiting.

Sam focused his *rohw* on the tip of *Ahimiro* and caused it to glow. The light opened up a circle in which Sam could see, but all that was visible was the floor itself. He couldn't see a wall or anything else. Rindu stepped inside the room and closed the door, causing the tunnel of light from the hall to wink out.

Sam figured the room had to be very large for him not so see the walls in his light. He walked toward the left and after several steps found a wall. It had a torch sitting in a sconce. Sam projected a sharp, intense burst of *rohw* energy onto the torch head and it flared to life. The new increased circle of light allowed Sam to see the next torch, ten feet away. He lit that one as well.

Looking askance at Rindu, and getting no response, Sam walked the perimeter of the room, lighting all the torches along the way. When he made his way back to where he started, he began to light the braziers. They were in some kind of housing, with glass set in a metal framework over the bowls and a shiny, reflective surface lining the bowl's walls. When he lit a brazier, the light bounced off the mirrored surface and then passed through the glass and illuminate a large area of the room. It was a lantern, he realized, but much bigger than any he'd ever seen.

He lit the last of the braziers and then looked around. They illuminated the whole area so that it was bright as daylight. The room was massive. The ceiling was not visible for the most part. Where it was, it was at least twenty feet high. The chamber was much longer than it was wide, probably over a hundred feet by maybe twenty-five. At the end, there were targets set in place. They were made of straw and had concentric circles painted on the cloth covering them.

"An indoor archery range?" Sam asked.

"It appears so," Rindu said, "but we will not be using it for that purpose today."

The Zouy went to a cabinet near the door and retrieved several clay pots. "Come with me," he said, and started walking toward the targets at the end of the room. Sam hadn't noticed, but behind the targets there were hooks hanging from chains. Rindu handed the pots to Sam, grabbed two of the hooks, and pulled them toward the front of the room.

Sam was surprised when they swung along like they were on a track. Setting the pots down to hoist *Ahimiro* high, and increasing its light by projecting more energy into it, he saw that there were indeed tracks in the ceiling running the length of the room and the chains were attached to some kind of roller, allowing them to be positioned smoothly anywhere along the track. It was ingenious.

Rindu picked up one of the ceramic pots. It was the kind usually used for storing water or other liquids, with a handle on each side of the spout. The Zouy put one of the hooks through the handles so the pot was hanging from the chain. He did the same with the next pot, moving it ten feet closer to the room's door, and likewise with the two remaining pots. When he was done, there were four pots hanging from the hooks, each approximately ten feet apart.

Rindu started walking back toward the door. When he was twenty feet from the first pot, he stopped and turned around. He looked at Sam. "This is your lesson today, Sam. Please watch closely and I will explain."

Rindu closed his eyes briefly and took a long, slow breath. Then he opened his eyes and fixed it on the pot twenty feet ahead of him. He made a quick gesture with his right hand, flicking the wrist as if striking something with the heel of his palm. The pot shattered.

Sam had seen the pulse of *rohw* energy as a flash of light. It was impressive that Rindu could project it far enough to damage something twenty feet away. Impressive, but not unexpected. He had seen the man do so many amazing things in the time he had been with him, this didn't seem to be outside the realm of possibility. Maybe he was just becoming jaded.

Rindu looked at him and raised one eyebrow. "Did you see the *rohw*?" he asked.

"Yes."

"Good. Can you duplicate this feat?"

"No," Sam said, but then added, "I mean, I can try."

"You will," Rindu said, a lightness in his voice. "But not yet. That is not the lesson I would teach you."

The monk faced the next pot, thirty feet from him. He repeated the process, shattering that pot as well. Sam was a little more impressed. Thirty feet was a fair distance over which to project energy like that.

Without speaking further, Rindu faced the third pot. His face grew more intense. He closed his eyes, as before, took a breath, and made the same gesture as he released his breath. The pot, forty feet away, made a thunking noise and swung on its chain as if pushed.

Rindu frowned.

The Zouy planted his feet—both pointing forward and parallel—breathed in a deep, slow breath and let it out. Then, he breathed in again deeply. His eyes slowly opened and he put his hand up, moving it slightly as if to track the swinging pot. In a sudden burst of exhaled air, he flicked his wrist again, harder than before, and the pot shattered. Sam was more impressed with this.

"As you can see," Rindu said, "that is the limit of my abilities to project my *rohw* forcefully enough to break the pot. In order to increase the distance, I must have more power. But from where can I get this power? Is not the universe full of *rohw* energy? Should I not be able to snatch just a bit more for my purpose?"

"Not if you have reached your limit," Sam said.

"Good. You are correct. It is not the lack of *rohw* that is available, but my ability to utilize it. In order to do so, I must be more than what I am. I must somehow increase myself, increase my abilities. But how can I do this?"

"Um," Sam said, figuring he knew where this was going, "harmony?"

"You are correct," Rindu said, clapping Sam on the shoulder. "But who is there for me to harmonize with?" he asked, looking around the room.

"Me," Sam said with a sigh. "What must I do, Master Rindu?"

"Ah. Thank you for volunteering, you among all those here." Rindu's smirk made Sam war with himself over whether he wanted to laugh or growl. "I will gather as much *rohw* as I can hold. You will try to join with my *rohw*, try to become one with me and that which I hold. If you do it correctly, you should be able to shatter the last pot, using your energy as well as my own. When two come into harmony with each other, they are more than either alone. Their *rohw* is added to that of the other, making it possible for them to perform feats neither could do by themselves."

Sam tried to meld with Rindu. He entered the *khulim* and found his teacher's mind easily enough, but he flailed about, trying to come into harmony with him. After trying over and over again, he was becoming frustrated.

"Stop," Rindu said. "I will be honest with you, Sam, I cannot understand why it is so difficult for you to do this. It is my failing that I cannot give you better direction. Perhaps if I show you how to accomplish it, from the other side, you may understand better.

"I want you to gather *rohw* into yourself, as much as you can hold. Gather it from the surroundings, from the heat of the fires, from me if you wish. Gather it and hold it. Do not attempt to use it in any way."

Sam nodded. He was already doing as instructed before

Rindu finished speaking.

Rindu breathed in deeply and then let loose with a burst of *rohw* so powerful, Sam could see the flash behind his closed eyes. He opened them just in time to see the pot shatter and fragments spray far enough to hit the walls on either side.

"What did you feel, just before I shattered the pot?" Rindu asked.

"I felt a calmness, like the stillness of the water in a deep well," Sam said. "I felt intent and then execution just before I sensed the flash and then saw the pot explode."

"Do you believe you could reproduce the feeling if we tried again, with you trying to come into harmony with me?" Rindu asked.

"Yes, let's try."

He tried for another hour, but was never able to get the feeling back. "I don't know why I can't do it. It's like something inside me is blocking it. I'm trying, Master Rindu. I really am."

"I know, Sam," the Zouy said. "Let us stop for now. I will meditate upon it this evening and see if I can determine what it is that I need to do to make you see the way. Disciples practice these exercises when they are very young. Perhaps since you were an adult when you began learning to use the *rohw*, your mind finds something foreign or objectionable about joining with another's energy. We will solve this mystery, though it may take time. For now, we must clean up our mess. As it is said, 'cleanliness is beside religion.' You will find brooms in the cabinet. Please take two out and help me get these shards together."

When they had returned to the part of the keep Sam knew and Rindu had gone his own way—back to his own room—he headed to where Nalia would be. Doing some sparring would be just the thing to clear his head of the disappointment of not being able to do what Rindu asked. He hoped the Zouy would figure out what was wrong.

Sam knew what he was being taught was important. It also bothered him that he couldn't seem to learn what children learned to do in the temple. What if his life depended on this skill someday? He would need to master it. But how?

50

The morning dawned gray and cold. Sam, Nalia, and Ix gathered their supplies and bundled into their cold-weather clothes and cloaks and headed back to the last spot on their journey. It was Sutow-Rup, the second month of winter and things could get chilly, even this far south.

The first jump brought them to an area with rolling hills and folds in the land. It made Sam think of a massive sheet that had been billowed out and then allowed to settle back down lightly, causing patterns that were smooth and pleasing to the eye. The vegetation was thinning, so Sam could see the terrain for miles in any direction through the trees.

After the second jump of the morning, Sam could see some kind of city or town in the distance.

"What is that city?" he asked.

"I'm not sure, but I think it's Somas," Ix answered. "It's a small town, with less than a hundred people, mostly relying on trade for their living."

"Somas," Sam said, trying the word out on his tongue.

"We should make it to the town on our mounts, instead of teleporting there," Nalia suggested. "We do not want to be seen displaying such abilities."

"Good idea," Sam said. "Let's get off the road and I'll go back and get them. It will only take me a few minutes once I have learned this place."

In less than an hour, the three had their mounts. Nalia and Sam had their rakkeben and Ix had a manu bird named Feather. It was an ironic name, Sam thought, considering the bird was the fattest manu he had ever seen.

As they neared the town, which seemed to spring up in the middle of the hills and folds in the land, it was obvious something was amiss. People were scrambling everywhere and there was damage to some of the buildings, including two that looked to have been on fire. The scent of wet, charred wood reached the trio as they came to the outskirts of Somas.

People stared at them as they made their way to a building that seemed to be a tavern, as indicated by the bright green door. Being a trade town, Sam knew it wasn't just that they were strangers that caused the others to take special notice of them. Something had happened to make the townspeople wary.

"Excuse me," Ix said to a man hurrying by. "but what happened here? Is there trouble?"

The man rushed by without a word. Ix sniffed.

The next two people she asked acted in the same way. Her mouth pressed into a straight line and her jaw clenched.

"You," she said as a young man passed her. He was close to a foot taller than the assassin, and Sam was sure he outweighed her by nearly two to one, but Ix grabbed him by the upper arm and pulled him toward her. "What has happened here? Why is everyone ignoring me?"

The young man's eyes widened at her audacity and a look of shock and fear ran across his face. He looked down and his expression settled into a more neutral one. "Sorry, miss," he said, ducking his head. "There was trouble earlier and everyone is still recovering. We mean no disrespect."

"That's fine," Ix said, eyeing him coolly. "What kind of trouble was it?"

"A large group of people came through here early yesterday. Or should I say, they started to come through early yesterday?" He fidgeted as if he wanted to escape. "It was an army, an honest-to-goodness army. The leader, some woman—a woman!—talked with the traders here and purchased a few things, but we didn't have what she was most looking for: food. We trade but we don't have many farms of our own. Being a small town, we didn't have nearly the amounts she wanted.

"She wasn't too pleased at that, but she didn't cause trouble, either. She and those with her continued through the town and out the other side, heading east. It wasn't until later that there were problems.

"The force took a long time to go through the town. As they passed, most of them minded their own business and just continued marching. Toward the end of the procession, though, were a few troublemakers. They demanded strong drink and began to get grabby with the town's women, including the carpenter's daughter. When he intervened to protect her, one of the soldiers killed him where he stood. Then everything went crazy, townsfolk and soldiers fighting, people dying—mostly us—and some of the soldiers started looting and setting fires.

"They didn't stick around. It wasn't because they were afraid of us. I think it was because they didn't want to get behind in the march. I don't think that woman who is their leader would have been happy with them falling behind. We just finally got the last of the fires out and we're trying to figure out who is missing and what was taken."

Sam looked at Nalia and at Ix. The former was expressionless, though he could see the fire in her eyes. The latter had a pinched expression on her face. "Thank you," Ix said. "I won't keep you any longer."

The young man ducked his head again and took off at a

brisk walk.

While the man was giving them the news, Sam saw that others had noticed them. As they headed toward the tavern's door, three older men were coming directly toward them. Sam took Ix's lead, dismounted, and went into the building.

All around them, there were pieces that had been tables, benches, and chairs as little as a day before. The three had no sooner settled in at one of the few remaining tables in the common room when the townfolk pursuing them came through the door. Ix waved to a man with an apron to get his attention.

"Good afternoon," one of the men said. He was tall, lanky, and had the silliest hairstyle Sam had ever seen. His black hair was long on top and was combed over to his left side, where it covered part of his eye and hung over his left ear. The hair all along the sides and back of his head was shorn short. "I'm Stumin Kile, mayor of Somas."

"Good afternoon, Mayor," Ix said.

"I hate to be rude," the mayor said, "but seeing as we just had a traumatic experience with strangers, I owe it to the people of Somas to ask about you and your intent. I hope you understand."

"It's no problem," Ix said, "we are not here to cause problems. One of your citizens was kind enough to explain what happened. We are sorry to hear you had troubles with outsiders."

"That's very kind of you. May I ask your names and your purpose for being here?"

"My name is Ix," she said. "My friends are Nalia Wroun and Sam Sharp. We are merely—"

"Sam Sharp?" the man said, his eyes growing wide. He eyed Sam's staff. "*The* Sam Sharp?"

Ix looked the mayor over as if he was an apple she was thinking of purchasing. "I'm not sure if he is *the* Sam Sharp, but he's the only one I know with that name."

"You pardon," Stumin Kile said. "I have family in the

west, in Bayton. We keep in touch by writing letters that we pay traders and other travelers to carry for us. I just received a very long letter about some important events along the coast. Turns out that a tyrant who had been spreading his influence far and wide was overthrown. The name of the hero who performed the task was Sam Sharp."

Sam tsked. The mayor looked at him, an offended expression on his face.

"I'm sorry," Sam said. "That wasn't meant for you. I just keep hearing about how I'm the one responsible when I did very little myself. My friends, Nalia here and her father, mostly, along with my hapaki friend Skitter, were the heroes. I was just along for the ride. I don't know how the stories got it so wrong."

The offended expression left the mayor's face, replaced by a smile. "It *is* you. Oh, what a great honor. Wait until I tell my brother about this."

Sam wondered why he couldn't seem to explain to others what really happened. He felt his face warming. Well, there was no use in trying to change the man's mind. "It's nice to meet you, too."

"Have you come to defeat the army that passed through here?" the mayor asked him.

"No, not right now, though we are working against the leader of the army, Ayim Rasaad."

Stumin Kiles beamed. "That's wonderful. Towns and villages the size of Somas are no match for a force that large. Many *cities* are not even a match for such an army. The letter I received said something about a new government, one that is unified. Is it true? Is such a thing being set up?"

"It is," Nalia said. "As we speak, Dr. Walt is discussing it with leaders from many different areas, trying to create a government that will benefit all."

"I received no notice, no invitation," the mayor said. "Is it only for larger populations? Do small towns have no say?"

"Oh, it's not that," Sam said. "It's just that it takes time for news to spread. Dr. Walt is concentrating on local areas. If he waited for all of Gythe to hear and respond, nothing would happen for years. All towns, villages, and cities are welcome to take part. No matter what size."

"Wonderful. I will send a letter immediately. No, I will go myself, just as soon as I am able to get things under control here."

"I'm sure Dr. Walt would love to have your input and support," Sam said. "In fact, I think I can help you to get there much sooner than you would expect." He explained briefly to the man about his ability, and Ix's, to teleport instantly to Whitehall. Sam offered to take him back with them when they finished their traveling for the day.

"That would be grand, and very much appreciated. It will take me a few days to do what I need to do here, however."

"That won't be a problem," Sam said as looking at Ix and Nalia. They both nodded. "When we are done traveling for the day, we can stop back here and bring you with us when we go back to Whitehall. Then, you can discuss whatever you like with Dr. Walt and when we start traveling again tomorrow morning, we'll drop you back here before setting out. You won't be gone for more than one night."

"Is such a thing possible?" Stumin asked.

"It is," Ix answered. "That is how we have been traveling. We return to Whitehall each evening and sleep in our own beds."

The mayor bought the three drinks the man with the apron brought them and discussed the new government with them. Sam peppered him with questions about Rasaad and her army also, but the mayor didn't know much more than the man they talked to earlier. He soon took his leave, his two shadows following closely, telling Sam where to find him when they returned.

Sam finished his drink with a smile. "That was fortuitous. Dr. Walt will appreciate an ally this far out. The more people involved in the new government, the better."

Ix and Nalia agreed. The three went outside, mounted, and headed out of town. When they were out of sight, Sam memorized the location so he could return in the evening, then Ix took over, jumping to the next location.

When they appeared in the middle of the road at their next stop, Sam noticed immediately that things were different.

"We're ahead of them," he said plainly, looking at the roadway that had just a few wheel tracks and a handful of impressions from the beasts that had pulled the carts or wagons.

"Yes, or they left the road and are taking another way." Ix said. "Now we can set the pace. We should easily be able to make it to Iboghan before Rasaad does."

There was enough time before sundown for two more jumps. The terrain Sam needed to memorize had transformed to a flatter geography with fewer trees. In fact, it was starting to look to Sam as if it was the Southwestern desert climate he was accustomed to seeing in this part of his own world, though he had never imagined it as being so cold. Then again, there had been some cold days and nights at his home in the desert, too.

"There aren't many trees here," he pointed out.

"It is so," Nalia said. "I have not seen such a lack of vegetation before in Gythe. Is the land sick?"

Ix as shaking her head. "No. It's just the way it is. It is drier here, with little rainfall. I have seen areas like this before. I don't think I would like living where there are no trees."

Sam smiled. Ix looked questioningly at him, but Nalia just nodded. She had seen where he had lived in Telani, in the desert of Southern California, before they had moved up north to Oregon.

"Okay," Sam said after he had meditated to learn the

vibrations of where they had stopped. "I'm ready to go back. Ix, do you want me to teleport us so you can save your strength?"

"Yes, that would be good."

Sam entered the *khulim* and in a few minutes, they were at the outskirts of Somas. After the short trip into the town, racing the setting sun, they met up with Stumin Kiles.

"Are you sure it's safe?" he asked them, "this jumping through the air to another place thousands of miles away?" He tried to hide his nervous trembling, but it was evident.

"We do it all the time," Sam assured him. "We did it several times since we talked to you last. It will be fine, you'll see."

"Okay then," the mayor said. "I suppose I am ready."

Nalia helped to direct and console the man while Sam entered the *khulim* once again.

Then they were at Whitehall, in the familiar area in front of the stable. At the sound of them talking, two of the grooms came out to take care of their mounts. All four of the travelers headed for Dr. Walt's library, Sam knowing that the old scholar would be there. Dinner time was an hour away, so they could make introductions before heading to the dining room.

"That was…remarkable," the mayor of Somas said. "It felt sort of—I don't know—slippery. Not unpleasant, but different."

"Yeah," Sam agreed. "You get used to it."

"I would think so. To travel so far in the blink of an eye, it is a small price to pay. Imagine what such a power could do for trade. Teleporting food and trade goods instantly from one place to another, one could become rich very quickly."

Spoken like the mayor of a trade town, Sam thought.

As the four approached the door to the library, Sam could hear Skitter's thoughts within, though he wasn't talking to Sam. What was Skitter doing in Dr. Walt's library?

To their knock, Danaba Kemp opened the door. Sam couldn't see much around the former leader of the Red Fangs, but he did see a bit of reddish brown fur. *Hi Sam*, Skitter sent to him. *I thought I sensed you nearby. Look who is back.*

Danaba moved out of the way and Sam got his first full view of the room. Dr. Walt was there, of course, as well as Skitter. A tall, muscular woman with black hair pulled tight into a pony tail was standing rigidly with feet spread and her hands clasped behind her back. The swords on her back looked formidable and Sam didn't think for a moment that she didn't know how to use them.

On the other side of the woman was his mother.

"Mom," Sam said, rushing to sweep her into a crushing hug. Her eyes went wide and she jumped a bit at first until she saw it was him and then she wrapped her arms around him and hugged him back.

"Hi, Sam," she said, when he released her and she could breathe again. "You look well."

Sam looked at her searchingly. "Mom, you're speaking Kasmali."

"I am. I've been practicing. I've also been practicing speaking with the hapaki. I feel comfortable doing both now."

"That's great," Sam said. "So I take it that your mission was a success?"

"It was." She pointed down and Sam noticed for the first time that there were three hapaki in the room: Skitter, Max, and another one. The new hapaki had dark brown fur, shot through with gray, almost skunk-looking. It was a little smaller than Skitter, with a nose that was longer and sharper. Sam wondered again if the different communities each had their own unique physical features.

Greetings, and welcome, Sam sent to the new hapaki. *My name is Sam.*

Oh yes, the new hapaki's thoughts pushed their way into

Sam's mind. *I have heard much about you. You are the Hero of Gythe and Friend of the Hapaki.* He heard Skitter chuckle in his mind.

Sam felt himself flushing again. That title again. He wondered what he had to do to make people—and hapaki—stop using it.

"We were just telling Dr. Walt about our trip," Nicole Sharp said. "Oh, and Sam, I want you to meet Captain Chisin Ling." She gestured toward the woman soldier. "She was a great help not only in escorting and protecting me, but also in helping me learn Kasmali. And other things." She gave the captain a conspiratorial look as she casually made a knife appear in her hand, twirled it in her fingers, and then made it disappear again.

"Hi, Captain Ling," Sam said, eyeing his mother's hand and wondering if he had just seen what he thought he had seen. "Thank you for watching over my mother and keeping her safe."

The woman nodded and smiled. "It was my pleasure. Nicole has told me the most wonderful things about your world. I especially enjoyed the stories of your armed forces and the—what are they called—the sea lions?"

"SEALS," Nicole corrected.

"Ah, yes. Remarkable. We have nothing like that here, though I am trying to talk General Kemp into starting a group patterned after them." She looked out of the corner of her eye at Danaba Kemp, who was wearing an exasperated look. Sam tried to hide his smile.

Realizing how things had gotten away from him, Sam cleared his throat and spoke. "Dr. Walt, everyone, this is Stumin Kiles, mayor of the town of Somas. His town is approximately where Nogales, Arizona is on Telani. He has heard of the new government being formed and would like to take part. He will also be rallying for support with the other local leaders where he is from. He was kind enough to come back with us to speak with you. We'll take him back home on our way out tomorrow morning."

"That is fantastic," Dr. Walt said. "Welcome, Mayor Kiles. Please, come in, sit. Would you like something to drink? There are several of the local leaders still in Whitehall. Perhaps we can have an impromptu meeting after dinner. I would love to hear about your area and your ideas on what we will try to accomplish."

As Stumin Kiles sat and began conversing with Dr. Walt, Sam and the others took their leave. "We'll see you all at dinner," he said as they walked through the door, but he wasn't sure if the scholar and the mayor heard him.

Sam spent the time before dinner talking with his mother and the hapaki. He marveled at her smooth communication with them. It hadn't been that long since she had departed on her mission and now she seemed like she had been in Gythe for years. It made him happy to see her like this. He couldn't remember ever seeing her so engaged, so committed to something. It was as if she had regained her energy and her reason for living.

Nicole stopped talking mid-sentence and looked at him. "What?" she said.

"Oh, I was just thinking how much Uncle Grayson would have loved to see you like this. His last words were that I do something good with the fortress. I think he'd be proud of you."

Her eyes became watery and she pulled him into a hug, kissing him on the cheek. "He'd be so proud of you, too, Sam. I think our family owes it to Gythe to do all we can. Besides, I feel like I belong here. I haven't felt like this since your father and I first looked at you sleeping in your crib when we brought you home from the hospital. It's just a feeling of—oh, I don't know—that we're exactly where we belong. I like it."

"Me too, Mom. Me too."

Dinner was a blur of stories going back and forth, interspersed with talk of the new government and how it would eventually spread to other locations from its humble beginnings in Whitehall. By the time it was done, Sam was full and happy and ready for a little training before bed.

Nalia had taken to asking the other Zouyim to help with Sam's physical training. Tonight, he was sparring with Palusa Filk and her triple staff.

"You are really very good, Sam," she said as she whirled and struck at him with one of the end sections of the staff. He blocked it with the dull thunk of hardwood striking porzul wood.

"Thank you," he panted, moving to try to strike her with an overhand swing of *Ahimiro* in its staff form. "Nalia has beaten at least some skill into me." He caught Nalia smiling out of the corner of his eye.

"Really, though," she continued, not even breathing hard, "for the time you have been training, it's remarkable. You have natural talent." She looked toward Nalia. "But shh, don't tell Nalia I said that." She laughed, blocked his strike with the center section of her triple staff, and somehow got the section in her right hand through his guard to strike him hard in the abdomen.

"Oof," was all he could get out.

"All right," Nalia said. "Enough. We do not want to cripple him this night. He must be able to move tomorrow."

Sam swung his staff around so it was nestled in one hand and he saluted Palusa Filk with the other, bowing to her. "Thank you, Palusa. It's nice to spar against a different style of fighting. It will make me better. After I heal." He winced as he straightened.

"Thank you for allowing me to practice with you, Sam," she said as she saluted back. "I am rusty and must regain my skills, but in no time, I think you will be besting me when we spar. I must take advantage of the time to train now, while I can."

"When is it my turn?" Ix's voice came from a dark corner of the training room. Sam started. He hadn't even known she was there. By the look on the faces of the other two women, they didn't either.

"When you show your true colors and try to betray us," Nalia said. "Then you will have all the combat you could ever desire."

"Nal," Sam said, "be nice. Ix hasn't given us any reason to doubt her motives. She's been a great help."

"Thank you, Sam," Ix said as she slunk toward them.

Sam watched her. She was very graceful, but in a different way than Nalia. Nalia was smooth, fluid, sexy in the way she was perfectly efficient in her movements. Ix was…dangerous. It was like the difference between a crane and a snake. Both were graceful, agile, and efficient. Both were lethal as well. He had never really thought of it before.

Nalia noticed his inspection of her as she came closer. He realized his mistake just a moment too late, when he saw her mouth thin to a tight line. He would have to discuss it with her later, let her know that he wasn't looking at her body, but that he was comparing the two of them, how graceful they were. No, that would not end well, either. He'd have to figure out how to explain it to her.

"Well," Sam said, "I'm tired. I think I'm heading to bed. We should get an early start in the morning. Goodnight everyone." He left the room quickly, telling himself he wasn't really running. He just needed sleep.

51

The next two days seemed to last much longer than should have been possible. Sam thought that maybe that time had slowed down and each day was actually forty or fifty hours.

He looked from Ix to Nalia and sighed. "Come on, guys," he pleaded. "We really need to just get along." They both looked back as if they didn't know what he was talking about.

He had tried, unsuccessfully, to explain to Nalia what he noticed about the way the two of them moved, but every time he tried to explain it in a different way, he seemed to make it worse. He finally gave up and instead told her how much he loved her and how every second with her made him happy he was alive, no matter what they were doing. It eased the tension a little bit, but not when Ix was around.

With a sigh, he pushed his quarreling companions from his mind. The area they were passing through was as it had been for the last three days, sparsely covered with vegetation, mostly the desert plants he was so used to seeing when he was where he grew up in Telani. There were a few large hills or mountains in the distance, but otherwise the terrain was fairly flat with rock formations dotting the landscape. The red-tinted rock reminded him of Arizona and New Mexico in Telani and for good reason. That was precisely where he was.

They had been following the road due east. Whenever they stopped and he looked around at the area, there was no sign of anyone else having been there for a long time. He was sure that the road was used, but he guessed that with the time of the year and the unpredictable weather, most travelers waited until the spring to utilize it.

By the time they got to the next settlement, the sun was setting and their surroundings were growing dim. It was starting to snow as well. They decided that it would be best to return to Whitehall and enter the city in the morning. None of them knew what it was called or what to expect, but they all agreed that they would better be able to handle anything they found there with a full day of light ahead of them.

By the time they returned to the fortress, Sam was exhausted. The traveling hadn't been anything extraordinary, but the constant tension between Nalia and Ix was weighing upon him. He ate dinner, saying little, and went straight to bed, his mind frantically trying to figure out how to help the women make peace. He hadn't even completed his first thought before he was asleep.

They found out the next morning that the name of the town was Kryzyq. It straddled a large river as if it was guarding it. Low mountains surrounded the buildings, pale and washed out with their light dusting of snow upon them. To Sam, the hills looked to be the soft, rolling type instead of the sharper, harsher kind, but it was hard to tell with their white blankets.

On second look, Sam revised his assumption of the place. He would probably classify Kryzyq as a city, not a town. It was much bigger than Somas. He thought for a moment about leaving them to their own devices, figuring that Rasaad's forces wouldn't attempt trouble with such a large population—he expected they had several hundred people judging by the size and number of structures—but quickly changed his mind. Any advance notice they received may well save lives. He couldn't selfishly leave them on their own without telling them what to expect.

"Are you thinking we should just let them find out about Rasaad themselves?" Ix asked. Sam looked over to notice she was staring at him, as if inspecting his thoughts.

"It occurred to me, but I decided against it," he said. "If warning them prevents what happened in Somas, lives could be saved."

Ix nodded.

"We must not spend too much time in this city," Nalia added, "just warn them and then continue on. Rasaad's forces are behind us, but it is a tenuous thing. We must hurry and get the artifact and then be gone before she is able to arrive. I do not wish to do battle with her entire army with just the three of us."

"Oh, you're no fun at all," Ix said with a smirk that deepened into a smile when Nalia glared at her.

"Please," Sam said, "don't bait her like that, Ix. Let's just be nice today and get our job done, okay?"

The miray of Kryzyq was easy enough to find. She was in the government center in the middle of the city. The first person the three asked directed them straight there.

"What is a 'miray?'" Sam asked.

"It is the title for a leader," Nalia answered. "It is much like a mayor but with more power. Some cities, even a very few towns, use this structure of governance. Whereas a mayor may be overridden by a city or town council, a miray may not. He or she is supreme, holding the office until resigning or until being removed by unanimous vote of the council."

Sam considered it. "Holding that much power, it seems that there would be abuses. I would think that sometimes it would transform into a dictatorship or other oppressive form of government."

"It is true," Nalia said. "That happens sometimes, but it is surprisingly rare."

"Regardless, we need to talk to the miray," Sam said. "We'll just warn the city and then we can move on."

Remarkably, they were ushered in immediately when they presented themselves at the city government office.

"The miray believes in communicating with her constituents and any others who seek her out for consultation," the short, skinny man sitting at the reception desk said as he brought them down a short hall to the miray's office. He knocked softly and, when a firm voice said, "Come" from the other side, opened the door to admit them.

Sam froze when he spotted the miray. She was just getting to her feet from behind her modest desk. Her appearance was completely unexpected. Sam tried not to stare, but couldn't seem to stop looking her over, couldn't seem to make himself move even though Ix ran into his back when he stopped.

She was of medium height, about two inches shorter than Sam, and wore what was probably this city's version of formal government attire. Snug pants that seemed to be made up of one long piece of cloth that was wrapped tightly from ankle all the way up the legs and around the waist and hips melded into some sort of tunic that Sam would think—if he didn't know better—was made of elastic or spandex. As he scanned her firm body, much too toned for someone who spent her time behind a desk, part of him knew he had been looking too long already.

When he looked into her eyes, he got another shock. Bright green orbs contrasted with her fire red hair and seemed to glow from the midst of a face more beautiful than any he'd ever seen, except for Nalia's. She looked as if she could have been related to Inoria and Emerius, with that hair and those eyes. By Gythe's standards, she must be very ugly. According to the conventions of beauty on

Telani, she was breathtaking.

Ix pushed him, laughing. He heard her mutter under her breath, something about "likes the ugly ones." Nalia glided in after Ix, looking Sam over coolly first, and then fixing her gaze on the miray.

"Good morning," the woman said, in a voice that was too alluring. "I am Miray Shiran Slayth, leader of Kryzyq. I understand you have something to discuss with me? Please, sit down. Would you like refreshments?"

"No," Nalia said curtly.

"Uh, no, thank you," Sam added. "We will be brief. You must be very busy."

"Nonsense," she said, smiling. "It's my job to be available for whatever matters may be important to the city. Please, sit. What is it I can do for you?"

There were several chairs scattered throughout the office. Sam sat directly in front of the desk, wishing the miray would sit down so he could stop looking at those pants, trying to figure out if they were all one piece of cloth or just that they appeared that way. It was distracting. Ix and Nalia sat down also, the assassin on his left and the Sapsyr on the other side.

"This," Sam started, "is Ix." He pointed to her. "This is Nalia Wroun, and I'm Sam Sharp."

"*The* Sam Sharp?" the miray asked, and Sam began to dread what she would say next.

"Yes," he sighed, "the only Sam Sharp I know of."

"And he said your name was Nalia Wroun?" she asked Nalia, whose mouth had become a tight line.

"That is correct," Nalia said briskly.

"Nalia Wroun, the Faceless Sapsyr? Nalia Wroun, veteran of not one but two battles against the Gray Man? Nalia Wroun, who is reputedly so ugly that she spent almost three decades of her life wearing a mask to hide it but then bravely decided to show her face so all could see? That Nalia Wroun?"

Sam saw Nalia's mouth drop open. For a moment, it

seemed as if she had completely forgotten her anger. "Yes, that Nalia Wroun," she whispered.

The miray leaned over her desk and took one of Nalia's hands. She brought it to her lips and kissed it repeatedly. "I have always wanted to meet you, since the first time I heard of you and your exploits. I can't begin to tell you how much you have affected my life. Everything I have done, I have patterned after your example. It is my great pleasure to meet you. My dream, really."

Realizing she was still holding Nalia's hand—the Sapsyr was so surprised, she hadn't even pulled it back—the miray patted it and released it. Sam realized his own mouth had dropped open and could see Ix's small smile out of the corner of his eye.

"I…uh…it is my pleasure to meet you as well, Miray Slayth," Nalia was able to get out.

"No, no, you must call me Shiran. I could never be addressed so formally by you. Not you. Please."

"Very well," Nalia said, regaining a bit of her composure. "Shiran."

The smile that grew on the miray's face made Sam feel warm inside. It wasn't just a smile from this beautiful woman—which would have warmed anyone from his world—but it was that, finally, some of the credit for great deeds was going where it belonged. To Nalia.

"I helped, too," Ix threw in. "She beat me up."

The miray looked askance at Ix.

"Forget I mentioned it," the assassin said.

"Oh," Shiran Slayth said, "I'm shaking. I'm so excited to meet you. But I must be professional. What is it I can do for you, the Heroes of Gythe?"

Sam looked to Nalia, hoping she'd understand that he was asking her to speak. She shook her head and began. "It is what we can do for you, Shiran. There is an army coming your way, traveling the road from the west. They will be here within a day or two. They brought trouble in Somas, causing a loss of life and property. We wanted to warn you so that you may make preparations."

"I see," the miray said. "Is this a large army?"

"It is," Nalia answered, "several hundred soldiers, possibly a thousand."

"Oh, that's too big for us to resist if they attack us."

"We don't think they'll attack you," Sam said. "They're heading east on a mission and don't want delays. In Somas, it was just the tail end of the force that caused trouble as they were passing through. If you talk to the leader, Ayim Rasaad, and cooperate with her, maybe you can prevent such a thing from happening."

The miray looked thoughtful. "Yes, I could see to that. Your notice will help us to prepare. We have a city guard, but they are not large enough to resist an army like that. Between my negotiations and their presence, we should be able to find a way to keep the peace. I'll get to work on it right away. I can't think of how to repay you for your help. You may single-handedly prevent deaths from occurring here. Will you stay to help us?"

"Sadly, we cannot," Nalia said. "We are on a mission of our own. As for repayment, we require none. It is our honor and obligation to aid those in need."

That radiant smile graced the miray's face again. Sam wondered at her misfortune in being in Gythe where she was considered so ugly when she would be renowned for her beauty in Telani.

"See," she said. "That's why I have patterned my life after you. Have I mentioned how great an honor it is to have met you, Nalia Wroun?"

Nalia's cheeks flushed, and Sam found himself wearing his own smile.

"Shiran," Nalia said, trying to fill the uncomfortable silence, "we would consider it a great favor to us, as well as the people of Gythe, if you would take part in the new government being set up by Dr. Walt and my father. Leaders local to what used to be the Gray Fortress are already taking part to make it a success, as is the mayor of

Somas. Your attitude and abilities would be most welcome."

"It would be my honor and privilege to do so," the miray said. "Once this crisis is averted, I will think on how best to do so, if by letter or personal travel. I promise you that I will do all I can."

"You have my thanks," Nalia said. "Perhaps we will return in a few days' time to discuss it with you. We may be able to simplify your decision considerably. For now, however, we must continue with our own mission. We thank you for listening to us and hope that our news will help your city."

Sam, Ix, and Nalia stood, as did the miray. Sam forced his eyes to meet hers as he thanked her for her hospitality.

"Thank you for bringing it to my attention, Nalia Wroun. And thank you also Ix, Sam. Let me walk you out."

She wrapped her arm in Nalia's and headed toward the door. Sam smiled at the scene. They looked like sisters or best friends gossiping or sharing some secret. The miray was animated in her speech and Nalia's attention was rapt. Ix elbowed him as they went out the door and down the hall. Sam thought that maybe this chance occurrence was just the thing Nalia needed to shift her mood.

52

Shiran Slayth told the three what she knew about the land beyond Kryzyq. She had heard of Iboghan but had never been there. It was to the northeast, though she couldn't tell them much more than that. The road that went through Kryzyq split and went to the north and to the east. As far as the miray knew, there were no roads to the cave. There may have been one hundreds or thousands of years ago, but if so the shifting land and blowing sands had covered it over.

Nalia seemed more like herself after the encounter with the miray. Sam teased her that he thought the woman was in love with the her, but Nalia just shrugged it off. Mostly. She had a gleam of pride in her eyes when they talked about it, that at least one person recognized that Nalia was carrying on the heritage of the *Sapsyra Shin Elah*. Sam kissed her and told her that she had always been his hero. That made her blush and smile and kiss him back with fervor.

"Okay, okay," Ix said. "Wait until we return to Whitehall and you can close a door before you go too much further." She was smirking and for a change, Nalia didn't snap back at her. She just kissed Sam one more time and then stepped away from him.

For the rest of the day and the following day, Ix skimmed toward where they thought Iboghan should be. Sam could feel that they were getting closer, but figured it was his anticipation and not anything real he could sense. Their traveling was something like throwing a dart at a map while blind-folded and then taking off the obstruction to look at where they the point stuck.

Ix was taking smaller jumps so they didn't miss anything. She headed generally northeast based on the sun's location, but as they covered mile after mile of sparse vegetation and hardy scrub brush, Sam began to fear they were off track. When he brought it up, Ix shrugged and said she was doing her best.

Two days after leaving Kryzyq, Ix transported them near a road, the first one they'd seen since leaving the city. That in itself was a surprise, but not nearly so great as what they found on the trail itself. There was trash, animal droppings, and many tracks. A large force had passed by, and recently. Sam looked at Ix with the obvious question in his eyes.

"I don't know," Ix said before he even asked it. "It doesn't make sense to me. There's no way Rasaad could have overtaken us, and we haven't gone backwards." She scratched her head and surveyed the area. "Look, you can see the mountain we've been using at a landmark over the last few jumps. We're still going northeast."

"Let's look around," Sam suggested. "Maybe we can find something that will tell us what's going on."

They spent several hours walking the road, looking at tracks and items that had been discarded along the way. Nothing told them what they wanted to know. As they traveled further down the road, which seemed to be heading due east, the surrounding vegetation increased. They appeared to be leaving the desert area they had been traveling through the last several days. Sam didn't know if that was good or bad.

The party had stopped to rest, sitting on a discarded husk of a wagon that had been dragged off to the side of the road. It was late afternoon and they didn't want to waste any more time looking for clues they were increasingly sure weren't there.

"We're wasting our time," Ix said. "Let's keep going. Maybe if I take smaller jumps, we won't miss anything. If there is anything to miss."

"I guess," Sam said. He was tired but felt that they were missing something. "I have a feeling we're off course somehow."

"Well, now," a voice came out of the trees a few dozen feet away from them, "that depends on where you're trying to go."

All three whirled and had weapons raised as a green-clothed man stepped out of the forest, a large bear at his side.

"Emerius!" Sam said. "I'm glad to see you alive. What are you doing here?"

The big hunter eyed Ix but didn't comment on her presence. "I've been following Tingai's force since we split up. I've almost caught up to him, judging from the age of these tracks. Just another day or two and I'll have him in my sights. It's been a long road filled with difficulties, but I'm close now. The question is, why are you here?"

Sam explained to Emerius their method of travel, with Ix's skimming and his own teleportation. The hunter looked at Ix as if inspecting her, but still didn't say anything to her. When Sam was finished, Emerius laughed.

"So, you're blindly jumping around trying to find Iboghan, huh? I'd love to help you, but I haven't seen it. All I've seen is the leavings of Tingai's force. I have to take time out each day to hunt or forage so I can eat, but I am still making headway."

"What will you do when you catch him?" Sam asked. "I mean, you're alone and there are hundreds of them. What is your plan?"

Green eyes drilled into Sam's face. "No plan. I figure I'll sneak in and kill Tingai. Maybe I'll be able to get out again, maybe not. I don't really care at this point. I just want to put a stop to the man." His voice was soft but dangerous.

Sam recalled the Emerius of old. He was boisterous and arrogant and loud. It was nothing like this man, who was quiet and had the pall of death hanging over him.

"I was thinking," Sam said. "We could really use your help with what we're doing. We—"

"No, I have my own goals."

"Please, let me finish. We could use your help, and with what I can see, you can use ours. There is no way you'll get to Tingai in the middle of his forces without being killed. You may be able to somehow kill him, but your life will be the cost.

"If you help us to finish this thing, then we can help you with your quest. We're almost to Iboghan, so it won't be more than a few more days. Then, with Ix and myself able to transport us, we can catch Tingai and put an end to him. What do you say? We can help each other and by so doing increase the chance we'll both succeed."

Emerius stared blankly at Sam. He seemed to be mulling it over.

"Plus," Sam said, "we'll be able to go back to Whitehall and eat each night, not to mention sleeping in a bed."

"I have your word that we'll take care of Tingai?" Emerius asked.

"Absolutely. We want to stop him as well. Once we have the next artifact and have stopped Rasaad's mission to collect them, we can attack Tingai's forces."

The hunter nodded and turned to Ix. "I'm Emerius Dinn," he said to her. "I guess we'll be traveling together."

Sam smiled at Nalia, who gave him a firm nod.

When they returned to Whitehall with Emerius and Oro in tow, Sam was beginning to feel better about the next day. With the remaining twin tracking for them, they would be able to find Iboghan more quickly. It didn't make a difference to Sam that it wasn't logical to think tracking ability would help in this. He knew he was grasping at straws, but accepted his buoyed mood.

At dinner, Dr. Walt welcomed Emerius back and listened intently when the big man gave an account of his tracking of the army. Sam sat back and listened, but he also watched. Emerius seemed to have changed, to have matured. That was good, though the reason for it was not. He felt a pang of loss for Inoria and hoped they could end this before anyone else lost their life.

Skitter came to join them late in the meal. *Those kittens are running me ragged*, he sent to Sam, but could not help but to have affection leak through in his sending. The hapaki had been spending a lot of time with the baby cats, allowing them to swarm him and attack him. Sam had heard about it from others as well as the hapaki himself, but now he could clearly sense in the hapaki's mind how much he loved the little monsters. He was like a proud parent.

They'll do that. How are Stoker and Molly doing? Sam sent back. He saw his old cat rarely because he had been so busy with his traveling. It had been a few days since the cat scratched at his door to visit with him, being busy with his own tasks, stalking the keep and hunting rodents.

They are fine.

Sam laughed at the way Stoker had taken to Skitter. They were the best of friends. He was glad his cat had adjusted so well to his new life. With the litter of kittens, it would be no time until there were many families of domestic cats in Gythe.

"Sam," Rindu said, "I would like to accompany you from now on when you go out to look for Iboghan. I feel that there is some hidden danger in this and would like to be there if it should prove to be true."

"That would be great, Master Rindu."

I want to come, too, Skitter sent. *I have been stuck here at the fortress for too long and would like to explore with you, if that's okay. I miss our traveling together. I can still visit with the kittens each night.*

I'd love to have you come with us, Sam sent. *It'll be like old times.*

53

The larger party gathered in front of the stables and prepared to leave. Rindu was standing a dozen feet away, looking out across the courtyard toward one of the parks when he saw Ix approach Sam.

"You know, with this many people, skimming will be tiring," she said quietly, so softly that Rindu had to strain his ears to hear. "I won't be good for more than maybe four or five jumps before I'm too tired to go on."

"I know, Ix," Sam said. "I'm sorry about that. We'll just have to do with shorter days. Let me know when you're tired and we'll call it a day. I'm with Rindu, it feels like we're on the verge of something. I asked Lahim last night, but he hasn't seen anything of use. He mainly sees the army and how big it's getting. Still, there's something…"

"Okay. I just wanted you to know we're sacrificing speed for increasing the size of our group."

Sam nodded. Rindu understood from what Sam had told him that Ix's ability didn't work quite the same way his teleportation did. She would become tired quickly with the extra people, even more so when they got closer to their destination and had to bring the mounts to search on foot. It was a tradeoff that was necessary, however. They were nearing the most dangerous part of their quest and he would be there beside Sam and his daughter.

The Zouy looked about as everyone gathered around Sam. He had called them to him and sat down in his cross-legged meditation position. He was even now entering the *khulim* and he would soon transport them to the location at which they had ended the previous day's travel. Rindu walked over to Nalia and put his hand on her shoulder. She smiled at him but didn't say anything.

In addition to Rindu and Nalia, Skitter was there, sitting on his haunches next to Sam. Ix was there, too, of course, looking as if she was shoring up her strength for a tiring day during which she would be doing all the work. Emerius Dinn was standing next to the assassin, his height in sharp contrast with the diminutive woman. Oro had been left to his own devices in one of the parks, much to his obvious disagreement. Six. It was not a large number of people if they found extraordinary trouble, but sufficient for most hazards, the Zouy thought.

Rindu felt the familiar energy, a shifting, and then he was standing with the others on a narrow road. It was warmer than at Whitehall, but the wind whistling through the small groups of trees made it seem colder. He looked around. To the west, there were large stretches of land without an appreciable number of trees. To the east, the direction the others seemed to be orienting toward, copses of trees seemed to be getting progressively thicker and larger. The blue sky seemed to stretch on forever, with very few wispy clouds racing across it.

"With the extra members of the party," Sam said, "Ix will not be able to skim all day long. It's too tiring. So, we need to be smart about where we go. I suggest we carefully decide into which direction we'll go and how far. We could easily miss the opening to the cave completely."

The others nodded or looked around, but remained silent.

"As close as I can tell, we're far enough north, so we should concentrate on going east now," Sam continued. "Emerius, do you agree? Have you seen anything while tracking Tingai that might indicate where we should go?"

Emerius considered a moment, then shook his head. "I don't really know where Iboghan would be. Tingai didn't seem to be concerned about it, only about going toward the north. East sounds as good a direction as any. Maybe we'll run into an old road or something else that will tip us off that it's near."

"Master Rindu," Sam said as he turned toward him. "Do you sense anything, anything at all, like you did at Gromarisa?"

"No, Sam, I am afraid not. I do not doubt that I will sense something when I am close, but I can feel nothing now."

"Okay," Sam said. "Well, unless anyone else has any other ideas, I think we should just go east. There are those sharp hills that way, so if we can jump to the foot of them, that seems like a good start. Ix, Nalia, any other suggestions?"

"Your plan seems the most reasonable way to proceed," Nalia said.

"I don't have any objections," Ix added. "Let's get started."

They made five jumps that day. After each, they scouted the area looking for any signs that might indicate there was a large cave system close. They found nothing.

Rindu tried to extend his senses for anything out of the ordinary, anything at all, but to no avail. The number of trees and thus living creatures increased at they moved toward the east, but there was nothing of the feeling he encountered when they were close to the first artifact.

"It seems like we're just shooting arrows into a bush, not aiming but poking around blindly," Emerius grumbled. "How do you track a hole in the ground? What do you look for? I have found caves before and there is nothing that indicates where a system lies. At least, nothing further than a quarter mile or so away."

Rindu saw Sam tense and the way his eyes narrowed, he thought the young man might snap at the hunter. Instead, he took a deep breath and nodded. "I know, Em. There's really nothing else we can do, though. I'm not sure how Rasaad is going to find the cave, but we can only do what we can do."

"Sam," Ix said. She was sitting on a rock, head hanging. "I may be able to make one more jump today, but that will be it. I'm very tired."

"No. You're done for the day. Let's go back to Whitehall. Maybe Lahim Chode can give us some information. You should rest so we can start again tomorrow."

The assassin nodded tiredly.

Sam meditated to learn the location and then teleported everyone back to Whitehall. Rindu saw that the monumental task was weighing heavy on Sam. As the others split up to go their own way, he put a hand on Sam's shoulders.

"Sam," the Zouy said. "Do not let the difficulties we face wear you down. We will find the cave and the artifact. We must remain positive and channel our energies toward the solution. Perhaps a little rest and meditation will improve our outlook on things."

"Yeah, I think that might help. I'm going to go check in with Lahim Chode and Dr. Walt first. We have several hours yet before dinner. Maybe we could work on my problems with harmonizing myself with others? If you have the time."

Rindu smiled at Sam. "That would be wonderful. I will think of another way I might explain it to you. Come to my room when you are able."

"I will," Sam said. "I'll see you in an hour or so." He walked off toward Dr. Walt's library.

"Is he still unable to harmonize with others' *rohw*?"

Nalia asked.

"I am afraid so," Rindu said, turning toward his daughter. "It is because he came to his training so late in life, I think. He will understand it, make it his own. Eventually. I can do naught but try different techniques until he understands it. The primitive mind is complex. Who knows what it will take?"

Nalia nodded, her gaze unfocused. "I will think upon it as well. Maybe I can find something that may help. I know how important it is for him to progress."

"Would you like to participate this afternoon? It may help Sam if you are there, taking part in his training."

"No," Nalia said. "I think it would make things worse at this time. We have not been completely at peace lately. It is my fault, but until I can correct it, I believe I would be a distraction."

Rindu looked at his daughter. "Very well, but do not delay in setting things right. We never know when the unforeseeable will happen and take away our ability to do so. As it is said, 'Only put off until tomorrow that which you are willing to die having left undone.'"

"I will, Father. Thank you." She kissed his cheek and moved off down the corridor.

When Sam arrived at Rindu's room just over an hour later, Rindu met him at the door. Instead of inviting him in, though, he stepped out into the hall. Torim Jet stepped out right behind him.

"We will be going to a chamber with more space," Rindu said to him. "Brother Torim has agreed to help."

Sam bowed to the white-haired Zouy. "Thank you, Master Torim. It is an honor. I really appreciate you and Palusa Filk helping me."

"You are one of us, Sam," Torim Jet said. "We have no official Zouyim Temple and at this time, there are only we three—if you do not count our newest disciple Chen Bao Ling—but once we are able to meet and decide, your precise place in the order will be determined. One thing is clear, Sam: you are our brother in the Zouyim Order. It is my obligation and my privilege to aid in your training."

The three went into a room just down the hallway. It was larger than Rindu's chamber, and empty of furnishings or obstructions. "This will suffice," he said.

Rindu turned toward Sam. "I would like you to remain motionless and soften your gaze. Brother Torim and I will generate *rohw* so that you may see clearly our energy signatures. Then, we will merge our energy and act in harmony, in unison. Pay close attention to our *rohw* and how it flows and interacts, one with the other. Do you understand?"

"I do," Sam said.

Rindu and Torim Jet both began generating *rohw*, extracting it from their surroundings. He looked at Sam to make sure he was seeing it. Once there was sufficient energy surrounding them so that he knew Sam could see its movement clearly, he motioned to the other Zouy to begin.

Using movements from the *kori rohw*, the two projected their energy, combining it with the other's, merging it. Torim Jet allowed Rindu to take the lead. He took control of the combined energy and moved it around the room, creating patterns and whirls in the air that he knew Sam could see. After doing so for a full minute, he gathered up the combined *rohw* and projected it toward Sam, pushing him back toward the wall gently, as with a strong wind. He smiled inwardly as Sam's eyes widened. Then, he separated his energy from the other Zouy and allowed it to dissipate into his body.

"Did you see?" Rindu asked.

"I did," Sam said. He gave a small smile and added, "I felt it, too."

"Did you see how we combined our *rohw*?" Torim Jet asked. "Was it evident that we, at the same time, surrendered part of ourselves while still maintaining control and thus became a harmonious whole?"

"I think so."

"Good," Rindu said. "Now it is your turn to try. You and I have tried repeatedly, so this time I would like you to attempt to come into harmony with Torim Jet."

"Okay." Sam immediately shifted into the deep, rhythmic breathing he had been trained to use when doing work with the *rohw*.

Sam gathered *rohw* with lidded eyes. He still, more often than not, closed his eyes to concentrate when doing something unfamiliar, but Rindu knew that he probably wanted to see Torim Jet's energy so he could try to merge with it.

"Now, Sam," Rindu said. "I want you to see the pattern of Torim Jet's *rohw*. More, I want you to feel it. Latch onto it, make it your own, but do not greedily snatch at it. Instead, control your own energy to match that of his. It is somewhat like when you teleport, changing your vibrations to match that of the location you wish to travel to."

Sam's eyes narrowed even further, locking onto Torim Jet's energy. To Rindu's *rohw*-sensitive sight, Sam glowed brightly, compensating for the strangeness of the situation by generating more *rohw* than necessary. He had the look of a child snatching at a favorite toy, only to have an older child pulling it away each time. Rindu could see him getting frustrated.

"Relax, Sam," the Zouy said. "It should be an easy partnering with the energy. Do not grasp for it too firmly or, as with a wet seed, it will pop from your grip."

Sam stopped, breathed more deeply, and relaxed his shoulders, which had tensed from the effort he was expending. He seemed to be doing better, relaxing and causing his own energy to flow around that of Torim Jet, but still he could not seem to come into harmony with it. Try as he might, Rindu could not see anything that prevented the melding of the *rohw*.

After half an hour, with Sam dripping sweat and exhaustion evident on his face and in his posture, Rindu stopped them.

"That is enough," he said. Sam's shoulders drooped as he opened his eyes.

"I'm sorry, Master Rindu, Master Torim," Sam said. "I just can't seem to do it for some reason.

"The blame is mine, Sam," Rindu said. "I cannot determine the problem. From what I saw, you should have succeeded. Brother Torim, did you see something I missed?"

"No," Torim Jet said. "I felt your energy, Sam, felt you channeling it correctly. I expected at any moment for our *rohw* to become one, but it did not. I, too, do not understand it. I have not encountered its like; it is a mystery to me. Perhaps it is due to you being from Telani. I do not know. I must think upon it."

Rindu wondered if Torim Jet was correct. "Do not despair, Sam. We will find the reason and you will succeed. It may be as the old saying, 'the cloak most difficult to find is the one you are already wearing.'"

Sam looked confused for a moment, but only sighed and remained silent. Rindu should have used one of the sayings from Sam's world. The young man just did not seem to understand the wisdom of Gythe.

"We will try again when we are able," Rindu said to Sam. "I believe it is time for dinner now, and I am hungry. Would you accompany us to the dining hall?"

"Yes," he said. "It would be my pleasure."

At dinner, Sam revealed that neither Lahim Chode nor Dr. Walt had any other information for them. They would just have to continue in their current endeavor, searching the area for the opening to a cave system that stretched on for miles underground. Rindu wished he could think of something to help narrow their search, but he could not.

54

The next day, they gathered at their normal location. Rindu had decided he would begin bringing *Sunedal* with him each day. He still had a feeling that some sort of battle or danger was impending and he wanted to use his new weapons if the need arose.

Ix seemed refreshed and rested from her efforts the day before. After Sam had teleported the party to their ending point from the day before, she was ready to get started right away.

"Today is the day," she said to no one in particular. "I have a good feeling about it."

Rindu wondered if the assassin had some sort of talent for premonition or if she was speaking from intuition. Often they were the same thing. In any case, he hoped she was correct. If they delayed too much longer, Rasaad and her army would catch them.

With the first of Ix's jumps, things were different. The road they had been following had all but disappeared between where they started and where Ix teleported them. Rindu looked around and saw the hills they had used as a reference. She had brought them exactly to the location they wanted to go.

Sam looked around and down at the faint remnants of the road they had been traveling. "What now?" he said. "Do we backtrack or continue on?"

Emerius shielded his eyes with his hand and looked toward the east. "There is a break in the trees where the road was. I think we should follow it. It's obvious the path continued on this way but has fallen into disuse. Isn't that exactly what we were expecting? Iboghan was a tourist spot hundreds of years ago but there isn't much call for people to go there now. I think continuing on is our best bet."

Rindu watched Sam as he looked at each of the others in turn, gauging their agreement. He got the blank expression on his face he normally wore when speaking with Skitter. Finally, he said, "Yeah, I suppose you're right. The road had to lead somewhere. Why not to the cave?"

Ix made three smaller jumps, hardly further than line of sight each time, before they stopped to rest.

Sam was off to the side, near a meadow area set in the midst of a stand of trees. He was shaking his head and rubbing his temples with his palms. Rindu walked over to him.

"Are you well?" the Zouy said.

"I…" he rubbed his head more firmly. "I have this horrible ringing in my head. It feels like a migraine coming on."

"Come, let us sit with the others in the shade and I will see if perhaps you have a blockage in one of your *rohw* pathways."

Sam followed Rindu for a few steps and then stopped. "Hm," he said, looking back toward where he had been just moments before. "It just disappeared. There's no trace of it now."

Rindu looked at him quizzically. "It just stopped? You do not hear the ringing, do not feel the pain any longer?"

"No," Sam said. He took a step back toward where he

was and Rindu could see in his eyes that the pain had come back. "Wow, there it is again." He took another step. "Yep, it's stronger now."

"Step away from there, Sam," Rindu said calmly.

When he did, Rindu went toward the area Sam had been, one slow step at a time. Within two steps, he felt what he had been too busy to notice before. There was some kind of resonance coming from the center of the meadow.

"Sam, you are fine. There is something there, in the meadow. It is causing vibratory energy to bounce back and forth between you and the source, increasing in intensity until it is causing you pain."

"Feedback?" Sam asked.

"I am not familiar with that word," Rindu said. "What does it mean?"

"Well," Sam scratched his head, obviously trying to figure out how to explain it. "When signals interfere with each other, they can cause a violent shrieking kind of sound. Oh, I don't know how to explain it. I've heard it before when a microphone, a sound transmitting device, gets too close to a speaker, a sound-emitting device. The sound signal goes through multiple times, repeating and causing a particular sound based on the resonance frequency of the original sound. Or something like that. Dr. Walt could explain it better."

"I see," Rindu said. "I will try something, Sam. Wait there." He walked a few steps toward where Sam had encountered the pain.

The Zouy stopped and closed his eyes, allowing the strange vibrations go through him, absorbing them and analyzing them as they did so. The solution came to him suddenly. Making small adjustments in his body's own vibrations, the irritating effects of the area stopped.

"Sam," he said, "I want you to match my body's vibrations exactly. Can you do that?"

"Yes," Sam said, "though you may have to nudge me if

I get stuck. Hold on."

Sam closed his eyes and began to breathe regularly and deeply. Rindu saw his energy signature spike as he entered the *khulim*. Then, Sam opened his eyes slowly and looked at Rindu, eyes unfocused, his gaze softened. Within a few minutes, he had matched the Zouy's vibrations exactly.

"Very good. Now, walk with me."

Sam, hesitant at first, took one slow step. When nothing happened, he took another. Realizing there would be no pain, he took the last few steps until he was standing beside Rindu.

"I am not sure what the vibrations signify," Rindu said. "Let us find out."

As they entered the middle of the meadow, Nalia and Skitter came toward them to see what they were doing. By the time Rindu noticed them, they were already well into the clearing. He was surprised to see that there seemed to be no effects on either of them. He would have to think upon that later. For now, he was more concerned about what had been causing the vibrations to begin with.

Sam's foot struck something and a metallic thunk sounded. When the other three went to see what it was, they discovered a half-buried sheet of some kind of metal.

"What is it?" Nalia asked.

"I do not know," Rindu said, knocking on the surface of the metal.

"I think it's a door," Sam said.

Skitter had gone off a few feet, looking at a strange hole in the ground. As Rindu turned to look for the hapaki, the furry creature disappeared into the blackness.

"Sam," Rindu said, "Can you talk to Skitter? He just disappeared into a hole."

Before Sam could answer, there was a solid click and a hiss and the metal at their feet shifted and slid out of the way, revealing a man-sized hole in the ground.

"What do you know." Sam said. "It must have been spring loaded and when Skitter hit the release, it opened.

Good job, buddy." Skitter was just now scrambling up out of the darkness, a smug look on his whiskered face.

Sam started through the doorway, using his *rohw* to cause the tip of his staff to light the corridor, illuminating a set of stairs. The hole Skitter had gone through was visible to the side, near the ceiling of the stairwell.

"Be careful, Sam," Rindu said. "I am unsure yet what caused the strange vibrations we felt."

"I will. I just want to look around a little."

Rindu shared a look with Nalia and then followed immediately after Sam. Gravel, dust, and the occasional rock cluttered the set of stairs they descended. At the bottom—Rindu had counted forty steps—there was a small landing with a single door. It was more conventional than the one at the top of the stairs, with a rounded handle that Sam grasped and turned. There was a click and Sam pulled it open. The door squealed loudly as the door resisted the movement.

Sam poked his staff into the blackness, lighting up a hallway that was similar to the corridors in Whitehall, but lower and not so wide. It was perhaps wide enough for two men to pass without brushing shoulders with each other or the walls, but just barely. The door Sam had opened was metal, as the one above, though different in design. The walls beyond it were some kind of stone, but not any variety Rindu had ever seen before. It looked like the crumbling walls of some of the ruins he had seen, but not quite so deteriorated. It had probably been sealed up for centuries, slowing its eventual demise.

As they moved down the corridor, the light from Sam's staff revealed walls displaying some sort of decoration, flat rectangular objects that seemed to be just hanging there. When he touched one, it disintegrated in his hand, the crumbling pieces falling to the floor.

In the globe of illumination, a door on the right side of the hall became visible. It was made of metal and had one of the rounded handles like the one they had just come through. Sam looked back at the others for a moment and then opened the door. It squealed, but not so loudly as the first.

It was not a large room, appearing to be a work area. A desk sat off to one side, made of the same type of metal as the door. Rindu knocked on it and it made a higher pitched sound than he was expecting. Pushing the desk, he found that it was much lighter than it should have been.

"It's some type of aluminum alloy, I think," Sam told him. "Do you know this metal? Do they use it on Gythe in the current time?"

Rindu shook his head. "I have not seen its like."

"I can understand that. It's really no good for making sharp weapons, doesn't hold an edge."

Rindu picked up a small cube resting on the desk. He turned it over in his hands. It was made of a material he had never seen. It was not quite metal, but not stone either, and definitely not made of wood. It was perhaps twice as large as his outstretched hand and had a hole in it as big around as his middle finger. He put his finger into the hole, but could feel nothing but the cold, smooth surface, the same as the outside. He set it back on the desk.

Another part of the surface of the table top projected upward, facing the chair in front of the desk. "Is that glass, Sam?" he asked.

Sam ran his finger along the flat surface of the square projection. "Yes, I think it is. It looks like a computer monitor. It's kind of like a book with pictures that can change. Instead of turning a page, a new one replaces it on the screen. This must have been sitting here since before the Great War."

"Computer monitor," Rindu repeated, trying the strange words out. "You must tell me of these things at another time. For now, though, we must continue our search for Iboghan."

"I know," Sam said. "Just give me a few more

minutes." He picked up the cube and put it in his backpack. "I want to bring this back to Dr. Walt. Maybe he can figure out how to use it. I don't see a plug, so I don't know where it gets its power."

They continued down the hallway, checking each door they came to. At least, they opened those that were not covered with rubble from collapsed portions of the ceiling. Most of them led to offices like the first one, but there were a few chambers that appeared to be storage rooms and one that seemed to be a recreation room or dining hall. It was difficult to determine because other than those items made of metal or that other strange material, when any of the party touched anything, it crumbled to dust.

They finally came to the last door at the very end of the hallway. It was unlike any of the others, though made of the same metal. It was twice as large, almost as wide as Rindu's outstretched arms, and high enough that he could not touch the top. It had no handle.

Rindu closed his eyes and sent out his senses. "Sam, the vibrations we felt above are coming from this door, or from beyond it."

"Yeah, I can feel it," Sam said. "I wonder how we can open it."

"Perhaps," the Zouy said, "the question is not *how* but *if* we should open it."

Sam did not seem to hear him. He was looking at the door intently. Rindu's gaze followed where Sam's searched all around the portal. It seemed that it did not open on hinges as with the others. Instead, it appeared that it somehow slid into the wall itself. There was no doorframe to speak of, only the cold wall made of that strange rock.

He saw Sam's eyes focus on a small square to the right of the door, almost at shoulder height. The young man put his face very close to it, looking for something.

"This looks like some kind of glass," Sam said. "It almost looks like—" Sam snapped his fingers and pulled his head back. He took a deep breath and slowly moved his hand to the plate, fingers splayed. Inch by inch, he neared it. Rindu saw Sam's *rohw* swirl, concentrating on Sam's palm, but he did not think Sam was doing it on purpose. He opened his mouth to tell Sam to stop when his palm slapped onto the plate and there was a sharp burst of *rohw* in Rindu's vision. At exactly the same time, Rindu felt the harmful vibrations he had sensed earlier disappear.

The door silently slid into the wall. There was a hiss of air escaping—or rushing in—and Sam pulled his hand away quickly and slumped against the wall. "It...it felt like it sucked energy from me. I'm so tired all of a sudden."

Rindu put his arm around Sam to support him, using his *rohw* to probe him for injury or blockage in his energy pathways. There was no damage he could detect. "I believe it used your energy, your *rohw*, to activate the device operating the door. I can sense no damage in you, however."

Sam straightened and shook his head. "I'm starting to feel better. It was just a shock, that's all. I wasn't expecting it. Let me try something." He put his hand on the plate again, more gently this time, and Rindu saw the energy swirl as before. Sam furrowed his brow in concentration and the door slid closed again. Prepared for it this time, Sam did not slump but he did take in a sharp breath.

"That's the strangest thing I've ever felt," he said as Nalia came and put her arm around him to help support him. He did not appear to need it this time, though.

Rindu was intrigued. Nudging Sam out of the way with an "excuse me, please" he put his own palm on the plate. It felt cold to his touch, but nothing else. He softened his gaze, but did not see any energy whorls as he had seen with Sam. He tried his other hand, but nothing happened.

"Nalia, if you would?" he said to his daughter.

He watched intently as Nalia put her hand to the square, but nothing happened. "That is strange," Rindu said.

Sam had been watching. He looked confused and Rindu did not blame him. He himself was confused. It may be a question of raw power, but he did not think so.

"Maybe it's dead now," Sam said. He put his palm back on the plate and the door hissed open. "...or not. Well, that's a mystery for another time. Let's see what we've found."

As Sam entered the room, the walls and ceiling glowed a blue-tinged light. The walls to each side and the back were barely visible, even in the illumination. While there were a few tables or desks scattered about, what caught Rindu's attention were the shelves.

There were two types. One held row upon row of small cylinders, looking like they were made of the same material as the box they had found in the first office. There were more of the boxes and the "computer monitors" on the desks in the room. The other shelves, however, made the breath catch in Rindu's throat. They were full of books. What looked like thousands of books.

The tomes arranged neatly on the shelves were not books as he was accustomed to seeing. They were tidy and obviously of good quality. The bindings appeared tight and there did not seem to be any wear on them. His mind swirled with the possibilities. They looked new.

"Oh my God," Sam whispered, the sound seeming a shout in the dead still air. "It's a library. One that probably hasn't been opened in hundreds of years. That hiss when the door first opened. I think the room was sealed with a vacuum. Look, there isn't any dust anywhere."

The others had already started moving about the room. Emerius picked up one of the cylinders and was tapping it against a shelf. Ix had pulled a book down and was flipping through the pages. Nalia was reverently caressing the spine of another.

"It's Old Kasmali," Ix said. "but a strange dialect. I can only make out every other or every third word."

Sam went over to the assassin and looked over her

shoulder. His eyes traveled down the page for a moment before he spoke.

"No, not a strange dialect," he said. "It's technical. The words you don't know, those are trade words. This must have been a reference library for whatever scientists or scholars worked here." He whistled. "These books may hold the secrets to the technology of Gythe before the Great War. We have to bring these back to Whitehall. There might be something that can help us in all these references."

"Look, Sam," Nalia said from the other side of the room. She was pointing to a painting hanging on the wall. The man in it had long, pale yellow hair hanging loose past his shoulders. He wore a strange tunic—looking to be made of a metallic fabric—which almost appeared to be shimmering in the picture. Beneath the picture, there was a name: Magry Andronis.

"He looks important," Ix said. "Maybe he was the leader here. I bet some of these books tell who he was."

Sam's excitement was evident. Rindu smiled inwardly. He understood having a thirst for knowledge. As pleased as Sam was with the find, Dr. Walt would be even more so.

"Sam, we must continue on," Rindu said. "We can come back when we are finished with our task and retrieve some of these books. For now, though, we must remember what is important."

"I know. We'll leave in just a—oh!" He had moved to the opposite side of the room, on the other side of many of the shelves, so Rindu could not see him. When he walked there, he saw Sam looking at another wall hanging. It was a map.

"I know where we are, now," Sam said, looking at the Zouy. "We're in Roswell."

55

"I do not recognize that name," Rindu said.

"Oh," Sam said absently as he was looking over the map, "that's just what it's called in Telani. Here, it was called Kawkibon, according to this map. "Star Rock" in Old Kasmali. The important thing is that we have overshot Iboghan. We're here," he pointed to a spot on the map signified by a large green circle, "and we need to be here." He pointed again, this time to the south and east of where they were. "We'll need to head there."

Ix and the others had come over to look at the map. The assassin studied it. "That will be helpful. We can get started right away."

"Ummm," Sam started. "there's one thing I want to do first before we get started. It'll only take a few minutes. I want to learn this place and then I want to transport the entire contents of this room to Whitehall."

Rindu looked around at all the others. Even Skitter had stopped and they were all looking at Sam as if he had lost his mind.

"What?" Sam said.

Rindu thought quickly about how he could phrase what

he wanted to say. "Sam, these books are important, but we do not have time to move them all. They will be fine while we continue on our quest. We must leave them for now. You can close the door and no one will be able to get to them."

"No. It *is* important that we continue on, but I think it's important to get these books to Dr. Walt as soon as possible, too. He may be able to find something that will end our conflict. It won't take long. Give me one hour. I'll learn this location, teleport back to Whitehall, find a suitable location to deposit all these books, and then move them all in one shot."

"That's impossible," Ix said. "No one has enough power to move this many things. You'd probably kill yourself trying."

"I won't," Sam said. "My teleportation ability doesn't work like yours, remember? I can do it; I know I can. One hour, that's all I ask."

The others looked doubtful, but they nodded their agreement. Sam gave his thanks and then sat down to enter the *khulim* and learn the room's location. After several minutes, he told them he would be right back and disappeared. He reappeared a quarter hour later.

Within a few more minutes, forty from when he had first started, Sam was ready to move the library. "I think everyone should wait out in the hall, or back up on the surface." He winked. "Unless you want to go along for the ride." Only Nalia and Rindu decided to go along with Sam. They went inside the room and Sam closed the door from the inside, using an identical plate as the one on the outside.

"Before I start, I just want to let you know that I'm actually going to try something…uh…different. I'm going to try to move the entire room. Walls, doors, and whatever mechanism exists to make the door work. Hopefully. There is some sort of indoor arena Doctor Walt showed me when I went to Whitehall just now. It's more than large enough for the entire room—I paced it out. I'll put it there. I've never tried to move a part of something this large into a space inside of something else, though."

Sam sat down in his cross-legged position and within minutes he opened his eyes again. "It is done." Rindu had felt the familiar shift of the teleportation, but it seemed less powerful, as if being in the midst of the room somehow buffered the experience. It was, he thought, the same as being in a boat on the sea: a larger boat seemed to move less with the waves than a smaller one.

The younger man used the plate to open the door and, when it opened, he let out a sigh of relief. "I'm glad it still works," he said.

When they went out the door of the library, Rindu saw the door to the arena in which they had placed the entire room. Sam opened it and Dr. Walt's face appeared. "Is it done?" he asked excitedly.

"It is," Sam answered. The old scholar rushed toward the library with a speed that belied his age.

"It's all yours," he said. "We have to get back to looking for Iboghan. We'll see you later tonight."

The older man didn't seem to hear Sam. He was busy looking through the shelves, emitting oohs and ahhs as he perused the books.

Sam teleported the three of them back to where the doorway of the library was. Some rocks had fallen into the void he created when taking the room, but there didn't seem to be a danger of total collapse. They made their way up the stairs to the others and soon they were on their way.

*****

Emerius was in a funk. The discovery of the library made him think of his sister. She had always loved books and would have been excited to see so many in one place, especially ones that were technical in nature. Even seeing that door and the way it moved on its own would have had her giddy. His mouth tried to force its way to a smile, but he did not allow it. He missed her. He missed her terribly.

The hunterstill wasn't sure about going with Sam and the others. The only thing in his life he seemed to have control over was his choice of going after Tingai. Or not going after him. He could see that, logically, going with them may actually increase the chance of success in not only catching Tingai, but in surviving it. He wasn't sure if that was a positive or a negative.

His old self would have gone with the others so he could play the hero, do something that would win him acclaim, if not just for the sake of helping others. With the deaths of everyone important to him, all but Oro, he just wasn't sure he cared anymore. He was so tired. If he thought he could get to Tingai and kill him alone, he would accept it as a one-way mission. Emerius Dinn sighed. He would help the others for now, in exchange for them helping him. Baron Tingai would die for what he had done. When that was complete, he would decide what to do next. If he was still alive.

Sam, the Zouy, and the Sapsyr had just come up the stairs, so it was time to go. He looked toward the assassin and the hapaki, who were getting to their feet, and did likewise. It would be good to get moving again, even better to be able to think about something other than the poor tale his life had become.

"So," he said to Ix, "how did we get so far away from where we were supposed to be? I thought you knew all about this teleporting stuff."

The assassin eyed him coolly. "It's not that easy. All I had to go on was a general direction and a vague description. With no specific landmarks to look for, we're lucky we're not further off than we are. How likely would you be to hit something with one of those arrows of yours if you had to do it by someone else's directions but couldn't see it yourself?"

"Okay, okay, I get it. Will we be able to find it now?"

"It should be easier," Ix said. "According to the map, we're almost directly north of where it should be. We can use the sun and judge where we're going. I will take small jumps so we don't overshoot it. I don't think it'll take more than a day or two."

The others arranged themselves around Ix so that she could touch them all. Emerius felt that strange feeling again, the one that accompanied teleportation. He didn't think he'd ever get used to it. He opened his eyes—he had developed the habit of closing them when they jumped—and saw that they had gone maybe ten or fifteen miles, judging from the proximity of the hills he had been staring at earlier. He immediately set out, spiraling from the others to search the area.

The day progressed, Ix moving them a handful of miles each time and each of them searching their new locations. By mid-afternoon, the assassin could hardly stand on her own feet. She rested on a flat rock as the others returned from scouting the area.

"We'll have to call it a day," Sam said. "You're exhausted, Ix."

"I can do one more jump."

"No," Rindu said. "One jump will make no difference for today, but it could cause you harm. We will start again tomorrow."

It was telling that the woman didn't object again. She was very tired, Emerius could see that.

Sam took some time to learn the area and they went back to Whitehall. Emerius mentally ticked off one more day Tingai lived, and became more despondent.

After eating dinner, the party split up. Emerius saw Sam head off with Dr. Walt, obviously toward the books they had found earlier that day, and the others went in their own directions. The hunter himself went to check on Oro, spending a little time just sitting silently with the big bear. With a final pat on Oro's massive head, Emerius went to his room and wrestled with consciousness until he drifted into an uneasy sleep.

After the first jump the next morning, Sam suggested they continue forward using their mounts, which they had brought with them. "I went to the caverns one time on my world. I remember driving up a big hill to get to the opening. The hills we're currently in look familiar, though it's hard to tell. I don't want to overshoot it again, though. Without searching on foot, we could bounce back and forth around it and never find it."

"I agree," Emerius said. He was tired of hopping around by magic. His own feet, and Oro's paws, were good enough for him. His ursine friend was so happy to be traveling again, Emerius could hardly keep him from jumping around and capering. It warmed Em's heart to see his friend happy, even if it was mainly nervous energy. He patted Oro's head and rubbed one of his ears as they set out.

They scaled two hills with no luck when Sam stopped them for a lunch break.

"I'm sorry, guys," he said. "The hills look so much alike, and I came from the other direction. I have a feeling we're getting closer, though."

No one responded. They were all tired, but even more importantly, no one had a better idea as to how to go about their search. They finished their meal and moved on.

An hour later, they came upon the road. Rather, they found what had once been a road.

Emerius was the first one to notice the odd way the hill was shaped, of course. He was a hunter and tracker, so his job was to find things that looked out of the ordinary. He kept it to himself until he was sure.

As the land sloped upward, there seemed to be odd patches where trees were missing in the tapestry of vegetation. That was nothing odd in and of itself, but it tickled Em's mind, calling out for explanation. He ignored it with the first few thin patches he saw. But while they were cresting a neighboring hill, giving him a chance to look at the whole pattern before him, it became obvious.

"There was a road here," he said to the others. "Not a road like we were traveling before. An old road, ancient."

"Where?" Sam asked, shielding his eyes from the sun with one of his hands and looking out toward the surrounding hills.

"There," Emerius pointed toward the south. "see how the hill is oddly shaped? Accounting for the wear and erosion of centuries, picture the strange cuts along the edges of the hill as sharper, more defined. Imagine the slopes on the inward side of the hill being more in contrast with the flatter parts. Can you see how it has been cut, not by wind or rain, but by something else? By humans?"

Sam nodded. "I do see it. It winds up the hill, making its gradual way to the top. It looks just like the road I took when going to the caverns back home. Do you think that might be it?"

"Only one way to find out," Emerius said and gestured for Oro to continue.

It took another hour to make their way up the hill. Oro and the rakkeben climbed the steep slopes quickly, but Ix's manu bird was flagging. So much for its name. Feather. That bird needed to go on a diet.

It would have taken much longer to follow the path the road had taken up the hill, so though the bird slowed the pace, Sam had decided that the steeper path would save time in the long run, even if it tired their mounts. They could rest when they got to the cave mouth, he said. Assuming this was the hill they were looking for.

Emerius looked toward the assassin. Her face was calm, but she was perspiring despite the chill in the air. She felt his gaze and looked back, flashing a toothy grin at him. He chuckled and looked away. She was interesting, that one. He'd have to ask her to tell him her story when this was all over. He didn't quite know how she fit into all of this.

They finally arrived at the top of the hill. On part of it, on the side opposite the one they scaled, a large portion of the tip had been sheared off and flattened. There were sparse trees and low plants growing there, but it was obvious it had been altered by people. Emerius wondered what it had been used for. Maybe there were buildings there before.

"Parking lot," Sam said. When the others, all except Nalia, looked askance at him, he went on. "Vehicles that were used to transport people, sort of like carts or wagons, would be driven here and then left so people could see the cave. Then, when they were done, they would get back into their vehicles and leave.

"Over there was the visitor center," he pointed to the crumbling remains of some type of building, almost unrecognizable in the midst of the bushes, shrubs, and occasional trees that had grown there.

"And if I remember correctly," Sam said, turning and walking alongside the ruins of the building, down the slope a little way and then facing to the right, "the opening will be over here. At least, that's how it was in my world."

Sam stopped then, as if he had just remembered something. Emerius could only see the side of his head, but by the angle of it he seemed to be confused. Or concerned. With a small shake, he turned back toward the west. "Uh oh," he said.

The rest of the party looked toward where Sam was directing his eyes. Putting a hand up to block the sun, which was almost directly above, Emerius saw the problem. There was a force of people coming toward them. A large force. Ayim Rasaad had almost caught up to them.

"Em, how long do you think it will be before they catch us?" Sam asked.

"It's hard to tell. With this terrain, I'd say maybe three or four hours, at the most. We better do what we need to do, or it will become very crowded in there, no matter how big the cave is."

Sam muttered something under his breath that Emerius couldn't quite make out, gripped his staff until his knuckles were white, and turned back toward the east. "Let's get going. We don't have any time to spare."

Emerius was second-to-last in line, ahead of only Ix. He heard Nalia gasp and Rindu say something to Sam. The hunter walked until he was even with them and then he understood. Tilting his head downward, he stared into what surely had to be the gateway to hell.

He had seen caves before, even been in a few, though he didn't like the feeling of being surrounded by dirt and rock. But nothing he had ever seen compared to this. From his vantage point, he could see down several hundred feet.

The red-tinted sandstone surrounding the gaping maw gave no sign of the cave beneath it from any side other than where they were standing. If they had come from the other side, they could have stood on the mantle above the opening and never known it was there. The top of the opening was flat, as if huge squares of rock had fallen off in ages past. From there, the mouth of the cave opened in an oval, with small ledges and holes peppering the surface of the walls. Birds wheeled and chirped and alighted on their nests in the crevices.

"What is that smell?" Ix asked, wrinkling her nose.

"Bat guano," Sam replied. "There is a very large population of bats here. It smells exactly the same in my world. You might be interested in it, Emerius. Lots of nitrogen. I bet you could use it for some of your mixtures."

Nalia drew her shrapezi and looked around as if she thought they were about to be attacked.

"No, Nal," Sam said. "Not the kinds of bats we faced in the Undead Forest. These are just normal-sized bats, this big." He put his hands close together to show the size, not even as large as an outstretched hand. "At least, that's how they are at home. They only come out at night, leaving the cave to hunt. We'll be fine."

Emerius looked down from the walls into the blackness below. The sunlight penetrated enough to see the hole narrow to what looked to be thirty or forty feet wide and then…nothing. He gulped. The inky dark looked impenetrable. Winding down into the cave was a thin path, broken in some places, grown over with weeds in others, but still serviceable for getting them to where they needed to go.

Sam started picking his way down the trail, his rakkeban just behind him.

"We're going to bring the wolves?" Emerius asked.

"We could probably send them off," Sam said, "so they aren't seen by Rasaad, but the manu would just stupidly wait here and get captured or killed. Besides, I plan on teleporting us all back to Whitehall as soon as we put our hands on Azgo. It's better if we keep them with us. The rakkeben have been in caves with us before. Will Oro be okay?"

Emerius felt a drip of sweat travel down the side of his face. It had nothing to do with temperature. "Yeah," he finally said. "He likes caves. He's a bear. I'll just have to poke him occasionally to keep him from curling up and hibernating." He forced a chuckle, but it sounded frail, even to him.

Ix looked into his eyes. "Are you okay, Emerius? You look pale."

He forced his green eyes to meet her brown, though it was uncomfortable. "I'm fine," he said. "I don't much like closed spaces."

"I understand," she said. "I don't much like gossiping women. Or dying. Or any number of other things." She winked at him, surprising him. He chuckled again. Weakly.

When it came his time to start forward, Ix patted his shoulder. "Just focus on the path ahead of you," she whispered. "Don't worry about anything else. You'll be fine."

"Thanks," he said, and picked his way over a small plant in the path and followed the others, eyes pinned to the gound directly in front of him. He swallowed hard and tried to think of pleasant things.

56

"The way down used to wind around like a giant snake," Sam said as they all headed toward the darkness. "At least, it did in my world. It looks like the blowing dust and sand that accumulated has smoothed it all out into a large ramp now, though."

Emerius could see what he was talking about. The surface on which they were descending was a path only in that there were not the large rocks and sizable trees that existed on either side. He wondered how long it had been since anyone came through this way.

They finally stood on damp stone just inside the covering of the cliffs above. The rock seemed to push down on Emerius. Had it just moved? He wasn't sure he was made for this type of adventuring. Leave the tunneling to the rats. He just wanted to be in the forest.

"Come on, Em," Ix said to him, nudging him, "they're starting to move again."

With a last mournful look at the sky and the sunlight, he followed the others into the opening, Oro and Ix trailing him.

As they went further into the cave, using light from

Sam's staff and from the few torches being held by the others, the sounds of the birds faded and finally stopped altogether. It was soon replaced by a silence Emerius had never experienced. There were no insects, no breeze, nothing to cause any sound except for the intruders making their way where they did not belong.

The light seemed a paltry thing in this kingdom of darkness. Emerius caught glimpses of rock outcroppings above him, but couldn't see the roof of the cavern. They continued to go down, keeping a fast pace to outrace the forces coming behind them, but could they outrace their doom? The hunter wasn't sure.

The surface on which they walked seemed to have been carved or at least manicured in the past. There were parts of rails in some areas, though they did not seem able to keep someone from falling if a person leaned against them. How old were they? He put his hand on one. It wasn't metal but something else.

"Plastic," Sam said when he noticed Emerius touching it. "That's probably the only reason it's still there. There were some metal rails over there," he pointed to a few deteriorated objects off to the right, "but they didn't last as long. With the moisture and the corrosive nature of some of the drippings, they're all but destroyed."

Sam looked Emerius over. "Are you feeling okay?" he asked, moving the light on his staff nearer to the hunter's face. "You look like you're ill."

"He's not fond of closed spaces," Ix answered for him.

"Oh," Sam said. "I'm sorry, Em. This probably isn't your idea of a pleasant adventure. At least it's a big cavern and not something we have to squeeze through like some caves are. Let me know if I can do anything to help out, okay? We'll get out of here as soon as we can."

Emerius looked over at Ix, wanting to be angry at her for telling Sam his weakness. When she smiled at him, he didn't have the heart, though. She was just trying to help. They all were. Why, he didn't know, but he appreciated it.

A couple of months ago he would have made fun of someone for having a weakness like this, for being a coward. It was funny how life taught you lessons.

Though the ground was damp in most places—water dropped onto the party's heads as they made their way downward—it wasn't slippery. The rock was rough enough to compensate for the moisture and moss didn't seem to want to grow there. Maybe it was simply that there was no light. Inoria would know.

The path wound around, going alongside and in between fantastical shapes that Emerius hadn't known existed anywhere in the world. He found himself being distracted enough by the shapes that he sometimes forgot he was underground, forgot he was having trouble breathing. There were fans and shapes that looked like droplets formed from the same rock the walls were made of. There were great pointed formations that came down from the ceiling a hundred feet above and ones that seemed to be growing up from the floor. He marveled at how some formations were ridged and sharp looking while others looked smooth enough to lie down on in comfort. And all the while they continued downward.

At one point, Sam held his staff up as high as he could and made the light increase until it was glowing like a small sun. They still couldn't see all of the ceiling. The part they saw, though, showed a jagged maze of shapes more than a hundred feet above them. Just how deep were they that the ceiling itself was that high?

Sam continued on, using his staff to light the way, talking with Rindu and Nalia the whole time. He seemed unconcerned how deep in the earth they were. None of them seemed to have any trepidation. In a way, it was comforting. On the other hand, it was a little frustrating, too, being the only one who was afraid. Even Oro lumbered along without a care. Worse, the stupid manu bird seemed to be at ease. It probably didn't have the brains to be scared.

They stopped when they got to an area that seemed to sprawl out on the same level they were at, not going up or down like the rest of the path had been up to that point. Emerius looked around, and up. He was surrounded by the same formations he'd been seeing for almost an hour. The only difference is that the path wasn't going down anymore.

"Over there is where the elevator is on my world," Sam said. We'll go there and see if we can find anything. Rindu, can you sense anything? Do you have any idea where we should go? This is a big place."

"I can feel something," the Zouy said, "but I cannot locate it yet. Perhaps when we get closer, I will be able to do so."

A few minutes later they were standing in front of a massive door. Sam looked it up and down. "This is where the elevator is on my world, but this doesn't look like an elevator. Maybe it's some other kind of transport. Who knows what they had during technological Gythe. Rindu? Can you feel anything on the other side of that door?"

"No, Sam. If anything, the feeling is weaker here."

"Oh," Sam said, obviously disappointed. "We're in what's called the Big Room on my world. It's one massive cavern, but the trail goes all around the perimeter. I guess we should just go around it as quickly as we can and hope Rindu can sense where we need to go."

The others all nodded. Emerius was feeling a little better because it didn't seem like he had a ceiling above him. He tried to imagine it was just a very cloudy night and concentrated on the path ahead of him. They would find the artifact, and then they could teleport out of this place. They would never have to come back here again. He suddenly realized how happy he was that two of their number could do that strange teleportation thing.

It took the party a little more than half an hour to walk quickly around the Big Room. When they arrived back where they started, Sam did not look happy. "Anything?"

he asked the Zouy.

"Nothing definite," Rindu said. "I am sorry. In fact, at one point, it felt as if the direction of the artifact flipped exactly in reverse. There is much I still do not know about these artifacts and the power they hold. Perhaps if we make another circuit, I may narrow it down to a general location."

The party made the circuit again. As they neared an area with a hole so deep that Sam could not light it no matter how he increased the power to the tip of his staff, Rindu stopped them.

"There is an echo of a feeling here," the Zouy said, "but it is not coming from the hole. It is from this general direction." He pointed toward the cavern wall.

The others moved toward the wall to inspect it, but Rindu stopped them. "However, if I take one more step toward it," he did so, "the direction shifts toward here." He gestured toward the center of the cavern where there were several of the large pointed pillars that looked to be growing up from the floor—Sam had called them stalagmites earlier. "I do not understand how it shifts in such a way."

Emerius could see Sam pondering, trying to figure out what it all meant. "Does the artifact itself move?" the hunter asked.

"No," Rindu said. "I feel no motion. The feeling is simply in one location and then it is in another."

Sam nodded and muttered to himself. "I have an idea," he said. "Everyone please stand over here." The others moved to him and waited. "I'm going to increase the light and try something. Watch the surrounding area and tell me if you see anything."

Sam did as he said he would and the light grew in intensity until it began to hurt Emerius's eyes. When Sam noticed the hunter shielding his face, he allowed the light to decrease slightly so that it was like daylight in a circle thirty feet in diameter. He then walked slowly from where

Rindu had first pointed until he was well on the other side of when Rindu indicated the change in feeling had occurred.

"Did you see anything?" Sam asked.

The others shook their heads or gave soft negative answers. All except Rindu.

"Please do that again, Sam," the Zouy said.

Sam did so. As he passed the exact spot where Rindu had said the feeling changed, the monk stopped him. "Wait there," he told Sam as he walked to stand next to him. Suddenly he let out a breath and his mouth twitched. Emerius thought that maybe the man was smiling, though he never seemed to have any emotion at all on his face.

"Ah," Rindu said, "you have found it, Sam."

"Uh, found what, exactly?" Ix asked.

"I think I saw a flicker, as if the surrounding stone was a flame," Nalia said. "I was not sure the first time, but the second, I was watching for it and saw it. I believe I did."

"Correct, *Iba*," Rindu said.

"But what does that mean?" Ix said, insistent.

"I believe," Rindu said, "that we have discovered a defense system for Orum, the drum artifact. Using some manner of energy I am unfamiliar with, the trap shifts perception away from the drum. In effect, it turns us around, causing us to go back from whence we came, though we believe we are walking forward."

"How is that possible?" Emerius said. "I have a tracker's sense of direction, but I don't feel turned around. How could it do such a thing?"

"I do not know," Rindu said, "but perhaps I may defeat it. To accomplish such a thing, there must be a trigger or a projection point. Please give me a moment. Now that I know better what I am looking for, I might be able to find it."

The Zouy closed his eyes but remained perfectly still. Emerius looked more closely at the man. He didn't even seem to be breathing. What was he trying to do?

The minutes dragged on, with only the sound of the mounts shifting, claws scrabbling on the floor in subdued tones as if in reverence for their location. The remaining party members looked at each other, but said nothing. Skitter appeared to have gone to sleep, curled up in his litter on Sam's wolf.

Rindu's eyes snapped open. He turned his head toward a particularly large stalagmite and walked up to it. The monk began to wave his arms in the air as if he were trying to catch insects, swirling and moving them with a mesmerizing rhythm. With a sharp exhalation of breath, he slapped his palm to the surface of the stone and there was a loud crack.

A chunk of rock twice the size of Rindu's fist broke off and dropped to the ground. He put his hand inside the massive cone and did something that caused a door to swing out, revealing that the entire stalagmite was hollow.

Sam immediately poked his staff into the doorway, lighting up an object inside. It was a simple box with some sort of words engraved in it, in a language Emerius had never seen.

"What is it?" Sam asked.

"It is the item of power that causes our perception to be bent." Rindu answered. "I have never seen its like."

"Did you disarm it?"

"Let us see." Rindu went to pick the box up, but it would not budge. He squatted low, wrapped both arms around it, and heaved. It still would not move.

"Please step back," the monk said. When everyone did, he took three deep breaths, letting each out in a long hiss. On the final exhalation, he motioned with both palms toward the box as if he was pushing a great weight. The box spun a half turn and stopped.

"I do not know how it manifests so much weight," Rindu said. "It is not attached to anything, but simply resting there. In any case, I believe I have moved it enough so that we may find the way. Shall we try again?"

The party, roused from watching Rindu find the hidden box, turned back toward the section of the pathway they had been walking. As Sam's light swung toward it they could see that there was now a passage against the cavern wall, a passage that had been hidden before.

"You did it," Sam said to Rindu. "That has to be the way to Orum. I had been wondering how such a thing could be hidden for all those centuries when there were people constantly exploring for new parts of the cave. Now it makes sense. Every time someone got close, they were turned around without knowing it. It was hiding right in front of them the entire time. Let's go get it." He started toward the passage.

Rindu put a hand on Sam's shoulder to stop him. "Wait, Sam. We must use caution. The first artifact had a guardian. I do not believe the ones who hid the drum would have used only a tool of misdirection. Let us tread carefully."

Emerius couldn't tell in the light of Sam's staff, which he had allowed to soften to a glow rather than harsh light, but he thought he saw the yellow-haired man flush. He felt empathy for him, though. He himself had become excited and would have rushed into the opening, though he could now see the folly of it.

"Of course," Sam said. "You're right. Better to be careful. Let's go."

57

Sam was starting to get excited. So excited he forgot himself and had to have Rindu correct him. He needed to curb his enthusiasm so he didn't make any stupid mistakes. What they were doing was serious, life or death. It wasn't just his life or death, either; all of Gythe was in the balance. If they didn't get the artifact and get away before Rasaad caught them…well, he didn't want to think of that. They had to succeed.

He wondered how long it would be until the army caught them. They had wasted quite a bit of time trying to find the hidden passageway. It was too bad that Rindu didn't know more about the box they found. If he did, they could use it to hide the passage again, thereby hiding them from Rasaad. They could just wait her out if she did catch up. Better not to think of what could have been, though, and concentrate on what they were doing.

"Are we ready?" he asked the others. Between the light from his staff and the new torches the others held—the first set had burned out long ago, as had the second—he could see them all nod. Skitter sent a *ready* straight to his mind. "Okay, let's finish this. I, for one, would like nothing better than to soak in a bath at Whitehall just before eating a good meal." The joke fell flat. The seriousness of what they were doing had settled in upon everyone.

They started down the passage, Sam in the lead, with Rindu right behind him, then Nalia, Emerius, and Ix. The mounts were scattered in between the humans, with Skitter still riding on Shoynb.

The corridor they were in was smaller than what they had seen in the rest of the cavern. It was only ten to twelve feet high and maybe eight feet wide. It allowed them to walk two abreast, but with its winding manner and the abundant projections, they found it was better going single file.

The stone was rougher here, too, probably the result of not having the thousands or millions of shuffling feet on its surface over the centuries, Sam thought. How many people had actually traversed this section of the cave? The ones who placed the artifact had, obviously, but had any other human ever used this passage? It was a sobering thought.

The tunnel widened suddenly, and the ceiling sloped up out of sight. Sam held *Ahimiro* as high as he could and increased the light coming from the tip of it until he could just barely see the stalactite-covered ceiling almost thirty feet above. The walls had raced off to either side so they were twenty feet apart. He let his light fade back to a soft glow.

Emerius sighed loudly. Sam had forgotten the big hunter's claustrophobia. He had been quiet the entire time while going through the narrow passageway. Sam felt a bit embarrassed that he hadn't considered it.

"You all right, Em?" Sam said.

He could hear the bigger man gulp. "Yeah. Fine."

Sam walked toward the left wall to see if there were side passages. There were not. He had only walked ahead for another thirty feet when he came to the edge of a precipice. Swinging his staff down, he could see the sharp edge and then blackness swallowed up the light.

"Uh oh," he said at the same time Nalia said, "Sam, we have a problem." She was on the other side of the chamber, following the right-hand wall as he was following the left. She swung her torch down into the void, showing everyone that her side, too, dropped off into nothingness. They walked toward each other on the edge of the pit and their worst fears were confirmed. It cut the room completely in half.

Sam held out *Ahimiro* over the abyss, increasing the light until the far side was visible. It was at least thirty more feet, too far to jump. Even for Rindu.

The other side was much like the side they were on. It had a scattering of formations, some large stalagmites, a few of which were actually joined to stalactites to form the beginnings of pillars. Just at the very edge of what he could see, it appeared that the passageway narrowed again ten feet or so from the edge of the pit. Sam could see nothing there that would help them get across, however.

"What now?" he asked as he sat down on the rough floor. "I refuse to believe that after all we've been through, we're going to be foiled by a hole in the ground."

"The ceiling is too high and too wet to scale and traverse," Rindu said, as if any reasonable person would have ever thought of scuttling across a ceiling thirty feet above a bottomless pit. Remembering the way Rindu had scaled the walls of the Gray Fortress, punching his fingers into solid stone, he thought that maybe Rindu thought he *was* being reasonable in thinking of trying.

"And it is too far to jump, even for my father," Nalia put in. Sam smiled at her. He liked it that she had exactly the same thought that he had.

"Even the rakkeben can't jump that far, right?" Sam asked.

"Perhaps with a bit of luck, one of the wolves could make a jump that far, with a running start, but I am not willing to risk it," Rindu said. "The uneven floor, the damp…no, it is too risky."

Ix was leaning against the wall, watching and listening with a smirk on her face. Nalia noticed. "Is something funny to you, assassin?"

"Yes."

"Oh," Nalia said, smacking her forehead with her palm—a gesture she picked up while in Telani—"of course. You can teleport to the other side."

"That's right," Sam said. "I always think in terms of how my teleportation works, but yours works differently. You can easily jump across with the rest of us in tow."

"Yeah," Ix said with a wink. "I was wondering when you would figure it out."

Rindu's face tightened. "Enough levity, Ix. We must get the artifact before Rasaad catches us. Please teleport us to the other side so we may continue."

"Okay, okay. No need to get huffy. I was just having a little fun. Everyone gather round."

They arranged themselves carefully, making sure the assassin was touching them all. She checked to make sure they were all accounted for and then looked toward the other side of the pit.

Nothing happened.

The party waited.

After a half a minute, Sam looked over to Ix. Her brows were drawn down and a frown was deepening on her mouth. "Ix?"

"I…it's not working. I don't understand it. I've never had that happen."

"Perhaps there were safeguards other than just the box of misdirection," Rindu said. "That is troubling. Sam, can you use your teleportation?"

Sam sat down on the floor and immediately entered the *khulim*. First he learned the location so he could get back. After that, he went through the familiar process, recalling the vibration of the area at Whitehall they used as a staging area. When he tried to match his own vibration to the location, it was like trying to play tug of war with a greased eel. The vibratory signature seemed elusive, not allowing him to reach it.

"No," he said, sighing. "That…complicates things."

"It does," Rindu agreed.

Sam could see Nalia's expression clearly in her torchlight. She was disappointed they could not get across, but the glitter in her eyes and the smirk that was fighting to burst its way through the thin, tight line of her mouth was evident to Sam. He would really have to figure out how to make the two women reconcile with each other. If they all survived this.

Sam saw that Emerius was staring at the other side of the pit. He could almost see the parts in his brain moving, calculating, figuring. "Em, do you have an idea?"

"Maybe," the hunter said. "I was just thinking. With the draw weight of my bow, I could easily put an arrow into one of the softer stone formations. I could tie a rope to the arrow, too, and with luck, still get it to stick. It won't be enough to hold anyone, but if we could figure out how to use that to get a loop of rope around one of the formations, maybe we could get across."

"That's a great idea," Sam said. "Maybe you could get an arrow to wedge into something so it's strong enough to hold one of us."

"An arrow won't hold a person, no matter how I wedge it in," Emerius said. "Let me think some more."

Me, Skitter sent to Sam. *Let me do it.*

What? Sam sent back. *What are you talking about?*

Let Emerius shoot his arrow with the rope. Then I will cross the rope to the other side.

No, Sam sent. *It's too dangerous.*

Sam, everything we do is dangerous, more so for all of you than for me. I want to do my part. I am the only one who can do it. Let me try. Let me help. Please.

Sam frowned. There was a chance, he guessed. He

didn't like it, but… "Skitter says he'll do it."

"Do what?" Rindu asked.

"He says Em can shoot the arrow and then Skitter will cross the rope and tie it securely on the other side so we can go across. Emerius, will it be able to hold forty or fifty pounds?"

"Yes, it should," the hunter said. "If I get a solid shot."

Do you know how to tie a knot? Sam sent to Skitter.

I have seen in your memories how to do it, the hapaki answered. *I have clever fingers. I can do it.*

"Okay," Sam said. "Let's give it a try. I'm going to tie another rope to Skitter, though, in case he falls. He'll get battered swinging on twenty or thirty feet of rope and hitting the wall, but at least he won't fall into a bottomless pit."

They took out two sections of rope, fifty feet long each, one from Emerius's backpack and one from Sam's. The ropes themselves were a marvel to Sam. They were thin and much lighter than the ropes he was used to, but still very strong. He mentally reminded himself to ask Dr. Walt about how they were made.

One of them they tied to Skitter and the other they tied to an arrow. The knot that Emerius secured was ingenious. As they pulled on it, it not only tightened, but the force was directed perpendicular to the shaft of the arrow so that they didn't have to rely on friction alone to keep it in place.

Even better, the hunter took out two arrows that had slits partway up the shaft. Through these, Emerius tied a fine thread—so strong that Sam couldn't break it after trying several times—and wove it throughout the rope. It was as solid a knot as Sam had ever seen, definitely strong enough to hold the weight of the little hapaki. Now the only thing that concerned Sam was the arrow itself, and if even with Emerius's strength it could make it across the chasm and strike its target with enough force to stick.

Sam held *Ahimiro* out and increased the light until it

reached the other side of the pit.

Emerius wasn't taking any chances. He rolled his shoulders and took a few deep breaths. His face lost all expression and his gaze drilled into one of the large fan formations on the other side of the pit. He stood in a wide, stable stance and nocked the arrow, averting his eyes to the coil of rope to ensure it would play out smoothly. Nodding his head, his eyes found his target again.

Massive shoulders bunching, the hunter drew his bow as he raised the arrow toward the target. The string and the wood creaked as he pulled the fletching to his cheek. He paused for only a moment, visualizing the target, then the chamber was filled with a sharp twang and the slap of the string, immediately drowned out by the whizzing of the rope playing out as it was pulled across the pit by the arrow.

The arrow struck the rock with a dull tchunk. A small smile crept its way onto the big hunter's face. "I think that'll do it." He pulled the rope tight. The arrow didn't budge.

All eyes went to the hapaki, standing on the stone floor, diminutive and shivering. *My turn now, huh?* he sent to Sam.

"Be careful," Sam said to him, while sending it mind-to-mind. He patted his furry friend and then tugged on the rope knotted around him. "Take it nice and slow."

Skitter's eyes were wide as tea cups as Emerius threaded the rope through a hole formed in a nearby rock formation and then wrapped it around another one. The hapaki climbed up on the rope with the ease and grace of a lemur.

With a quick look back at Sam, Skitter started forward on the rope. He moved easily, maintaining his balance much like the squirrels Sam used to watch running across telephone and electrical lines back home. At least he didn't have to be afraid of the hapaki stumbling or falling off the rope.

As Skitter went forward, Sam played out the rope attached to him. He was starting to feel better about what they were doing. He had been afraid for nothing. His friend would make it across with no problems and then they would move on.

Just as Sam was finishing that last thought, the arrow came loose. He watched in horror as Skitter fell into nothingness. All of the others gasped.

Sam was too surprised even to react. Thankfully, he had a tight grip on the rope as he felt it go taut. There was a small impact through it and he winced to think that it was his friend hitting the wall of the cliff.

Skitter, are you all right? he sent.

Yes, I am fine, the hapaki sent back. *I only fell a few feet. I hadn't gone far. It scared me more than hurt me.*

Even as he was sending his thoughts to Sam, the hapaki was climbing the rope Sam was holding. He pulled himself up onto the ledge and scuttled across the floor to curl into a ball at Sam's feet, shivering.

That's it, Sam sent. *We'll find another way. It's too risky doing this.*

No, Sam. There is no other way. I'll try again. Tell Emerius to shoot another arrow.

Are you sure? Sam sent. *You don't have to do this.*

Yes, I do. Please tell him.

Sam didn't want to put his friend in danger again, but he was right. There was no other way they could think of. "Skitter asks for you to shoot another arrow. He'll try again."

Emerius nodded and set about pulling in the rope from the pit.

And Sam, Skitter sent, *tell him to do a better job of it this time.*

Sam laughed out loud, more from the tension than anything else. When everyone looked at him strangely, he said, "Skitter says to do a better job of it this time." The others wore expressions ranging from mild amusement to relief.

As they waited for Emerius to shoot the rope across again, Shonyb came up to Skitter, still curled in a ball and shivering, though less than earlier. The big wolf nudged the hapaki with her nose. Skitter curled more tightly into a ball and tried to ignore her.

The rakkeban, insistent, nudged him again, pushing him a few inches across the floor. When the hapaki poked his head up, Shonyb licked him so thoroughly that it pushed him another few inches across the floor. Skitter hugged the wolf's nose. He seemed to have stopped shivering, but Sam could still feel trepidation in his thoughts. He could also feel his affection for the wolf and his thanks for her support. His little paw reached up and rubbed the ear that was many times its size.

Emerius, wanting to be sure of the strength of the arrow this time, got on his back and put both feet on his bow. He drew the arrow back with both hands, the bow creaking so loudly that Sam thought it might break. When he released, the sound was much louder than before, the rope playing out so quickly it seemed the entire coil might take off into the darkness. A loud crack confirmed that the arrow head had struck stone.

Ready? Sam sent. *Are you sure you want to do this again?*

Yes. It was kind of fun swinging on the rope like that. I might do it again sometime, as long as I don't have to hit a wall. Not now, though. Not now.

Sam smiled and rubbed the hapaki's head.

After Emerius secured his side of the rope, Skitter climbed up and began to go across the chasm again. He moved so quickly Sam could hardly keep up with letting the rope out. As Skitter got halfway across, the drag on the rope, and its weight, caused the hapaki to slow down. Sam started to fear that the weight of the it would tug his friend down and make him fall. Skitter just lowered his body and crawled on, slower but still steady.

Sam had wedged *Ahimiro* into a space between two

rocks, projecting out into the chasm, but even its light had limits. Skitter had passed out of the ball of the illumination. He looked into the blackness but couldn't see a thing except the silhouettes of the rock formations.

Are you okay? Sam sent.

Yes, Skitter answered. He was panting. *This rope tied to me is getting heavy. I'm almost there, though.*

There was a moment of panic, shared by Sam, when Skitter missed his footing because of his fatigue. The rope didn't seem to be where it was supposed to be, so his right front paw met empty air and the hapaki stumbled. He tried to compensate by shifting his balance and it only caused him to become more unbalanced. Sam could feel the hapaki's stomach drop as Skitter knew he was going to fall but couldn't do anything about it.

Sam cried out as he shared the feeling the hapaki was having, pitching headlong into the blackness. One tiny paw was able to grasp the rope to keep Skitter from plummeting. For the moment he hung on, little claws straining to hold a weight they were never meant to hold. Sam didn't know how long his friend could maintain his grip. Skitter didn't know himself.

One. Two. Three. Four seconds. At five seconds, Skitter's strength gave out and thoughts that he might die rushed through his head. Sam was surprised the hapaki didn't make a sound. Not a scream, not a whimper, nothing.

Skitter's back paws hit something immediately after his grip had given way.

He had only been a few feet off the ground. On the other side of the chasm.

Sam slumped against one of the cave formations, trying to control his breathing. "He's...fine," he said to the others' questioning looks. "He fell, but he was already on the other side." Rindu slapped Sam's back while Nalia kissed him. Ix and Emerius breathed out in relief and smiled.

It didn't take long for Skitter to tie both ropes in knots around good, solid rock formations. When Sam and Emerius tightened the ropes and secured them on their side, they were ready to go.

"The mounts can't go across," Sam said. Remembering how the passage narrowed again on the other side, he turned to Emerius. "Will you stay with them, to guard them? We should be able to get through to the artifact and get out of there in no time."

"Yeah," Emerius said. "I can do guard duty. Someone's gotta cover our backs." His mouth formed a sly smile. "Thanks, Sam."

Okay, so he was transparent. It was the thought that was important anyway, right? He slapped the hunter on the back. "Any time."

"I'll stay, too," Ix said. "If Rasaad catches up to us, wild man here won't be able to hold them off."

"That sounds good to me," Sam said. "We'll be back as soon as we can. Relax, have something to eat. Enjoy yourselves." He winked as he started across the ropes. They were taut and solid and before he knew it, he was on the other side. Nalia came over and then Rindu, and, just like that, they were ready to go get Orum.

58

Sam looked back across the pit to where Ix and Emerius were digging through their packs for food. Their features flickered by the torchlight, making the scene surreal. He pulled his eyes away from them, starting at the sudden feeling that the party was splitting up, no matter how briefly.

It was silly, really, but he had become accustomed to his new friends. Nalia would give him that patient you-just-don't-know-how-things-are look if he told her. Maybe she was right. He had no reason to trust Ix, or even Emerius for that matter. But he did. He hoped that when this was all over, they could get to know each other without the constant threat of danger hanging over their heads.

He looked longingly at his friends, including his rakkeben friends, one more time and turned to go forward.

I have become rather fond of everyone myself, Skitter pushed into his mind. *Even if you all are an inferior species.* His humor recalled the old joke they bandied back and forth.

Yes, Sam sent back. *Even if. Are you ready?*

I was thinking that maybe I should rest here, if that is okay,

Skitter sent with a feeling that Sam thought was close to embarrassment. *My heart is still beating quickly from thinking I was going to die and I am very tired from it. I can go with you if you like, though.*

Sam patted the hapaki's head. *No*, he sent. *Rest. We will probably just stroll down the passageway and collect the artifact. We'll be back in no time.*

Okay, I will be waiting here.

"Are we ready to finish this thing and get out of here?" Sam asked Rindu and Nalia.

"We are," Rindu said. "Lead on, Sam."

Nodding firmly and smiling at Nalia, Sam started down the passageway. It was almost exactly as the passage they came through, the one on the other side of the chasm. He soon lost his sense of direction. It was disconcerting, but he didn't worry. There were no side passages, just the one narrow winding tunnel. They couldn't get lost.

After a few hundred feet, the passage they were traveling widened out again, more gradually than before. It roughly doubled in size in ten feet, then doubled again in another twenty. By the time they had gone thirty paces, the walls disappeared within the inky blackness. But that wasn't what concerned Sam.

Well into the chamber, they came to the first object. It looked as if it had grown from the stone floor itself. Roughly spherical, it was large enough for Sam to stand up inside, and shone a dirty white in the light of *Ahimiro*.

"What—?" Sam began, but stopped when Rindu put a finger to his lips. The Zouy pointed out two more of the shapes that were barely visible on the edges of the light. He motioned with his other hand, opening his fist and raising it up and away from himself.

Sam understood and increased the light at the tip of his staff. As he did, the breath caught in his throat.

They were in a cavern that was maybe fifty feet in diameter, with both sides pinched into smaller passageways. He could just see what looked like the end to the tunnel across from where they entered. In the dead center of the chamber was a glass case and under the glass, clearly evident, was what looked like an ancient tribal drum. It had to be the artifact they were looking for.

Orum was roughly the size of a basketball, a rigid cylinder that appeared to be made of wood. The top was covered with leather drawn so tightly that Sam could almost hear it hum from where he was. Laces that were similar to leather, but looked stronger and more durable, kept the drum covering taut. On either side of the main body of the instrument were sticks mounted on brackets. They were simple, with a ball of hardened leather stuffed with some kind of padding. Sam wasn't sure if it was his imagination or if the artifact actually glowed slightly.

As impressive as it was, though, Orum was secondary. Surrounding the glass case, more than twenty feet from where Sam and the others stood, there were many more of the soft-looking, dirty white objects scattered across the floor. As he watched in stunned disbelief, he saw movement in one of the shapes. A shadow seemed to be flickering through the barely translucent wall of the sphere.

Three sets of eyes were locked on the movement. The tip of an appendage thrust through an opening that Sam hadn't even realized had been there. It was as thick as his wrist, covered with coarse hair and, once it had emerged enough for Sam to see it, displayed joints or segmentations.

An involuntary shiver ran up Sam's spine. *Please don't be what I think you are,* he thought, afraid to even whisper it. Watching intently, hardly breathing, he didn't blink as the hairy appendage was joined by another, and then two others just like it. Each segment above the ones on the ground grew in thickness, all moving in perfect synchronicity, exiting the den of the creature.

Sam looked around at the other spheres, seeing now what he had missed. They were spun, like cocoons. Or nests. Thankfully, the only movement so far was from the one he had been looking at, the one showing half of the massive body of a spider as it moved slowly out into the open.

The creature was huge, as big as Sam. The same coarse hair covering its legs made a thick layer over the entire bulbous body of the arachnid. The shape of the monster was the same as tarantulas Sam had seen, thick strong legs, fur, and a fear-inspiring face. The color was strange, sort of a pale green, almost translucent, with the hair a slightly darker shade

As the spider exited its den completely, Sam couldn't help but notice how graceful it was. The front walking legs of the creature probed ahead of it, seeming to feel its way around. The pedipalp, the set of legs directly in front of the monster's face, waved as if feeling the air.

Compound eyes stared blankly ahead above two wicked-looking curved fangs and chelicerae, plump with poison ready to inject the deadly venom into any prey it found.

Sam froze, mesmerized by the motion of the creature. All thought left his head but his fear of being struck by those fangs. He had always had a tenuous relationship with spiders. While not really having a phobia, they made him uncomfortable. He was fine with the smaller versions, as long as he knew where they were. When they surprised him, however, such as one that had jumped on him when he was a child, he lost all sense of sanity and panicked. He was feeling that panic now.

"Sam," Rindu whispered. "Do you remember the snakes? The ones in the caves the last time you were in Gythe? Sam?"

He hadn't even realized Rindu had spoken until he played it back in his head. "Yes," his whisper sounded more like a croak. The spider was moving toward them. Slowly.

"Spiders can see with their eyes," the Zouy whispered, "but they rely more on their vibratory sense. They have fine hairs that detect vibrations and give them information about their surroundings."

Rindu was silent for a moment. Sam could not take his eyes from the slowly approaching monster to look at him. Finally, the monk whispered again. "I will try to do what I did with the snakes, or at least try to distract it. While I do so, get the drum. We must escape before the others sense us and come out of their nests as well."

Sam willed his body to move, but it was not cooperating with him.

"Sam?" Nalia whispered, close against his right ear.

With as great a feat of willpower as he had ever displayed, he tore his eyes from the spider and swung his head toward Nalia. Her green-tinged blue eyes captured him, cradled him, calmed him. He took a breath, the first he had taken in hours, it seemed, and he shook his head. "I'm good," he whispered to her, trying to force a smile, but failing, displaying instead a sickly grimace. He swallowed hard. "Let's go."

"Slowly," Nalia told him, and then suited her words by turning at a glacial pace and shuffling toward the glass case in the center of the cavern. Sam was reminded of the drills Rindu had forced him to perform, the *kori rohw* exercises that he had to move through with such a slow pace that the butterflies would not fly off him. He was suddenly glad the Zouy had insisted on perfection.

As he and Nalia moved toward the drum, Sam cast a look to Rindu, who was trying to find a vibration that would pacify the spider less than ten feet in front of him. So far, it didn't look like he was having success.

When they were four paces—normal walking paces, not the slow shuffle they were now engaged in—from the case, Sam saw a quick movement out of the corner of his eye. The spider in front of Rindu had reared up on its back legs, first two walking legs in the air and the pedipalp waving madly toward the monk. Sam's stomach dropped when the creature unfolded the chelicerae and extended fangs as long as Sam's forearms out in front of it, ready to strike. The venom on the tips of the fangs shone cruelly in the light of Sam's staff.

With a look and nod at Nalia, they quickened their pace. There was nothing he could do to help Rindu right now other than getting the drum as soon as possible. In a few fast steps, they stood before it.

Sam reached for the glass case and then pulled his hand back. What if it was trapped? What if touching it set off some sort of device, making things even worse for them? He looked to Rindu, standing in a ready stance to dodge the deadly fangs in front of him, to the spider, waving its appendages to and fro and looking ready to strike, and finally to Nalia, face wearing a tight expression, her mouth a thin line and her eyes ablaze. What should he do?

They are here, he heard a very faint whisper in his mind, so faint he wasn't sure it was there.

Sam, Rasaad is here. We will need you. It was Skitter, sending a thought to him, further than they had ever communicated before. They were trapped, with death all around.

He had to make a decision. There was no time for deliberation. Taking a deep breath, he did what he had to do. He reached out and touched the glass case protecting the drum artifact Orum.

Nothing happened.

Sam thought that was probably a good thing. Then he saw movement from all around him. The other denizens of the cavern were rousing. From each side, hairy legs were making their way out of their spherical abodes, bulbous bodies trailing. Sam gulped and looked to Nalia.

"We must get the artifact and leave quickly, Sam, before the creatures are fully in motion." Nalia was looking around them as if gauging an upcoming battle.

One of the spiders closest to the pair was fully outside its nest. It was looking right at Sam with those multiple eyes. It seemed to sense something and suddenly hunched down low, its legs ready to spring.

Sam traded a look with Nalia. He wasn't sure if his expression showed the fear he was feeling, but the empathetic look on her face told him that it probably did. He took a breath and let it out slowly, then moved around the glass case with a purpose, not at a snail's pace but not rushing either. As he did, the spider that was staring at him scuttled and pivoted so it was always facing him. It seemed ready to jump on him at any moment, but it had not extended its fangs yet. Sam took that as a good sign.

He made a complete circuit of the glass case, which was sitting on a stone pedestal. The glass was in an octagonal configuration, coming to a point at the top. It rested at just above waist level to Sam and was probably three feet tall. As he moved around it, looking for some type of door or hatch, he found it to be perfectly crafted, each side identical to the others. The spider was still locked onto him, acting as if it thought Sam would attack it.

With no way to get into the glass, Sam caught Nalia's eye and motioned toward his staff. She understood. Her shrapezi were already in a guard position. She tightened her grip and nodded. Sam struck the glass as hard as he could with his staff, averting his eyes at the last second to prevent having glass sprayed in his face.

There was only a dull thud, as of a heavy wooden mallet striking a large boulder. The glass wasn't even scratched. At his sudden movement, the spider watching him hunched lower, on the edge of springing, but waited.

Nalia stepped toward the glass and motioned for Sam to watch the arachnid guarding them. When he turned from her, she struck the glass with her shrapezi. A high-pitched metallic ring filled the air and the monster in front of them scuttled a foot closer. Sam could see its appendages trembling in anticipation and something moved below its eyes. It had decided to bring its fangs out.

The glass was still unblemished, despite Nalia's strike. Rindu was still in his faceoff with the spider that was rearing toward him and threatening to strike. The other creatures, while not seeming too interested in the humans, nevertheless were moving around with more energy. If Sam didn't do something soon, they would be surrounded and outnumbered, a battle they could never win with these giant poisonous monsters.

Sam had a thought then, so ridiculous that he was embarrassed even to think it. Despite that, he acted. Putting *Ahimiro* in the crook of his arm, he reached over and put both hands on the glass case. He could see Orum just inches from his hands, on the other side of the transparent covering. With a heave, he lifted up on the case. It raised easily off the pedestal and over the drum, exposing the artifact.

"Huh." He rolled his eyes to Nalia and set the case down on the floor. The spiders still didn't seem to be interested in them. All he needed was to pick up the drum and they could leave.

As soon as his skin touched Orum, the spiders all whirled toward him, every last one of them raising the front halves of their bodies up and extending their fangs.

"Run!" Nalia said to him, leaping in front of one of the more anxious spiders that had jumped at them. Her shrapezi spun in the air and two of the arachnid's legs became significantly shorter.

Sam didn't want to do as she said, but he did. He took off running as fast as he could back toward where they had come. If he could get into the narrower passageway, the creatures would have to come at him one or two at a time, instead of all together. Relying on Nalia's skills to keep her safe, he ran as if his life depended upon it. He knew that it did.

A spider off to his left jumped at him as he passed Rindu. Sam projected his *rohw* from the end of his staff and swung it awkwardly with one hand. It was enough to buffet the hairy body away from him before it could bite him. With his staff in one hand and the drum in the other, he weaved his way through the cave's features and slipped into the narrower tunnel.

When Sam turned to look, he felt despair. Nalia was moving like a snake, dodging jumping and striking spiders, whipping out with her shrapezi to remove parts of the creatures where she could, but always focusing on defense. One scratch of the venom from a spider this big and she might not survive to kill the creature, Sam thought.

Rindu, too, seemed to be fighting for his life. His swords were out and he was causing legs and pieces of hairy flesh to fly as well, but they were vastly outnumbered. There were at least thirty of the creatures and it would only take one mistake for them to be poisoned. Sam set the drum down and began to go back to help.

"No, Sam," Rindu yelled. "Go further down the tunnel. We will seek an opening and flee this battle into the more restricted area. You will only be in our way. Go."

Sam picked up the drum, wishing he could do more, and headed down the tunnel. Before he went out of sight, he saw Rindu nod to Nalia and then flash brilliantly for a moment as he used his *rohw* to push all the spiders around him. They took advantage of the lull and ran toward him, so quickly he had to turn, duck his head, and sprint for all he was worth.

The three came out into the open area almost at the same time, the spiders hot on their heels. Sam had already sent to Skitter that he should cross the ropes to the other side, so the hapaki was halfway to Ix and Emerius when they came out of the mouth of the tunnel.

All three whirled and readied their weapons, determined to cut down the monstrous arachnids as they came out of the narrow tunnel one at a time.

There was no need.

The spiders stopped at the end of the narrow passageway, looking right at the three, but they came no nearer. One by one, they turned and made their way back to their own chamber at an unhurried pace. One final spider, missing half of one of its front legs at the third joint, waved its setae briefly as if confirming that the humans were still there, and then it too retreated, leaving only a thin trail of wetness where it had bled.

"Huh," Sam said, almost as an exhale. "I guess they're not allowed to leave their home. What do you suppose they eat? They, or their ancestors, have been there guarding the artifact for thousands of years."

"I do not know," Rindu said. "Perhaps Dr. Walt has an idea. We can ask him when this is over. I am just happy to be alive and curious."

"A little help!" Ix yelled from across the chasm. The assassin, the hunter, and the rakkeben were engaged in battle with soldiers trying to force their way out of the narrow passage on the other side of them. Sam nodded to Rindu and Nalia and the three went to join their friends.

"Sometime soon, I'd really like a break," Sam said, as he finished securing the drum in his backpack and moved over the ropes to the battle on the other side.

59

Sam stepped off the rope into chaos. Emerius was twenty feet from the passage opening firing arrow after arrow at the soldiers trying to break through. Each arrow was so precisely placed that it was fatal. Ix, the rakkeben, and Oro were cutting through the soldiers who managed to get past the arrows. There were just too many for Em to handle.

As he watched, Ix cut the throat of an archer who was preparing to shoot back at Emerius. In one smooth motion, she ended his life, twisted his dying body, and slipped the quiver off his shoulder as he fell. She turned quickly and threw the full quiver of arrows toward Emerius, who in turn snatched it out of the air, set it down, and continued firing arrows from the quiver he was already wearing, all without a pause.

The three rushed into battle beside Ix and the mounts. Emerius was able to slow his firing, choosing his shots in a more leisurely manner and, more importantly, rest so he did not become exhausted. There was no telling how long the battle would last, so they all had to conserve energy. Luckily, the bodies of the soldiers were already piling up, making it more difficult for the others to push clear. If it wasn't for the choke point of the narrow passage, the party would have been overwhelmed.

In the cramped conditions, Sam split *Ahimiro* into two sticks. Even so, movement was difficult without bumping or striking his friends. When a sword slash cut a shallow slit in his backpack, he immediately stepped out of the battle, halfway to the pit. He took the backpack off, set it in between two rock formations, and entered the battle again. He didn't want the artifact to be damaged while he was fighting.

Sam cleared his mind and let himself feel the battle's song. His body began to move, almost as if of its own accord, performing impossible evasions and maneuvers and striking out with perfect efficiency. He wasn't sure how long the battle would be, but he felt as if he could keep the pace up forever. Sparing a glance at the others, he saw them all moving smoothly and efficiently. They too looked as if they would be fine for the long haul.

A flicker of movement along the edge of the passage opening caught his eye. With a blur of motion, a shape flew over the heads of the soldiers and Ix, turned a perfect somersault, and landed lightly on its feet. It was only after landing that Sam got a clear look.

It was a woman holding a bell in one hand and a short staff in the other. The staff looked to be made of metal, and as for the bell, Sam had no doubt that it was the artifact Azgo. This had to be Ayim Rasaad.

He wasn't sure why exactly, but Sam hadn't pictured his enemy looking like the woman he was seeing now. She didn't appear more than a few years older than he and though he knew she was evil, she looked like someone he would have been friends with. Her face was pretty, but short of beautiful, by Telani standards. It was all angles with a strong jaw, but still soft somehow. Her almond-shaped eyes scanned the chamber lit by the torches wedged into rock formations.

Rasaad's clothing was strange, flowing britches tied

with cord at the knees and ankles, a tight blouse that left her midriff open but had long sleeves of the same lightweight material as her pants. Soft shoes that were tied tightly with a length of cord covered her feet and her ankles. She was a tall woman, and from her body shape and her movements, Sam could see she was a skilled athlete, a warrior on par with any he'd seen. That was to be expected of a former Zouyim monk, he supposed.

The strange thing about the woman, though, was her head. She was bald, but not completely hairless like the Arzbedim. All across the tight skin of her skull were colorful tattoos, swirling, curving shapes that made the eye dizzy to follow them. She still had dark eyebrows, which were drawing down as she caught sight of Rindu. There was recognition in her hazel eyes.

Too late, Sam realized what she was doing. She had the bell in her hand to teleport away—would the teleportation of the artifact work here?—and she was planning on grabbing the drum artifact. He began to move toward where it was, but then stopped himself. It would be stupid for him to go toward it and reveal its location. Dodging a knife strike and the swing of a mace from nearby soldiers and counterattacking without thinking, he kept his eyes on Ayim Rasaad.

She headed right for where he had placed the drum. Sam chastised himself. Of course, she had been watching him, she had seen where he put Orum down. Now she was heading toward it to take it away. Dropping all pretense of not paying attention to her, he started running toward the woman, knowing as he did so that he would be too late.

Don't worry, Sam, Skitter's thoughts edged their way into Sam's mind. *I have taken the drum and moved it to another hiding place. She will not find it.*

Thank you, Skitter. You have saved me from myself once again.

Rasaad got to where the drum had been and confusion painting itself across her face. It was quickly replaced by rage. She calmly put the bell into a pouch on her waist, spun her staff in her hands, and turned toward Sam.

Sam realized he would be unable to stop, so instead he continued running at full speed, preparing his sticks for Rasaad's attack. He didn't expect what the woman did next.

With a smirk, Ayim Rasaad lowered her staff as Sam was rushing headlong at her. She raised her left hand, palm out, and gave it a little twitch. The next thing Sam knew, he was flying through the air and striking the back of one of the soldiers who was fighting with Rindu. The man cushioned his fall, but it still knocked the wind out of Sam.

Shaking his head, he climbed to his feet and started back toward the former Zouy. As he went, Rindu and Nalia finished off the soldiers they were fighting and joined him, having seen the situation.

"Be careful, Sam," Rindu said. "She is a powerful *rohw* user. You must be mindful of using your *rohw* for defense, as we have practiced."

"Okay," Sam said. "I'll remember."

The Zouy, the Sapsyr, and Sam surrounded Rasaad. Though outnumbered, she did not seem concerned. "Make it easy on yourselves and just hand over the drum. I promise you a swift, painless death if you do so. It will go much harder for you if you refuse."

"Ayim Rasaad," Rindu said, "you always did have an arrogance that was unjustified. You cannot prevail. Surrender and we will not have to kill you this day."

A smile that was wholly incongruous with her attitude lit up her face. "You do not know the power I hold, Master Rindu. It is a power that the Zouyim have always feared to wield, a power that is superior to the pitiful *rohw* you hold in such reverence. You will behold my power, the power of the *awkum*. You cannot stand against it."

Sam saw Rindu motion to him and Nalia, a subtle gesture that only had meaning because of how many times the three of them had fought battles together. He prepared himself for what was to come.

As if by a verbal cue, Sam, Nalia, and Rindu attacked Rasaad at once, from three different directions. Rindu flew through the air with a kick directed at the woman's head. Nalia dashed in, shrapezi spinning, ready to cleave. Sam ran straight for the woman, sticks up and ready to strike. Ayim Rasaad simply stood there, casually raised her hand, and then firmly closed it into a fist.

It was as if an explosion had emanated from that raised hand. All three of her attackers were thrown back a dozen feet. Sam crashed hard into Cleave, Nalia's rakkeban, both falling to the ground. Nalia spun off and struck the wall of the cavern with a grunt. Rindu cartwheeled toward the pit, only just catching himself on the ropes so he did not go in. When Sam got up and looked, Rasaad stood there with a wry smile on her face.

Sam concentrated, forming a shield made of *rohw* around him. He saw that the soldiers had all but stopped fighting and were watching the four combatants further inside the chamber. Rindu flipped back onto the stone floor, a bright shield of his own *rohw* springing up around him. Even Nalia was limned in energy, though not as brightly as her father.

"Your pitiful energy cannot stand against the *awkum*, Rindu," Rasaad sneered. "Your precious *rohw* is motion and light and life. The *awkum* is of solidity, non-movement, darkness, and death. You will see."

While she was speaking, Rindu and Nalia had circled her until the three of them were facing Rasaad. Sam looked to the Zouy, but found no direction there.

"But I tire of this. It is time to end it. Goodbye, Master Rindu." Ayim Rasaad raised both her arms, staff still held in her right hand, and pointed them at Rindu.

Sam couldn't see anything more than a simple distortion, but he knew some power was emanating from her hands. He watched in horror as Rindu's *rohw* shield shattered and he flew backward as if struck. His cry of pain told Sam all he needed to know. Ayim Rasaad was too powerful for them.

Rasaad relaxed and Rindu slumped to the floor, breathing hard.

"Sam," he whispered, too softly for Rasaad to hear, "you must come into harmony with us. It is the only way to defeat her. Together, we may do so."

Their enemy was raising her hands again, getting ready to finish Rindu off.

Sam's thoughts swirled. He had to combine his power with Rindu and Nalia. If he didn't, they would all die. Not only that, but if they failed, Rasaad would get the other artifacts and all of Gythe would be subjected to her cruel reign. But how, how could he do something that he had not been able to accomplish before, no matter how hard he tried? He had only seconds, he knew.

Nalia was looking at him, her expression pleading with him. The firm set of her jaw, the soft look in her eyes, they told him that she believed in him, that she knew he could do it. She had faith in him. So much faith, in fact, that she knew that her very life was in his hands, and she trusted him with that life. His vision got blurry as he blinked the wetness from his eyes. She was so much a part of him, sometimes he couldn't tell where he ended and she began. They were like different parts of one person.

Different parts of one person. The thought echoed in his mind. They were the same. There was really no difference. So what if they were physically separate? That wasn't the important thing. They had a connection that could not be broken any more than it could be defined. Yes.

Sam's mind tried to catch up with itself. He was confused, but there was something important in there. If he was the same as Nalia, if they were connected, then how much harder was it for Rindu to be connected to them as well? He loved the monk as a father and had a strong *rohw* connection with him as well from all the training they had done together. What if he had been trying too hard all this time? What if it was really as simple as letting his feelings guide him?

He remembered when he had first started training with Rindu, trying to learn combat with Nalia. What was it Rindu had said? *The first and most important thing is that you must stop thinking and start feeling.*

Sam took a breath, trying to ignore Rasaad as she prepared to kill Rindu with this other power of hers. Exhaling, he relaxed completely. With his eyes closed, he could see in his mind the energy surrounding Nalia and Rindu. Reaching out, he touched Nalia's aura with his own *rohw*. Tentatively probing, then caressing, then finally embracing it, he let himself melt into her as she melted into him. It was such a shock that he almost lost his focus, almost opened his eyes. Instead, he forced himself to maintain the connection, something similar to how he and Skitter communicated, something intimate and comfortable. He felt himself smiling.

Immediately, he reached out to Rindu and did the same thing. It took more focus and a few more precious seconds, but finally the Zouy's *rohw* slipped into the stream surrounding the other two and then they were one. Their energy was merged and much more powerful than when they were apart.

Sam felt Rindu's eyes snap open, felt the monk smile, and then get onto his feet. When Sam opened his eyes, he saw the Zouy glowing like the sun, felt the power that was rushing through all three of them. He knew he must look the same to the other two.

Rasaad thrust her hands toward Rindu. Her eyes went wide when her power was absorbed into the shield now surrounding the man. "How...?" she said.

"Your power is discordant," Rindu said. "The *rohw* is accordant, harmonious. You cannot prevail."

The woman threw energy at Rindu, at Nalia, and at Sam, but the shared shield protected them from her attacks.

"Very well," she said. "I will simply have to destroy you in a more…conventional manner." She spun the staff in her hands and rushed to attack the closest foe. Nalia.

"*Iba*," Rindu said, "we must maintain the harmonious energy. If we all do battle, it will be lost. We will maintain it so that you may fight her without fearing her power. It is your contest now."

Nalia nodded and raised her shrapezi. After the briefest of pauses, she rushed into battle with Rasaad.

60

Sam thought the battle would be over quickly. Nalia, after all, was Nalia, and he had the utmost confidence in her abilities. Though he knew that Ayim Rasaad had been one of the Zouyim, thus trained well in combat, he figured that without her abilities to attack with energy, she would be easily defeated. He was wrong.

Though the harmonic energy he and Rindu were channeling protected Nalia from Rasaad's attack using this new strange energy, the *awkum*, they could not keep her from using it to enhance her own performance. Rasaad moved far more quickly than Sam thought she should be able to, and judging by the few hard blocks Nalia had performed, the woman's strength was increased as well. Sam noted that Nalia had shifted to using exclusively parrying and evasion techniques.

Rasaad used that metal staff of hers expertly. As Nalia whirled and slashed, the weapon seemed always to be there, deflecting the shrapezi and then counterattacking. Nalia evaded or in other ways defeated the counterattack, of course, but it was maddening to Sam that it had already taken so long.

"Relax, Sam," Rindu said to him. "Your tension will affect the flow of energy. Trust in Nalia's abilities and focus on maintaining the shield against the *awkum*."

"Sorry," Sam said, purposely relaxing his tense shoulders and neck. He did trust Nalia's abilities. Nevertheless, it was hard watching the battle and not joining.

Sam looked around the chamber. The main battle had essentially stopped. Emerius stood with an arrow nocked, but not drawn, taking turns in scanning the edge of the forces arrayed against him and watching the battle with Nalia unfold. Ix, too, was dividing her attention between the battle and the soldiers standing only a few feet away, mesmerized by what was happening. The rakkeben and Oro were likewise immobile. It was highly improbable, Sam thought, but he was seeing it for himself.

Rasaad spun, throwing kicks so perfectly and rapidly that Nalia could not get her blades around to strike at the legs. As the former Zouy spun around again, she whipped the metal staff out, aiming toward Nalia's head. The Sapsyr brought both swords up and deflected the blow, sparks rocketing from the point of impact and showering the opponents. Then, without any break in the motion, Ayim Rasaad squatted low as she turned again, sweeping one leg out to strike at Nalia's feet. Nalia seemed almost off-balance from the flurry of strikes preceding it, but managed to leap into the air, turn a twist, and land lightly on her feet while striking down first with the sword in her right hand and then following immediately with her left.

Rasaad angled her staff so that the first strike slid off to her left and then brought the staff up in time to slap the second strike, making it go wide to the right. A high-pitched ring reverberated in the cavern. It seemed to last for several seconds. In the meantime, Rasaad changed her grip on the staff.

It was shorter than any staff Sam had ever seen, though not so short as a fighting stick, maybe four feet in length.

The grip the woman was using now looked like a modified sword grip, hands at one end and the tip and most of the shaft being used for striking. She whipped it around and caused Nalia to backstep then angle off to the side to try to evade it and find an opening so she could strike.

The two lunged back and forth, one or the other moving to the side rather than linearly to try to get around the other's guard. Sam thought of some of the fencing matches he'd seen in the Olympics. When there were two particularly skilled fencers, a match may go several several seconds before a touch, with most of the movement in straight lines. What these two women were doing was so complex, Sam almost couldn't believe it. And still neither had been struck.

Nalia had been backed against a large stone formation and was barely deflecting Rasaad's blows. Sam's breath caught in his throat. He wasn't sure how she would get out of that position. The two seemed to be so equally matched in ability that any little advantage seemed a huge obstacle. He saw Rasaad say something to Nalia and the Sapsyr's eyes flashed. He felt a tremor go through the energy he and Rindu were maintaining.

As she was parrying aside an overhand strike meant to crush her skull, Nalia's foot came up, impossibly fast and at an angle that flesh and bone should not have been able to accomplish, striking Rasaad in the jaw. The *awkum* master's head snapped back and she was propelled backward.

Sam's elation was cut short, though, as Ayim Rasaad converted the motion into a graceful backflip. As her body became right-side-up again, her left hand flicked out and there was a flash of several objects shooting toward Nalia. Sam heard himself gasp when he realized what they were: razor-sharp darts. Rasaad had thrown them, landed with too much backward momentum, and rolled to dissipate the energy, coming smoothly back to her feet.

Nalia's shrapezi blurred as she levered them in front of

her. Sam heard twin twangs as two of the darts were deflected, one spinning off to strike one of the soldiers standing by. The third, unfortunately, made it through. Nalia's grunt as it hit her left shoulder made Sam wince.

Despite the injury, Nalia pressed the attack. Rasaad was barely able to get her staff up in time to block the first blow. She narrowly avoided the kick that followed. Nalia was whirling faster now, taking advantage of her momentum to whip out her blades to try to strike her opponent. She leaped in the air and wheeled around to drop a kick onto Rasaad from overhead, changing her motion from the side-to-side twirling to an implacable downward force. The former Zouy was hard-pressed to escape the attack.

Sam saw, as Nalia was coming down, that the kick was a diversion. As her body pin-wheeled around to launch the kick, she moved her injured left arm and then released the shrapezi to allow it to hang motionless in the air for a fraction of a second. Then, as her body rotated, she swung the blade in her right hand and caught the other blade, hook to hook. Continuing her spin, the free sword whipped out like a chain weapon, going toward Rasaad's head.

Ayim Rasaad's eyes went wide as she held her staff with both hands in a powerful block meant to stop Nalia's sword. She realized, too late, that she was, in fact, facing two swords, end to end. The shrapezi in Nalia's hand was blocked, but the other sword whipped around, pivoting on the hook, and went over Rasaad's guard. The sharpened spike cut a deep furrow in the *awkum* master's skull, the blade continuing down to part her nose cleanly in two and separate the flesh of her lips. A sort of strangled gasp escaped as she tried to back away. But it was too late.

Nalia caught the handle of the shrapezi with her left hand, wincing at the pain it caused in her shoulder. Before Rasaad could react, she thrust both swords toward the woman, arms crossed with the sword in the right hand going to her left and the sword in her left hand going right. As Ayim Rasaad tried to spin the staff up in time to block the strikes, Nalia pulled her swords back toward herself and outward.

There was a sickening wet sound as the razor-sharp inside blades of the hooks caught Ayim Rasaad's neck. Her head flew free from her body and the woman who had once been a Zouyim monk but who traded it for unscrupulous power, dropped to the stone floor, headless and very dead.

The cavern grew silent as a tomb. Sam could hear Nalia breathing hard, something he didn't think he had ever heard before. He looked around and saw his friends, mouths open, jaws slack, staring at the headless form of Ayim Rasaad. For a good five seconds, there was no movement, no other sound.

Then, as if waking from a dream, Sam saw heads shaking and eyes snapping into focus. The soldiers who had been watching the battle to see their leader victorious suddenly realized things had shifted. Half of those on the front line turned to run. The others brought up their weapons to try to kill the party. They all fared the same.

Sam, Nalia—moving her left arm carefully—and Rindu joined the battle once more. The soldiers trying to escape were cut down easily, trapped between their fellows further into the passage and the warriors dealing death from the chamber. It took only a few minutes until all the forces changed their direction and began to flee.

"Allow them to flee," Rindu called out to the party. Sam, Nalia, and Ix stopped immediately. The rakkeben stopped very soon after. Even Oro, after looking around at the others, figured out what was going on and stopped mauling the fleeing soldiers. Emerius, though, was still shooting arrow after arrow at the retreating foes, screaming at them incoherently.

"Em!" Sam yelled to the big hunter. "Em, that's enough. We've won."

Still the hunter fired his arrows rapidly, each one striking a vital area, taking another life. It wasn't until Ix slipped up behind him and put her arm on his shoulder that he looked up and noticed that no one else was fighting. Arms dropping, he slumped. He had a haunted look in his eyes. Sam hoped something had not broken in his friend.

Sam looked around. Half the cavern was full of bodies. The passageway had narrowed considerably because of the corpses piled there. There would have been many more, he knew, without the choke point of the narrow passage, some of them theirs. He sighed. So much death. Why did there always have to be so much death? He felt his stomach roil, but fought it. He had to make sure everyone was safe.

He went first to Nalia, to check on her shoulder. He found her sitting on a smooth rock formation, pulling a small dart from her flesh. She was bleeding, but not profusely.

"Are you okay?" he asked her.

"I am well," she answered. "It is just a scratch. I do not think there was poison on it. We can dress it when we get back to Whitehall. Check on the others."

Sam did as she suggested. Oro and the rakkeben all had minor cuts and some bruises, but nothing that was serious. Ix, surprisingly, had a few shallow cuts also.

"What do you expect?" she asked. "While you were enjoying yourself and taking your time getting here, I was the only one fighting at close range, and without my ability to teleport. I'd like to see you do better."

Sam put his hands up in surrender. "Okay, okay. I was just surprised. I have seen you fight. It seems difficult to strike you, that's all. I'm glad you're not seriously hurt."

Her eyes lost some of their fire. "Yeah, well, okay. It's possible to hit me. Just ask your girlfriend." She nodded toward Nalia. "Anyway, I'll be fine. I just want to get out of here. These caves are kind of giving me the creeps, with their teleportation blocking powers and all that."

"I agree," Sam said. "I want to make sure everyone is okay and then we'll collect the artifacts and go to where we can teleport home."

Uh, Sam? Skitter sent.

Oh my God, Skitter, Sam sent back. *In all the excitement, I forgot to check on you. Are you okay? Are you injured?*

I am not injured. I hid. There is something else, though.

Something else? Sam sent. *What is it?*

The drum is gone.

"What?" Sam said aloud. The others all looked at him.

"Skitter just told me that the drum is missing. He hid it, but now it's gone." He ran to where Ayim Rasaad's body still lay. Trying to avoid the blood as much as he could, he rolled her body over and checked the pouch on her waist. He had seen her put the bell, Azgo, in there. The container was empty.

"No," he said. "No!" He connected his two sticks so that *Ahimiro* was a staff again. He created the light on the tip and made it as bright as he could. Pure, white light flooded the cavern, making the scene look even more grisly than it had before. "Everyone, both artifacts are missing. We have to find them. One could have been knocked out of its place, even into the pit, but not both. The one from Rasaad's pouch is missing, too. Someone took them."

The party searched the cavern and the passageway for over two hours, moving bodies, looking for any sign of what happened to the artifacts. They found nothing. Rindu was not even able to sense them any longer.

I'm sorry, Sam, Skitter sent. *I was standing right near where I hid the drum. Even during Nalia's fight, I was only a few feet away. I don't know how someone was able to take them.*

It's not your fault, buddy, Sam consoled the hapaki. *None of us saw who did it.*

The party had moved out of the passage into the Great Room, near where the machine that misdirected centuries of tourists sat.

"I knew Tingai wouldn't be here," Emerius said, "but I thought that mutated assassin would have stayed with Rasaad. I want him dead almost as much as Tingai. Maybe they're together."

"Yeah, maybe," Sam said, not really paying attention to the conversation. He was already trying to figure out what the missing artifacts meant. He was pretty sure whatever it was, it wasn't good.

Rindu came up to Sam, moving carefully. "Sam, there is nothing else we can do here. Let us go back to Whitehall so we can determine what our next steps will be."

"Yes, you're right," Sam said, eyeing the way the Zouy was moving. "Are you injured, Master Rindu?"

"I am sore, that is all," the Zouy answered. "That blast of the other energy, of the *awkum*, was very powerful. I will be fine with some rest."

There was nothing to do but to go back to their home. They could discuss what their next steps would be then. Sam gathered the party and within a few minutes he was teleporting them back to the fortress. He was glad to find out that the power blocking their teleporting abilities was limited to the secret passages.

No sooner had they arrived at Whitehall than Lahim Chode, looking much healthier than he had the last time they saw him, came walking up quickly, still using a staff for support but not seeming to rely on it. "Oh, I'm glad you're back. I've had some viewings. Please come with me to Dr. Walt's library. I'm afraid we have a new enemy, one that is worse than Ayim Rasaad."

61

"You lost track of the artifacts?" Dr. Walt's bushy white eyebrows looked ready to take flight and leave his forehead completely. "That is dire news indeed." They were in one of the meeting halls, the closest one to the teleportation area.

Rindu looked back and forth from Dr. Walt to the seer. The latter had a forced neutral look on his face. "This does not surprise you, Lahim Chode?" Rindu asked. Surprise leapt onto the seer's face, but then was smoothed away quickly.

"I…did not know, but it's not surprising," Chode responded.

"He wouldn't tell me of his viewings until you were all here," Dr. Walt said. "Maybe now we can get some answers."

"First," Chode said, "please tell me what happened. I may be able to piece some things together that way."

Sam told the tale, from the last time they were in the fortress until they returned. Everyone was there: Dr. Walt, Lahim Chode, Danaba Kemp, Nicole, all three hapaki, Torim Jet, Palusa Filk, and Chisin Ling were silent as he described what they had been through.

"I see," the seer said. "It makes more sense now, but it is still not completely clear. I will tell you of the strong visions I had. They were even clearer than is typical, for some reason.

"I was not trying to view anything. I was simply meditating to relax and to ease my anxiety. The viewings came unbidden, something that has not happened in years. It was of a large chamber, the walls of stone but almost completely covered by tapestries depicting battles. I did not recognize the style of the weaving nor any of the scenes themselves.

"At first, I was seeing from the viewpoint of one of the people in the room. I saw to whom this person was talking, a very tall, thin creature that resembled a man, but was not. It…he was completely hairless, wearing only a breech cloth. His head was larger than it should have been for a man, and his arms were longer than seemed natural as well. His long, almost skeletal fingers ended in sharp nails that were very nearly claws."

"That's the assassin who tried to kill Dr. Walt," Danaba Kemp said.

"Yes, that was my thought also," Lahim Chode said, "from the description you gave after the attack, and from the glimpse I got of one in my previous visions.

"The voice of the person whose point of view I was sharing said, 'Vahi, we have much work to do. Ayim Rasaad is no more and so it is up to us, you and I and Tingai, to complete what she started. We must get the final artifact.'

"As Vahi, the assassin, nodded his agreement, my point of view swung around until it was able to take in the entire chamber. The one who had spoken, from whose eyes I had been watching, was an old man. A very old man.

"He was a taller than average man, though not nearly as tall as the assassin. His body still seemed rugged, thick of limb, not at all like most very old men I have seen. He had a full head of white hair, except perhaps for some that was missing from his larger-than-normal forehead. He wore a close-cropped beard. The lines and wrinkles on his face lent him an expressive quality as he spoke to the assassin.

"'Yes, master,' Vahi said. 'We will find it and then all three will be in your possession. Then all of Gythe will know its new ruler, Chetra Dal.'"

Rindu's throat constricted and he found he could not finish the breath he had started. "Chetra Dal?" he said after he had fought to seize a breath. "Did you say Chetra Dal?"

Lahim Chode looked to Rindu with concern, taken aback by the urgency in the Zouy's voice. "Yes, that's what they said. Chetra Dal. Does that name mean something to you?"

Rindu looked to Torim Jet. The older Zouy had a look of shock on his face as well. It reflected perfectly what Rindu felt.

"That...is not possible," Torim Jet said. "Master Chetra Dal has been dead for thirty-five years."

"Chetra Dal was the heart of the Zouyim order," Rindu explained. "When the old Grandmaster died, he was the unanimous choice to succeed him. Master Dal declined. Still, for decades, through two other Grandmasters, his counsel was sought. He was the wisest, the most powerful among us. He it was that taught me Syray, the language and art of calligraphy. He it was who, more than any other single person, is the reason I am who I am today.

"He was the best of us, and when word of his death on a mission that to this day remains shrouded in mystery came to the temple, it was as if the sun had been blotted out. Master Chetra Dal could not be alive, could not be this villain who has set himself against us. It must be someone else, someone using the name of our great master. That he does so doubles his crimes."

"Yes," Torim Jet breathed, "an imposter. That is it. You heard the men speaking, Lahim Chode, but you cannot ascertain the truth of what they spoke. We will uncover this liar when we defeat him and the honorable name of our master will continue to shine without this shadow of accusation."

"I'm sure you're right, Rindu," Dr. Walt said. "We will learn the truth. However, that brings up the subject of what we shall do next. Will we try to find the man, wait for him to come to us, or something else? We still have the army being arrayed against us."

Rindu's mind was still reeling over the news about Chetra Dal. There was not a day that went by without something reminding him of his old master, something recalling how wise he was. He had spent his life trying to emulate the man. Who would use that name, and to what purpose?

He realized that no one had spoken. Shifting his attention on the matter at hand, Rindu did so. "Lahim Chode, have you seen anything that would indicate where this army is, or the imposter? Or do you know where the third and final artifact is?"

"I have not seen anything that I recognize as a location, no," the seer said, "I'm sorry. I will try to find more information."

Dr. Walt cleared his throat. "I have been looking, but have not found anything to help us in this. I too will keep trying. I believe our best chance lies in trying to find the artifact, since I have already found reference to Bruqil, the tuning fork artifact. Perhaps with what we have and any new information we can find, we could figure out where to look. On the other hand, I wouldn't know how to even start finding our enemy or the army. Unless Lahim has some viewings, going after the artifact seems to be the thing to do."

"I agree," Sam said. "Dr. Walt, has anything in the new library we brought helped?"

"What?" Dr. Walt said as if he was surprised by the question. "Oh, the new records. Or, rather, the very old records that are new to us. I have been searching through them, looking for clues that will help us in our predicament. Fascinating information.

"The facility from which you obtained the records was a research facility of sorts. The leader of the group, Magry Andronis, was apparently the heart and soul of the work there. As close as I can tell, they worked on technology that would help them in the war effort. In a sense, I suppose it could be said that they made weapons. Highly technological weapons, though their definition of technology would be different than ours.

"But anyway, I have found nothing there that relates to the artifacts. There are several books that appear to be biographical in nature, all about this Magry Andronis, but I have more pressing subjects to research. It might be that I will find something in the library, but for now I will focus on the records we already had in the fortress. In fact, it is past time for me to get back to my research. Time is of the essence if we are to find the last artifact. Please excuse me."

Dr. Walt left, going back to his library. Lahim Chode left immediately after, saying something about trying to get helpful viewings. The others left also, one by one, until only Sam and Nalia were left with Rindu.

"We are perhaps at the most dangerous point yet," Rindu said. "Whoever this imposter is, I do believe that he has the other two artifacts. With all three, he would not need his army. We must get to the last one before he does."

"We will do so father," Nalia said. "We will find it, end his plans, and unmask him for who or what he is."

"Yes, I'm sure Nalia's right, Master Rindu," Sam said. "I'm sure we'll be on our way to finding it within a couple of days. We really have no choice, after all. Saving the world is what we do."

Epilogue

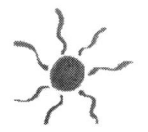

Chetra Dal sat in a large stuffed chair in his library. The light from the fireplace mingled with that from the braziers set at the corners of the room, illuminating his face at odd angles, making the shadows leap from line to line in his ancient visage. He held a cup of tea, all but forgotten in the swirling mist of his thoughts.

He had lived a long time, seen many things. His life, at times, seemed to consist solely of his plottings, of his research and discoveries. There were moments when he felt tired, so tired. There was not much left for him to do. He would ensure that the information he had so painstakingly worked to obtain would not die with him when he inevitably went to the grave. He was old and had little time.

The death of Ayim Rasaad was a setback. He had been training her for more than eight years and she had been progressing nicely. Now she was gone. To whom would he impart his knowledge now?

When he had first discovered the little hints that there was power beyond the *rohw*, he had carefully concealed his dabblings. As his knowledge and abilities grew, it became clear that he must go off on his own to dedicate his full attention, and all his time, to discovering more and more about the *awkum*.

In the thirty-five years since he had faked his death and left the Zouyim temple, he had learned much. About himself, and about the power that had been used in ancient times. Rasaad was to be his tool to secure his power on Gythe and then she would be his means of ensuring the knowledge about the *awkum* would never again be lost. Ah, but now that was impossible.

When he snuck into the chamber and stole the first two artifacts, he had thought of destroying those who had been hounding Ayim Rasaad and who had succeeded in killing her. He could have done it. Using surprise to his advantage, he could have prevented them from using whatever technique or power they used to defeat his apprentice. He could have killed Rindu and the others would have toppled easily. He should have done so, he thought.

What had held him back? It was true that he needed another disciple, another to learn the *awkum* and carry on his work. Rindu would be ideal. Was it for that reason he spared the other, insignificant members of their party? Perhaps.

There was something about the other one, the younger man with the yellow hair. They called him Sam, he recalled. Yes, he would make a fine tool for his purposes. He was younger than Rindu, with a potential that was probably greater than his old friend.

But that was not really the reason he did not destroy them all. There was a slight chance they could have rallied, surprised him, defeated him. If that happened, all his work would have been for naught. No, it was better to be safe.

He would get the last artifact, defeat the new government, and put in place an order that would see humankind rise from the muck in which it found itself wallowing. He would do this, and then they would see. He and his chosen would usher in a new golden age of technology and power that would make the pre-war Gythe look like a group of children pretending to be heroes. All he had to do was to obtain one more powerful artifact and kill all opposition.

Chetra Dal took a sip of his tea and found it had grown cold and bitter while he mused. He sighed. He was tired, but he had strength enough for this. Strength enough to accomplish what he had been working more than forty years to do. Nothing could be allowed to stand in his way. Nothing would. He set his cup down and got up from his chair. He had work to do, a world to change, to take. His steps, still steady and graceful, took him to the books on his planning table. He opened one where it was marked and began to read, thoughts of the end of Gythe, and the beginning, swirling in his head.

Be sure not to miss the sneak peak of the first chapter of Resonance, the third book in the Harmonic Magic Series (at the very end of this book).

Thank you for reading my book. I hope you enjoyed sharing Sam's (and his friends') adventures in Harmonics, the second book in the Harmonic Magic series. If so, please consider taking a moment to post a review where you purchased the book. Reviews are important in helping other readers find exciting books and help authors to continue to write them, as well as providing valuable feedback for the author. Your honest review would be very much appreciated.

If you would like to get information on upcoming books, such as the next book in the series (titled *Resonance*, an excerpt of which is in the section following the glossary, please visit my web site at pepadilla.com and join my mailing list.

I also appreciate any comments I receive, so please feel free stop by my web site and comment on the site itself or to send me an e-mail at pep@pepadilla.com.

Adventures in Gythe

Vibrations: Harmonic Magic Book 1

Harmonics: Harmonic Magic Book 2

Resonance: Harmonic Magic Book 3 (to be released)

Tales of Gythe: Gray Man Rising

Glossary

Agago (*ah·gah'·go*) – Baron Tingai's compound at approximately the same location as Kingman, Arizona. In Old Kasmali, the name means "emaciated" or "wasting away."

Ahimiro (*ah·hee·meer'·oh*) – the name of Sam's porzul wood staff, meaning "fire pole" in Old Kasmali.

Ahu (*ah'·hoo*) – a small bird that takes its name from the Old Kasmali word for "funerary monument" because of its habit of digging holes into which it lays its eggs.

Akila Gonsh (*ah·keel'·ah gonsh*) – one of the two co-leaders of the city of Patchel's Folly. Her husband, Raire, is the other co-leader.

Ancha Dinn (*an'·ka din*) – the seven-year old brother of Emerius and Inoria Dinn.

Arzbedim, *singular* **Arzbed** (*arz·bay'·deem, arz·bade'*) – a group of rogue Zouyim who place their own selfish desires for power above all else; they are the natural enemies of the Zouyim.

Awkum (*ow·koom'*) – The strange power used by Ayim Rasaad. Instead of being based on peace and harmony, it is based on chaos and disorganization.

Ayim Rasaad (*ah·yeem' rah·sod'*) – a former Zouyim who defected to become one of the Arzbedim and narrowly escaped the extinction of that group by the Gray Man. The chief antagonist in the story.

Baron Tingai (*tin'·guy*) – Rasaad's chief scientist, responsible for the creation of mutations to be used for combat.

Bayton – a fairly large city (for Gythe) that is in the exact location as San Franciso in Telani.

Bhorgabir (*bor'·gah·beer*) – stealthy assassin-type of mutants genetically created in the Great War and of which there are still a handful. They are called "bhor" as a shortened form of the name, the full name meaning "twilight man" in Old Kasmali.

Chen Bao Ling (*[ba·oh]' ling*) – a nine-year old girl of the Chen clan (Ix's clan). She has come from Zhong, where Ix grew up.

Chen Feng Dao (*fong'·[da oh]*) – fighting monk from Telani who accidentally transported himself to Gythe and founded the clan to which Ix belongs. Feng Dao means loosely "wind knife" or "wind sword"

Chetra Dal (*che'·tra dahl*) – a legendary Zouyim master who is believed to have died while on a mission more than three decades ago.

Chi (*chee*) – the name for internal energy in Chinese martial arts, such as kung fu. It is the equivalent to *rohw* on Gythe.

Chisin Ling (*chee'·sin ling*) – a captain in the forces of the new government, tasked with leading the force escorting Nicole Sharp in her quest for the hapaki community.

Cleave – Nalia's rakkeban.

Danaba Kemp (*dahn'·ah·bah*) – former leader of the Red Fangs, a group of bandits that lived in the area called The Grinder. He is now the general of the forces of the new government.

Dead Zone – an area where there is essentially no life because of devastation hundreds of years ago. This area is approximately what surrounds Olympia and extends to the north of Seattle in Telani.

Dr. Walter Wicket – a physicist/archaeologist who was arguably the top expert in ancient societies' use of vibrational energy, when he was in Telani. Now he heads the effort to establish the new government on Gythe.

Emerius Dinn (*eh·mare'·ee·us din*) – twin to Inoria Dinn. Both are hunters and tinkerers of supreme skill. Emerius focuses more on engineering devices while Inoria concentrates on herbs and other plants.

Fulusin Telanyahu (*foo·loo'·seen tell·an·yaw'·hoo*) – the leader of the city of Seamouth.

Gawzay (*gah'·zay*) – the artisans who make ceramic glass items, especially weapons.

Georg Santas (*gay'·org san'·toss*) – the leader of the town of Wethaven.

Giswych (*giss'·witch*) – in a legendary story about the hero Suka Templar, a magical item that endows people with superhuman attributes and everlasting life.

Gray Man – the successor to the Arzbedim, a tyrant who had plans to control two worlds. He is now deceased.

Grayson Wepp – a paleontologist who was transported to Gythe by the Arzbedim and who became the Gray Man. He was also Sam's uncle, brother to Nicole Sharp.

Gromarisa (*grow·mah·ree'·saw*) – the name in Gythe for the Grand Canyon. In Old Kasmali, the name means "bed of bones."

Gutu (*goo'·too*) – Ayim Rasaad's fortress. The name, in Old Kasmali, means "lip" or "snout," no doubt referring to the mouth of the valley where it is situated. The location is approximately where Hermosillo (in Mexico) is in Telani.

Gythe (*gaith*) – the world in which Sam found himself accidentally (in the book Vibrations), and to which he returned (in the book Harmonics). The name, in the Old Kasmali language means roughly "the physical world."

Hant Marr (*haunt marr*) – one of Chisin Ling's soldiers, a scout.

Hapaki (*ha·pah'·kee*) – a race of furry telepathic creatures that looks somewhat like a lemur mixed with a badger. Skitter is hapaki.

Iba (*ee'·bah*) – the term of endearment Rindu uses for his daughter, meaning "heart" in Old Kasmali.

Iboghan (*ee'·boe·gahn*) – the name for Carlsbad Caverns on Gythe. In Old Kasmali, the name means "heart of hell."

Ikalau (*eek'·ah·la·oo*) – a small fishing village around where Eureka, California is on Telani. The name means "large fish" in Old Kasmali.

Inoria Dinn (*in·oh'·ree·uh din*) – twin to Emerius Dinn. Both are hunters and tinkerers of supreme skill. Inoria concentrates on herbs and other plants while Emerius focuses more on engineering devices..

Ix – formerly the Gray Man's chief assassin. She took her name from the 8th letter of the Old Kasmali alphabet. The name of the letter meant roughly "fence in," or "destroy."

Kasmali (*caws·mah'·lee*) – the language spoken on Gythe.

Kawkibon (*caw'·ki·bon*) – the name for the location of Roswell, New Mexico on Gythe. The name in Old Kasmali means "star rock."

Khulim (*khoo'·leem*) – the state of consciousness just on the edge of going into a trance; "dream" in Old Kasmali.

Kimatar (*keem'·ah·tar*) – a pear-like fruit with a sweet taste.

Kokitura (*koe'·kee·too·rah*) – The mountain on which the main temple of the Zouyim was located before being destroyed by the Gray Man. The name means "Storm Mountain" in Old Kasmali and is called Mount Shasta on Telani.

Kori rohw (*koe'·ree roe*) – sets of movements or forms for bringing the body into harmony with the surrounding *rohw*; in Old Kasmali, "*rohw* play."

Kryzyq (*kri'·zik*) – in Gythe, the town in approximately where El Paso, Texas is in Telani.

Lahim Chode (*lay'·him chode*) – the only surviving prisoner from the dungeons of the Gray Man. He has a talent for remote viewing.

Manu (*mah'·noo*) – large birds, somewhat like an ostrich but bigger, typically used as mounts.

Marge Tousin (*too'·sin*) – the primary healer in Whitehall

Mark Sharp – Sam's father, deceased, previously husband to Nicole Sharp.

Martin Steeves – one of the guards at Whitehall, a sergeant.

Marybador (*may·rib'·ah·door*) – the location of the headquarters of the *Sapsyra Shin Elah*. The location is called Crater Lake on Telani. The name means roughly "Bowl of Fire" in Old Kasmali.

Max – a hapaki, Skitter's nephew.

Molly – a stowaway cat that was transported to Gythe while hiding in Sam's woodbin. She had a litter of kittens, the only ones in Gythe.

Nalia Wroun (*nah'·lee·ah roon*) – one of the *Sapsyra Shin Elah*, perhaps the last one living, daughter to Rindu Zose and Ylleria Zose.

Nicole Sharp – Sam's mother, wife to Mark Sharp.

Old Kasmali (*caws·mah'·lee*) – an ancient language of Gythe, not spoken any longer except in fragments, much like Latin is on Telani.

Onekai (*own'·eh·kai*) – a vegetable that grows close to the ground; the name means "earth fruit" in Old Kasmali.

Palusa Filk (*pah loo'·sah filk*) – one of the three known surviving Zouyim monks, a woman of an age with Nalia.

Pantor – large predatory cats, much like the panthers or cheetahs on Telani.

Patchel's Folly – a city in the area of the Dead Zone, located approximately where Olympia, Washington is on Telani.

Porzul (*pore'·zool*) – wood from the tree of the same name, having properties of metal and very conductive to vibrational energy.

Rabadur (*rah'·bah·dure*) large four-armed humanoids that were created genetically from humans as weapons during the great war and some of which are still around today.

Raire Gonsh (*rare gonsh*) – one of the two co-leaders of the city of Patchel's Folly. His wife, Akila, is the other co-leader.

Rakkeben, *singular* **rakkeban** (*rah'·keh·ben, - bahn*) – large, intelligent wolves that can be ridden as mounts, if the rakkeban bonds with the rider.

Riati (*ree·ah'·tee*) – small, thin, hairless mutated humans most often seen in the Dead Zone

Rindu Zose (*reen'·doo zoze*) – a Zouyim monk, one of the last, husband to Ylleria Zose and father to Nalia Wroun.

Rohw (*roe*) – the energy that pervades all life in the universe, from Old Kasmali for "spirit" or "wind."

Sammy – a hapaki from a different community than the one to which Skitter and Max belong.

Sam Sharp – a man who accidentally transported himself to Gythe and became known as a hero because of actions he took trying to return home. Many people call him "the Hero of Gythe."

Sapsyra Shin Elah, *singular* **sapsyr** (*sap·seer'·ah sheen ee'·lah*) – an order of women warriors, the finest person-to-person fighters on Gythe, pledged to honor, justice, and helping others. Nalia Wroun may be the last surviving Sapsyr.

Seamouth – a town in approximately the location where Everett, Washington is on Telani.

Shen Nan – the husband of one of the deceased Sapsyra, Eoria Nan.

Shiran Slayth (*she'·ran slayth*) – the miray (a leadership position similar to mayor but with more power) of the town of Kryzyq.

Shonyb (*shoe'·nib*) – Sam's rakkeban; the name loosely means "fang" in Old Kasmali.

Shrapezi (*shrah'·peh·zee*) – Nalia's favorite weapon, hooked swords with razor-sharp crescent handguards; from Old Kasmali meaning "iron moon."

Silicim Mant (*seel'·ee·seem maunt*) – leader of the Arzbedim when they captured Grayson Wepp.

Skitter – a hapaki who got caught up in Sam's original

adventure in Gythe.

Somas – the town in approximately the same location as Nogales, Arizona in Telani.

Sondria (*sawn'·dree·ah*) – in a legendary story about the hero Suka Templar, a city and region in which the adventure takes place.

Stoker – Sam's housecat.

Stumin Kile (*stoo'·min kile*) – the mayor of Somas.

Suka Templar (*soo'·kah tem'·plar*) – an ancient hero, one whom Emerius Dinn idolizes and patterns himself after.

Syburowq (*si'·boo·roke*) – the area that is the Olympic Peninsula on Telani. The name means "green finger."

Telani (*tay·lah'·nee*) – Earth, the world from which Sam comes. In Old Kasmali, the word means, roughly, "shadow."

Torim Jet (*toe'·reem jet*) – one of the three known surviving Zouyim.

Tramgadal (*tram'·gah·dahl*) – The village that served as a doorway to Kokitura Mountain, located at the base of it.

Vahi (*vah'·hee*) – the leader of the bhorgabir, a race of mutant assassins.

Wethaven – the city in the location where Seattle is on Telani.

Zhong (*jzong*) – the area where Ix grew up, founded by

Chen Feng Dao and in the location of the Salt Lake Valley in Telani.

Zirquay River (*zeer′·kway*) – the name of the Colorado River in Gythe. The name, in Old Kasmali, means "blue snake."

Zouyim, *singular* **Zouy** (*zoo′·yeem, zoo′·yah*) – a class of monks or mages who use vibrational energy (the *rohw*) and are experts in combat. Their purpose is to aid the citizens of Gythe in living peacefully and honorably. The main Zouyim temple was at Kokitura mountain before being destroyed.

Zumra (*zoom′·ra*) – Rindu's rakkeban. The name means, loosely, "singing" in Old Kasmali. He was named thus because of his habit of humming.

Zyngim (*zeen′·geem*) – the artisans who are able to make steel, the only ones who can do so on Gythe because of the peculiar difficulty of making alloys of iron.

Zyrqyt Lake (*zeer′·kit*) – The lake surrounding the island of the former Sapsyra headquarters of Marybador. The name is derived from Old Kasmali and means "blue glass."

About the Author

A chemical engineer by degree, air quality engineer by vocation, certified dreamer by predilection, and writer by sheer persistence, P.E. Padilla learned long ago that crunching numbers and designing solutions was not enough to satisfy his creative urges. Weaned on classic science fiction and fantasy stories from authors as diverse as Heinlein, Tolkien, and Jordan, and affected by his love of role playing games such as Dungeons and Dragons (analog) and Final Fantasy (digital), he sometimes has trouble distinguishing reality from fantasy. While not ideal for a person who needs to function in modern society, it's the perfect state of mind for a writer. He lives in Southern California.

Preview of Resonance:
Harmonic Magic Book 3

Zouyim Master Chetra Dal had narrowly escaped death. His fellow monks had not. He was not in the clear yet, though. The creature, some sort of guardian, had found them searching where they did not belong. It hunted him still. He could hear its heavy footfalls, the inrush of air as it sniffed for him, searching. Dal was not sure he would survive being found.

The master monk stopped and drew in a deep breath. He let it out slowly, soundlessly, allowing it to leave his body on its own, not forcing an exhalation. As the breath exited, his body relaxed and his mind cleared. He could not match his hunter in physical combat. He knew his only chance was to outthink the beast. Another deep breath in and another peaceful out-breath and he was completely calm.

Dal's eyes swept his surroundings. He was in a crumbling stone corridor somewhere below ground. He was not sure of his exact location because of the battle and his frantic escape after the monster had killed his three brothers. The creature had destroyed them in so short a time. It was impossible to believe that anything could defeat three Zouyim monks so expediently. But he had witnessed it.

The Zouyim were masters of combat, experts at a martial system that had been developed over hundreds of years. More, though, they were adept at using the *rohw*, the vibrational energy that was pervasive, suffusing all life and surrounding everything at all times. The monks' *rohw* attacks seemed to have bounced off the creature, having no effect at all. That was puzzling, and more than a little disturbing.

The stomping grew closer. Chetra Dal could hear the grunts of the monster's breathing now. He would have to formulate a way to defeat his adversary soon or he would die as quickly as his brothers.

The corridor held nothing that could be used as a weapon. As the Zouy began running again, looking back over his shoulder, he cut a turn too closely and struck the edge of the wall hard with his shoulder. Pain shot through his arm as if he had been struck with lightning. So hard was the collision that part of one of the stone blocks rattled and moved a few inches, causing stone dust to shower down on top of him. Though he was able to keep from coughing, the sound of the collision itself was loud enough to capture his enemy's attention. It grunted and the thump of its footfalls grew more rapid.

The monk ran as fast as he could, not bothering to look behind him any longer, only looking ahead. He took three more turns down random corridors before he stopped short. He was in some kind of chamber. It was twenty feet on either side, square, and had one opening. The one he had just come through. There was no escape, with stone blocks surrounding him and the monster quickly coming upon him. He could not see it yet, but he heard it getting closer. It seemed as if his time in this life was now done.

Deriding himself for thinking so negatively, the Zouyim master snapped his mind back into focus. He went through all his available options and decided upon the one that would give him the best chance of surviving. Without another thought, he ran at top speed. Back toward the approaching creature.

He had barely made it out of the chamber when he caught sight of the greenish brown scaled beast. It was massive, seeming to fill the entire corridor. Close to seven feet tall and at least five feet wide, it was squat but it moved with a fluidity that belied its form. Its feet were thick and triangle shaped, coming to a point at the toe. Dal had seen what that toe had done to Chilk Triss just moments ago. The creature had kicked the Zouy and the toe had acted like an ax, splitting the monk almost completely in two, killing him instantly.

The tree trunk legs of the beast pumped, moving the barrel-shaped body toward Dal. Its arms, each carrying a multi-bladed weapon, readied themselves to strike when it saw the remaining Zouyim monk. A wicked grin split the fang-filled mouth that took up more than half the bestial face. Yellow, gimlet eyes locked onto Dal and glittered.

Chetra Dal dove past the creature, spinning in mid-air and barely dodging the blows from the weapons aimed at him. He rolled smoothly to his feet, and was running again before his adversary had even turned. Its bellows pursued him down the corridor.

Dal knew he had only moments to live unless he executed his plan perfectly. Glancing quickly toward the beast, he darted through a short corridor and under an archway he had seen just moments before. Here was where he would make his stand.

His senses told him to duck and he did so, feeling the wind of one of the monster's weapons pass just above his head, hearing the whistle of the blades that made up a pattern much like a pine tree along the main shaft of the weapon. The next blow could not be dodged, the Zouyim master knew. He would have to act now.

Going down deep into his core, focusing on his center of energy just below his navel, Chetra Dal drew up all the energy he could muster, both from himself and from his surroundings. With a sharp exhalation, he channeled all the *rohw* through his hands and struck at the archway with both palms, one over the other, hoping he had acted in time.

The strike of the creature's other weapon was unable to land on Chetra Dal. As soon as the Zouy struck the archway, the massive blocks making the top of the opening began to fall, one of them deflecting the blow that would have ended his life. The world seemed silent and calm for just a moment, and then the roar of stone falling all around sounded and the monk dove clear, desperate that he himself would not be trapped.

He landed roughly on his side, pain shooting up through his torso and making his vision narrow at the sides, but then he regained his perception. Looking around, he saw the results of his ploy. The creature was pinned by tons of rock, only parts of one leg, a shoulder, and its head showing up through the stone. It wriggled, trying to free its arms, but for now, it was unable to get loose. Its grunts were as much from frustration as from anger.

Chetra Dal knew what he must do. He had seen his fellow monks trying to pierce the creature's hide with their swords, to no avail. Its skin was too thick to be cut. There was but one thing to be done. He hoped it would be enough. He knew that eventually, the beast would free itself and then nothing would stop it from killing him.

Walking slowly to where his adversary was trapped, the monk wary and looking for any sign it could actually move to attack, he looked into the creature's eyes.

"I am not sure if you understand my language or not," Chetra Dal said in Ancient Kasmali, a language that had not been spoken in hundreds, if not thousands, of years. By the cessation of its movements and the narrowing of its eyes, it seemed that it did understand.

"I know you are performing your task, your duty. You are to be commended on your commitment. However, I cannot allow you to kill me. I have work still to do in this life. Please know that I respect your task and honor you." The monk saluted the beast, right fist cradled inside the left hand, both held out in front of his chest as he bowed.

The Zouyim master breathed deeply for a moment, generating as much energy as he could. He felt his body warm and saw that his hands were glowing. The creature's eyes widened at first, and then relaxed. It knew what was to happen next.

Dal made a few motions with his hands, concentrating his energy even further. Then, with lightning speed, he struck the top of the beast's head with the open palm of his right hand. The monster's eyes became unfocused, but still held the light of life. Three more strikes to the same spot, alternating the right and the left hands, did more damage. Finally, the last strike broke through and the monster's head caved in, its eyes glazed over, and it ceased moving altogether.

It was done. The monk regretted that he had caused the creature pain, but using his energy to the full could still not kill it in one blow. He had done the best he could.

Chetra Dal bowed weakly to the corpse once more and looked around. It would take quite a bit of exploring to regain the chamber in which they had first found the creature, but he would persevere for as long as it took. It was obvious that the guardian was left to protect something of great value. Now that it had been defeated, he would see what it was.

Three hours later, Master Chetra Dal found his way back to the small chamber in which the bodies of his fellow monks still rested. Sadness radiated through his body like a winter chill. If only they had thought more quickly, perhaps one or more of his friends would still be alive. There was a lesson there. He would meditate upon it when he returned to the temple and he would make sure to note it in one of his books. Wisdom was hard-gained and the honorable man shared it with whomever would accept it.

Master Dal turned to the end of the chamber, where they had first spotted the guardian. There, on a simple shelf carved into the stone wall itself, was a box. He ran his fingers over it, feeling the carvings. It was wood, but it seemed that it had turned to stone because of its vast age. Only three handspans wide and perhaps two high, it seemed a small thing for the death it had caused. Grasping the cover, the monk opened the lid. As he raised it, there was a hiss as of air escaping.

Within, there were five scrolls. They were rolled upon wooden cylinders, which also felt as if they had tured to stone, like the box itself. The scrolls were exquisitely made from some natural fiber, but it seemed to be woven of many fine threads, tight and perfect and in the same condition as the day they went into the box.

The Zouy read over the scrolls, skimming them to get a general sense of what secrets they revealed. They were written in Ancient Kasmali, which made him recall that the guardian had understood him when he spoke that dead language. He was only part-way down the first scroll when his eyes widened and his heart began to beat faster. The scrolls explained an energy, related to the *rohw*, but superior.

He had never heard of this energy, called *awkum*, before. He knew he would have to study these scrolls carefully. Perhaps he would be responsible for expanding the Zouyim order's understanding of universal energy. He would study them in secret, master the knowledge written there, and then he would share it. Until then, he would not tell anyone about what he had found. He would, most of all, have to make sure it was safe for others. He was a master, with the experience and wisdom to investigate things such as this. If it was safe to use, then others would benefit from what he had learned, but not until then.

Bowing to his fallen brothers, Chetra Dal put the scrolls into his pack and navigated the twisting corridors to the outside world. He would have much to study when he got back home to the Zouyim temple. Anxious to begin, he forced his weary feet to speed him home.

Printed in Great Britain
by Amazon